TERROR TRADE-OFF

Paula Dubois could barely watch as Jaeger dragged her thrashing daughter toward her mother. Then he placed a heavy boot on Katy's stomach and stepped down. The girl's screaming was stifled, and he made a snorting sound.

Paula's eyes were imploring. "She's a child," she screamed in rage. But Jaeger, grinning, ignored her. He was lowering his trousers.

Charbonneau, his breath coming faster, remembered their objective. He leaned close to Paula. "The folder—where is it? Tell me, and I'll stop my friend."

Paula knew the importance of the folder—but how much was that worth now . . . ?

D0288287

FINAL THUNDER

Tom Wilson

A SIGNET BOOK

SIGNET
Published by the Penguin Group
Penguin Books USA Inc., 375 Hudson Street,
New York, New York 10014, U.S.A.
Penguin Books Ltd, 27 Wrights Lane,
London W8 5TZ, England
Penguin Books Australia Ltd, Ringwood,
Victoria, Australia
Penguin Books Canada Ltd, 10 Alcorn Avenue,
Toronto, Ontario, Canada M4V 3B2
Penguin Books (N.Z.) Ltd, 182–190 Wairau Road,
Auckland 10, New Zealand

Penguin Books Ltd, Registered Offices:
Harmondsworth, Middlesex, England

First published by Signet, an imprint of Dutton Signet,
a division of Penguin Books USA Inc.

First Printing, October, 1996
10 9 8 7 6 5 4 3 2 1

Printed in the United States of America

PUBLISHER'S NOTE
This is a work of fiction. Names, characters, places, and incidents either are the product of the author's imagination or are used fictitiously, and any resemblance to actual persons, living or dead, events, or locales is entirely coincidental.

This work is dedicated to Lillian L. Wilson, a pioneer of the Canadian far north who never forgot her Southern heritage. She taught me to revere the written word, but passed away before seeing the results of her efforts. Wish you were here to set me straight about my prose, Mom.

ACKNOWLEDGMENTS

While *Final Thunder* is a work of fiction, much research and collaboration were involved before and during the writing. Steffie dug up source material, and applied a critical eye for detail and drama. The people of Browning, Montana, shared insights to Blackfoot and Plains Indian heritage. Friends in Idaho (including those in the Air National Guard at Gowen Field) lent snapshots of local color. Mac and Sallee Calico provided friendship and daily moral support. The aviators of the Red River Valley Fighter Pilot Association, the CBSA, and the Aspenosium shared aircraft data, flying experiences and war stories. Literary agent Ethan Ellenberg gave sound advice and direction. Mr. Joseph Pittman (this was our fourth effort together) applied his keen editorial eye, trimming away excess fat and mercilessly sloughing off unnecessary scenes and characters like poor forgotten children—and made it a better book. Thank you all.

PROLOGUE

Manhattan, New York

The Weyland Foundation was privately held by a handful of individuals, but its purposes were not at all private.

Success, a penchant for anonymity, disgust at the taking of human life, fierce patriotism, and the ability to reach difficult decisions quickly—were prerequisites for the group of people Cyril Weyland had gathered at a quiet dinner when the Great World War was raging in Europe and across the Pacific. As the meal ended, he'd asked that only those willing to risk all of their possessions for the betterment of mankind remain.

A majority decided they were unwilling to gamble everything. When those had gone and he was left with "the handful," Cyril Weyland placed his corporations and considerable lifetime's earnings, together worth some forty million dollars, into trust, withholding only a modest amount for the maintenance of his family and residences. The others had done the same.

The founders had been self-made. Most had been first- or second-generation Americans, but all had been first-generation rich. That evening they made their first decisions and, to the benefit of the free world, the Weyland Foundation was born. Since then the foundation had accomplished many things. Their human-excellence council promoted artistic endeavor and initiated great charitable causes, and their wildlife and flora council bought large tracts of ruined lands, deserts, and swamps in the Americas, Africa, and Asia, and returned them to nature.

Without the financial board, consisting of the five original members or their heirs, none of those things would have been possible, and they were extolled for their fine efforts. But it was their other, much quieter projects that changed the world into a better habitat for humans.

Through prudent investment their fortunes had grown a thousand-fold, and through their most secretive decisions the earth became a safer, more benevolent planet. Their underlying tenet was that democracy and capitalism were the best possible institutions for mankind, and the United States, although it had its warts and terrible problems, was an excellent model.

They strove to make human life sacred. Two of those in the room had been Jewish, with European roots and close relatives in Nazi Germany's death camps. They'd agreed that it must not happen again. They opposed tyrants everywhere, especially those who treated the lives of fellow humans with contempt. When elements within the American government became corrupt, those too were quietly exposed, and credit given to various agencies or members of the press who seemed to stumble onto truth. That periodic interference in domestic issues had created arguments, and in the mid-seventies the handful turned exclusively to international issues.

If economic freedom in Country X depended upon the formation and capitalization of certain companies, and if the governing infrastructure was appropriate, the companies and capital quietly appeared. If human interests in Country Y were threatened by the greed of a few, the handful made appropriate disbursals so the few were denied and the people benefited. The handful was not always successful in stopping tyrants and atrocities, or in encouraging governments to turn to democratic capitalism, but they helped.

The handful were non-partisan and non-political, and Cyril Weyland had quietly announced their purpose to every president since Franklin Roosevelt. They'd provided and were given information, support, and anonymity. Twice they'd been requested to make questionable investments, and their support had been withdrawn until the next executive came to power.

"The board will come to order," said Cyril Weyland in a voice that betrayed his ninety-three years. In its half century of existence the staff of the Weyland Foundation had grown tremendously, but the numbers of the handful remained constant.

The summit room, on the twenty-seventh floor of the Weyland Foundation Building, was massive. At the far end, beyond the small conference table, were plush chairs and a small bar, where the participants could take water, juice, tea, coffee, or—in the evening—wine or a cocktail. On the wall at one side were portraits of American presidents. On the other were likenesses of the five original directors of the financial board. Two of those were in the room. Three others had died and been replaced by heirs— the youngest a woman who had been born the same year the foundation had been established.

In its fifty-three years, two hundred and ninety covert projects had been considered by the financial board, but only half of that number had been pursued. Of those, eighty-six had been considered successful. Twelve were ongoing. Six more were presently under consideration.

The secretive projects were assigned codes, consisting of a color and a number. Blue projects were undertaken to assist the U.S. government. Green denoted financial assistance to peoples of foreign nations. Black projects were designed to expose, disrupt, or topple tyrants. Projects assigned the color scarlet were emergencies, with the potential for dire consequence. Those assumed the utmost sensitivity and importance, and few had been so designated.

The five members sat about the same heavy yet modest-sized oaken table they'd used in 1944. Cyril Weyland's thirty-six-year-old grandson—a non-member, but an executive vice-president entrusted with their most difficult projects—was seated at the side of the room, dressed in a dark blue suit. He looked weary, an appropriate appearance for a man who'd flown in from half the world away and spent much of the previous evening preparing for the meeting.

Cyril Weyland pressed an intercom button set into the oak table. "Send in the secretary and the project leader for Green two-seven-nine."

The secretary of state, the honorable Vernon M. Calico, was ushered into the room. Calico called himself a country boy from Texas and, unlike many in government, the American public trusted him. When he'd been the President's campaign manager, he'd been as likely to show up at a political rally in a gaudy line-dancing shirt as a white one. Today he was dressed conservatively, his button-down look marred only by sharkskin Western boots and a glistening silver belt buckle. He'd been selected by the President as his intermediary with the Weyland Foundation, since most of their secret projects fell into his realm at State.

Vern Calico greeted the handful with a raised hand, then grinned hello to the grandson as he took a seat beside him to hear the status of two projects of importance to the government.

"We'll cover Estonia first," Cyril told the secretary of state, "then the Russian affair."

The first project leader took the podium, smiled nervously at his audience, and began.

The breakup of the Soviet empire had not gone without casualties. Russia and the Ukraine were basket cases, but the worst sufferers had been the smaller fragments. One of those was tiny Estonia, located on the Gulf of Finland.

The Estonians had been ecstatic about their new independence, and their economy had prospered for a few false glory years until ugly reality set in. Their industries were paralyzed by inefficiency and ancient equipment. They used bog peat for heat, and produced food in poor yields. Their fishing industry was destroyed, for the voracious Russian processing fleet had gillnetted so thoroughly that food fish had all but disappeared from the gulf.

Now Russia was pounding on their door, urging them to step back into the fold, lusting after their lost oil-shale fields and the seaport of Tallinn. Since Estonia had a large and politically vocal Russian minority, the U.S. State Department had all but written the country off.

The project leader had visited there—had toured the countryside and walked the impoverished land. He'd spoken to despairing families and dispirited officials, but he'd also listened to those who still dreamed. He'd picked industries the Estonians knew. They'd processed shale and heavy oil in one way or another for the past century, but their techniques were ancient. It was the same for their phosphate and cement industries. He'd used the best engineers available to devise plans for new petroleum facilities at Kohtle-Järve, and new plants to produce fertilizer and concrete building materials. The volume and quality of their products would be dramatically increased—as would their shares of the European market.

The construction projects would be massive, and new prosperity would instantly reach across Estonia. After two years production would raise their living standard even higher.

The project leader concluded by recommending timely approval.

"The President wants to assist 'em," the secretary of state drawled."but the votes just aren't there. He'd be happy as a hound pup if you could help out."

Cyril Weyland regarded Calico evenly. "Perhaps the cause is just, Mr. Secretary, but this single project would involve nine billion dollars of capitalization."

"We'd only provide a third of that in capital outlay," the project leader hastily interjected. "The remainder would be in guarantees."

Cyril slowly shook his aging head. "The fact remains that a large amount of foundation funds would be tied up and perhaps placed in jeopardy."

As the project leader left the room, Vern Calico looked on glumly. He'd been denied his previous green project recommendation, and approval of this one seemed no more likely.

The handful refilled water glasses as the grandson took the podium and arranged his notes. Cyril Weyland nodded for him to begin.

"Project Blue two-eight-three." Cyril's grandson enunciated clearly, for the elderly board members could not hear as well as they once had. "Four weeks ago, U.S. intelligence monitored Russian military transmissions as a convoy left Yakutsk, in northern Siberia. The movement was a routine one—Russian strategic rocket forces relocating SS-18 missile reentry vehicles to a weapons storage area four hundred miles to the south. On their second day, the National Security Agency overheard messages relayed to Moscow indicating that a transporter was missing.

"The Defense Intelligence Agency briefed that each transporter carries two nose cones—both weighing two tons and containing four MIRVed thermonuclear warheads. Each warhead has an equivalency of forty-five million tons of high explosives. The State Department wanted to know where they'd been taken, and by whom—but the National

Reconnaissance Office had no satellites in position, and the CIA has been restricted from HUMINT operations in Russia. Since the Weyland Foundation has ongoing construction efforts in Siberia, the secretary requested that we investigate the matter. Mr. Calico also suggested that I be placed in charge of the effort."

The secretary of state smiled. "The choice was easy as picking pecan pie out of a truckstop menu, Frank. You speak the language and know about nukes."

The grandson went on. "I was replaced on another project, flew to Washington for my inbriefing, then traveled to Siberia with our team of investigators. Two of those were Russian nationals, and two others were nuclear weapons experts. When we arrived, I appropriated a helicopter from one of our construction sites and flew to the suspected location of the theft. We distributed funds to locals freely, and were finally told about a truck and closed trailer that had been seen traveling east on a frozen road, remaining hidden under trees during daylight hours.

"A Russian military team was also searching, and we found them two hundred miles along the road. After a few thousand rubles changed hands, the officer in charge, a major, became cooperative."

One of the handful frowned. "You bribed a military officer?"

"Today's Russian army is ragtag . . . so underpaid they lead a hand-to-mouth existence. Their conscripts are viewed as those too stupid to avoid the draft. There's no respect, little discipline, and corruption from top to bottom."

He continued his story. "The Russian major knew nothing about warheads, just that he was to track down a stolen tractor-trailer and its contents. As we returned to our helicopter, one of our team pointed out an oddity. Their search team wore the red collar flashes of the army's combined forces—not the blue of their rocket forces.

"We continued, landing at each settlement and cabin, and found that the driver of the tractor-trailer—which was not at all similar to the transporter suspected by the DIA— had also worn the red collar flashes. At that time I relayed word to the secretary of state that it was unlikely that the trailer contained nuclear warheads."

Vern Calico drawled: "By then the Department of Defense was involved, and they were nervous as cats. Still are. No one likes the idea of a bunch of renegades getting their hands on all those megatons. They felt the warheads might have been transferred to another trailer."

"So we continued looking and asking questions," said the grandson. "We traced the trailer several hundred more miles over back roads, and finally to the port of Magadan, on the Sea of Okhotsk. When we landed at the Magadan airport, the local customs chief had us picked up and almost incarcerated, and restricted us from going near the harbor area.

"Even when I told him seismic equipment had been stolen from one of our projects and we wanted to find it before it could be shipped out, he refused to cooperate. I had the feeling that someone had already gotten to him with a bribe.

"When the customs chief continued to balk, and also made sure no one else would answer our questions, we contacted officials in Moscow. Although the Weyland Foundation is viewed favorably by the Russian government, they delayed us for several more days. *Finally* we were given the information. No large cargo flights had left Magadan. The bay was still partially iced in, but icebreakers had escorted three cargo ships into port."

The grandson displayed a chart, with vessel names, tonnages, and sailing times. One ship was from Kobe, Japan, another from San Francisco. The third had brought construction equipment from Marseilles and was scheduled to return there.

"I queried the foundation's office in London for more information," said the grandson, "and they researched maritime records. On its last five voyages, the French ship made unscheduled stops in North Korea, Vietnam, Libya, and Iran."

"That's it," blurted the secretary of state. According to the chart, the French vessel had sailed that morning. Vernon Calico rose to his feet, charged with excitement.

The grandson raised a restraining hand. "I suggest you do nothing rash, Vern. At the most I'd place the ship under surveillance, at least until you know the destination."

"That's up to the President, Frank. If North Korea or Iran get their hands on eight nukes that big, they'll become gorillas overnight."

"I'm convinced there are no nukes involved."

"Considering the alternative, that's still a hell of a gamble."

"If you board their ship, it will be an act of war. Contact Paris and let them handle it."

"The French are hardheaded as plow mules. By the time we came to agreement, if we could agree, the ship might already be in North Korean waters."

"There are *no* nuclear weapons aboard the ship, Vern." Cyril looked at his grandson. "You're convinced of that?"

"Yes, sir. One, the stolen tractor-trailer was too different from the transporter described by the DIA. Two, the Russians would have searched more diligently if warheads were missing. Three, both the search team and the thieves were in the wrong military service. Finally, we had all three ships under surveillance most of the time they were in port, and nothing went aboard that vaguely resembled reentry vehicles."

Cyril nodded resolutely. "I'll go along with Frank's judgment," he told Vern Calico. "Tell the President we believe it's a false alarm."

Others of the handful voiced agreement.

"I'll relay your suggestion," said the secretary. He grinned at the grandson. "Thanks again, Frank."

"Let us know how it goes with the President," said the grandson.

"Sure will."

Cyril Weyland smiled, the expression stretching the parchment-thin skin of his face. "We have other business to attend to now, Mr. Secretary."

Vern Calico thanked the handful and left. It was no disgrace to be dismissed by Cyril Weyland. Presidents of the United States had been asked to leave the room while they discussed private matters or took their votes.

The next project was considered too sensitive for the secretary of state's ears. The government was susceptible to leaks, a fact recently emphasized when a disgruntled member of the House Intelligence Committee had blatantly released CIA secrets to the press.

The project leader for Black 277 had requested an emergency session with the handful. When the grandson had learned the details the previous evening, following his return from Russia, he'd changed the project's status to scarlet—emergency status. Except for the handful, only he was authorized to make such decisions.

As the project leader entered and took the podium, Cyril's grandson looked on with proprietary interest. He had managed 277 until being transferred to the Russian effort.

"As you know, I was a late arrival to the project," the leader said, then shook his head wryly at the grandson. "Thanks a lot, Frank. I didn't anticipate anything like this."

The project's purpose was to investigate the activities of a man named Salvator DiPalma, an obscenely wealthy Argentinean who had once been the youngest member of the Colonel's Revolution of 1944. As head of El Soleil, the largest banking institution in South America, DiPalma had become rich, and now threatened to militarize Argentina and influence the entire continent. His handpicked senior staff at El Soleil would wrest power during the upcoming national elections by eliminating and terrorizing the opposition. On three occasions, numbers of key officials and potential candidates had been murdered or simply disappeared. Insiders within El Soleil called the nights *truenos*, and there would be more of them.

If Salvator DiPalma was not stopped, he would become a tyrant of the worst kind, driven by a lust for power and a righteous spirit of ultra-nationalism.

The briefing would be short, an update to reveal the latest revelations, for the handful was familiar with the project. The project leader pressed buttons on the podium, and a map of Argentina appeared on a large television screen. Red circles flashed around two locations.

"There have been two developments," said the project leader. He pointed at the southernmost circle, highlighting a location just inland of bleak and windblown Punta Medanosa in Patagonia. It was the El Soleil research and development campus, funded by DiPalma's banking conglomerate soon after the end of the Falklands War.

"One of our informants at the campus passed the following photograph to us yesterday. He explained that two months ago a trailer-van was transported from the El Soleil campus to their test range. There it was given final check, and at seven a.m., when the wind was calm . . ."

The project leader pressed another button. An image of

a mushroom cloud appeared, rising high above the barren landscape. Several in the small audience drew gasps.

"Although it *appears* to be a nuclear explosion," said the project leader, "it is not. It is, however, a device of obvious power. We've learned that this was their fourth such test."

"It's not an nuclear weapon?" asked the woman on the handful.

"No, ma'am, but the device—whatever it is—releases a great amount of energy. As Frank pointed out to me, their intent may be to use it for mining excavation or some other peaceful purpose, but he still felt you should know what they're coming up with."

"Could the weapon be delivered by one of their rockets?" the woman asked. Scientists at the campus had developed modest-sized rockets to boost communications satellites into orbit.

"No, ma'am. The explosion came from a large trailer, and their Bolivar rockets don't have that sort of payload capability. Still, Frank's suspicious."

"I studied Salvator DiPalma at length," the grandson said from the side of the room. "He is amoral. I do *not* trust him, and believe he's capable of anything." He looked somberly at the group, then nodded for the project leader to continue.

The leader motioned to the second flashing red circle, about the metropolis near the mouth of the Rio de la Plata. "An informant planted in El Soleil's offices in Buenos Aires has failed to make contact for the past week. We checked her apartment, and she's missing. We believe DiPalma's people took her, and may now realize that someone's gathering information."

"The investigation is compromised?" Cyril asked.

"To some degree, yes, but Frank personally set the woman up so her contacts would be compartmented and she wouldn't know others involved."

"You met with the informant?" Cyril asked his grandson, showing concern.

"I was there at the time, and felt it was necessary. In the event of something like this, I didn't want her to be able to identify our people in-country. She used computer E-mail to pass her information to a blind source, and we paid her with deposits into an account."

"Did she know you were from the foundation?"

"It wasn't mentioned, but if DiPalma's people took her, they've got the resources to put it together. Still, they shouldn't be able to identify our investigators. They're all under deep cover."

"Stay away from South America until this is over," Cyril Weyland warned him.

"Yes, sir."

"How many people do we have in-country?" Cyril asked the project leader.

"Thirty-nine. Five in Patagonia, twelve in Buenos Aires, and the remainder scattered around the other major cities."

"How many informants?"

"Seventeen, not including the woman who's disappeared. Two are inside the campus, working on the rocket program. The photograph of the explosion came from one of them."

"Now they're all in harm's way. How quickly can you wrap up the project?"

"We've got some documentation on El Soleil's part in the assassinations and rigging the upcoming election, but we'll need more. Within three weeks we should have enough."

"Your recommendation?" asked Cyril Weyland.

"Continue until we've got the answers, then stop them prior to the elections."

"Do you agree?" Cyril asked his grandson.

"Yes, sir. It's critical that we prevent DiPalma from taking over."

"I'll let you both know our decision," said Cyril.

The project leader and the grandson left the room, for none but the handful could remain during the deliberations and vote taking.

Cyril waited until the door closed, then smiled. "Frank conducted himself admirably."

There were murmurs of assent.

"We'll begin with Green two-seven-nine."

The decision was difficult, for an enormous sum was involved and there were other worthwhile causes. Yet after a short discussion, then a vote, Estonia had been placed on a new course of prosperity. It was a minor country in the global scheme, but two powerful companies were about to be formed there—their backing and ownership untraceable.

Next they discussed the Argentine problem, Scarlet 277. While Colonel DiPalma was dangerous, and their personnel were in peril, the project was too important to drop. They decided to complete the investigation, then expose DiPalma and El Soleil before the national elections.

The handful stood to limber their aging muscles. Two of the men lit cigars, and the woman went to the bar, where she poured hot water from a porcelain pot over loose tea.

"Now we must decide the final issue," Weyland said. "My replacement as chairman."

The woman laughed lightly. "You've been setting us up for the past six years, Cyril."

"Frank is indispensable," said a member.

The issue was quickly decided. Weyland's grandson would not only assume Cyril's position on the financial board but would also take over as chairman. If the handful had known of the bloody consequence of their decision, they would have made it differently. But they did not, and a relentless chain of events was set into motion.

When the meeting was adjourned, Cyril Weyland returned to his office, where he was met by a vice-president who acted as his personal aide. Cyril also called in his senior secretary, a woman of proven loyalty who had been with him for more than twenty years, and told her to have the records department bring certain sensitive documents. They should use appropriate security.

As she went to her task, Cyril told his aide about the brief he wanted prepared. He would work in an adjacent, secure room. Once the brief was complete, it must remain under tight control. When he explained the purpose for the brief, the aide smiled.

As he finished, Cyril noted that the secretary had reentered his office and was standing nearby, appearing shaken. "A doctor called from Wisconsin," she blurted. "My mother's suffered a stroke." She had trouble continuing.

"Were you expecting it?"

"No." Her voice faltered. "I spoke with her on the phone just last night."

Cyril turned to the aide. "Tell transportation to prepare an airplane and crew for immediate departure, then have someone drive Ruth home to help her pack."

Northern Wisconsin

As soon as Ruth Batterhorn deplaned from the Learjet at the Rhinelander airport, which served the north woods of Wisconsin, she hurried into the terminal. She'd decided to rent a car and drive to Minocqua, the small town thirty miles distant where her mother had been hospitalized.

A very tall man, balding, with a prominent hawk's nose, approached. "Miss Batterhorn?"

Ruth blinked with surprise.

He introduced himself as the doctor who had spoken with her earlier. He was cadaverous and had a distinct European accent. "When I called back, your office was kind enough to give your arrival time."

Ruth feared the worst. "My mother?" Her voice trembled.

"I think it would be wise if we go there quickly. Let me help with your bags."

She followed almost blindly as they went out of the terminal and turned to their left, where a sedan waited. A pleasant-looking man with brown hair placed her luggage into the trunk as Ruth and the doctor took their seats in back.

"The truth," Ruth said in a low voice. "I must know, Doctor."

"I think it's best that we wait," said the physician.

A blond man in the front passenger seat turned to observe her, as if she held some odd fascination, then raised his hand to brush an unruly forelock in an effeminate gesture. He was young, thirtyish, and Ruth determined that he was an associate of the doctor's.

The pleasant man got into the driver's seat and wordlessly started the engine.

As they turned onto the highway, Ruth looked out through the darkened side glass at the heavily forested countryside. There were few permanent residents in the Wisconsin north woods. On weekends most of the vehicles had Illinois plates, driven by Chicagoans getting away for a few days of quiet respite. In mid-week like this, the traffic was light.

"It was thoughtful of you to come for me," Ruth said in a strained voice.

The doctor did not respond, just stared forward, his lips pursed.

When they'd driven for only twenty minutes, the driver slowed, then turned off on a side road. A sign read Tomahawk Lake.

As Ruth started to question, the doctor smiled. "*Now* it is time for truth."

She had not known anything could be so terrible, or so painful. They'd been in the lakeside cabin for less than an hour, but Ruth had already been subjected to unspeakable cruelty. She had told them secrets she'd vowed to tell no one, yet she had not known answers to the specific ones asked by the cadaverous man the others called Jaeger.

Ruth lay naked, sprawled on the floor in a bath of urine, feces, and blood. She'd swallowed several teeth, and felt bones snap as they'd been twisted and levered. There was little method about it. Whenever she failed to respond, Jaeger would hit her or break another limb—fingers or an arm—or step down hard on one of her already broken knees and pull upward on her foot, pausing only when the blond man asked another question. Ruth knew more pain than she'd experienced in a lifetime's accumulation. It came in great waves, like a relentless, surging tide, each more awful than the one that had come before. There was no respite, no hint of mercy.

The excruciating waves continued as the effeminate blond man knelt at her side. His voice was high and held a lisp. "There's no reason for this to continue, Miss Batterhorn. I am a businessman, and I'm thoroughly repulsed. Tell me what I want, and I'll order him to stop and have you taken to a hospital."

Ruth was crying, as she'd done since Jaeger had begun to destroy her body, but she was also desperately trying to listen.

"It makes sense that you wouldn't know everything we've asked for, but surely you know where we can find it."

She choked out the words. "In the . . . Weyland Foundation . . . Building. In . . . the records . . . department."

"We can't go there, Miss Batterhorn. There must be another place."

She continued to cry.

"Perhaps a courier service? An executive? Perhaps one of the those called the handful, who takes records home with him?"

"It's ... not allowed."

The effeminate man sighed. "Then he will continue until your memory improves."

Jaeger came closer, his mouth twisted in a smile that held no mirth. Ruth Batterhorn cringed, then cried out from the agony the slight movement had brought.

She thought of the project assigned to Cyril Weyland's aide.

"There's a brief," she blurted.

"Tell us about it," said the man called Jaeger in his rumbling voice.

When she'd told them everything about the brief, and had explained her understanding of where it would be taken, how, and by whom, Ruth begged to be taken to the medical facility as the effeminate man had promised.

The others left the room then, and Jaeger unbuckled his belt and lowered his trousers. His crooked grin grew as he knelt.

She did not mind the forced sex nearly as much as the agony when her broken limbs were twisted and jarred. When he'd finished, Ruth begged again, this time for death.

It was not that easy.

Part I

The Leather Folder

1

FRIDAY, JUNE 7

6:05 A.M.—Washington National Airport

Lincoln Anderson parked his aging pickup in one of the reserved spaces in front of the building, and looked up at the new sign. The lettering was gold, on a background of royal blue, the same shade as their new flight jackets and the airplanes owned by the company.

Executive Connections
PRIVATE CHARTER AIRLINE

Henry N. Hoblit, chief operating officer of the firm, pulled up in his DeVille, and got out beside him.

"It looks nice, Henry." When business had begun falling off, Henry had blamed at least part of it on their mundaneness and lack of class, and had kept harping until the other partners agreed that the logo, signs, and uniforms could be replaced.

"How's Lucky doing?" Henry asked. Link's adoptive father, a retired three-star general and majority owner of the firm, was suffering from a heart condition. Henry had known Lucky Anderson when they'd served together in the Air Force. Their entire staff—including pilots, flight attendants, mechanics, and even secretaries—were ex-military, from the different services.

"About the same." Link reached into the seat to retrieve his canvas flight bag. He was tall and athletic—with even features, dark hair and eyes, and an easy smile. He was a private man, not profuse with words.

Henry stared at the pickup, working to keep something akin to a sneer from his expression. "Young bachelor like you needs a status symbol, Link. I know where you can pick up a two-year-old Corvette at a sweetheart price."

Link locked the truck's door, then slammed it closed. He was amused by Henry Hoblit's uneasiness about the elderly, somewhat battered pickup occupying a reserved parking spot near his new sign. Lincoln Anderson did not spend his time worrying about such things. The truck was paid for, functional and adequate for his needs.

"Think about it. A bachelor pilot with a Corvette?" Henry laughed. "The Washington matrons would be dragging their daughters off to convents."

"My fiancée might disagree, Henry. Anyway, you keep me too busy to get into mischief."

Henry Hoblit gave up the argument as they started for the front door. "There's a change in today's schedule. You'll be flying to Teterboro with Billy in the G-four."

Teterboro Airport was located across the George Washington Bridge from New York City. Although they also had another Gulfstream, two Learjets, and three propeller-driven aircraft, the G-IV was the most luxurious of their fleet.

Hoblit tried the door and found it open, then held it wide for Link. "You'll pick up the Dubois family and fly them to Monterey, California"

Link found himself smiling. It would be the first time they exercised the new contract, and he'd been looking forward to meeting with his old friend.

Hoblit lowered his voice, as if revealing a secret. "I asked around about Frank Dubois after you pulled off the deal. Big money on both sides of his family. They say he'll be one of the wealthiest men in America when his grandfather dies."

"Should be a good contract," was all Link said.

Frank had been a squadron mate in his fighter unit in the Gulf War, and they'd shared a room. It had been common knowledge that Dubois was well off, that the males of his family served an obligatory tour of military duty before moving into the security of their riches, but Frank Dubois had been a regular guy and they'd become close. Henry was likely overstating his worth, but even if it was true, Link couldn't imagine his friend changing. Frank had been an easygoing type who took things in stride.

Henry gushed on. "Dubois' secretary called in the flight request yesterday afternoon. She said they arrange things at the last minute like that for security reasons."

Link thought it must be a pain for Frank's family, having to live in fear of kidnapping.

"Mr. Dubois requested you specifically. He also wants time at the controls. That's why I'm sending Billy along." Billy Bowes was their chief pilot and flight examiner.

"Frank's a good pilot," Link said, "and Billy's even better. They'll get along."

"His secretary said he's qualified in the Gulfstream. Still, we may have to nursemaid him some, and Billy's . . . you know . . . a bit rough around the edges, and we *need* this contract. See if you can make sure he doesn't say something to upset Mr. Dubois."

Link smiled. "Pig-foot Dubois is hard to upset."

Henry's jaw drooped.

"That was Frank's nickname because of the way he stomped on the rudder in flight school. When we spoke on the phone, I reminded him."

Henry preferred to keep things in more proper perspective. "*Mr.* Dubois asked for an experienced attendant, because his wife gets nervous when she flies. I'm pulling Jackie Chang off another flight." Henry went to his office looking apprehensive, as if he was sure there was something he hadn't thought of that they might screw up.

Manhattan

Frank pulled on his robe, quietly closed the bedroom door, then went to his study. As he entered he glanced at the door mirror and grimaced. He looked forward to seeing his old squadron and room mate Link Anderson, but wished he was in a semblance of the physical condition he'd been in when they'd flown together. Anderson likely would be. Frank remembered his friend as agile and efficient at everything he tried, the rare kind of no-nonsense person who reached decisions quickly, then moved with fluid, athletic grace to accomplish them.

Tomorrow he vowed to begin a new regime. As soon as he awoke at the bungalow in Big Sur, he'd do the morning exercises he'd ignored for too long, then take a run on the beach. Cap off the morning with eighteen holes at Pebble Beach. There'd be three weeks of golf, tennis, and loafing with his wife and daughter. Paula and Katy had been at odds recently, bickering over inconsequentials, and he hoped the time might also draw them together.

He heard noises outside. The cook was up. Frank often joined the household staff for breakfast before going to work. Paula and Katy normally awoke later and ate in the second shift. This morning was different. For the next twenty days they'd do everything together.

There were several photographs in the study. On the wall beside him were informal shots of the important people in Frank's life. To his right were family photos, with individual views of Paula and Katy, and a recent one with the three of them together. Next were his grandparents, the Weylands and Duboises. Left-most were two older photographs, reminders of a former, gentler existence.

Frank's eyes paused on the aging photos. The first was of a sturdy man and a slight woman, a self-conscious girl and a pleasant-faced boy. In the second, the same man and boy stared back, carrying shotguns, wearing padded shooting vests and wide smiles. The man was his father, the boy himself. The photo had been taken on his thirteenth birthday. His father had made each of birthdays special. A gift was always presented and an impression made.

His father's family lived and breathed old traditions. A custom handed down from the first Dubois in the New World, who had arrived in Louisiana from pre-Napoleonic France, was that once each year parents should impress an important lesson upon their children. That thirteenth year he'd been given the Citori over-and-under shotgun he'd clutched so proudly in the photograph. His father had flown the two of them up to the lodge for an afternoon of trap shooting. The lesson had been about responsibility. He was approaching manhood, and there were obligations that a man must bear. Foremost, he must provide for his family and those he employed, and make sure they were safe from harm and mental anguish.

A month later he'd asked to remain behind in Baton Rouge while his father flew the rest of the family to New Orleans for a sailing excursion into the Gulf of Mexico. On their first day out, fumes had accumulated in the auxiliary engine bay of their sailing yacht, and been ignited by an errant spark. His parents, sister, and the two crewmen had been killed in the explosion.

Frank had blamed himself. Over the years the guilt had

receded as he'd realized how presumptuous he'd been, but a niggling belief remained that if he'd gone they wouldn't have perished.

He had not remained in Louisiana. His mother had been an only child, and as the sole surviving Weyland grandchild, Frank had come to his grandparents' Long Island estate to live. He'd been immersed in their lifestyle—and his grandfather's belief that when the dignity of any man was destroyed, all men were threatened. His grandfather had understood commitment, and when he'd finished his graduate degree at Princeton, Frank had served in his country's military service, as Dubois men had done since the War of 1812. He'd become a fighter pilot, as his father had been before him. Six years later he'd returned to work at his grandfather's side in the Weyland Foundation.

The door to the study opened and his daughter peered in. Katy was barely fourteen, but she was maturing at a mindboggling pace, which accounted for some of the friction growing between herself and Paula. The vacation meant she'd miss an important competition—she was a superb swimmer, approaching championship ability. Katy said she understood, but Frank doubted that was so. He vowed to make it up somehow.

"Mom's up and breakfast is almost ready. Are you hungry?" she asked.

"We'll eat together this morning." He'd missed his wife and daughter when he'd been away in Russia, chasing after the phantom nose-cone transporter.

"For the next three weeks, let's do *everything* together, Dad."

He slapped her raised hand as he got to his feet. "That's a deal."

"No work, Dad?" She thought he spent too much time at it.

"We'll leave all that toil back here for the work slaves."

The three of them chattered away during breakfast, talking about the wonderful time before them. Then Frank took a phone call and smiled apologetically. "I've been asked to drop by the foundation before we go. They're sending transportation."

Twenty minutes later Frank climbed aboard a helicopter, which was waiting—rotors idling—on the rooftop helipad.

As soon as he'd buckled in, the pilot took off. The ride took less than five minutes. When they landed atop the Weyland Foundation Building, the eighth largest structure in New York, he was met by the vice-president who served as his grandfather's aide.

"What's it about?" Frank asked as they walked toward the rooftop entrance.

"They set up the meeting yesterday. That's all I know, Frank." The aide was having difficulty suppressing a smile, and Frank believed he knew more.

The private elevator was paneled in northern California oak, as were many of the foundation's offices, for Frank's grandfather liked the particular shade and grain. They got off at the twenty-seventh floor and approached the guarded entrance of the financial board's summit room. The aide wished Frank good luck, opened the door for him, and remained outside. No one was allowed in the summit room unless specifically bidden.

The handful were at the opposite end of the room, seated in overstuffed leather chairs set about a large, thick Persian rug. As usual the men were in suits, the woman in a dark dress. Frank had dressed hastily, pulling on the casual clothing he'd wear on the flight to California. As he approached, he wished he'd selected something more formal.

Cyril Weyland regarded him with a sly and capricious look. "I see you're ready to go out and lie in the sun while we continue slaving."

Frank grinned, thinking of similar words he'd spoken to his daughter. "Yes, sir, and I promise not to feel guilty."

Cyril's eyes twinkled. "Well, go on out there and get the laziness out of your system. When you return we're going to put you to work."

"A new project?"

"You might say that."

Frank started to take a vacant chair.

"I think you should remain standing, Frank. We've got something to tell you."

The board members had flutes of Dom Perignon set on their side tables. His grandfather motioned him toward an extra one, similarly filled.

"This occasion marks only the fourth time in our history that we've dragged out champagne this early."

Frank picked up the glass and held it to his chest, wondering as the board members—except for one who was wheelchair-bound—all rose.

Cyril raised his flute. "I present the new chairman of the Weyland Foundation."

Frank looked about. They were all staring . . . at *him*.

"As for me," his grandfather said, "I plan to go fishing. This moment belongs to you."

"Here, here," said an octogenarian, and they all—except Frank—drained their glasses. Frank was too stunned to join them, frozen into position with his flute half raised. He'd known he would become a member of the handful upon his grandfather's retirement, but the chairmanship? Other of the financial board members, older and—he believed—more astute, were gathered in the room.

"You'd better drink your champagne," the only woman said impishly. "Otherwise they'll think I made a bad selection. I picked the year very specially, Frank."

Frank Dubois remained speechless. When he finally downed the champagne, the others chuckled and politely clapped.

"You've got your three weeks of freedom before you take over," Cyril told him, "but the responsibility starts now. As you'll soon learn, you can't get away from it."

He explained that the chairman couldn't allow his knowledge to become dated, even while on vacation. A brief had been prepared, showing the foundation's past and current projects. Frank was to study it and digest the full scope of their endeavors. There'd be daily encrypted faxes sent to the bungalow, keeping him posted with up-to-the-minute developments. Upon his return Frank would be expected to be prepared to assume the chairmanship.

"This afternoon we'll advise the President of our decision," said his grandfather, then went on . . . but Frank hardly heard him over the shock and enormity of the situation. He went from one to the other, shaking hands and accepting congratulations, but still only half believing.

"Now, get on out of here and enjoy your vacation," said Cyril Weyland.

When he reached the door, Frank turned back. The members were watching, smiling smugly as if pleased with themselves. "Thank you," he said earnestly.

Outside, his grandfather's aide was waiting. "There was

a message from the secretary of state," he said. "He'd like a call over a secure line."

Frank hesitated, still heady with excitement. He'd hardly thought of the projects all morning and considered ignoring the call. Finally he sighed. "Have the folder for Blue two-eight-three sent to my office."

"You won't need it, sir. Cyril had me prepare a summary of all of our projects. It should contain everything you'll need." He introduced him to Gary, a burly young security officer who carried a monogrammed leather folder, gave him a last wide grin, and returned to his office.

Frank walked down the corridor, the guard close on his heels.

"So you're in charge of the folder?" Frank asked amiably.

"Yes, sir. I'm to look after it so you won't have to lug it around."

"Tough duty," Frank said. "I guess that means you'll have to come along to Big Sur and take in all those bikinis."

The security guard grinned as they entered Frank's outer office.

"Get the secretary of state on a secure line," Frank told his administrative assistant, then took the folder from Gary and stepped into his inner sanctum. He was leafing through the brief when the assistant's voice came over the intercom.

Frank picked up line ten, and waited until the Secure light blinked on.

Vern Calico's voice was tinny. "The navy jumped on it like a blue-tick hound after a scared rabbit, Frank. They boarded the vessel about six hours ago."

Frank was incredulous. "The President ignored our recommendation?"

"Yeah." The secretary of state released a breath. "There was nothing illegal on board."

Frank had trouble maintaining a calm voice. "I told you, Vern. It was a false alarm. There were *no* nukes involved."

"The French ambassador's livid, and I'm having trouble keeping a lid on things. Our President's going to make a personal call to theirs to brief him on what we were looking for."

"That should have been done before the boarding."

"Maybe. Anyway, the President's asking for more information, and he's not very happy. Could be, he'll be looking for a scapegoat."

"Did you tell him our recommendation was for surveillance only?"

"Sure I did. But I also said you hadn't watched the ship *all* the time, and they *could* have loaded the nukes without your people seeing."

"We're not taking responsibility, Vern. Period. Both you and the President ignored our recommendations."

"I took a gamble, believing it was for good purpose. I'll need your support, Frank. I've got to tell the President something so he won't think we were rash."

"Not we, Vern, and I do think you were rash." Frank glanced at his watch. "I'm on my way to California with my family. When I get there, I'll give you a call."

Calico paused, then dropped to a quieter voice. "There was another thing I wanted to bring up yesterday, Frank, but I forgot in all the excitement. A certain agency of ours has an ongoing investigation in Argentina. I hear you have a similar one under way."

Frank hesitated, then spoke calmly, trying to mask his surprise. "If there is one, it's not my project, Vern." That was the truth. He was off the project.

"Look into it, would you? Maybe call off what you're doing so our efforts won't interfere."

Frank continued to frown as he hung up. Since 1951 the foundation had been provided with an administrative tie within the CIA to ensure duplications did not occur—a *hidden* link, so if queried the director could deny all knowledge or involvement. It was unlikely that Vern knew about the arrangement. Frank wondered if he should take the vacation, with all that was going on. His decision was quickly made. He could think just as well on the cliffhanger fifth hole at Pebble Beach as he could here in New York. Likely better.

When he passed through the outer office, both his grandfather's aide and the young security guard—now carrying a hang-up bag—fell into step. As they walked the aide briefed him about a new development in Scarlet 277. The female informant's body had washed up on a beach between La Plata and Buenos Aires. She'd been in the water for several days, but it appeared that she'd been beaten to death. El Soleil was now conducting a methodical witch-hunt for other turncoats within their ranks.

Frank nodded grimly and started to pass on what Vern Calico had told him—that there might be a duplication of efforts with the government—but decided to wait until he'd thought about it more.

As they boarded the elevator to return to the roof, he was told that Gary was aware of their communications nets, and would remain in constant contact with the Weyland Foundation. Guards would escort Frank and his family to the airport, and others would meet them at Monterey and drive them to Big Sur. Access to the bungalow would be restricted by teams of security agents. They were to protect the family, but the guards had also been told about the folder. If there was a problem, the contents were to be destroyed, preferably by burning.

Flight EC-992, Washington National Airport

The royal blue Gulfstream IV taxied to the number one position at the end of the runway. The queen mother of luxury jets was low-slung and sleek, with swept wings and sharply angled winglets to provide added stability. Powerful jet engines were mounted in pods, one on either side of the aft fuselage, and they whispered as they idled.

When the tower operator cleared them for takeoff, Link Anderson released brakes and eased the throttles forward. There was no hesitation. The Rolls Royce Tay turbofans were built with the same profound precision as the legendary cars that bore the RR emblem. At the proper speed he rotated the nose with a steady grip on the yoke and moved his right hand to the stainless steel throttles, a habit to ensure neither crept back during the critical takeoff phase. The gear stopped their rumbling noise, and the airplane sprinted skyward like an eager greyhound.

"Not bad," Billy Bowes commented from the right seat.

Link knew it was a damn good takeoff, but he couldn't crow. The Gulfstream was an honest lady, so easy to fly it *made* her pilots look good. He turned on the auto-throttle and let the computer handle the power settings as they climbed.

Billy's tone changed to business. "I've got a seven-sixty-seven at our two o'clock high, descending. Probably landing at Dulles."

Departure Control directed him to contact Baltimore and gave a frequency. Link switched to the second radio and told Baltimore Control that Echo Charlie Niner-Niner-Two was airborne out of National, turning to a heading of zero-three-zero degrees and climbing for flight level two-niner-zero. Destination was Teterboro Airport.

Baltimore had him on their radar and told him to continue the climb.

Abraham Lincoln Anderson loved to fly. He'd completed his orientation flights with a Gulfstream factory instructor pilot, and also the series of mandatory check rides that had to be accomplished before he could be turned loose as a flight captain.

Billy Bowes watched as he began the long loop around the Washington prohibited area. "Keep up the good work and maybe the company will keep you around."

Billy joked about Link's father being the majority shareholder of Executive Connections. Lieutenant General Paul "Lucky" Anderson, USAF retired, was president. Glenn Phillips, the senior senator from Florida and a longtime friend of Lucky's, had made the second largest investment, but he'd placed his shares in a blind trust to eliminate the possibility of a conflict of interest charge. Henry N. Hoblit was chief operating officer, and a partner. Billy Bowes held the least shares, but he did a lot of the flying and his business card read "chief pilot." His father had told Link to listen closely to Billy. It was sound advice. Bowes was a superb pilot.

Jackie Chang leaned forward in the jump seat behind Link. She was tall and trim, with soft Eurasian eyes. "Either of you need anything from the back?" Jackie was known for her diplomacy and the way she could handle difficult clients. Link was pleased she was along. They'd be spending the night in Monterey, and Jackie was a good conversationalist. In 1991 she'd been an Army lieutenant, a helicopter pilot forced down in Iraq when her chopper had been damaged. She'd been sexually abused and terribly beaten. When she'd returned to the States and been discharged, Link's father had hired her to take charge of their flight attendants.

"I'll take coffee," said Billy.

"Link?" she asked. He shook his head, and Jackie went back.

They passed through ten thousand feet, now steady on the northerly heading.

"Who are these clients again?" Billy asked, watching as Link continued the climb-out.

"Guy named Frank Dubois and his wife and daughter. It's part of a contract we signed with the Weyland Foundation."

"Henry says they're big," said Billy. "What do they do?"

"Give grants to needy artists, put on benefits for the poor, buy and sell small continents—crap like that. Frank Dubois' grandfather is Cyril Weyland, and he runs it."

"How did we get hooked up?"

"Frank and I were in the Air Force together. We served in the same squadron in Saudi and shared a room. Frank's highly intelligent, maybe brilliant. He's a good pilot and a good friend, the kind of guy you can rely on."

Billy nodded. "Combat builds friendships that last. That's why your father pulled Henry, Glenn, and me into the company. He'd flown with us in wartime."

"When Dad said the company needed a boost, I called Frank to ask if he knew anyone in the shaker-and-mover circles who might want to use us, and he said he'd get back. Next week, out of the blue, we were offered a big retainer and a contract from the Weyland Foundation. They guaranteed five hundred thousand a year so long as we drop everything at a moment's notice to cart their executives' families wherever they want to go."

"You'd think an outfit that big would have their own fleet."

"They do, but Frank wanted us for some of their private hauling."

"Sounds like a sweetheart deal, like Henry said."

"Dad wasn't sure. He didn't like the idea of screwing up other clients by having to jump when they decide to fly somewhere. I tried to stay neutral, but Henry wanted the contract bad."

Billy chuckled. "Henry loves to rub elbows with anyone whose name he can drop at a party. I'll bet he was laying on all the charm to convince your dad."

"He's very persuasive."

"Henry's sorta like baby shit. Smooth, but sometimes there's a hell of an aftertaste."

Link grinned at the description.

"Henry was damned good in combat," Billy added, to soften his joke.

"Anyway, Dad knew we could use the business and he didn't argue for long."

Jackie came back into the cabin to give Billy his coffee. "If you need anything," she said, "call over the loudspeaker. I'll be in back, making sure everything's ready."

"Have a nice nap," Billy called behind her.

"Hey, I do all the work and I get flak from a bus driver?"

"Link's driving. I'm just along to make sure you both do everything right."

"Keep your eyes on the road," Jackie said cheerfully, and went on back.

Billy shook his head. "If I was a couple years younger, I'd be loping along behind her."

"I'd advise against it. Jackie's boyfriend's the size of a standard doorway and doesn't smile much." As he leveled out at twenty-nine thousand feet, Link notified the flight center and was told to continue on course.

"How's Lucky these days?" Billy asked. "I've been meaning to go out to the Farmhouse to visit him for the past week. I guess the roto-rooter didn't work so good."

Link's parents lived on a rural Falls Church property, in a grand old home they called the Farmhouse. Two months earlier, his father had undergone laser angioplasty to blast away the gunk in his arteries. They'd also implanted a new, smarter kind of pacemaker.

"His heartbeat's still irregular," Link said. When Lucky Anderson had called him in Montana and asked him to come to Washington to look after his end of the business until he was better, Link hadn't hesitated. His father didn't ask favors frivolously.

Billy shook his head glumly at the turn of events. "I met your dad in Thailand, when we were flying combat over North Vietnam. Lucky was a hell of a flight leader. Best I ever had."

Link had heard the story from his father. Captain Billy Bowes, a Cherokee Indian from Oklahoma, had been one of his favorites, even though he'd tended to get into inordinate amounts of trouble.

Baltimore Control radioed and asked them to give their Executive Connections office a call on a different frequency.

Henry Hoblit responded to their radio call with guarded words. Billy's niece had been in an automobile accident. "A nurse phoned from the hospital," Henry said. "Your niece's leg's broken and she's banged up. Nothing life-threatening, but she's asking for you, Billy."

After his brother had died, Billy had raised his niece and two nephews. They were close. As Billy mulled it over, Link told Henry they'd return to National.

"I'd rather you continue on course," Hoblit said. "The Beech Baron's at Teterboro, where we left it for radio repairs. Billy can bring the Baron back to Washington, and I'll send another pilot to take his place on the G-four. Shouldn't be more than an hour's delay."

Billy asked Henry Hoblit where his niece had been taken.

"A hospital in Arlington. Only the broken leg and a few bruises and scratches."

Billy made up his mind. "I'll take the Beech and see you back there at"—he computed in his head—"fourteen-thirty hours."

Link remembered something. "Henry, the client's a fully qualified pilot, and he's current in the Gulfstream. How about letting him take the right seat?"

"The contract reads that we'll supply two pilots and a flight attendant."

"Let's give him his choice. He wanted time at the controls anyway."

Hoblit paused as he digested the words.

Billy keyed the radio. "I'll give you a call from Teterboro after we talk with Dubois."

"Do that. But make damned sure we meet all the rules."

Manhattan

Frank came back through the front door and made his way past luggage piled in the foyer, still numbed by the news of his appointment. The bodyguard trailed closely behind, carrying the leather folder.

He'd decided to tell Paula ... then changed his mind. He'd wait until they arrived at Big Sur and start out the vacation right. She would be as stunned as he'd been. Frank had spent much of his lifetime preparing for the task, but she'd shared the last fifteen years and put in her own efforts. Big Sur would be a good place for a fitting celebration.

With great difficulty he switched from business to his home role. "Everything ready to go?" Frank asked cheerfully.

"All except Mom's bags," Katy said with a tinge of causticness. "She's *still* dressing."

Frank ignored the innuendo, closed a catch on a suitcase, and looked about: two carry-on bags, six large suitcases, and two golf bags. Paula would bring as much herself.

Katy spoke to Vanessa, their household staff director: "Tell the doorman to have them bring three luggage carts." Her voice was authoritative and sure.

Paula swept into the room, hair coiffed, makeup in place, wearing low heels and a clinging blue silk dress that accentuated her sensuous body. To Frank she remained as breathtakingly beautiful as she'd been when they'd met, although in a subtly different, softer way.

"Do you like the dress?" Paula asked.

"It's very pretty," Frank said truthfully. He'd advised them to dress comfortably for the flight, and he and Katy had opted for loose-fitting sportswear. He started to remind Paula, but stopped himself. She'd been like that for the past month, overdressing and never emerging from her room unless everything about her was precisely in place. The change had come after her last birthday, so it likely had something to do with vanity and fear of aging. He couldn't complain. Paula was intelligent, understanding about his peculiarities and incessant work habits, and the only human with whom he shared his secrets. In their years together, they'd grown comfortable with each other, and much of the credit was hers.

Katy was not as charitable. "We're going on an *airplane*, not to a wedding." She rolled her eyes dramatically.

Frank glanced at his watch. Their transportation would arrive at any moment—two limousines, for a second vehicle would be necessary for the luggage. Another vehicle would follow, carrying their ever present security guards.

"Check to make sure we've got everything," Paula told Vanessa.

Katy grimaced. "Any more and we'd need a semi to carry it to the airplane."

Paula gave Gary a quizzical look, so Frank introduced them. Neither Paula nor Katy seemed surprised. Bodyguards were an integral part of their lives.

As they waited for the limos, Frank wandered into his study, his mind lingering on the momentous news he'd received. As he took a final look about, his eyes paused on the old photos.

Frank wished his parents were alive so he could tell them about the appointment. He touched the glass over their image. As a young man, several times he'd flown down to visit his relatives in Louisiana and tried to fit in, gone bass fishing and bird hunting with them, but he'd only found that his accent had grown harsher and his mind filled with Yankee impatience. Regardless of his efforts, he'd been unable to recapture the magical time of his childhood.

"Do you miss them?" Katy had entered quietly and caught him in his contemplation.

"Sometimes," he admitted.

"Your mother was pretty."

"So's yours, sport."

His daughter carefully maintained a neutral face, and Frank decided that he'd touched upon yet another sensitive subject between mother and daughter. He understood little of it, and remained an outsider in their ongoing squabble.

"Katy?" Paula called from the other room.

"Oh, yeah. Mom said the drivers are on their way up, and she's all nervous." Paula had a small case of fear of flying, another fact that drew Katy's scorn.

"We're all on vacation. Try for a little less sarcasm and more cooperation."

Katy sighed, as if he had just given her a Herculean task, as he followed her into the foyer, where Paula was briefing the staff about what was to be done during their absence.

He went to their bedroom and began lugging his wife's suitcases to the foyer. There were five, most very large and so heavy he wondered if she hadn't included her exercise weights. Gary, the powerfully built bodyguard who would accompany them, entered the room from the kitchen as Frank hauled the final piece of luggage into position.

"Good timing," Frank said as he blew out a breath.

2

1:35 P.M.—The White House

The President was irked that a damage-control meeting was necessary so early in his term, but unless something was done his administration could suffer a black eye for a perfectly well-intentioned act.

The previous evening he'd reluctantly approved the interception and boarding of a vessel of French registry, believing a source of information he'd previously considered unimpeachable. The threat of nuclear weapons in the hands of unstable regimes was unthinkable, however, and his Secretary of State, while equally hesitant to order the military option, had briefed that coordination with the government of France would take an unacceptable amount of time. So the President had approved the action, and his National Security Council had met through most of the night as the U.S. Navy had carried it through. But there had been no nuclear weapons aboard the ship, and the captain—and now the French government—were livid.

Seated about the conference table were his White House press spokesperson, chief of staff, national security adviser, and his international affairs adviser and secretary of state, Vernon M. Calico.

"I suggest we downplay the affair," the chief of staff was saying. "Explain that a mistake has taken place, apologize to the French, and just let it blow over. There are too many other things happening in the world for John Q. Citizen to worry about it for long."

"That would be great," said the press spokesperson, "if the media would go along. The honeymoon's over, gentlemen. They're looking for an excuse to barbecue us as they do all administrations. I'd prefer that we be as open as possible, tell them how the information came available to the

CIA, then how the President acted in the best interest of the world community."

The President almost corrected her about the intelligence source, then held his tongue. Soon after he'd taken office he'd been briefed about the contributions of the Weyland Foundation and agreed that all contact with them was to be maintained in secrecy. Hell, FDR and all of the presidents since had taken the same pledge, and all had benefited from the arrangement.

He wished Vern Calico would join the conversation. He'd been invaluable with such advice since early in the presidential campaign, when he'd switched from backing the front-runner and brought his expertise to the camp of the dark horse. The election committee had been electrified with Vern's energy, and adopted his dictum that "Maybe winning ain't everything, but it's sure to hell better'n the alternative." More than anyone, Calico was responsible for his victory, and he trusted his judgment in critical matters.

His chief of staff spoke. "It might just be better to let the French and the press take the lead, then build a counterargument. Maybe there won't be much to it."

"I disagree," said the press spokesperson. "We should take the initiative and be first with the truth. That way there can be no surprises." She preferred openness in all things, and felt that the worst possible option was to be caught in a lie.

For a moment the President wondered if she wasn't right. Yet the situation was sensitive and what he'd authorized had turned out dead wrong ... and a more politic approach was likely required.

Vern Calico formed a wry smile. "Maybe both of you're right. We got a saying in east Texas. When a blue norther heads your way, get ready, then hunker down and let her blow."

"Do nothing?" the spokesperson asked incredulously.

"I didn't say that, honey. Get ready means to do what's necessary, but not *too* much. Maybe prepare a short statement how we acted for the good on available intelligence."

"It would be better if we were candid. Explain how the decision was made."

Calico shook his head. "We got another sayin'. Tell folks about your mistakes often enough, and they'll start believing all you do is make 'em. Best thing to do right now is act like we did the right thing, and we'd do it again if it's called for."

Twenty minutes later, the meeting broke up. The press spokesperson would prepare a short statement to the White House media that the President, reacting quickly and upon the best intelligence available at the time, had ensured that nuclear weapons had not been placed in the hands of irresponsible nations. To have done less would have been an abdication of his role as leader of the world community. He had forwarded his regrets to the French president. There would be nothing more said about the event.

As the others departed the room, Vern Calico remained in his seat, a sign that he had something for the President's ears alone.

The President waited until the door closed, then released a breath. "Thank you for the input, Vern. I just wish it hadn't been necessary."

Calico nodded. "Neither one of us is gonna come out of this looking good. The foundation gave us a bad recommendation."

"We'll have to examine what they say much closer in the future."

"Maybe." Calico raised an eyebrow. "I just got a message they wanted passed on to you. They named a new chairman, old Cyril's grandson."

"Is that good?"

"Frank Dubois is smarter'n a treed coon. It was the codgers on the handful that insisted you send in the navy. They're getting senile and prone to make mistakes. If it weren't for Frank taking over an' keeping them calmed down, I'd say we wouldn't be able to trust 'em a little bit."

Teterboro Airport

Link looked out the cockpit window as two limousines pulled in beside the jet. Another vehicle drove up beyond them, and four uniformed guards looked on. As the drivers went to the rearmost vehicle to unload luggage, a gangling teenage girl bounded out and walked toward the nose of the airplane to observe the airport operation. *Frank's daughter?* he wondered.

He continued the cockpit pre-flight. The EFIS—

electronic flight instrument systems—checked properly on the six CRT displays. Link entered that there'd be six persons aboard, glanced out at the tremendous amount of luggage, and made it eight for calculation purposes. The computer would add the weight of the fuel and provide optimum takeoff and cruise data. Satisfied, he started back to greet the clients and tell them the bad news about the delay.

A stunningly beautiful woman peered through the hatch into the lounge area, and Link vaguely remembered photos Frank Dubois had shown of his wife. Her features were delicate and even, her lips full. She had green eyes and honey blond hair, gathered about her face and gracing her shoulders so naturally that he knew every position of every lock had been planned.

She showed white teeth and a nice smile. "You must be Frank's friend."

"Yes, ma'am. Link Anderson."

"Paula Dubois," she said, and shook his hand in a delicate grasp.

"Welcome aboard," Link said with a correct smile that would have pleased Henry Hoblit.

The girl he'd seen previously entered, glanced around, and jauntily went on back.

"That little tornado was our daughter, Katy."

The heavier luggage would be placed in the baggage hold at the rear of the aircraft, but a driver struggled in with an armload of carry-on bags. Close behind him came a pleasant-looking man with brown hair and eyes, dressed in blue jeans, loafers, and knit polo shirt.

"It's been awhile, Frank," Link said in greeting.

Frank Dubois's eyes crinkled in recognition. He laughed lightly as he shifted a leather folder and shook his hand. "Good to see you, Link. You're the captain?"

"It's turned out that way. Our chief pilot's niece was in a car accident and he's been recalled to Washington. The company wants to fly another pilot up from Washington."

"Forget it. I'll be your copilot and we'll share gossip."

"I'd like that, but Billy'd have to approve. He's in flight ops, checking on the weather."

Jackie Chang appeared near the bulkhead. "Everything's ready for you back there."

"Could I trouble you for a Perrier water?" Paula asked.

"Certainly, ma'am. Anything for you, sir?"

"No, thank you."

As Jackie hurried to her task, Paula made her way toward the rear cabin. Frank Dubois' eyes followed her, and Link couldn't help noting the warmth in his expression.

Billy Bowes came through the entry hatch. "Is this Mr. Dubois?"

"Call me Frank," Dubois said as he shook his hand.

"Sorry I took so long. A storm front's moving up from the four corners into your flight path, so I refiled to take you farther north. I left the takeoff time as it was, so Link will have to radio them about the delay while we fly up another pilot."

"There's no need," said Frank. "I'm checked out and current in the Gulfstream."

"Link mentioned that, but our office thinks it may violate our agreement."

"I dictated the contract, Mr. Bowes. Now I'm making a verbal change. We'll stick to the original takeoff time . . . unless you're concerned about my flying ability."

Billy shook his head. "Link vouched for you. You'll have to take the right seat for takeoff and landing, to make sure you're clear of air traffic. FAA rules require it."

"I'll spend most of the flight in the cockpit. It's safer and I need the flying time."

Billy regarded Link. "You and Jackie hole up in Monterey until we get a backup copilot out there. That may take an extra day."

"The Weyland Foundation will pick up any extra costs." Frank Dubois turned back to his friend. "Stay with us, Link. We've got plenty of room for your flight attendant too."

"We'll do that." Link looked at Billy. "What's our new route?"

"Pittsburgh, Kansas City, Boulder, Ogden, then try to beat the front to Tonopah and head direct to Monterey. I show five hours-forty en route, but you'll be able to shave some off."

"I'd better check the baggage bay," Link said, glancing outside.

"Already taken care of and buttoned up," Billy told him. "I'll get my flight bag and head back to Washington." He disappeared into the passenger compartment, where Link heard him introducing himself to Paula and Katy Dubois.

Link noticed that Frank was grinning. "You're looking awfully happy."

"I just got some news that makes me want to skip around like a kid."

"Care to share it?"

"I can't. Not yet, anyway. In a few weeks you'll be invited to the party."

Billy came forward from the cabin, a hang-up bag slung over his shoulder, and regarded Frank Dubois. "I'll tell the office about the verbal change. Maybe we should alter the contract so you can do this sort of thing in the future."

"I'd like that."

A sturdy young man, wearing slacks and a blazer, entered and stood quietly nearby. Dubois handed him the leather folder. "Watch after that, Gary. I'll be going to the cockpit."

"Is he on the passenger manifest?" Billy asked.

Frank made a face. "Sorry. I forgot."

Billy added the bodyguard's name to the form, crossed his own name off, and showed Frank Dubois as second pilot. After initialing the changes, he handed Link a copy and took the other two.

"We want to do this right," he said.

Frank Dubois sat in the right seat as they taxied in the conga line of airliners and private jets, looking on as Link finished the before-takeoff checklist.

Link glanced his way. "So you've kept your license current."

"I've flown most of my life. My father taught me the basics when I was a kid. I'd had a private ticket for five years when I joined the Air Force."

"Keep an eye out for air traffic," Link told him. "There'll be a lot of weekend flyers out. We'll have crowded skies all the way to California."

When they were number one for the active runway, the tower operator read takeoff instructions. Link Anderson replied, selected auto-throttle, paused briefly as the engines ran up, and released the brakes. The jet shuddered very little as they accelerated down the runway.

* * *

Frank Dubois observed the two large CRT's before him. Various functions could be brought up, according to their phase of flight. For the climb through the crowded airspace, he'd selected collision-avoidance radar on his right display, flight status and positioning instruments on the left. They were stair-stepping up to thirty-five thousand feet at the direction of the various regional centers, remaining under close observation on the radar scopes of the flight followers.

The weather remained clear and Link Anderson wasn't likely to need assistance for the next few minutes, so Frank felt it was a good time to check on his family.

"I'm going back to the cabin for a few minutes," he said as he unbuckled.

"Take your time," Link replied pleasantly.

Frank paused in the lounge area behind the enclosed cockpit to speak with the flight attendant, who was preparing hot beverages, then continued back.

Gulfstreams were tailored in different configurations, according to the desires of their buyers. This one was a show of luxury. Behind the lounge were four rows of plush, leather-covered passenger seats, one on either side of the aisle. Aft of the passenger area was a well-appointed bathroom, complete with dressing area and stand-up shower.

Katy was seated at the very back, chatting with Gary, the new bodyguard. Frank stopped beside her and nodded at the porthole. "We're five miles up and still climbing."

Katy displayed a map Link Anderson had provided her before takeoff. "We're passing over Philadelphia," she said knowledgeably. "Pittsburgh's next."

"You're right on, navigator."

He observed Paula, seated two rows forward, appearing deep in thought as she stared out at the sky. Although they flew often, she was not fond of airplanes. He'd learned to gauge her anxiety level by studying the corners of her mouth, which were now moderately pale.

"Stay buckled in until we've finished climbing," Frank told his daughter, "then go forward and sit with your mother."

Katy rolled her eyes in a show of disgust, but Frank ignored it and went forward.

He rested his hand lightly on his wife's shoulder. After

sixteen years they still enjoyed physical contact with each other. Paula said they were *touch* persons, and he agreed.

"How's the flight?" he asked, keeping his voice light.

She wrinkled her nose. "I'd prefer a good horse."

Frank smiled. "Might take a while to get to Big Sur."

Paula cocked her head. "You've got something to tell me."

"What makes you think that?"

"You've had the look since you returned from your meeting. It's *good* news, right?"

"I wanted to keep it as a surprise." He bent close and told her.

Paula's face drooped with astonishment. "The *chairmanship*?"

"You helped make it possible, Paula."

She shook her head, pride glistening in her eyes. "It was their confidence in your capability, Frank. They know you'll do an excellent job."

"I can't do it without my right arm, Paula. We're a good team."

Katy made her way up the aisle and sighed heavily as she took the seat opposite her mother's. When Frank grew tight-lipped about her display, she spoke quickly. "Mr. Anderson turned off the seat belt sign, and I want to talk to Mom. *Girl* talk."

Frank relaxed. She was cooperating. "That's unfair," he said. "No males allowed?"

"Men don't understand us." She peered closer, first at one parent, then the other. "Anyway, I got curious. What were you both grinning about?"

"Your father just got a very big promotion," Paula said, "but we can't tell anyone yet."

"Oh," said Katy, as if she wasn't particularly impressed. A couple of years before she'd believed that her father was Superman, and nothing he accomplished came as a surprise. He wished she felt the same about Paula.

The flight attendant arrived, knelt in the aisle, and locked trays into position at Katy's and Paula's sides. She placed ceramic mugs—the same blue and gold colors as her uniform—onto the trays and filled one with hot chocolate, the other with coffee.

"Thank you, Jackie," Paula said primly.

"If either of you need anything more, let me know."

Jackie Chang smiled pleasantly, then continued back to give the bodyguard his beverage.

Frank explained what Link had told him. How Jackie had been an Army helicopter pilot, and was about to begin training to become a staff pilot for Executive Connections.

"That's neat," said Katy, craning her neck to look back. She was an admirer of the "new American woman," and Jackie fit that bill. She viewed her mother as an anachronism from a past century. On the other hand, Paula wished her daughter could be at least a little more traditional and proper. Frank tried to mediate, but the schism between them was growing wider.

The airplane shuddered as they passed through a small pocket of turbulence, and Paula tensed, then looked out the porthole and frowned.

Katy reached across her. "The light's too bright, Mom." She said it without her normal rancor, and slid down the cover so the view was blocked. When Paula didn't object, Frank decided things were under control. When she wanted, Katy could be helpful.

He gave Paula's hand a final light squeeze and started forward.

"Everything all right back there?" Link Anderson asked as Frank took the right seat.

"Yeah. You've got a good attendant."

"We're at thirty-five thousand, passing Pittsburgh and on our way to K.C. I'm having intermittent problems with the avoidance radar, but everything else checks out."

Frank scanned the sky, then examined the instruments shown on the full-color displays to regain his bearings. "I'd like to hand-fly it. I need the practice."

Link Anderson switched off the flight-augmentation systems. "You've got it."

The G-IV was responsive. Frank quickly got the feel of it, then made a slight adjustment to the trim wheel, which positioned tabs at the rear of the T-tail surface.

Kansas City called with an advisory. Pilots near Cedar City, Utah, were reporting towering cumulous clouds and moderate to severe clear air turbulence at flight levels above thirty thousand feet.

Frank motioned to draw Anderson's attention. "My wife gets nervous in turbulence. I'd like to avoid it if possible.

After a short discussion they decided on a lower altitude

and a more northerly route. Link spoke on the radio, requesting to deviate from the flight plan and proceed from Ogden to Reno—to avoid the worst of the storm front—then to the Fortuna, California, VORTAC, where they'd turn south for Monterey. He also asked that they be able to descend to twenty-nine thousand feet after passing over Boulder, Colorado, to remain out of the turbulence.

The controller approved the deviation, but said the requested altitude was congested. At Boulder they could descend to twenty-three thousand. It was much lower than the Gulfstream's optimum cruise altitude, but Link accepted the change.

Monterey, California

Two men sat in a nondescript sedan, looking out at the airport operation. Simon Charbonneau was immaculately dressed in a buff-colored, collarless shirt and gray sports jacket. The tall, gaunt man beside him wore the rough clothing of a working man.

"When are they scheduled to arrive?" Simon asked in a high voice that betrayed a lisp.

"A little after five, unless they run into weather." Jaeger spoke in an indefinable accent that gutturalized his vowels. "One hour before landing time, Dubois' security will dispatch a limo and a panel truck from Big Sur, with a driver in the limo, a driver and guard in the truck."

"Three?" Simon was surprised. "That's all?"

"Webb tapped into their conversation. They felt the airport was secure, and no one would try anything on Highway One, with all the weekend traffic."

Charbonneau watched and listened closely.

"The drive from Big Sur will take twenty-eight to thirty-six minutes, depending on traffic. When they get here, they'll line up beside the terminal to wait. Webb and I will be in the van parked beside them. He'll be monitoring the radio, listening in on the tower frequency for the Gulfstream pilot."

Charbonneau leaned forward, looking at the airport layout.

Jaeger continued. "Webb will give the word when the airplane begins its descent. That's when we'll get out and approach their vehicles. I've got a couple of ruses in mind to get them to open up. I've done it before."

Charbonneau narrowed his eyes, visualizing it. Although pressed for time, Jaeger seemed thorough. He was called the Hunter, and had come highly recommended. He was also the most dangerous man Simon had ever met. When asked if he needed more men for the task, he'd curtly turned them down. He knew his capabilities and trusted no one, not even Webb. Perhaps not even Charbonneau, who was his employer.

Jaeger nodded. "I'll force the security guards into the back of the van, have them strip, then deal with them. Webb and I'll change into their uniform shirts, take their places, and wait for the airplane. It's a royal blue Gulfstream with gold script lettering. The pilot will taxi to the parking area on the other side of the tower, and we'll drive both vehicles out to meet them."

"How about the security guard aboard the airplane?"

"First thing he'll do is check the vehicles. I'll deal with him in the panel truck while Webb's unloading the baggage. By then I'll know about the brief. The guard will likely have it."

"What about Frank Dubois?"

"Once the family's in the limousine, I'll drive them to the back of the parking lot, deal with them, and secure the brief."

"If anything goes wrong," Charbonneau said, "just eliminate Dubois and take the brief. Those are your priorities."

The cellular phone in Jaeger's pocket gave a low buzz. "Go ahead," he said into the receiver. He nodded at what he was told. "Good."

"What was that?" Charbonneau asked as Jaeger folded and put away the phone.

"Webb didn't have time for complete profiles on the crew, but he got enough to know the captain might be trouble." Jaeger formed a smile. "One of my old contacts called the charter airline and said his niece was in an automobile accident. The captain's returning to Washington. Dubois will be flying the airplane with the other pilot."

"You've very good at staging accidents," Charbonneau said with approval. He looked out at the airport. "What if the crew give you trouble?" he asked.

"I'll leave them alone unless they suspect something. If

that happens, I'll deal with them. When I leave the airport in the limousine, Webb will follow in the panel truck and contact me on radio if he sees a problem. We'll continue north to Aptos, drop the limousine and bodies off a dock in the dark, then meet you in Santa Cruz and hand over the brief."

Charbonneau smiled. "When the Duboises don't show up at Big Sur, the police will suspect that they've been kidnapped."

"Yes." Jaeger pursed his lips and looked about the airport with narrowed eyes. He'd said he was unhappy about making the attack so overtly, but there seemed to be no better option.

"What about the van with the dead security guards?"

"We'll leave it parked at the airport. It will add to the mystery."

Charbonneau ran the scenario through his mind. "It sounds simple enough."

"That's the best kind." Jaeger mused for another moment. "The only unknown is the second pilot. All we know is the name shown on the flight plan: A. L. Anderson. Webb's trying to access more computer records. If there's anything dangerous about him, I'll want to know."

3

2:10 P.M.—Butte, Montana

Doc Aarons parked his car and hurried into the airport operations desk, where an attendant was posting notices on the flight advisories board. "How's the weather to Salt Lake City?" he asked.

"There's a big storm about to pass through there, Doc."

"How long have I got?"

"The front'll hit Salt Lake any time now. Better put your flight off until morning."

"Can't do that. Got a patient down there they've talked into an operation he doesn't need, and I'll be damned if I'm gonna let those knife-happy yahoos get away with it." The other man grinned, and Aarons supposed it was because of his reputation as a hardheaded old coot. Didn't matter, though, because he wasn't about to let a bunch of money-hungry surgeons talk his patient into something that should be handled by a daily aspirin, a healthy diet, and exercise.

"Unless you filed an IFR flight plan, there's no way to fly to Salt Lake, Doc. The way that storm front's being reported, they may even have to shut down the airport there."

"Nasty one?"

"You bet, and it's coming in a big stream that stretches down to the Gulf of Mexico. Weather service has advisories out to batten down. Towering cumulus up to forty thousand feet, with severe turbulence and big anvil heads spittin' hail the size of baseballs."

Aarons was not qualified to fly on instruments. He'd barely passed his last flight physical to keep his visual flight rules rating. "Blood pressure's a little high," his colleague had rightly told him, and Aarons had called in a favor to squeak past the requirement.

"How far can I get in the one-seventy-two before the weather turns bad?"

"Maybe Pocatello. According to how quick you get off the ground and how fast that front moves. You may even have to hole up at Idaho Falls."

Aarons started for the door, then stopped and turned. "Call down to Pocatello and have 'em reserve a rental car, would you? I'll land there and drive on into the city."

"It'll be a good two-, maybe three-hour haul to Salt Lake by car."

"Better than losing a patient for no good reason," Doc grumbled as he went out.

Aarons got off the ground quickly, flew eastward for nine miles, and made a low pass over the house to let his wife know he was on his way. He turned south then and climbed to six thousand feet. He'd not gone fifty miles when he saw the low clouds ahead, and beyond them the first billowing monsters. It wasn't going to be as easy as he'd hoped.

Still, he'd been flying for six years, had well over four hundred flying hours, and hadn't yet gotten into trouble he couldn't handle. He wondered how much farther he could go and still be able to see the ground. That was the rule for VFR fliers; you had to be able to see the ground, and there had to be an airport you could get to without getting into weather.

He approached the first low bank of clouds. Although higher than his present altitude, they appeared broken and he felt it was likely there were clear patches beyond. Aarons estimated that the tops were no higher than eight or nine thousand feet. He argued with himself for a full minute, then set power and began to ascend.

He'd begun the climb late and soon passed into the clouds. Doc considered turning back, but decided he wouldn't be in them long enough to have to worry. He'd climb on through, get on top, then look for the clear patches and hope to hell Pocatello was in one of them.

A flutter of uneasiness ran through him; he studied his instruments carefully before realizing he was in a bank. Aarons set his mouth and concentrated on keeping the wings level, and climbed at a steeper angle.

It seemed forever before he broke out above the clouds.

By the time he did so, his heart was pounding. Calm yourself, he chided, and decided to climb a bit more so he could see the clear areas he knew were there. He set the trim and checked that the throttle was at full power.

Aarons felt light-headed. He glanced and discovered he was at thirteen thousand feet. Too high, but not seriously so. He still couldn't see the clearings he'd anticipated, so he continued the climb. Just a little more, he told himself. A few spots danced before his eyes, so he blinked hard until they diminished. He saw a clearing to his right and wondered if he shouldn't turn there, but knew he'd not come far enough for Pocatello.

He stared ahead, looking for another hole in the clouds, still slowly climbing. The small airplane was laboring in the thin air, even at full throttle.

Aarons passed a hand over his face and did not realize it was trembling, for hypoxia had begun to play tricks on his mind. He leaned back and told himself to relax.

The light blue Cessna 172 passed over a final five-mile expanse of clearing, but although Doc Aarons saw it, it did not register. Pocatello, Idaho, was clearly visible at the far end of the clearing, but he did not see that either. His oxygen-starved brain was functioning in strange ways, feeding false information, telling him everything was fine.

When the Cessna crossed the border into Utah, the high, roiling cumulus clouds were directly ahead. Doc Aarons' head was lolled back, his normally reddened face turned a bluish hue. His respiration was ragged and his heartbeat unsteady. Five minutes later the aircraft was at nineteen thousand feet, far above its operational ceiling but still struggling gamely to maintain the climb. Aarons heart fluttered wildly for a few dozen beats . . . and stopped as the aircraft entered the towering cumulus clouds and was lost to view.

Approaching Ogden, Utah

They were at twenty-three thousand feet, passing through heavy clouds. While the Gulfstream was on autopilot, and it was a smooth ride, they were flying blind, in near-zero visibility. Except for the intermittent avoidance radar, all aircraft systems were functional.

They'd been talking about their time in Saudi, and the long period of boredom after they'd arrived. Like the others, they'd been relieved when the combat flying had begun. Frank told him the other pilots had considered Link to be the best aviator in their organization.

Link mused. "You didn't do bad yourself, for a pigfoot."

"Not *bad*? I was the one who got credit for the kill."

They'd been flying together, Link leading and Frank on his wing, when he'd spotted a Soviet-built Hind helicopter down low over the desert. They'd taken turns, trying to line up with the elusive quarry that darted wildly while their thirty-millimeter cannons spewed lead over the countryside. Frank had been closing for his third pass when the Iraqi pilot flew into the ground.

Link shook his head, as if disgusted. "Pure luck, Frank. I scared the crap out of the guy. It just took him that long to realize it."

"A kill's a kill," Frank said.

"Yeah, Pig-foot, but some are more graceful than others."

Frank chuckled. During the past hours they'd bantered, talked about old times, and renewed their friendship.

Link looked out at the solid clouds, then at Frank. "This is a lousy cruising altitude."

Frank observed the fuel flow, which was excessive, and agreed.

"The tops of the clouds are reported at thirty-nine thousand. If you don't mind, I'm going to ask to climb over this stuff. We may pass through some turbulence on our way up, but I don't like flying in weather when we don't have to, especially with the radar out."

"I agree," Frank said. Paula wouldn't like the turbulence, but they shouldn't be in it long.

Link called Ogden Air Traffic Control Center. He said they were approaching their station, and asked for permission to climb to forty-five thousand. He was told to stand by.

Anderson turned to him. "I'm going to take a short break. We're dead on course and the bird's trimmed up and on autopilot. All we're waiting for is permission to climb."

"Understand." Frank touched the control yoke. "I've got the airplane."

Anderson unbuckled, then stepped around the seat and disappeared from view.

Dubois let his hands ride lightly on the yoke, feeling the thing move at the dictates of the autopilot. On the G-IV even the throttle settings could be automated. The time would soon come when they'd need no human pilot, he thought. Electronic brains would do it all.

Talking with Link Anderson had made him realize the depth of their friendship, and how much he missed having someone like him with whom he could share things. At the present there was only Paula, and while he savored their closeness, it would be good to be able to speak about the weighty secrets he harbored. After he became chairman of the foundation, he decided to ask Link if he'd consider working with him—at least on the most crucial of their projects. After all, they'd once agreed to come to each other's assistance whenever the need should arise.

The events of the past months increasingly plagued and troubled him.

The urgency of the matter regarding the missing missile transporter had reached almost hysterical proportions in the top echelons of the State Department, yet from Frank's first days in Russian Siberia it had seemed apparent that there'd been no nukes involved.

Vern Calico's people had been convinced that Frank was the only one who could find the stolen transporter, and Calico had *insisted* that he be assigned to the effort. Had Vern been influenced by someone eager to pull him off another project? Away from Scarlet 277, perhaps, which he'd been managing at the time?

The Argentina project replayed in his mind. People had been killed there—horribly so—and before it was over there would undoubtedly be others. The organization called El Soleil was powerful, and Frank was convinced that the man who ran it—Colonel Salvator DiPalma— was more evil and determined than the handful at the Weyland Foundation realized.

He'd given his initial briefing to the handful not long after his first trip to Argentina, to convince them to open the investigation. At first they'd seemed less than fully interested, but as he'd continued they'd grown attentive.

* * *

"In April of '95," Frank had told them, "the night after the bombing in Oklahoma City, two police officials and an investigative reporter disappeared in Patagonia and were never found."

In October of that year, the night after the Simpson murder trial verdict, three more people—a newspaper publisher, a television personality, and the Buenos Aires chief of police—disappeared overnight. All were ardent supporters of the Argentinean president and his policies.

In November of '96, the Argentinean Minister of Internal Affairs was assassinated in Buenos Aires. He was the architect of their president's anti-inflationary policies, and his likely successor. The shooting occurred the same evening as the American national election, and was scarcely mentioned by the international media.

The political overtones hadn't been overlooked by Weyland Foundation analysts. The Argentinean presidency had been severely weakened, and it was likely the incidents were related.

"When I flew to Buenos Aires to look into the crimes," Frank briefed them, "I found their officials reluctant to talk. Then one evening I took a phone call in my hotel room. A woman—she was soft-spoken and I believed well educated—said her husband had been one of those who had disappeared. As soon as she offered the name of the man responsible, the line went dead."

Memory of the woman's cultured voice troubled Frank, for the next day the missing publisher's wife had been killed in an auto accident. He hadn't been able to learn more about her death, but when he'd returned to New York he had looked into the background of the man she'd accused. It had been revealing.

He'd shown the handful an image of several pompous-looking, uniformed men.

"In 1944 Salvator DiPalma was youngest of the colonels who overthrew the Argentinean government. As Juan Perón solidified his popular base, they continued the policy of quasi-neutrality in the war, tilted in favor of the fascists. When the Third Reich crumbled in Europe, German officers and businessmen fled to Argentina, bringing their families and abundances of artistic treasures and gold—which Colonel DiPalma *temporarily* seized as they came ashore.

"In 1945 Perón declared support for the Allies, and DiPalma convinced certain of the frightened Germans to buy the failing El Banco del Soleil Eterne, a respected banking institution established in 1678. These had been some of German's most brutal wartime murderers, and they were totally at his mercy—not yet Argentine citizens and unwilling to publicize their presence—so none complained when DiPalma named himself president of the bank and used their impounded gold to create a substantial financial reserve. The German families were moved onto modest estates in the Gran Chaco plains, and avoided travel to Buenos Aires.

"By 1969 the bank, popularly known as 'El Soleil,' had major branches in New York, San Francisco, Tokyo, Bonn, London, and Paris. A decision that year was to expand the New York office and base all transactions upon the U.S. dollar. A few years later, DiPalma's wisdom was proven when Argentine inflation rose above a thousand percent, and remained in that vicinity for the next several years. By then El Soleil had expanded into thirty-six countries, and their middle managers were graduates of Harvard and Oxford. They provided venture capital for a new industry, bankrolling cocaine operations in Colombia and Peru, and laundering the tremendous amount of American dollars coming from drug dealers in the United States.

"Colonel Salvator DiPalma avidly supported the 1982 war with England over the Falklands—called the *Ilas Malvinas* by Argentines—and viewed the defeat as a national tragedy. He vowed it would never happen again, and demanded that General Galtieri resign in disgrace."

Another image appeared, of a bleak landscape and a group of large, modern buildings.

"The following year El Soleil constructed a campus and research facility near Punta Medanosa, in Patagonia, and brought in scientists from France and Italy."

An image of a sleek rocket, unbilicaled to a launch tower.

"In 1987 the first Bolivar rockets—named after the general who defeated the Spanish and dreamed of a united South America—were unveiled. Suspiciously similar to the French Ariel, and limited to modest payloads, Bolivars have now boosted seven communications satellites into orbit. The program is a source of pride to Argentineans. It's also a financial disaster, but money is no problem for El Soleil because of the lucrative drug industry."

Frank had gazed steadily at the handful. "Five years ago El Soleil began to hire Russian nuclear physicists, offering salaries and living conditions Muscovites would kill for. They now have a total of twelve such scientists working in a high-security section of the campus, as well as a large number of engineers and technicians."

One of the handful interrupted. "Is DiPalma actually building a nuclear capability?"

"Yes, and he's close to having it. His problem was getting high-grade fission material. We now believe an El Soleil European subsidiary was involved in the theft of a large amount of U-235 in Kazakhstan. They're likely only months away from having a weapon."

"Can the Bolivar rockets reach the United States?" Cyril had asked quietly.

"Not the old models, but for the past three years they've been working on a more powerful version, and they're building new launch facilities in northern Argentina.

"Now El Soleil is offering candidates for both the presidency and the legislature, and their most vocal opponents have already been eliminated. If they succeed in gaining power in September, we can expect a military buildup, and an acceleration of the weapons programs. That would create a loose cannon at our back door. Another Cuba, only much' worse."

The handful had approved Frank's project to stop Salvator DiPalma. Yet he did not believe they were nearly as alarmed as he'd become. Perhaps it was because he'd studied DiPalma and had met him once. Frank deemed himself a good judge of men, and he'd come away convinced that Colonel DiPalma was inherently evil, the kind who would likely agree with the idea of Hitler's death camps to achieve his purpose.

The word *trueno* echoed in Frank's head. Thunder. The word was used by top people in El Soleil to describe the times when prominent supporters of the president had disappeared and when the minister of internal affairs, the right arm of the Argentinean president, had been assassinated. *Thunder* was the loud, echoing rumble created during an electrical storm. The events had occurred when the press and the public were preoccupied.

Analysts at the Weyland Foundation had begun monitoring breaking news stories, and alerting the investigators in Argentina on those days, but so far there'd been no more *truenos*.

Frank remembered the morning's conversation with the secretary of state. The boarding of the French ship seemed utterly irresponsible. *Why* had the President ignored their caution?

There was yet another enigma. Vern Calico had learned about the Weyland Foundation investigation in Argentina, when even the CIA's director of intelligence was unaware.

Frank replayed the puzzles in his mind as the control yoke moved smoothly in his grasp.

The covers over the adjacent portholes were still closed, and Paula was at ease. While Katy was sometimes disdainful about her mother's uneasiness with flight, she was working to keep her spirits up. Paula knew what her daughter was doing, but it didn't matter. They'd been at odds entirely too much recently, and the truce was enjoyable.

"I really would like to go to Spain," Katy said. Whitmore School had a program that featured living a year in various European countries and attending similar exclusive schools.

"You're very young," Paula said.

Katy suppressed her normal angry rebuttal, but not without obvious difficulty. "I'll talk to Dad," she finally said.

"Why don't we *all* talk it over?" Paula said.

"Because you never listen," said Katy, breaking the pleasantness.

"I just don't automatically agree," Paula snapped, and immediately regretted her tone. She softened her voice. "Let's wait until we get to Big Sur and all discuss it together?"

"Forget it. You don't want me to do *anything*. If it was up to you, I'd just hide somewhere. You want me to be a sissy like . . ." She stopped herself and took a breath.

Paula sighed and shook her head. "I don't want you to be like anyone, Katherine, and you won't be. You are quite unique."

"I'm going to do things, be whatever I can be, like Dad says, and you can't stop me."

"I agree, darling, and when the time comes I won't try. But for now you have to endure being fourteen years old. You'll be amazed at how quickly that will pass."

4

After relieving himself, Link stretched and shuddered deliciously, then returned to the passenger cabin. Everything seemed normal there. The G-IV was a true lady, much smoother and quieter than most birds, pushed along by the Rolls Royce Tay jets mounted at the aft end.

The girl and woman were sitting together, but studiously ignored each other. As he passed them, Paula Dubois caught his attention. "Could you tell me where we are?"

"We should be passing over Ogden, Utah, about now. We'll be climbing, and there may be turbulence as we pass through the intermediate altitudes, but it shouldn't last long."

"Thank you," she said pleasantly.

Link stopped in the small galley, where Jackie Chang was working, and exercised his shoulders again. He loved flying but, like most fighter pilots, disliked long flights.

"Here's your sandwich," Jackie said, pulling a foil-wrapped packet from the oven.

The muscular bodyguard—Frank had told Link his name was Gary—was leaning against a nearby bulkhead, acting as if he hadn't been trying to hustle Jackie. He carried the leather folder, and Link wondered what was inside that could be that important.

Jackie placed his hot pastrami on rye on a plate and handed it over. Link nodded in thanks and stepped around the small bulkhead into the lounge, still close enough to overhear their conversation.

"You don't sound too serious about your guy," Gary told her.

Jackie was stacking pastries onto a tray. "I just said he's the jealous type. I like having someone to come home to."

"Here's some advice," Gary said seriously. "People are like wine. It's an individual thing. Go for the right vintage."

"And you were born in a great year, right?" She finished with the tray, examined her work, then headed for the back.

Gary's smile faded when he saw Link looking on.

Link deadpanned and took another bite of sandwich as the guard started for his seat in the rear. He turned and stared out a porthole at the bleak weather. Lincoln Anderson enjoyed life, and since there was no such thing as an old, bold pilot, he did not enjoy flying in the soup. He took another bite and peered harder, wondering about Frank. From all indications, he was as wealthy as Henry Hoblit had said, yet he seemed hungry to renew their friendship.

As he was finishing the sandwich, Jackie returned to the galley.

It happened in the flicker of an eyelash. He'd glanced back out the porthole in time to see a light blue object flash into view. The impact was tremendous—as if they'd smashed into a stone wall. The aircraft shuddered and yawed, and as the lighting went out Link was thrown hard into the bulkhead, his forearm taking the brunt of the violence. Close by, Jackie started a scream, but there was a meaty thump as her head impacted the counter and the shrill sound was truncated as quickly as it had begun. Dust and debris flew about wildly, and for the few seconds until the pressure equalized, it was sucked through an opening somewhere aft.

Link tried to lurch toward the cockpit compartment, but the aircraft slowly rolled onto its side, then twisted and slewed again. "Damn!" he yelled as he was slammed against a couch, his voice lost in a loud, roaring sound from the rear of the fuselage.

He pushed to his hands and knees, pain shooting through the battered arm. Then he crawled across the floor in the dim light until he was blocked by Jackie's supine form. As he attempted to crawl past her, the dive angle increased and he began to slide forward, half riding on the attendant's limber body until they slammed into the closed door to the cockpit.

The nose of the aircraft continued to pitch over.

"Jackie," he yelled, but there was no response as the dive angle became more acute. Link raised himself back onto hands and knees, then grasped over Jackie's body until he found the handle. He twisted, and as the door swung open, he slid in alongside Jackie—kept sliding until they both lodged against the back of his empty seat.

Frank Dubois was desperately fighting the controls, but the dive angle continued to steepen, ignoring his efforts.

"Autopilot," Link yelled. He pushed Jackie's body away to his left, groaned with the bolts of fire that shot through his arm, then grasped the seat back and painfully pulled himself around, holding fast as he reached over and disconnected the flight-augmentation systems. With the autopilot off, the aircraft immediately entered a slow roll.

"Left aileron," Link shouted, and Dubois fought the control yoke to the left.

Link held fast to the shoulder strap, keeping himself from falling against the yoke as he slid into the seat. With an effort he fastened the belt about his waist, shoved the bayonet connector home to secure himself into the seat, then reached forward and grasped the wheel. With Dubois's help, he was able to decrease the dive angle.

"Again!" he yelled, and they pulled . . . and the airplane leveled more.

The cockpit was bathed in red—the emergency lighting activated with generator failure. The electronic instrument panels had dimmed, so Link peered hard. They were at fourteen thousand feet and descending, although slower than before.

They pulled together, and again the control yoke begrudgingly responded.

"Let's try to level her one more time," he shouted over the din of rushing air, and they strained with new effort. When they relaxed their grip, the altimeter read twelve thousand, seven hundred feet, and the rate of descent was much slower.

"We lost power on the right engine, and it's like the left flap's dropped down!" Frank Dubois shouted. "What happened?"

"Midair collision," Link yelled back. "I got a glimpse of another aircraft, then something sliced through the back, somewhere near the tail. She's built to fly on one engine, but I think part of the other airplane's lodged underneath, creating a lot of drag. That's why we're having so much trouble trying to control the bird."

"We had a rapid decompression." Frank Dubois's comment was unnecessary. They were shouting over the sound of wind blowing through the aircraft.

Link's heart pounded as he checked gauges and systems status. The master caution light glared. The primary Pitot system and both hydraulic systems were out, and they'd lost A.C. power. With the generator-alternators off line, they were operating on battery only. All navigation and communications equipment was dead. They were steadily descending, although only slightly, and could not turn to their left.

"Hydraulics are gone," Link yelled. "We're flying on cables and backup."

Frank grunted with effort. "Something's binding in there."

They were in dire trouble. The Gulfstream wasn't designed to land on anything except a proper runway. Even if they found an open field to put down in, the airplane would break up.

"Think we ought to go on oxygen?" Dubois shouted.

"Go ahead if you're feeling light-headed. I'm okay at this altitude."

Dubois pulled a mask from its holder, held it over his face, and took deep breaths.

"We've got to find the nearest airport and get this thing on the ground," Link yelled.

Dubois nodded in response, teeth clenched tautly, straining to hold what they had.

Rain began to stream across the windscreen as Link again tried to trim the airplane. There was little response to his inputs, and he had to keep both hands on the controls, although bolts of pain continued to shoot through his left forearm.

"We won't be able to see to land!" Dubois shouted.

"What's our heading?" Link Anderson continued his heavy grasp, ignoring the pain.

Dubois leaned forward. The small magnetic standby compass was functioning, but was difficult to decipher in the gloom. "Two-five-zero degrees!" he finally yelled.

Link nodded. "Let's try for Elko. They've got an acceptable runway."

The hatch behind them closed and the din diminished.

The girl's head appeared at Frank's shoulder, her face pale, eyes wide with fright.

"Katy!" Dubois reached back and grasped her hand. "How's everyone in back?"

She held on tightly, visibly trembling and unable to speak.

"How are they!"

"Gary won't answer when I call for him. He's in the back next to a hole in the floor of the airplane."

"How about your mother?"

"She's scared, but she's not hurt. She was screaming for me to stay in my seat."

"Honey, she's right. I want you to go back, and for both you and your mother to stay buckled in, no matter what. If we get low and it looks like we're about to land, both of you lean forward, keep your head down, and hold your hands around your legs real tight."

His daughter's face was crinkling, as if she was about to cry.

"Go on back, Katy." He repeated the position he wanted them to assume.

"What about Gary?" Her voice cracked and she shook more violently.

"Stay by your mother, and don't go anywhere near the hole. We'll check on him later."

Link was impressed. Dubois' voice was steady, and his instructions were right on.

The girl's eyes darted about the gloom of the cockpit. When she saw Jackie's lifeless body, the head turned an impossible angle, she released a shriek and scurried toward the doorway. Frank noticed the flight attendant for the first time, and his own face grew taut.

"Go on back," he said evenly.

The girl didn't answer, but a few seconds later the hatch closed behind her.

Frank Dubois cast another look at Jackie Chang.

"She's dead," Link said firmly. "We've got to concentrate on the living."

Dubois leaned forward, peering at the standby compass. "Two-sixty degrees. We're in a slow but constant right turn. That'll take us north of Elko."

"Let me see if I can ease in enough rudder to stop the

turn," Link said. He pushed on the pedal with effort, although it seemed jammed. "That do anything?"

"No. We're turning through two-sixty five degrees now."

Link checked the global positioning system, hoping to pinpoint their location so he could estimate a heading to another airfield—*any* airfield—to their right. That system was as dead as the others. While they were flying much slower, they did not know their airspeed, and with the constant turn there was no way to determine where they were.

Link looked at Frank. "Maybe you should go back and comfort your family."

Dubois wagged his head. "I can help more here."

"We're in deep shit, Frank."

"I'm staying."

Link remained impressed. His friend has lost none of his steadfastness.

"Remember the agreement we made in Saudi?" Frank asked.

Link did not hesitate. "I remember," he said. They'd promised to look after each other and, if anything happened to either of them, to look after the welfare of their families.

"We're passing through eleven thousand feet," said Frank Dubois. "Our heading's two hundred-ninety degrees."

"Let's try the rudder one more time."

They'd fought the controls for over an hour, constantly descending, and Frank held fast onto the controls with Link Anderson, his teeth gritted and bared as they tried to hold the nose up for as long as possible. The Gulfstream had emerged below the dark clouds, but rain continued to stream across the windscreen.

They skimmed over a high ridge, and the world below became a gloomy sea of trees.

"Damn," Frank muttered, for another ridge loomed in the distance, and there was still no place to attempt a landing.

"We've got to put it down," Anderson said. "We can't make it out of the valley."

Frank looked about desperately, then shouted, "Turn right! We can't turn left, but we can take it to the right and down the valley."

Anything to delay impact.

Link immediately pulled hard and twisted the control yoke. New firebolts shot through his left arm as the mortally wounded Gulfstream sluggishly responded. They lost more altitude . . . and leveled at five hundred feet above the treetops.

"Nothing out there but more trees," Link said hoarsely.

"There's something!" Frank jabbed his finger toward the rain-swept gloom at their two o'clock. "Looks like a lake."

"Got it in sight!" Link was already turning. Again they slipped earthward before they could recover. They skimmed above treetops, right wing slightly drooping. As they passed over the last conifers at the water's edge, Link hauled the throttles back and fought to keep the bird upright as they began to settle.

The engine sounds diminished. "We're about to land, Mom!" Katy squealed as she looked out the window.

"Stay braced like your father said!"

As they slowed, the sound of rushing wind at the rear of the airplane diminished to a whistle, and Katy saw the silver glint of water beneath the aircraft. "Oh God! Oh God! Oh God!" she repeated, crying but trying not to get sick to her stomach, then bent forward and clutched her legs in a death grip.

There was a loud, grinding sound from behind as metal contacted the water's surface. Then, as the airplane's nose dropped, the metallic sound was everywhere around them. They skimmed, then settled deeper and rapidly decelerated. Katy was pressed forward so hard that the seat belt threatened to cut her in two, but she continued to hold desperately onto her legs.

The aircraft shuddered and slewed wildly as they impacted an obstacle—a loud *crack* sounded as something broke away. The forward momentum diminished and the airplane twisted about, rocked over once, then settled.

There was a moment of utter quiet with the rushing air and engines silenced—and Katy felt so frightened and numbed she forgot the taut seat belt that was cutting into her stomach.

Sounds began to filter through, dimly at first, then becoming louder: creaking and popping noises of the airplane as it adjusted to its new environment, then an eerie swishing, gurgling sound. They bobbed gently, like a ship adrift without power. Only then did the fact register that she was stretched so far forward over the belt that she probably had a two-inch waist.

Katy felt cold water at her feet as she pushed herself back and grasped at the seat belt lever, hearing her mother making little sucking sounds like *"Unh, unh, unh,"* as if she were inhaling but couldn't breathe out.

The belt released and Katy took in a precious gulp of air, still shuddering with emotion.

Water lapped higher, now at her ankles. "We're sinking!" she screamed as the realization came.

Paula finally found her voice. "Katy!" she cried in a shrill voice.

"I'm okay, Mom," she managed, then started to be sick to her stomach again.

"Up here." It was the pilot's voice, and Katy could hear him splashing through water up forward. He grunted several times until there was an outline of light from a freed hatch.

Paula tried to stand, fell back, then rose and reached out for her daughter.

Katy stood cautiously, hardly trusting her legs, trembled violently once, then pulled herself to the aisle and took her mother's hand. They sloshed through frigid water together, heading toward the vague frame of light.

"Hurry," the pilot said in a pained voice.

"Where's Frank?" Paula asked in a high, tremulous voice.

"See those rocks?" the pilot yelled, pressing something at Paula. "Go there!"

"Is Frank okay?" Paula tried to edge back, but he pushed her to the open escape hatch. "Go to the rocks," he yelled again and unceremoniously shoved her out. He hunched protectively over his left arm, then pulled Katy forward, and pointed. "The rocks there. Pull one of the flotation cushions loose and take it across."

She froze, and her heart skipped a beat. "Where's Dad?"

"I'll bring him. Go on, you can make it." He disappeared into the eerie darkness.

Katy peered through the wind-swept rain. The island was only fifty yards distant.

Something bobbed in the water near her knees, and Katy

grabbed for it—it was one of the cushions he spoke about. Several others floated nearby.

"Dad?" Katy called anxiously, but there was no response and the water was rising relentlessly. She grasped the cushion and held her arms tightly around it, then lunged forward.

The water was shockingly cold. She bobbed once, then began kicking, propelling herself toward the rock island. Her mother was nearby—holding to her cushion with one hand as she reached out for Katy with the other.

"Come on, Mom," she yelled and continued to kick, avoiding her mother's grasp but leading the way through the water. In the water Katy was in her element, but she knew how people could panic and pull others under.

It took several minutes to make it to the rocks. Katy scraped her knees as she climbed onto them, then stood trembling. Paula scrambled ashore behind her and crouched, panting, on hands and knees. Katy helped her to her feet, then led her.

It was a tiny island, no more than twenty yards across, with a small sandy area at its center. As soon as Katy had deposited her mother on the sand, she started back for her father.

"Frank?" she heard Paula cry out in a mournful voice.

Katy paused at the edge of the rocks, still trembling hard as she peered through the rain. The airplane had settled lower. A dark shape separated from the fuselage. She slogged in, shuddered at the cold, and pushed away, then swam hard until she was close.

"Katy?" It was the pilot's weary voice.

"Yeah?" she managed.

"I've got Frank. He's unconscious, and I'm having trouble."

Katy's heart pounded. "Let me take him."

"I've got cushions strapped around his arms, but you'll have to keep his face out of the water. Watch his forehead and his legs. He's hurt."

Katy grasped her father's clothing, then held his head up as they started for the rocks. She was a good swimmer—better than good—but her father was bulky and heavy, and difficult to maneuver. The pilot stayed at her side as she struggled with the weight and kicked.

Katy heard him groan. "You okay?" she huffed.

"I'll do. Keep going."

Link was tiring badly by the time they reached the island, both from the exertion of pulling Frank free and swimming with one arm.

"Watch the rocks," Katy told him. "They're sharp." The girl guided her father's body onto a rocky shelf and held him there while Link crawled ashore crab-like, careful to protect his injured arm. Paula Dubois joined them, asking questions he was too weary to answer. He reached back with his right hand, and together the three of them strained and hauled Frank out. It took several long minutes to get him to the sandy area.

Paula crouched over her unconscious husband, wanting to do something to help him, asking more unanswerable questions as Katy sank to her knees nearby, exhausted and blowing breaths. Link's own heart pounded wildly. He was huffing, his breaths roaring loud in his ears, and he didn't notice that Paula had gained her feet and was tottering toward him.

"You've got to do something about Frank," he heard, and had half turned when she grasped his dangling left arm. It was as if a searing fire bolt had struck. He yelled out hoarsely and pulled free.

The pain in his left forearm was overpowering—a nauseous, sick-from-the-bone-out agony that surged with each heartbeat. He cradled the arm and staggered back toward the water, away from the others. An eternity passed before the pain subsided to a sharp throbbing.

He sensed a presence behind him. "Sorry," he managed through gritted teeth, then stopped himself as a wave of nausea swept over him.

The girl, Katy, cautiously came closer.

"My arm," he explained. "I think it's broken."

"Dad needs medical attention, Mr. Anderson." Her voice was distraught.

"I'll be there in a couple of minutes." He doubted there was anything to be done for Frank. During the landing they'd smashed into jutting rocks that had crumpled the right side of the cockpit. It was a wonder that he was still alive.

A loud gurgling sound drew their attention. Beyond the

sheets of falling rain the airplane's shape began to settle. The nose bobbed up, then dipped, and the long shadow slid beneath the dark water.

"Gary's inside!" Katy cried.

"I checked him," Link said. "It's too late." The rear of the cabin had been blood-spattered. The bodyguard had been killed in his seat by whatever had sliced through the airplane.

"Help him," Paula cried piteously from her husband's side.

A shuddering sensation swept through Link. "Go to your mother," he managed through gritted teeth. "I'll be there in a moment."

As the girl's footsteps faded, he settled to his knees. Emotion flooded over him. It wasn't something he could control. The aftermath of his trepidation. Fighting the controls and expecting the airplane to pitch over and dive into the ground. Landing in the lake and knowing the airplane would come apart or . . .

He steeled himself to be stronger, for the others would rely on him to get them through. Yet he knelt longer, huffing tortured breaths as the emotion returned, more powerful yet.

They were alive!

5

DAY ONE—Saturday, June 8

1:30 A.M.—Arlington, Virginia

The previous day Billy Bowes had returned to Washington in the Beech Baron, then hastened to the Arlington hospital—only to find that his niece was not there. No one using her name had been checked in, and none of their nurses had telephoned Henry Hoblit. To make sure he'd gone to her home, and arrived there as his niece came home from work. Except for a moderate case of jangled Washington traffic nerves she was fine. She said there'd been no accident. Then her husband had come in with their two kids from the day-care center, and they'd all scratched their heads together. It had either been a mistake, or an unfunny prank. In his relief Uncle Billy had taken their tribe to dinner at McDonald's.

Bowes had returned to his apartment in Arlington, popped open a Coors, and called Lucky Anderson. The aging warhorse said he was moving slower with his heart condition, and that he seemed exhausted most of the time. Billy had told him how his son had experienced no problem with the checkout in the Gulfstream, which came as no surprise to either of them. Then he'd brought up the lucrative Weyland Foundation contract.

"Link did us a favor with that one," Billy told him.

"Probably, but I don't feel easy working with anyone that big."

"Link says we can trust Frank Dubois. Right now I'm more concerned about Henry's penchant for spending money when everything's so tight."

"We need him, Billy. Can you imagine yourself at a black-tie dinner, trying to deal with a senator who's so self-centered he thinks the only difference between himself and God's a few years of tenure? That's where we need Henry

Hoblit, because he knows what it takes to impress people like that. But would he enjoy rolling up his sleeves and helping a mechanic chase down a hydraulic leak?"

"It's hard to imagine."

"You like that sort of thing. You're both good at what you do. Toss in Link to keep an even keel, which is what I try to do when I'm there, and it'll work out."

Lucky Anderson was often correct twelve times out of a dozen, Billy Bowes thought.

They'd talked about the infusion of youth Link brought to the operation. He was twenty years younger than Billy's fifty-three years, thirty years younger than Lucky, yet he was canny beyond his years. Lucky's pride was apparent in his voice, and Billy couldn't fault him.

After hanging up, Billy had cleaned the apartment and turned in early. The next morning he'd fly to Monterey and help Link herd the Gulfstream back to Washington.

Billy was sleeping soundly when the telephone jangled. He looked at the clock—it was half past one—and fumbled with the receiver.

It was Henry Hoblit, speaking in a somber voice. "I just got a call from an FAA night duty officer. Nine-nine-two is missing."

Bowes sat upright, instantly awake.

"They lost contact west of the Great Salt Lake. That's all they know so far."

"Jesus!" He groaned aloud at the terrible news.

"I'm in my car, on my way to the office."

"See you there," Billy Bowes said in a hoarse voice as he reached for his trousers, praying it was a terrible mistake.

When Billy arrived at the Executive Connections building, Hoblit was already in the flight-planning room, lips pursed as he separated aircraft forms into neat stacks. He was fully dressed, wearing a monogrammed blue blazer, white shirt, and club tie.

"Coffee's ready," Henry muttered, hardly looking up.

"What do you know so far?" Billy's mind had run rampant on the drive to the airport.

"Nothing except what I told you. I've made half a dozen phone calls, but so far there's no word. I got hold of the

Monterey airport, and all they knew was that the bird didn't show, Link hadn't called in, and no one in their flight region's reporting them on the ground."

"Why the hell did they take so long with the notification?"

"There was a communications blackout in the Western system for about twelve minutes yesterday, and a lot of things slipped through the cracks. A guy from the FAA's on his way over, and I'm hoping he can fill us in."

Billy went to the coffee urn and poured himself a cup. "It is normal for the FAA to be involved? Shouldn't it be the National Transportation Safety Board?"

The Department of Transportation was in the midst of a shake-up from top to bottom, and divisions of duties were murky between the NTSB, FAA, and the privately held companies performing many of their former roles.

"The FAA stays in control until they know there's been an accident. I suppose they want a look at our maintenance and flight records, and we're close by."

The Federal Aviation Administration, the division of the Department of Transportation that regulated American airspace, aircraft, and pilots, was headquartered on Independence Avenue in a confusing maze of government buildings.

A fat man, dressed in baggy slacks and open-neck white shirt, came through the door.

"Over here," said Henry.

"I'm Tom Oliver, from the Office of Aviation Safety."

They shook hands. "Henry Hoblit. This is Mr. Bowes, our chief pilot."

"What happened?" Billy blurted.

Oliver ignored his question. "Are those the aircraft records?" he asked, looking at the growing mounds in front of Henry Hoblit.

"They were mixed in with others. I'm almost done separating them."

Oliver went closer. "I'll take them back to the building."

"I'd rather they not leave the office."

As Oliver's look darkened, Billy identified yet another Washington bureaucrat unaccustomed to being questioned by mere citizens.

"I can have them subpoenaed."

"I doubt it." Henry finished sorting, stood back, and

looked up. "How about I copy anything you want? You can take those and we'll keep the originals."

Oliver was tight-lipped. "That will do for the present, I suppose."

Henry pushed a stack over. "Pick out the ones you want and I'll run them off." He switched on the Xerox machine.

As Oliver began making selections, Billy offered coffee but he turned it down.

He couldn't wait any longer. "What happened to the Gulfstream?"

Oliver didn't look up. "Last known position was ninety miles northwest of Salt Lake City."

"That's all?"

Oliver sighed deeply, as if he was being deterred from more important duties, and opened a manila folder. "Last recorded radio call to Ogden Control was, ah, a pilot request at 1601 hours to climb from twenty-three to forty-five thousand feet to get above heavy weather. At 1614 the alarm sounded and a controller reported their IFF transponder return had disappeared from his screen. When Ogden tried to contact them on radio, there was no response. That was also when the communications net went down, so there was a great deal of confusion in the system. No way to contact the aircraft, other traffic control centers, and so on."

"What caused the communications breakdown? The storm?"

"That's still under inquiry and none of your concern."

Oliver closed the folder and returned his attention to the forms and notebooks.

"That's all?" Billy prodded. "No radio call, emergency IFF squawk . . . nothing?"

"Several aircraft were momentarily lost while the system recovered." Oliver tersely pushed the forms he'd selected across to Henry. "You can start with those."

Henry began copying. "They were in weather. Lightning strike?"

"Possibly," Oliver said.

"That could explain the loss of radio and IFF."

Billy stared at his coffee, thinking about the pilot's nightmare—the thing they hated to even mention. "Midair collision?" he finally asked.

Oliver continued going through the forms. "It's doubtful.

There were no other aircraft noted within twenty miles of the Gulfstream, and none for a hundred miles within a thousand feet of their altitude. No one else is missing and nobody reported anything unusual."

Billy was relieved. "No other aircraft missing," he echoed.

"None in the system. Maybe I will take that coffee. Cream and two sugars."

Billy started for the urn, then stopped. "How about aircraft *outside* the system?"

"Most light aircraft can't get that high. They don't carry oxygen and they'd need it at twenty-three thousand. Also, the area was socked in, so you wouldn't find recreational pilots up there—no one but professionals flying on instruments."

"Bird strike?" Henry wondered. "I've seen Canadian geese at thirty thousand feet."

"Birds are smart enough to avoid really bad weather." Oliver squinted, about to share something. "If there *was* an accident, the pilot likely became spatially disoriented, entered a descending turn, and impacted the ground."

Billy was adding cream and sugar. "Not possible," he said without hesitation. "Link's too good. I've flown with him in weather, and I gave him his instruments recurrency check. He doesn't get disoriented in weather."

Oliver took his coffee and raised a pudgy eyebrow. "It can happen to anyone."

Billy shook his head doggedly. "Not to Link Anderson."

Henry Hoblit leaned on the counter. "Have *any* aircraft been reported missing?"

"Probably several dozen nationwide, as there are every day. Light aircraft pilots land at alternate airfields and spend the night, sometimes days, and forget to report in."

"How many are missing in that sector?"

Oliver sighed. "As I said, the possibility of a midair is remote."

"I'd like to know."

Oliver gave him an irritated look. "We'll look into it. It's standard procedure. With the communications breakdown we're looking at a lot of things." He took a single sip of coffee, then put the cup down as Henry handed him the final copies.

The FAA officer picked up the aircraft records and

cocked his head thoughtfully. "What was the condition of the Gulfstream's ELT?"

Emergency locator transmitters, designed to send electronic signals over emergency radio channels in the event of harsh impact, were required on commercial and most private aircraft.

"Ours were all inspected last month. We replaced a battery in the Baron's black box, but the others checked out."

"We've had no reports of a signal, so we can't eliminate the possibility that the pilot landed somewhere. We're querying all airports in the system."

"How long will that take?"

"A couple more hours. If there's no response, we'll initiate a search at first light."

Oliver started for the door, then turned. "I'll stay in touch. Where will you be?"

Henry motioned his head grimly. "Right here."

"Why was there only one pilot aboard, Mr. Hoblit?"

"One of our men was called back to Washington due to an emergency. Our client's a fully qualified pilot. He preferred to take the right seat rather than wait for a copilot."

As soon as the FAA officer departed, Henry pulled out a directory and began to leaf through the pages. "I don't like that guy."

"He seemed like a lot of other bureaucrats I've met here."

"He was too damned eager to get his hands on the aircraft records." Henry ran his finger down a page and paused, his eyes narrowing. "T. F. Oliver, deputy director for Aviation Safety. They didn't exactly send a clerk."

"What do you think?" Billy asked.

"Their system went down and they were scurrying around to cover their tracks. Then some duty officer recognized the passengers' names on our manifest, figured this one had better receive special treatment, and got the big wheels involved."

"We should begin notifying next of kin." Billy said. "Tell them about the disappearance and the search getting underway."

"I'll make the calls in the morning, after the FAA checks all the airports."

"How about Lucky and Linda?"

"Yeah." Henry Hoblit ran a nervous hand over his balding head. "That might be touchy, with Lucky's bad ticker and all."

"I'll handle it."

Henry nodded, obviously relieved.

After a few seconds of silence Billy said, "I should have been aboard."

"Should-have-beens are baloney. You know that. This is going to get big, Billy. There'll be repercussions because of who Dubois and his grandfather are. With Lucky laid up I'm going to need your help, and I don't need you worrying about things you can't do anything about."

It didn't help his growing guilt. "I'll help any way I can," Billy Bowes told him .

The White House

At seven o'clock that morning the President's breakfast was interrupted, and he was given an encrypted fax, marked for his eyes only. An aircraft carrying the Weyland Foundation's new chairman was missing, along with a file containing a synopsis of their, and the U.S. government's, past and present clandestine activities.

He immediately called in three men: the attorney general, the secretary of transportation, and Vern Calico, secretary of state and his liaison with the foundation. When they arrived, he provided no rationale, but told them to provide all possible assistance in finding the downed aircraft and retrieving, unopened, a brown leather folder. The effort was not to be released to the press. He told them that the matter involved national security—and no more.

When the first two men had left, he remained stonefaced as he regarded the verdant lawns outside the window, for the revelations in the Weyland files could destroy the final threads of the already cynical and fragile trust of the American people for their government.

The secretary of state seemed equally reflective, and then reminded him of what he'd told him the previous day. "Without Frank Dubois, there'll be no balance at the Weyland Foundation. They're likely to make questionable decisions."

"We'll help the foundation recover their folder. In the meantime, try to keep a close rein on them, Vern, and make sure there aren't any problems. We don't need more embarrassments for the administration."

"I'll stay close as a flea on a blue-tick hound," said the colorful secretary of state.

Boise, Idaho

Leslie Rocklin awoke, glanced at the clock, and bounded out of bed. There were things to do and it was no time to be sleeping in. Lazy journalists didn't win the Pulitzers, and this lady not only wanted one so badly she could taste it, she was by God going to get one.

She'd concluded that Boise was not the place to get it. There'd never once, in the history of the newspaper, been a Pulitzer prize awarded to a member of the *Times-Journal* staff.

After her father had died the previous month, she'd decided to offer her skills to one of the big Eastern papers. She'd thought of it before he'd passed away, but hadn't mentioned it. The thought of his daughter preferring to live in the East would have dispirited him. Westerner to the core, he'd distrusted anything tainted with Eastern ways. He'd already been let down that she'd become pushy and determined—new things in her life since her divorce.

Gotta move on, Leslie told herself, and that meant she'd need a few more good bylines—or maybe just one great one—for her résumé. Then hello, *Times, Tribune,* or maybe the *Washington Post* like Mort Yoder, one of her friends at work, had done six months before. Not Seattle, though. Her ex-husband was there, making a fool of himself over his twenty-five-year-old replacement wife.

She felt pity for the poor girl.

Leslie was thirty-seven—she'd wasted fourteen years of her life married to the male chauvinist bum who'd felt it unseemly for an attorney's wife to work as a lowlife reporter, even though her income had helped put him through law school and get him started—but she *felt* young and that was the difference.

She was also good at her work. At times Leslie could wring an interesting column out of very little. Make chocolate cake out of cow paddies, as Mort Yoder had put it. But there were also times when she'd let good ones slip by.

Great reporters had a sixth sense about stories; they knew which flashy stuff to leave to the tabloids and which of the mundane to turn upside down, dissect, and put on display. Leslie was still developing hers. Before Mort had left he'd told her she had the potential to become one of the best. Sometimes, like this morning, she believed him. She just wanted the opportunity—she'd handle the rest.

Leslie launched into her morning huff-and-puff exercises—stopped halfway through to put a bagel in the toaster—then finished with gut-wrenching, high leg lifts, feeling *good*.

About herself. About the day that was beginning.

Leslie was happily unmarried and had no desire to change that status. When she dated it was usually a one-time dutch-treat thing so she could get a good meal, maybe go dancing, and not be bugged by macho apes who hit on divorced women out alone. Like the previous night, when she'd dated a local television news announcer. When he'd turned on his ego, started talking like he was about to re-place Peter Jennings, she'd refused to clasp her hands and bat her eyes, so the guy had shifted his masculinity hang-up into high gear and Leslie had done the unpardonable. She'd laughed at him. It would be their last time together and good riddance.

Leslie daubed cream cheese and apricot jam onto the bagel halves. A quarter pound off, half a pound on. Not a winning formula, but this was her day and she'd diet next week.

As she munched on the doughy bagel she tapped keys on her laptop, connected with the *Times-Journal*'s news-share computer, and checked for overnight developments.

She culled through the wire-service inputs. International news was first, and while she doubted it would be useful, she refused to let anything go by.

The President had released a short statement and form-ally apologized to the government and people of France because the U.S. Navy had mistakenly boarded one of their vessels in international waters off the coast of Japan, searching for nuclear contraband. There was nothing else to that one except the President had appeared angry when asked about the incident, but no one knew at whom. She skipped over that one and went on to the next.

A new atrocity discovered in Bosnia. Nothing to be

added. A new burst of inflation in Argentina, and an opposition party promising stability if they were elected in September. No interest there either. French, Italian, Japanese, and South American politics were *supposed* to be turbulent.

Next were domestic news items, and she scanned past East Coast stories of local interest.

Leslie paused. There'd been an early morning drug bust in Seattle, involving a major gang who also dealt in Boise. A possibility.

The FAA's Rocky Mountain flight-following system had lost communications for a twelve-minute period the previous day. Their Flight Safety office was looking into the matter.

An aircraft had been missing since the previous afternoon, and a search was getting underway out of Salt Lake City. The airplane was a Gulfstream IV (she'd have to look it up) owned by a company called Executive Connections, which was headquartered in Washington, D.C., with six SOB (she knew that meant "souls on board"). Departed from Teterboro, New York, destination Monterey, California. Names of passengers and crew hadn't been released.

Leslie hedged, wondering if anyone important had been aboard. Salt Lake City wasn't that far, and was in their area of interest because of the numerous Mormons living in Idaho. Another maybe, she decided. If there was nothing bigger she'd look into it. Then she said to hell with that. She would look into *everything*. This was *her* day. There was a story out there with her name on it. All she had to do was find it.

As Leslie entered the news room, she was cornered by the city editor, who was her immediate boss, and asked when she would wrap up the "airport noise" assignment she'd been given.

"Soon," she said airily and went to her corner nook. She didn't like the woman, and the feeling was mutual. The city editor was relatively new, but she'd already called Leslie a pushy bitch to the other staff.

She wouldn't have to put up with her for much longer.

Leslie made her first phone call—a follow-up on what was supposed to be a drive-by shooting of a young woman. She suspected it was really a guy's way to rid himself of a pregnant girlfriend. A lieutenant cop friend agreed, but on the phone now said he was having a hard time breaking the guy's alibi. He said he'd keep her posted. Like how about over dinner tonight?

He wanted into Leslie's frillies and L'Eggs—she could tell by the way he sneaked looks at her breasts when they talked. She'd strung him along so he'd be cooperative, so she wasn't upset. *Dumb male,* she thought and put him off with a line about having to work late.

Mort Yoder said being an accomplished liar was a required trait of a good reporter. He felt it was their constitutional right to bend rules, even the law, to get to the *real* truth, and present it to the American people.

A woman called over a bad telephone connection and gave a name: Joan Cecil or something, acting like she should know her and complaining that an airplane had buzzed them the previous afternoon. Down so low—like it was going to land on the roof—that the place shook. Leslie sympathized, entered her name and number into her electronic memo maker in the unlikely event she'd use them, and hung up. Another follow-on to the dumb airport noise series. People moved near the airport because the prices were right, *then* complained about the noise.

Leslie called Mort Yoder in Washington—it was after eleven o'clock there, and she wanted to catch him before lunch—and asked what he had on the missing executive jet. Mort was working the story and gave particulars about how the plane had disappeared from radar screens at Ogden, then said he'd call a buddy at the FAA. He'd phone her back if there was anything of substance.

She felt hunger pangs and pulled a box of Cheese Doodles from the bottom drawer, and munched as she dialed her father's familiar number. The Filipina nurse who had been with Old Gerald during the final months still lived in a room at the rear of the big house. The trust was still being settled by her father's old crony lawyers.

"Are the hyenas there?" she asked. The law firm was taking a final inventory of the estate this morning, and Leslie was supposed to be present.

"Not yet, ma'am."

"I'll be by later," she said, and hung up. "Old Gerald" Rocklin had dreamed of leaving his empire to his only child, but there wasn't much empire left. Only two

mid-sized grocery stores and a king-sized debt larger than
their worth. Ten years before there'd been nine stores
stretching from Idaho Falls to Boise to Coeur D'Alene, a
meat-processing plant, and the largest bakery in the state.
One by one they'd been closed or sold off, devoured by
bad times and competition from cut-rate warehouse outlets.
By the time Old Gerald had died, his holdings had been a
shell of what they'd once been.

She'd put away the Cheese Doodles when Mort called
back about the airplane story. His voice was coming rapid-
fire, a sign that he was excited. They still didn't have
names of passengers, but something big was going on.
"The people at FAA are running around like the President's
missing," Mort said. His FAA contact wouldn't talk, so
something was afoot. Mort said he'd feed her information
from his end if she'd snoop out details of the search effort.
If it was big, as he was beginning to think, they'd share
what they dug up.

Without thinking twice Leslie agreed. It was her day and
she'd had a premonition that this was *the* one. As soon as
she hung up she felt a trill of excitement. "Yeah!" she
yelled.

A minute later, when she told the city editor what had
transpired and that she was going to fly to Salt Lake City,
her grin hadn't faded. The editor chewed her ass about the
idea of sharing news, ending with: "I don't give a damn
that Yoder worked here. He's competition."

"In Washington, D.C.? That's silly."

The woman's face reddened. "Your request for travel
funds are denied."

"I'm going," Leslie said. The owner of the *Times-
Journal* had been a longtime crony of her father's, and she
could get away with editor baiting, as long as she didn't go
too far.

The Lake

Katy sat beside the pilot named Lincoln Anderson, who
stared solemnly out at the water. She looked at her watch.
It was eight thirty-five. The rain had ceased, but the sky remained blustery and it was chilly on the windswept rock
island.

Paula had remained quiet throughout the night and morning, just huddled beside Dad's still body and shivered, bedraggled and cold in the crumpled silk dress.

Her father seemed barely alive. Now and then he'd awake enough to make low moaning sounds, but Katy didn't think he could possibly last much longer, which was the worst possible thing she could imagine. She loved her father fiercely, and couldn't help remembering how the day before he'd been so full of life. Katy had helped Paula clean the blood from his face, spread from a deep gash on his forehead. He'd received a hard blow there, and Mr. Anderson said his legs had been crushed when the airplane had smashed into rocks.

Yet regardless of how Katy prayed her father would get better, she knew they couldn't just sit around and mourn, as Paula was doing. They desperately needed food and shelter, and to get those they'd have to somehow get to the distant shore.

Mr. Anderson hadn't suffered a compound fracture of his arm—there was no bone protruding or bulging beneath the skin—but it was surely broken. She could tell it hurt, because he grew pale whenever it was jarred or he moved too suddenly.

With Paula preoccupied, he talked things over with Katy, trying to think of a way to get everyone to shore. The lake was four or five miles long and pear-shaped, with their island at the middle of the pudgy part. The problem was getting across. They'd tried tying flotation cushions together, but they made a poor raft. Katy felt she could make it to shore, but with his bad arm Mr. Anderson was a lousy swimmer, Paula wasn't that good, and Dad was dead weight.

The pilot had been eying the single part of the airplane's T-shaped tail that protruded above the water, all that remained visible of the sunken Gulfstream. It was at a forward angle, as though the airplane was in a dive, so the rear part of the fuselage was likely resting on submerged rocks on an incline on the lake bottom.

"There's a raft bundle inside the rear hatch," he said in a quiet voice.

"Big enough for all of us?"

"Bigger. It can support twelve people. There's oars and a survival kit inside. Everything we'd need to get across."

"How about a pump or something to blow it up with?"

"It's inflated automatically by a bottle of compressed gas." He continued looking out at the exposed part of the tail he called an elevator. It was deep blue in color and looked like the dorsal fin of a killer whale on its side, about to dive for the bottom.

"I'm an awfully good swimmer, Mr. Anderson." Katy had shelves of medals to prove it. She was on the swim team at the Whitmore Middle School, competing in both free-style and back stroke, and her coach said she was a small step from being Olympic material. She'd learned to swim early. At six, Dad had called her his minnow. Later she'd become his mermaid.

The pilot stared, his dark eyes periodically filled with pain.

"It's in the back end?" she prodded.

"At the rear escape hatch, in back of where you were sitting," he said. "The engine on that side was damaged and it's blocking the hatch, so you'd have to lug it all the way forward." He mused and shook his head. "It would be too heavy for you. I'll have to do it."

"I don't think you can with your bad arm."

"Things are lighter in the water because of their buoyancy."

"That's why I think I can do it. Anyway, the tail of the airplane's sitting higher than the nose, so I'd be pulling it downhill. I'd like to try, Mr. Anderson."

"The water's cold. You could get hypothermia." He scanned the sky. They'd all been doing that a lot, looking for airplanes. "There'll be a search underway."

"We're all cold, and we're going to get hungry," Katy argued. "And you said you're not sure where we are. Maybe they don't know either."

The pilot didn't comment as he rose to his feet. He looked troubled as he paced and looked out at the airplane. Katy hoped he'd decide pretty soon. They had to do *something*.

Monterey

The man called Simon Charbonneau walked down the hallway of the hotel, found the room number, and rapped cautiously on the door. Jaeger had phoned him the previous evening. They'd waited at the airport according to the plan, but the airplane hadn't shown.

"Yes?" came Jaeger's low voice.

"It's, ah, Simon." He'd almost forgotten the name he was using.

The door cracked, then swung open.

Charbonneau entered. "Are they still coming?"

The big man spoke in his rumbling tone. "All I know is they took off on schedule from Teterboro and didn't show. Perhaps they diverted somewhere. We're looking into it."

A rapping sounded at the door, and Jaeger let in a stocky man with tousled brown hair. Charbonneau remembered him as the one called Webb, Jaeger's pilot.

"I called the airport twice," Webb said. "The first time they said they didn't have a new arrival time on the Gulfstream. When I called back they wouldn't discuss it at all." He shook his head. "I flew for the FAA for a while, inspecting airfields. Something's definitely wrong."

Charbonneau felt his face flushing with emotion. The previous day he'd contacted New York and told them he was about to succeed with his task. "I *promised*." he blurted angrily.

"Perhaps we'll have to delay our plan," Jaeger said confidently, "but we'll get the file."

Jaeger took a phone call, and handed the receiver to Charbonneau. "For you."

He took the telephone and listened carefully. A moment later he said, "I see," and hung up, his face ashen, his voice low and trembling. "Our source in Washington was just briefed. The Gulfstream went down west of Salt Lake City. He confirmed that the Weyland file was aboard."

"They crashed?" Webb asked incredulously.

Charbonneau nodded.

Jaeger remained collected. "Have they found the wreckage?"

Simon was unable to respond. He rolled his eyes helplessly. They'd been so close!

"The wreckage," Jaeger prodded. "Have they located it?"

"They're just now setting up a search operation."

"As soon as we get there, we'll rent a helicopter and stand by while Webb monitors their in-flight frequencies.

When the wreckage is found, we must be first to reach it and remove the brief. If Dubois is dead, that part of your problem is already solved. If not . . ."

Charbonneau shook his head woefully, hardly listening.

Jaeger placed a reassuring hand on his shoulder. "It can work. We must hurry."

Simon hardly dared to believe they still had a chance of success.

Jaeger's voice was firm as he spoke to Webb. "Is the airplane ready?" The Piper Navajo was parked at the Watsonville airport, a few miles distant.

Webb nodded at the mist-streaked window. "The visibility's too low for takeoff, but the ground fog should lift in another hour."

6

10:45 A.M.—The Farmhouse, Falls Church, Virginia

Billy Bowes pulled off the road onto the meandering lane that snaked up to the house. The hilltop home was large, surrounded by emerald fields cross-fenced in white. A horse barn and corrals were set off to one side. On the other was a fenced tennis court. Two Irish setters loped toward his car, then trotted happily alongside.

Lucky and Linda Anderson owned the country property south of Falls Church, at the edge of the megalopolis that extended northward past Baltimore. It was Billy's second trip to the Farmhouse. The first had been at first light, to tell his friends that the airplane, with their son at the controls, was obviously down. He'd returned to the Executive Connections office to await developments. So far there were none. This trip was also out of duty, for Billy felt he should be with them when the wreckage was located, and share a portion of their agony.

The first time Billy had visited the Farmhouse, more than twenty years before, Link had been ten—the Andersons had adopted him at four years of age—and had stared at Billy sullenly and refused to speak to him. Later they'd discovered it was because of Billy's Cherokee blood, and the fact that Link hadn't been able to accept that he was part Indian himself. It had taken twenty more years before Link had resolved his shame of his Indian heritage, but in the past months he and Billy had grown to know each other and become friends.

Link was likely dead, and Billy Bowes blamed himself—sending him out so soon after being upgraded, with Frank Dubois' flying ability an unknown quantity.

As he stopped before the large, offset garage and killed

the engine, Linda Anderson walked out from the house. "Anything new?" she asked as he opened his car door.

He shook his head.

She was unable to smile. "Come on inside, Billy."

"How's the general taking it?"

"Hard."

Lucky Anderson was one of the most capable men Billy had ever known. In the Air Force he'd gone on to earn three stars, and Billy still thought of him as "the general." During two tours of combat Lucky had saved his life on more than one occasion. He'd also been a factor in Billy's rise to colonel, helping him overcome his penchant for pissing off brass when he felt they were being obtuse. Billy did more than owe him—he loved, admired, and honored the man.

"How about you?" Billy asked Linda.

"I'm coping. I just wish we knew more."

As they went inside, Linda said the general was asleep. He'd not rested well, so she'd shooed him back to bed. She deposited herself in her overstuffed chair. Billy sat nearby. When the maid—her name was Nadine, he remembered—came in, he said he'd take coffee.

Linda motioned at an opened letter on the side table. "That's from Marie. She was on her way out for a visit."

Marie was Link's fiancée, a bright and pretty girl in Montana.

"I called her," Linda said. She didn't add more.

The telephone rang, and Billy could hear Nadine answering it in the kitchen.

Linda looked squarely at him. "I lied to you, Billy. I'm not coping. Our lives are on hold until we find out about Link."

Nadine came in, bringing a portable telephone. "It's Mr. Hoblit," she announced, "for Mr. Bowes."

Billy felt a wave of foreboding. "Henry?"

"A search-and-rescue C-130 just located wreckage northwest of the Salt Lake. It's not the Gulfstream and doesn't even appear to be a complete airplane. Just part of a light airplane's fuselage and what looks like a wing a quarter mile away."

"Midair," Billy muttered.

"Maybe. They're sending a chopper from Hill Air Force Base for a closer look."

"It had to be a midair. Nothing else computes." Billy took a breath. "Anything else?"

"A gang of lawyers from the Weyland Foundation are on their way from New York, and the Department of Transportation's jumping through hoops. All of it very quietly, though, and they're putting a lid on everything. Tom Oliver called me before he left for Salt Lake to run the search effort, saying we're to protect the identities of the passengers. Soon as he hung up, a foundation representative called, asking why we hadn't had two pilots aboard. When I told him Frank Dubois had wanted it that way, he said they were reviewing the contract. Then he repeated that we are *not* to release the passengers' names."

"Henry, we'd better start looking at the fine print in the contract too."

"I did that at four o'clock this morning. It says we'll provide a minimum of two pilots and one attendant for all flights."

"Even if they request differently?"

"I couldn't find a provision for a change. Our company lawyer's looking into it." Henry spoke to someone off the line. "Got another call coming in. Jackie Chang's mother." Henry's voice was strained.

"Keep me advised."

"Yeah." Henry hung up.

Lucky Anderson's voice sounded from the doorway. "Have they found the airplane?"

"No, sir." Billy explained the conversation. "Now Henry's worried about litigation."

The general slowly took his seat, and it was apparent that even that small effort was tiring. "You heard Dubois say he wanted to fly with Link?"

"Yes, sir. He said he'd change the contract to allow for that sort of thing on a routine basis. The problem is, he didn't have time to pass it on to anyone at the Weyland Foundation."

"I don't *care* about all that," cried Linda. "What about Link?"

Although Billy wanted to assuage her fears, a lump grew inside his throat and would not allow it. Not because of Executive Connections' troubles, but about Link, Jackie Chang, and the Dubois'—and his guilt for not being with them.

"I'll be in my studio," Linda said, and left the room with glistening eyes.

At 11:15, Henry phoned back. The chopper was returning from the wreckage site. One body had been recovered from the cockpit of a four-place Cessna. They'd found both wings and luggage scattered about the area, but were still looking for the tail section, where the ELT was located. They were still puzzled because they weren't getting a signal.

"It was a midair collision," Billy Bowes said to Henry. "Had to be."

"Yeah, but they're not admitting anything, and they don't want anything getting out."

"Henry, I'd like to fly the Baron out to Salt Lake." He didn't add his reasoning—that they should find the Gulfstream not much farther along the flight path.

"I need you here. The Weyland Foundation lawyers are on their way over, along with a couple of yes-men from the Department of Transportation, and no one's sounding pleasant. It would be hard for me to face it all alone."

"Give me the phone," Lucky said quietly.

The general allowed Henry to explain it all again. After a moment he said. "I'm sending Billy to Salt Lake. You can both do what you're best at." He hung up, and Billy stood to leave.

Lucky Anderson regarded him closely. "Find him, Billy. Henry can handle things here. Find our son and bring him back."

"I will." Billy had followed Lucky's bidding since he'd been a young man, and felt honored that he'd maintained his trust. When they'd flown together, he would have given his life for his friend, and now he wished it was him and not Link they were searching for. The two were alike, Lucky and Link—both of them natural leaders with uncanny flying abilities. Billy was no leader, not in their category anyway. He'd looked forward to working with Link as he'd once done with Lucky, and had felt fortunate to have such an opportunity arise twice in his life.

A few minutes later, Billy was back in his car, heading down the lane with Lucky's words echoing in his head. He knew what they'd find in the Utah desert. He'd seen the aftermath of other airplane crashes, some containing remains so mutilated they were reduced to chunks of charred, pink flesh. He would bring Link home. It was appropriate that he be the one to do it. He should be one of them in the airplane.

The Lake

"Katy's a good swimmer," Paula Dubois said in a voice filled with concern, "but she might become trapped in the airplane." She remained beside her husband, eyes red from lack of sleep.

Link Anderson listened quietly, unable to say the venture would be without peril. Katy had convinced him she had a chance of retrieving the raft. When they'd told Paula, she'd immediately said no. She was now wavering, for he'd explained that they must have food and shelter, and it must be done before they were too weakened by hunger to function.

Katy snorted impatiently. "She's being chicken, like always."

It was not the first time he'd heard her use a scornful tone when speaking of Paula. The last thing they needed was dissension.

"No, your mother's right. It could be dangerous. I'll give it a try."

Link had removed Frank's and his own belt. Katy helped him buckle them together, then made two loops about his torso to secure the injured arm to his side. The slightest movement was painful, and he didn't want it bumping into anything needlessly during the dive.

Katy's voice was angry. "You've got a broken arm and Mom's being *ridiculous.*"

"She's concerned."

Paula approached them. "Are you sure you can do it safely, Katy?"

"Yes," the girl said confidently.

Her mother hesitated. "Then go ahead, and help, but be careful," she finally said.

"I will, Mom."

Link walked toward the rocky shore, the fourteen-year-old girl trailing behind. "The water's going to be cold," he cautioned.

Boise

Leslie was in a hurry. She'd returned to her apartment, packed, and driven to her father's house. The inventory takers—a bonded security company hired by the lawyers for the task—were already in the old home, walking through each room and listing everything.

"We were told to begin at nine sharp," the man in charge explained when she arrived. He scratched his jaw, then looked about. "Want us to start over?"

"No. I'm not going to be here for long, anyway." Leslie had avoided the big house since her father's death. "I'll just want to see the final list."

"The inventory goes to the law firm."

"That's fine." Old Gerald's friends had included several of the older, established attorneys in town. It was unthinkable that they'd try to cheat her.

Leslie walked around the house, looking at the items that had made up her father's life. There were several photographs and a large painting of her mother, who had passed away when Leslie was twelve. Then it had been just herself and Old Gerald in the big house. When she'd decided to marry, Old Gerald had disapproved of her choice. Leslie had believed he was being spiteful, and had defied him. She'd done that a lot, she remembered. Even after she'd been divorced, she'd been too proud to admit her father was right.

A brand was burned into a slab of knotty pine that hung over the fireplace.

The Rocklin name had been known in Idaho for the past 132 years, since a feisty ex-Confederate sergeant had been lured from the Ozarks by discoveries of gold. Idaho Territory had been vast then, including present-day Montana and Wyoming, and opportunities abounded. Tiring of fruitlessly wielding a pick and shovel, Sarge Rocklin had laid claim to twenty sections of grassland south of Idaho Falls, fought a few bloody skirmishes with Mormon zealots sent by Brigham Young to run him off, and raised beef cattle to sell to hungry gold miners. He'd called his ranch the Rockin' R, and the brand, as well as the name Rocklin, had become synonymous with stubbornness and tenacity. In 1890 Sarge had been elected to the new state legislature, and he'd built the large home in Boise for use when the

body was in session. In 1898 Old Sarge's son had disembarked for Cuba with his friend Teddy Roosevelt, and been
temporarily promoted to captain for the campaign to
"whup up" on the Spanish. Cap Rocklin had returned to
win the governorship in a landslide, and for the next eight
years the home had served as the Idaho executive mansion.

When Old Cap died, his son Gerald Rocklin had sold the
family ranch, used the money to open the first Rocklin
food stores, and moved permanently into the home his
grandfather had built. The historic brand had become the
logo for his stores and businesses.

Leslie decided to take the branded slab of wood with her
when she went East, although she had trouble envisioning
it in a high-rise apartment.

The Filipina was standing nearby, and her words burned
through Leslie's awareness.

"You're leaving?" she asked.

"Yes, ma'am. My fam'ly in Portlan'."

"When?"

"Mebbe tomorrow, ma'am."

At first the Filipina had come only during the daytime.
When Leslie's father had grown worse, she'd moved into
the guest room to be available around the clock. Old Gerald had been able to stay at home right up to the end. It
was the fourth time the nurse had watched over terminally
ill cancer victims, so she'd known what to expect and how
to provide the care such patients required. Leslie wouldn't
have traded positions for anything in the world.

The Filipina answered the doorbell and admitted the
managing partner in the law firm, who had been a pall-
bearer at Old Gerald's funeral.

"Everything going okay?' he asked Leslie.

She told him the nurse would be leaving the following
day. "Dad would have wanted her to receive a bonus," she
added. Old Gerald had been fastidious at making sure his
employees received their due.

"I'll have a check sent over." He graciously didn't mention the hundred thousand dollars of indebtedness as he
looked about. "Are you planning to move in, Les?"

"No." The home was expensive to maintain, and there
were too many self-reproachful memories.

"Then we should put it on the market right away. Older
homes are moving slow."

She could almost hear her father's explosion. "I'd rather wait," Leslie told him.

"That's up to you." His tone implied she was being foolish.

"I'm going to Salt Lake for a few days," she said. "On assignment."

"The estate should be established within the week. We'll handle the inventory, but before you leave I'll need instructions. There are two rather large obligations that must be settled."

Leslie glanced at the time. Only an hour remained before her plane departed.

The cellular telephone in her purse emitted a shrill buzz. She flipped it open. "Rocklin."

"Hiya." Mort Yoder's voice was hesitant.

"I'm dealing with a problem, Mort. What have you got?"

"I'm not sure. A group of Weyland Foundation people flew in from New York and went directly to the Department of Transportation building. I got back to my friend at FAA and asked if they had anything to do with the Gulfstream, but he still won't talk."

"So what does that mean?"

Mort sighed. "I dunno, unless someone from the foundation was on board. They do a lot of work with the arts, so maybe it's someone they're sponsoring. I've got a lot of ideas, but nothing firm. All I know is it's something big and no one's talking."

"So what's the official word from the Department of Transportation?"

"Nothing about when they'll release names of passengers, and they're not even talking about the rescue effort, except to say one's in progress. I've got a feeling about this one, Les. Everyone's gone too deaf and dumb at FAA, even my buddy there, and he owes me. It's either an official cover-up or a stall, and there's high-level people involved."

"Maybe," said Leslie. Mort was prone to believe in wild-eyed conspiracies.

He sounded wounded. "Look, if you're not interested . . ."

"I didn't say that. I'll go to Salt Lake and see what I can

dig up at the search-and-rescue effort. How about you? Will your boss let you work on it exclusively?"

"No way. He heard a rumor it's a group of attorneys from New York, and I've gotta have something firmer. Plug your computer into a phone connection so I can send some ideas I've been working on. Then maybe you can help with confirmation."

She glanced at her watch. Fifty minutes until takeoff. "I've got to catch an airplane, Mort. I'll call from Salt Lake City on a hard line."

Leslie punched the End button on the phone and collapsed it, wondering if they had anything. This morning she'd climbed out of bed feeling it was her time for the "big story", but she'd had other mornings when she'd felt the same rush. An *awful* thought struck her. What if Mort was wrong? What if it *was* a bunch of New York lawyers on the airplane?

Jesus, what a let-down *that* would be. No one would care if they lost a jumbo jet full.

She started for the door.

"What about the instructions?" the aging attorney reminded her. "The two debts?"

"You know more than I do about these things. Just do what's best for the estate."

He sighed at her frivolity as she left.

As Leslie drove away, she avoided looking back at the home of her childhood. She was tired of sadness, of worrying about what her father would have wanted her to do. It would be good to leave it all behind for a few days.

The Lake

Katy took a breath in the air pocket at the top of the cabin, then dove for the third time.

She'd found the raft—a heavy bundle at the rear of the submerged aircraft—and her problem wasn't the weight but the terrible cold. It was frightening in the dim fuselage, and she was terrified when she saw Gary's body, still strapped in the seat, or thought about the dead flight attendant up forward. As Katy tugged, her foot struck something, and she had the fleeting thought that she might get caught up and drown. She almost departed right then, and

it took all of her resolve to continue dragging the bundle
down the aisle past Gary. When she rose to the top for air
again, the life-raft bundle lay in the inclined aisle, a third
of the way toward the hatch.

There were several pockets of air in the fuselage, as the
pilot had predicted, and she'd learned how to use them.
When she felt the need she'd push up to the ceiling, take
a breath, and go back to work.

She shoved away from the pocket, grasped about in the
gloom until she found the raft, and dragged it along the
sloped aisle. Twice the bundle became hung up, but both
times she was able to pull it free and drag it ever closer to
the open hatch.

Katy floated to the top again for air, tiring badly but
pleased that she was no longer close to Gary's corpse. The
thought of him being dead there with her . . .

Something brushed her hand in the murky darkness.
Katy froze, petrified with the unreasonable fear that Gary
had freed himself from the seat and was reaching out.

It touched her again. It was diaphanous and clinging,
and could not possibly be a body, but . . . she drew gingerly
away. When it followed, she shrieked into the dark air
pocket. The echoing sound was itself terrifying—and all
reason left her. Katy kicked wildly for the open hatch, and
it was still following, now wrapping itself about her leg!
Her foot struck hard against the hatchway as she kicked
free of the fuselage and scrambled for the surface.

Link was waiting for Katy, holding onto the small flotilla
of cushions they'd bound together, when she burst wildly
to the surface, clawing with her hands and trying to climb
higher.

He grabbed her arm with his good hand. "What's
wrong?" he shouted

She choked and flailed, and began to shriek, "He's got
my legs!"

"Who?"

"Gary!"

Link released her and ducked below the surface. A few
seconds later he emerged and held a woman's scarf before
her eyes.

Katy spat out more water, trembling, eyes still wide and
mouth opened. He grasped her and held her close to impart

body heat. "You're fine," he told her repeatedly. She slowly calmed, then began to shiver violently. When it diminished, he released her. "Can you make it to the island?"

She looked and nodded. Her mother had heard her screams and was calling to her.

"Go ahead."

"What about the raft?"

"I'll get it. Swim to the island and warm up." He took a breath and went under.

It was difficult maneuvering, using one arm, but he found the open hatch and made his way inside. The raft bundle was only a few feet distant. He braced and tugged with his good hand, ignoring the bolts of fire that swept through the broken arm.

He was chilling badly by the time he'd hauled the raft to the lip of the opening, then lifted and shoved with the good hand. The bundle fell over, onto the muddy lake bottom.

Link pushed up to a pocket and took in a breath of air, then went out to the bundle. He laboriously unbuckled two nylon straps and loosened them, then felt until he found the Velcro fastener. Link yanked the flap open and immediately kicked toward the surface.

Katy had not returned to the island. She was waiting, holding onto the makeshift raft of flotation cushions, as he pulled in precious breaths of air.

"I'm ready to go down again," Katy said. Her fright had obviously waned.

"I've got it outside the airplane," he managed. "Move out of the way."

Link took a final breath and went under. He found the bundle, then the cord and handle under the loose flap. After anchoring his feet firmly on the lake bottom, he pulled hard.

The rubber life raft began to bulge and extend as he pushed clear to watch. It began to expand and unfold, then slowly rose from the lake bottom, like some eerie creature taking a deep breath as it came to life. He ascended with it, watching it grow—too tired, his arm too painful, to feel elation.

When he broke the surface, Katy was laughing exuberantly. "You did it!" she cried.

The raft was big, eight feet long and five feet wide, and was *still* filling with air.

"Climb aboard," he told her.

Katy grasped rope handles and pulled herself up and over, then fell inside onto a hard plastic, bright orange survival kit. "Ouch," she yelped.

He held the flotation cushions against the raft. She hauled them inside, then helped pull him into the raft. He looked about, shivering and cradling the arm.

"You did it," she repeated.

"We did it." He forced a smile. "I wouldn't have been able to disconnect the brackets on the bulkhead."

"Yeah, but I chickened out." She looked angry at herself.

"Telescopic oars," he announced, examining two lengths of sturdy, high-impact plastic. She helped him extend them. "Now let's get the rest of your family," he said.

"Wait." She paused for a brief moment, then slid over the side and went under.

They'd discussed what they should take from the airplane. After several long minutes she bobbed to the surface with the first item, the large first-aid kit from the galley.

He took it without comment. Katy was proving something, both to him and herself.

She emerged next with food from a locker in the galley area, two packets of it. As he stowed them, Katy held onto the side for a short rest.

"Don't overdo it," he said. She did not answer but went down again. This time she emerged with an armload of clothing, which he pulled into the raft.

"I got 'em ... from Dad's ... hang-up bag," she wheezed. They'd discussed bringing in other items, but she appeared spent.

He spoke firmly. "That's enough."

Katy started to protest, then looked at his face and held her tongue. He hauled her into the raft, where she collapsed, blowing breaths and trembling. As she rested, he held her close for warmth until he judged her breathing to be normal and could feel no more shivers.

Katy took up an oar and began to paddle toward the island, as Link examined the food packets. "Sandwiches," he announced. "Five pastrami and six ham and cheese."

"I could eat a ... Clydesdale horse," Katy said as she paddled.

"Water's seeped into most of them."

"That's okay. I could eat a *soggy* Clydesdale."

As they neared, Paula came to the edge of the rocks to watch.

"What do you think?" Katy called out proudly as they came close.

Her mother could not conceal an expression of relief that her daughter was safe.

Airborne over San Francisco

Takeoff from Watsonville had been delayed by a rain shower. They were in a dual-engine Piper Navajo on their way to Salt Lake City, but Charbonneau had asked for a brief side trip.

Webb was flying, Jaeger occupying the right seat. Simon sat immediately behind them, staring at the picturesque bridge below. "I'd like a closer look," he said, and Webb banked into a descending turn.

"There's not as much traffic as I'd thought," Jaeger observed.

"It's Saturday," Charbonneau said. "Commuters are bumper to bumper during the week."

Simon's pulse quickened as he looked farther north, toward the city of San Rafael.

"The trailer arrives tomorrow," he said, "and I already have ten people working. The ingredients have all been shipped. It will be ready in two weeks."

"That won't leave much time," said Jaeger.

"We don't dare let it sit idle. It's too unstable."

He searched until he found the fenced compound. Vapor rose from the main building, indicating the liquid oxygen plant was already operating. Everything was on schedule.

"That's good," he said to the pilot, and they turned eastward, toward Sacramento and, far beyond, Salt Lake City. The flight would take more than three hours.

Simon Charbonneau settled back into his seat, then let his eyes linger on the tall, hawk-faced man in the copilot's seat who had arrived from Argentina the week before. This was the first time he'd really studied the assassin since he'd seen him in action in Wisconsin, but he had met him once in Argentina and had been briefed in detail before he and Webb had arrived. He had reservations, especially about Jaeger's blood thirst, which some said he could not control.

The big man sat quietly, brooding as he stared out the windscreen of the Piper Navajo. Jaeger—called the Hunter because of his skills at tracking and killing men—was balding, very tall, and while he appeared cadaverous, the impression was deceiving. The hunter was quick, both mentally and physically, and powerful. He spoke English with a European accent, yet he'd never been on that continent. He'd been born in 1956 in northern Argentina of German émigré parentage—his father once a senior S.S. officer who had fled his country before the defeat of the Third Reich. Eight years after his birth, his parents' farm near Añatuya, in the high Gran Chaco plain, had failed, and his father had donned his dress uniform and called his son in to speak with him. Nothing was known about the conversation, for as soon as the child left he'd put his Walther P-38 pistol to his head. Afterward, Jaeger's mother had labored as a seamstess and maid when she could find work, and her son and two daughters had often been left to wander the dark streets of Añatuya. There was little more known about his childhood.

It was obvious that he'd spent time in the U.S., for he had contacts here and spoke the language well, but it had been in Colombia that the Hunter had been discovered and hired by El Soleil. In 1995 he'd planned the abductions and killings, and the following year the assassination of the Argentinean minister. Those had been the first *truenos,* and Charbonneau had cause to remember them well. He had presented the idea and then had even determined their timing.

Except for the blood lust, a failing that concerned Charbonneau but few others within El Soleil, Jaeger was efficient. If things went as planned, the man who ran El Soleil had determined that the Hunter would be placed in charge of the Argentine secret police. That was the prize that motivated him, and Charbonneau was one of those who judged him.

When they'd first met, Jaeger had asked that he take a false name, a security measure he preferred for himself and those who worked with him. Diego DiPalma had settled on his alias frivolously—he'd despised a woman professor at Harvard named Simone Charbonneau.

The Hunter had turned in his seat, and Simon motioned him close. "While we were waiting for the rainstorm to pass, I received another call. Our contact in Washington says a man named Tom Oliver will lead the search for the Gulfstream. He'll be staying at the Hilton."

Jaeger was pleased with the information. "I'll radio ahead and make reservations for us there so Webb can monitor his room."

Charbonneau had been told that Webb was good at such things. Webb was a licensed commercial pilot, and more—a jack of all trades who had bounced from job to job while searching for his niche. He was a trained medical technician, was good with electronics, and seemed more at ease when engrossed in his laptop computer than with the world outside. He was serious-minded, and Charbonneau had noted a troubled expression when they'd waited outside the cabin in Wisconsin as Jaeger had beaten the secretary to death.

Simon repeated his concern: "How will we get to the aircraft before the authorities?"

"After they learn where the Gulfstream's located, it will be a matter of reacting more quickly." Jaeger—the man called the Hunter, who trusted no one—smiled. "They must act within their restrictions. My rules are much simpler."

7

1:15 P.M.—The Lake

Paula padded awkwardly, dipping the oar into the water on
one side, then moving to the other side and rowing there.
It seemed they were not progressing at all until she'd periodically glance back at the rock island that was slowly diminishing in size.

She could not think of a worse hell. The awful terror on
the airplane . . . realizing that Frank was at the verge of
death and nothing could be done . . . worrying while Katy
dove into the airplane. Now there was the ignominy of being so damned helpless at such a simple task.

"A little to the right," Anderson said, an understatement,
for she'd maneuvered them into a right angle from her intended path. Paula huffed an exhausted sigh—her hands
were turning hamburger-raw, but she was determined to
continue.

"Let me help," Katy said for the second time. She'd
been first to paddle, but Link Anderson had shooed her to
the bow to rest when he'd noticed she was trembling, admonishing her that cold and exhaustion could combine to
build pneumonia, and sickness must be avoided at all costs.
The pilot had gamely tried paddling, but after a few
attempts—and although he'd awkwardly used only his
good arm—his face had paled and he'd given up, sitting
very still and clutching the broken arm. So Paula had
wordlessly taken the oar and began to try.

She would ply the oar for a while, rest, then start again.
The soreness in her shoulders was mounting, but she refused to give up. They must get to shore if her family was
to survive.

"You're doing fine," he encouraged as she rested, but

she knew she was not. She simply could not make the raft continue on a straight course.

She began to catch her breath.

"We're closer," he said, eyeing the shore that still seemed miles away.

"Mr. Anderson?" Katy said. "I feel rested now."

Paula regarded her daughter. "I'll do it."

Katy persisted. "The sandwich helped, and I'm warmer now."

The pilot relented. "You can try, but don't let yourself get too tired. We can't afford another invalid."

Katy moved to the right side of the raft and hefted the second oar. "Put your oar into the lock, Mom. It'll be easier with a rower on both sides."

Paula watched what Katy was doing, and snapped her oar into its swivel mount.

"Ready when you are, Mom." Katy's voice was uncharacteristically cheerful.

Paula began to row, using both hands as Katy was doing, trying to ignore the blisters that had developed on her palms. After a bit of practice they stopped going in circles.

It was three o'clock before they approached the shore. By then tears of pain trickled down Paula's cheek. "Head toward the sandy beach," Link Anderson told them. "We don't want to puncture the raft on rocks."

"A little farther right, Mom," Katy said.

"I'm *trying!*" she blurted, holding back an urge to cry. Then she felt ridiculous and shook her head angrily at herself. "You're right, honey. A little farther right."

When they were close, Link swung over the side, grasped the tow rope in his right hand, and began to haul the raft ashore. He stiffened, as if taken by a jolt of pain, then forced himself to continue.

Katy was quickly out and at the pilot's side, grasping the rope. Paula slumped, trying to relax her tortured shoulders and back, grateful for the respite. Then she too crawled over the side, yelped involuntarily when she encountered the icy water, and joined in.

"That's good," the pilot told them when the rubber craft was out of the water and on the sand. Next they carried the raft's contents onto a lawn-like patch of grass in a small gap in the trees, stumbling with exhaustion. Finally they carried Frank. After they'd laid him out as comfortably as possible, they all collapsed onto the grass.

"We did it!" Katy exulted, but Paula was too tired to feel victorious. She watched as Link Anderson bent over her husband to observe his breathing.

"How is he?" Paula asked. Frank looked terrible, ashen-faced and hardly breathing.

He rose, wearing a neutral expression. "No change," was all the pilot said as he knelt over the things from the raft. "While I'm sorting these out, I want you ladies to go to the beach and look for driftwood. We'll need sturdy sticks ten to twelve inches in length. Thin and flat ones."

"What for?" Katy asked.

"We have to set and split my arm if I'm going to function."

Paula frowned. "We don't know anything about that sort of thing."

Link looked at her. "We're going to have to all pitch in. I know what to do to survive, but I can't do it all."

Katy pushed to her feet, a task not so easy for Paula, and they went to the beach. There they walked slowly and stared at the water's edge, Paula still catching her breath.

While they'd drawn apart during the past months, Paula was always awed by her child's energy and resourcefulness. Katy was becoming an image of herself, but all Paula remembered at her age was being awkward and shy. Katy was neither of those.

"Mr. Anderson's in a lot of pain," Katy said.

"I know." Paula's thoughts were mixed toward her husband's friend. He was quiet, almost unnaturally withdrawn, yet he seemed to know about survival, and for the present they were forced to rely upon his resourcefulness.

Link watched the women searching, then returned his attention to the things they'd brought from the raft. He began by laying out the articles of clothing. There was a hodge-podge: a man's undershirt, a pair of lightweight trousers, a dress shirt, two polo shirts, and a golf rain poncho.

Link went through his pockets and pulled out a fingernail clipper and butane lighter. He did not smoke, but carried the emergency source of fire when he flew, as he'd learned in the military.

Next a small Swiss army knife, which he could not open

since his left hand was useless. The knife had a blade, can and bottle opener, and small scissors.

He searched Frank Dubois' pockets and found nothing except a set of keys, money clip, and slim wallet. He returned them, for they were of no use.

A sharp pain stung from the core of the broken arm, so he held it closer as he tackled the hard-cased survival kit, pulling off the adhesive waterproofing strip that held it together. Inside he found a twelve by sixteen-foot orange plastic tarp, which he laboriously unfolded and spread on the grass.

He began placing items from the survival kit onto the tarp.

There was a small first-aid kit, which he put aside, for they had the larger one. There were three smoke flares and a metal mirror for signaling; a brass-cased compass with a luminous dial; a hunting knife with a seven-inch, razor-sharp black-steel blade in an olive drab plastic scabbard; two fifty-foot bundles of nylon cord; a dozen fishhooks of assorted sizes, and twenty yards of fish line; a roll of thin wire, labeled: 25 FT. .20 GA., SNARE; two tins, one of cocoa mix, the other instant coffee; twenty tea bags; packets of salt and pepper; six nesting cups and six metal plates; a small cooking pot and skillet, and a detachable handle that fit both; six packets of metal flatware; four cans of liquid heat and a tiny, fold-out stove that used them; a plastic cylinder containing wind and waterproof matches, with a scratcher on bottom; twelve wads of chemically impregnated cotton tinder; a tube of liquid gel soap; a bottle of water-purification pills; a plastic two-cell flashlight; six pairs of woolen socks, size large; and six thin survival blankets made of stitched layers of aluminized polyester.

There was also a hundred-page survival manual that showed how everything worked, identified animals and edible plants, and at the back showed basic first-aid practices.

The women returned with a collection of driftwood, similar in that all were long, thin, and flat on two sides.

Link gained his feet, and Katy helped him remove the contraption of belts that had secured his arm. Next she helped him slip off the shirt, a feat that was more painful.

Katy's mouth drooped as she noticed the two symmetrical, gnarled scars that marred his upper chest. "Those are old," he explained, but the girl had trouble dragging her eyes away.

The forearm was taut, swollen twice its normal girth, and he slowly lifted it above his head, enduring several sharp bolts of pain. "This should let the blood drain and reduce the swelling some," he explained. Then, as he instructed, the women went to work.

Katy opened the large first-aid kit and pulled out a brown-colored sling, two rolls of gauze, adhesive tape, a pair of surgical scissors, and an elastic bandage.

Paula picked up her husband's damp undershirt from the tarp, flapped it in the air several times to dry it, and cut off the sleeves, neck, and bottom.

"We don't want any seams to chafe the skin," he explained.

Paula cut the shirt into three equal-sized pieces of soft cotton cloth, then wrapped one about a piece of the flat driftwood, taped it, repeated the process on two others, and was left with three sturdy, well-padded contrivances. She placed them onto the collection taken from the first-aid kit.

"Now the hard part," Link said. He explained what they were to do, then cautiously lowered the arm.

After much encouragement Paula still refused to pull on his extended hand, for each time she touched it he grimaced.

"I can't," she finally said in a quavering voice.

"It's got to be done," he told her patiently. "If it's not set, it's going to heal improperly."

Paula Dubois held her eyes tightly closed for a long moment. Finally she opened them and grasped his hand gingerly, avoiding looking at his face.

"Pull slowly and evenly," he told her.

"Harder," he grunted as the pain increased.

She did so, leaning back with more of her weight.

"Yeah," he whispered. "Your turn, Katy."

The girl was not as hesitant. She wielded gauze, securing the padded sticks on top, bottom and outside of his forearm. Finally came the elastic bandage. When she wrapped too tightly and Link released a painful grunt, Paula Dubois bit her lip, but she continued to apply pressure. When only his fingers were left unwrapped she released him, and Link doubted that he was half as pale as she.

After helping him into his shirt, Katy fashioned the sling, adjusting Velcro straps until the arm was comfortable, his hand positioned high over his sternum.

Link smiled at both of them. "It already feels a hundred percent better." It was no lie. Cloth and gauze now cushioned the arm, the invisible driftwood formed a protective barrier should he bump into anything, and it was all held securely in place.

Katy's craftsmanship was not done. She retrieved his flight jacket, folded up the left sleeve and secured it with safety pins from the first-aid kit, and helped him pull it on. Finally she stood back and observed proudly.

"Thank you," he said, meaning it. He looked at the dwindling sun, then around the clearing. "We'll build a fire over by that old log. Paula, you dig a pit while we gather wood."

Paula would fare poorly in the woods, for she'd lost her shoes in the swim from the airplane, and bare feet showed through hose that were ragged and tattered.

"What am I supposed to dig with?"

Link retrieved one of the discarded flat-sided sticks, handed it over, then walked to a spot equidistant between the log and the saplings. "Right here. Make it four inches deep, and about three feet in circumference. Then we'll line it with stones to retain the heat."

Paula sighed.

"We all have to pitch in," he tried.

"I'm *tired*," she blurted. "And I *don't* appreciate being bossed around."

Katy rolled her eyes in exasperation. "Aw, Mom. Don't be difficult."

Paula glared. "Do *not* speak to me in that tone." She closed her eyes tightly and took in a breath, on the verge of tears. "My husband is *dying!*" she cried, then released a shuddering sob.

Paula Dubois had led a sheltered life, and her frayed nerves were understandable. In normal times Link might have sympathized, but the situation was not at all normal.

He used an even tone. "Right now we need warmth and shelter. It's not going to be easy on anyone, but it will be better if we work together."

A long moment later Paula approached with the flat stick

and stared at the still-wet earth. When Link and Katy left she was on her knees, digging halfheartedly.

Fifteen minutes later, when they emerged laden with sticks and fallen branches, Paula was seated on the log, staring mournfully at her husband as she nibbled daintily on a sandwich.

Link dropped his one-arm load and grabbed for the half-eaten sandwich. "*Damn* you!" he exploded as Paula dropped the sandwich and raised her hands defensively.

Then Paula's own anger ignited. "My *hands* hurt," she said shrilly. "I *started* digging your damned hole, but my hands were raw from rowing."

Katy deposited her wood near the firepit site, picked up the sandwich, and carefully cleaned away foreign matter.

"Why in hell's name did you take the sandwich?" Link asked.

"I was *hungry*," she retorted. "Is something wrong with eating when you get hungry?"

"There's not that much food. We've got to—"

"Dad just said something!" Katy exclaimed.

Link Anderson abruptly knelt, looking closely at his injured friend. Paula crouched on the opposite side, biting her lower lip in concern.

Frank's eyes blinked weakly.

"Someone get water," Link Anderson said quietly.

Katy grabbed a cup from the tarp and hurried toward the lakeshore.

Frank's eyes almost closed but remained slitted.

"Where does it hurt worst?" Link tried.

"Feels like an ... anvil's on ... my head," Frank released a low moan. "My family?"

"Katy and Paula are fine. We made it to shore and we're setting up camp."

His eyelids fluttered.

"Frank?" Paula whispered, but he didn't respond, just made another mournful sound, as if wracked by pain, and fought to remain awake.

Katy returned with the water-filled cup, which Link held to his friend's lips. Frank swallowed as he poured in small doses. When the cup was half-empty, Link put it aside.

"I've been thinking ... about *trueno*," Frank whispered between gasps.

"What's that?" Link asked, puzzled.

"April of ninety-five . . . Oklahoma City . . . *trueno* . . . That one . . . was first."

Link's Spanish was spotty from disuse, but he remembered that *trueno* meant thunder. It made no sense. Frank was hallucinating.

"We've got food," Link tried to tell him, but Frank gasped a couple of times, the eyelids closed, and he slipped back into unconsciousness.

Link Anderson slowly stood and stared at the sky. "Dammit," he muttered. "Where are the *airplanes*?"

Paula Dubois gently touched her husband's face. Link observed her bare feet, went to the tarp, and returned with a handful of woolen socks. When she looked up, he handed them over.

"Put them on. The second pair's for Frank."

"Thank you." Her voice was subdued.

He turned to Katy. "Next we gather rocks. Anything bigger than our fists."

A few minutes later, they returned from the lakeside, laden with rock, to find Paula digging resolutely with the stick. The earth was moist and not difficult to penetrate.

"How much deeper?" she asked.

"Another inch," Link said as he deposited his load.

Paula sat back. "I'm sorry about before," she said. "I was being a brat."

"I was out of line too. Our tempers are all raw, and we'll have to watch for that sort of thing. We've got to focus our energy on survival and getting out of here."

When the firepit was sufficiently deep and they'd gathered a moderate-sized stack of stones, Link knelt and arranged them around the earthen bowl. As soon as he'd finished rock laying, he built a base of twigs, then added a wad of impregnated cotton tinder. He used the lighter. The cotton caught and emitted a blue blaze. The twigs, then the sticks burned, but the wood was rain-soaked, and as soon as the tinder was exhausted, the flame died.

Link doggedly built another base of twigs and added a second wad. This time the fire blazed brighter. When he was certain it had caught, he cautiously rose.

"We'll need more wood," he said to Katy as he gained his feet. When she grimaced he sympathized, for he too was bone-weary.

"I'll help," Paula said, but he shook his head.

"We're wearing shoes. You tend to Frank."

For the next half hour he and Katy periodically emerged from the forest with laden arms. The stack had grown to six feet in length and four in height before Link called off the effort.

He watched for a moment, pleased at the sight of the crackling fire, then sat heavily on the log, drained of strength and emotion.

Paula stood near the flames, hands held out for warmth against the growing evening chill. "It's a nice fire," she said quietly.

"I'll keep it going," chimed Katy. She took her seat on the log beside Link, already recovering from the exertion. "I've been to summer camp every year since I was eight. They said I was good in the woods," she told him proudly.

"You'll be using everything you learned. First, though, you've got to look where you're stepping. Did you see the rattlesnakes?"

"Snakes?" Paula looked alarmed.

"I saw the one you warned me about," Katy said.

"There were two others, and you don't want to tangle with them. Be careful and aware. They'll normally warn you if you get close, but don't bank on it."

Katy regarded the forest somberly.

"Next we hang the clothes to dry," he said. "Then we're done for the night."

"I'll do it," Katy said, and bounded off the log toward the packets of nylon cord.

As Paula followed her daughter, determined to be helpful, Link regarded the saplings in the gathering shadows on the opposite side of the fire. Tomorrow they'd build a shelter from the elements, and dig a trench for their waste.

"How's this?" Katy was standing beside a tree, holding up the rope.

"Is that high enough?" Link Anderson asked Paula, wanting her to participate.

Paula looked at Katy's upstretched hand and nodded hesitantly. She held the cord in place as Katy tied the end around the tree. When they'd finished stringing line, then flapping and hanging the wet clothing from Frank's bag, Link called them back.

"Let's have another half sandwich to keep our energy up."

"I've had mine," Paula said sheepishly, and he didn't argue. They had to conserve food until they found a new source.

When she'd finished eating, Katy examined the remaining food. All but one sandwich were waterlogged and mushy in their wrappers. "I think we should open them and place them near the fire," she offered. "When they're dry, we can wrap them again."

"Makes sense," Link said, hardly listening as the reserves of his energy drained away. As Katy unwrapped the sandwiches, Link went to the tarp to retrieve the survival blankets. He took one for himself and handed the remainder to Paula.

"Think the clothes'll be dry by morning?" Katy asked him.

"Your mother knows more about that than I do," Link tried, but Katy dropped the issue. The division between mother and daughter had not ended.

Paula began to unfold the thin blankets. As she tried to pull a side of one under Frank, Link approached to help.

"I'll do it," she said gamely.

Link curled up in his blanket on the opposite side of the fire, thinking about the difficult time they faced. He didn't know how long it would be before they were rescued, but they must be prepared for the worst. He would do his best to keep Frank Dubois and his family from further harm. For the present, though, he was badly in need of sleep.

Airport Hilton, Salt Lake City

Tom Oliver opened the door to let in the three men who had arrived from Washington before him. He'd landed three hours earlier and spent most of the time in the dining room. Since he anticipated a busy day tomorrow, Tom did not intend to let the meeting to go for long.

He sat at the small table, but did not invite his subordinates to join him. "What have we got so far?" he asked.

"The rescue operation's set up at the airport. The Air Force is flying nighttime infrared coverage, as of a half hour ago. Tomorrow morning we'll have fifteen light aircraft and two C-130's from Hill Air Base flying grid-search patterns."

"Who are we dealing with?"

"Fourteen pilots and observers from the local civil air patrol, and one pilot from the charter airline company. They're all—"

Oliver raised a hand to interrupt. "The charter company? Executive Connections?"

"They sent a pilot named Bowes. He's flying a Beech Baron."

"What the hell is he doing here?"

"He's got experience at this sort of thing, and raised holy hell when we tried to tell him we had enough searchers. Then we got a call from the administrator's office in Washington telling us to let him in. A U.S. Senator named Phillips laid on pressure to get him included."

Tom Oliver snorted disgustedly. "Jesus. That's all we need. How about the press?"

"There are a few locals hanging around, but not much national interest."

"I wish we could shut them off completely."

"Then they'd know something's up. We thought we'd tell them about the light airplane in the morning so they can chew on that, and maybe back off about the Gulfstream."

"Are they asking for the passengers' names?"

"Repeatedly. We've put them off, but we can't get away with it forever."

"You know our instructions. No names are to be released until the wreckage is located, and no information is to be given out that might help anyone else find it."

"It's going to be difficult to continue denying it was a midair collision."

"Don't deny or confirm anything, *period*," Oliver said. "And when the Gulfstream wreckage is located, we cordon it off and wait for the people from the foundation."

A rapping sounded at the door, and one of the FAA reps let in a man wearing a dark suit. He introduced himself: a lawyer representing the Weyland Foundation.

Tom Oliver rose and formed a warm smile. "We're getting our war plan together."

The man took the other chair and listened as Oliver iterated what they'd covered thus far. He did not seem displeased that Executive Connections had provided a pilot and aircraft.

"We'll hit the ground running tomorrow morning," Oliver told him cheerfully.

The Weyland lawyer nodded. "Let's go back to the time of the disappearance. We're puzzled about how an aircraft could disappear so completely from your radars."

"That one's easy," said one of Oliver's assistants. "First there was the computer shutdown and loss of communications just before the accident, and everything was switched to manual mode. The controllers were scrambling to get back on line, and were stretched too thin to look at returns from clouds, large birds, et cetera, so they viewed only IFF squawks from aircraft. If the Gulfstream's IFF was suddenly shut down, like maybe destroyed in a midair collision, it would simply drop off the screen."

"*No* one was monitoring the actual radar returns?" Oliver interrupted. "There were unmonitored radars that recorded aircraft skin paints. I'm having the tapes sent from Ogden in the morning."

"They haven't examined them yet?" the lawyer asked incredulously.

"They're contractors, and we were told not to let *anyone* else learn about the Gulfstream's location. We'll view them first thing in the morning, at the rescue center."

The lawyer took his feet. "If you don't mind, my colleagues and I would like to observe them too."

"Certainly," Oliver said to the representative of the foundation, to whom he'd been told to provide every possible assistance.

The Weyland Foundation lawyer left them, and a few minutes later Tom Oliver excused the others. He had a single drink of bourbon over ice then, and wondered about the upcoming day. If the search proved successful, the credit would surely come his way. He intended to do everything possible to make that happen.

Tom Oliver prepared for bed early, unaware that four different audio-monitoring devices occupied the room with him.

Webb was listening from a room two floors above. As he heard the sounds of Oliver showering, he took off the headset and removed the cassette tape from the recorder.

Jaeger, who occupied the adjacent room, would be interested. If the videotapes of the raw rader returns were to be viewed by the authorities the next morning, they would not have long to act.

The Lake

Katy was awakened by a shout.

Link Anderson had curled up across the fire, on the opposite side of the log. Now he was standing, gesturing with his free arm. He yelled again and grabbed a piece of firewood.

Katy pushed back the survival blankets and tried to blink sleep from her eyes. Then she froze, for a large, dark shape was moving about the dim periphery of the campfire light.

When the pilot brandished the stick, the shape grunted and reared onto hind legs.

"Get," Link said, then moved so quickly Katy hardly believed it, and thumped the bear squarely on its snout. The animal released a painful squeal, then dropped to all fours and scampered into the darkness.

The pilot examined the rock where she'd left the sandwiches out to dry. All but one were gone.

"What's happening?" Paula asked, rising up beside Katy.

"A bear ate our sandwiches," Katy explained. "Mr. Anderson whopped his nose."

"A *bear*?" Her voice was incredulous.

"I slept too hard," the pilot said, glaring at the forest.

Katy regarded the shadows. "At camp they told us to let a marauding bear have the food."

"Your councilors weren't as hungry as we are." He angrily piled wood on the flames, making sparks fly. "I should have hung the food out of his reach."

Katy and Paula were standing, casting cautious stares at the darkness.

Link picked up the pot, then went to the line and felt. "The clothes are dry. You ladies get them down while I go to the lake for water. Hot chocolate sound good?"

"Yeah!" exclaimed Katy.

As he disappeared, she and Paula went to the line, keeping a vigil for the bear, and carried armloads of clothing back to the log.

When the pilot reemerged from the gloom, he placed the pot at the edge of the fire, then knelt to wait for the water to heat. "Go ahead and change. Just tell me when I can turn around."

Paula cast a suspicious eye at Link, and didn't move as Katy replaced her thin blouse with one of her father's knit shirts, then pulled on a long-sleeved shirt to wear as a jacket.

Katy glanced at her mother with an exasperated sigh. "I'm through," she said.

The pilot turned and regarded Paula, still in the thin dress. "Aren't you cold?"

"I'm fine." She stared into the fire.

The pilot motioned at the still form. "Frank's a special friend, Paula. In Saudi we became close, like men do when they grow to rely on each other. We made a pact to watch after one another's six o'clock. Did Frank tell you what that means?"

"I don't think so."

"It's a fighter pilot's way of saying we'd look out for each other. We didn't put limits on it, didn't say it only applied to that situation. Last month when I told him my father's business needed a boost, he helped. Now Frank's in trouble, and I intend to get him through it."

It was a long speech for the normally reticent pilot.

"Our pact extended to our families," he said quietly. He walked to the clothing, picked out the golf poncho, and tossed it onto Paula's lap. "At least put that on so you won't freeze."

She stared back with an even look, then deftly slipped the poncho over her head.

"Darned bear," Katy groused. The tails of her father's white shirt hung past her knees, so she tied them at her waist. "It fits *purr*-fectly," she said, rolling up the sleeves. Katy walked stiffly for a few steps, then turned back, as if she were on a fashion show runway.

Link Anderson added wood to the fire. "As soon as we've finished our chocolate, we'll get more sleep. There's a lot to be done tomorrow."

"What about . . . him?" Paula sat on the log, eyeing the forest.

"He's a two-year-old black bear, and shouldn't have trouble getting food this time of year. I doubt he'll come back tonight. He was just being a pig, and we made it easy for him."

"I don't know . . ." Katy said dubiously.

The pilot looked at her, then nodded at the shadows. "In the old days, Indians named the animals they saw around their camps."

Katy cocked her head. "How do you know so much about Indians?"

"I'm part Piegan—that's one of the Blackfoot tribes. The scars you saw on my chest were from one of their sacred ceremonies."

"Wow," said Katy, impressed.

"Another part of the ritual was learning their legends and beliefs, and how they lived in the old days." He regarded the forest. "They learned to live in harmony with their closest neighbors, the animals around them. Now, what do you think we should name that guy?"

Paula pulled up the poncho hood and huddled inside her mound of clothing. After a moment of silence she offered: "How about Smoky?"

"Smoky looks different," Katy said with authority. "He's got a brown muzzle."

"You come up with one," Link challenged.

Katy thought about it for a moment. "Fuzz-butt," she said.

Link Anderson chuckled, and even Paula smiled.

"That's his name," the pilot said. "Fuzz-butt."

"What about the sandwich?" Katy asked. "Unless we hang it out of his reach, he's going to come back and get it. Want me to do it?"

"Nope. We'll just do away with the bear bait." He nodded at the remaining sandwich and handed the survival knife to Paula. "Thirds," he said.

Paula divided the sandwich as he stirred instant chocolate mix into the pot of hot water, then filled their cups. They sat on the log, sipping chocolate and eating in tiny nibbles, as if that would make the portions bigger.

Link told them a Blackfoot myth about Scarface, an ugly, badly disfigured young man in love with the chief's beautiful daughter, and how he'd enlisted the support of Otter, Badger, Bear, Swan, and other animals to climb mountains and cross wide waters to find the home of Old Man and his wife, the Moon. When Scarface saved the life of Old Man's son, he returned to the People and was handsome in the eyes of the princess, and they lived happily thereafter.

"Who was Old Man?" Katy asked suspiciously.

"The Sun. The one who made it all."

"Like God?"

"Not really. Old Man wasn't very perfect. He'd get lost or confused like anyone else, and the Blackfeet told jokes about how his wife Moon got the best of him. But he was a good guy."

It was a neat story, and Katy realized she wasn't looking for the bear or worrying about the forest as much. When she'd finished with the last crumb of sandwich, she spoke up.

"In the morning I'd like to take the raft out to the airplane and get more of the carry-on bags. Mom and I have jackets and jeans there, and she's got tennis shoes."

"That would be wonderful," Paula said. "Is there more food?"

"I think so," said Katy. "Is it okay, Mr. Anderson?"

The pilot nodded. "But this time I'll do the diving."

Katy shook her head adamantly. "I'm the best swimmer here, and I'll have dry clothes when I crawl back in the raft." She was still ashamed of her display of cowardice, when she'd come clawing her way out of the water.

"I'll help row," Paula said.

"We can't leave Frank unattended," said the pilot. "Anyway, I've got something else in mind. You're going to become the fisherman of the group."

Paula's mouth sagged as he continued.

"There's hooks and line in the survival kit. We'll need food—more than we'll find in the airplane—and I've seen fish in the lake."

Katy noted her mother's look of concern and almost laughed. Then she thought of handling a slimy fish and adroitly changed the subject. "Do you really think they're searching for us, Mr. Anderson? Shouldn't we have seen an airplane by now?"

"They're looking and they'll eventually get to this valley, so we've got to be ready. We'll prepare a signal fire to set off when we see a rescue airplane."

"How long will that be?" Paula asked.

"Could be tomorrow or next week. There's no way of telling. But things aren't all that gloomy. We're a lot better off than we were this morning."

"I'm still hungry," Katy complained.

"Tomorrow we'll dine on all those fish your mother's going to catch."

8

DAY TWO—Sunday, June 9

12:30 A.M.—Ogden

Webb was astounded that getting into the Ogden air traffic control center was so easy. When they'd flashed the fake ID's Jaeger had provided, claiming they were Department of Transportation inspectors, he'd waited for a challenge, but the woman who admitted them appeared even more nervous than he was. The on-duty night supervisor wasn't at all surprised—in fact, he acted as if he'd expected them. Following the communications blackout, both of the other shifts had received similar inspections. It was his turn.

Just as Jaeger had told him, all they had to do was act as if they knew what they were doing—and the surprising part of it was that Webb *did*. He knew his way around ATC centers and was sure he'd be able to understand the recording equipment.

They started with an abbreviated tour of the building, then accepted a cup of coffee in the break room and chatted. A few minutes later, Jaeger went with the supervisor to check the currency of their regulations, leaving Webb behind.

After a couple of minutes he slipped down the empty hallway until he found the room containing the video bank, which the supervisor had pointed out. Inside were rows of twelve-inch magnetic tape reels, each appropriately stamped with times and dates.

A large envelope—marked T. F. OLIVER—was set out on a table. Inside Webb found two reels—covering medium- and low-altitude regimes during the time in question. Webb took both, replaced them with tapes from the previous month, then removed a magnetic degaussing wand from his pocket and plugged it into a nearby receptacle. For more than a minute he passed the wand over the replacement tapes. Satisfied that both were erased, he transferred the markings from the originals to the replacements and re-sealed the envelope. Finally he slipped the reels intended for Oliver into his briefcase and hurried back to the coffee room.

Twenty more minutes passed before Jaeger and the supervisor returned.

"Get those regulations updated," Jaeger said in an officious tone.

As they drove away from the center, Webb burst out laughing. "It worked."

"Yes," said Jaeger.

"Now we need to find a video player that can handle this kind of tape."

"That's not necessary. The supervisor gave me the address of a laboratory here that will convert them and put them on VHS cassettes for us."

"You came out and *asked* him?" Again Webb was astonished.

"Of course. The laboratory opens at seven-thirty in the morning. Tell the manager you're from the Ogden air traffic control center and show him your government identification. They'll want you to sign a work order."

"What if they suspect something?"

Jaeger sighed in exasperation. "All they'll be interested in is making sure they get paid. You worry about the wrong things, Webb. Have the tapes converted and get back as soon as possible so we can find out what happened to the Gulfstream."

Salt Lake City International Airport

When Leslie had called the *Washington Post* that morning, Mort Yoder still didn't have anything except his suspicions that the FAA was up to skullduggery. His speculations about the identity of the Gulfstream's passengers included everyone from the vice-president's mother to various rock stars. He was also still convinced that the Weyland Foundation was somehow involved.

Leslie Ann Rocklin waited in a small room of the airport building claimed by the FAA as the search and rescue coordination and control center, or "RCC" as the handout called it. The Federal Aviation Administration was using new procedures and new terms for the search operation. Many of their former functions had been privatized and turned over to contractors, and they were scrambling to retain the Aviation Safety function, much of which was already usurped by the National Transportation Safety Board. A handout told the reporters about the FAA's newfound efficiency and explained how effective their new procedures would be.

Leslie wasn't impressed. The handout was written in such gobbledegook that it was scarcely understandable. She was still trying to decide who was in charge.

It was ten after nine, and while the morning press conference had been scheduled to start at eight-thirty, the briefers still hadn't arrived. The media people present were grumbling, and a few talked about having better things to do. There were only three cameras set up in the rear, and only herself and six other reporters up front. Four of those were from local newspapers and television stations. Two were stringers, one for CNN, the other for the Associated Press. She could not believe her good fortune—if it really *was* a big story—that there was so little competition. On the other hand, it seemed odd that she and Mort Yoder would be the only ones feeling it might be anything other than routine. It was one of those *Everyone's crazy except you and me and I'm not so sure about you* things.

So far she'd gotten no indication that anything about the missing airplane was unique. She'd even had trouble finding out about the press meeting, having to call the *Deseret News*, a local newspaper, and ask until she found the woman covering the rescue effort. The reporter had been surprised that Leslie had come all the way from Boise. Leslie had told her, with a slight twinge of conscience, she'd just happened to be visiting relatives here. Mort said an attribute of a good investigative journalist was the ability to lie well, but it made her uneasy.

She'd spent the early morning at the airport, watching military and civil air patrol airplanes take off to join the search—and on the phone with Mort. He'd provided what information he had on his various speculations, both by voice and computer link.

The vice-president's mother hadn't been seen in public

for the past few days, and she might have been on her way to visit a daughter in California.

As for the Weyland Foundation, Mort Yoder had very little about the potential passengers, but he'd done some digging on the organization. The extent of their wealth was difficult to pin down, for they were privately owned, but he'd found that they were very big and very rich. There were estimated holdings of twelve billion dollars in the U.S. alone. Then there was the international picture, which was more difficult. Thirty-five percent of Siegmund Press, in the Republic of Germany—the largest publishing firm in the world—was held by a foundation subcompany. So were nine percent of Sony, in Japan, seventeen percent of Italy's Fiat, and thirty percent of the Canadian Teck Industries. Those added several billion more, and the list was growing. Now he was working on conglomerates, held by companies that were owned by yet others. The foundation was controlled by their financial board, a group called the *handful*. It was unknown who would take over as chairman, but Cyril Weyland had made firm retirement plans.

"How about the rock star?" Leslie had asked him.

"Mick Jagger was in New York with some of his buddies about then, and I'm still having trouble locating them all. That one's sort of way out," he admitted.

Leslie's reverie was broken as three men strode into the briefing room, exuding officiousness. She switched on her mini-recorder and poised a stylus over the screen of her electronic notepad. The era of broken pencil nubs was fast passing in the new world of reporting.

A man tapped on the microphone. "Hear me okay back there?" he asked, looking at the cameraman at the rear of the room. He introduced himself, a public affairs officer, then the two others: the search and rescue coordinator, and an obese man named Thomas Oliver from the FAA's Aviation Safety office. All were from the Department of Transportation's headquarters in Washington, D.C..

"Before we begin," the spokesman said, "let me say we've found nothing regarding the Gulfstream, which remains the primary subject of this search. This morning we'll discuss other aircraft wreckage discovered northwest of the Salt Lake. While it has nothing to do with this effort, since you're already here we felt we could get it out of the way."

He passed out press-release forms, then began to read the words in a droning voice that would have immediately put anyone but a devoted reporter into a comatose state.

The wreckage of the light airplane contained the body of a medical doctor by the name of Samuel G. Aarons. He'd taken off in a privately owned Cessna 172 from Butte, Montana, at 2:35 P.M. on Friday, on a local flight to Pocatello. They had aerial photographs of the wreckage and others taken from the ground, courtesy of an Air Force photographer. Those would be distributed at the end of the press conference. The FAA spokesman showed several images of the crash scene on a large television monitor, paused, then asked for questions.

The CNN stringer spoke first. "If the light plane went down two days ago, why are we only getting the word now?"

"We didn't find it until yesterday, and we attempt to notify next of kin before releasing names of deceased."

"Even without the pilot's name, why weren't we notified?"

The spokesman turned to the fat man. "Mr. Oliver?" He handed him the mike.

"We didn't wish to unduly alarm the families of other private pilots. There's been heavy air traffic all weekend, and we didn't want a lot of loved ones worrying."

The public affairs officer took the microphone back and pointed toward a local newsman.

"You said Aarons was on his way to Pocatello from Butte, but he crashed not far from the Great Salt Lake. That seems to be a long way off course."

"I agree. Is there a question in there somewhere?"

"The Cessna went down near the flight path of the Gulfstream. Could there have possibly been an air collision?"

The fat man from the FAA's Aviation Safety office took the mike again. "The normal operating ceiling for the Cessna is well below the flight level of the Gulfstream."

Leslie noted that he'd not answered the question.

"What was the cause of death for Dr. Aarons? Was he alive when the Cessna impacted the ground?"

"The body was found in, ah, partial dismemberment. The doctors are attempting to determine the cause of death."

The AP stringer spoke up. "Who was aboard the Gulfstream?"

Leslie crossed her fingers, hoping . . .

"That information isn't releasable at this time. We're still having difficulty with some of the, ah, notifications."

Yeah! Leslie exulted. *They're still stalling.*

"You've had two days," another local reporter grumbled. "That's enough time to notify families in Kenya."

A round of laughter rang out.

The CNN stringer raised her hand. "I've been advised by the network that a Miss"—she read from a note—"Jacqueline Chang was the flight attendant on the Gulfstream. Is that correct, or are the names of the aircrew as holy as the passenger list?"

Oliver grimaced at the continued frivolity. "The air carrier is free to release the names of their crew members. We're still researching the, ah, accuracy of the passenger manifest. There have been certain discrepancies noted in corporate records. We'll advise you as soon as we're sure, and after appropriate notifications are made."

There was a stir at the hint of scandal.

The CNN reporter pounced first. "What kind of discrepancies?"

"We're still investigating."

"Are you considering bringing charges against the carrier?"

'The matter is under investigation, and I can't go any further." He set his jowls firmly as he handed the microphone back to the spokesman.

The public relations man smiled, showing great teeth. "This press conference concerns the crash of the Cessna. Are there further questions regarding *that* matter?"

Leslie was looking around at faces. A new man at the rear of the room near the video cameras caught her attention. He wore a button-down shirt, dark suit, and club tie, and as her father would have put it, he looked like an Eastern "big city lawyer."

She nudged the *Deseret News* reporter. "Who's the new guy in back?"

The girl looked. "Never saw him before. Maybe another FAA rep?"

The public affairs spokesman was talking about the

doctor's family. He was survived by a wife in Butte. They had two adult sons and three grandchildren living in . . .

Leslie edged toward the rear of the room, where another new man had entered and was speaking to the first. As she neared them she acted as if she was examining the pan angle of one of the video cameras. The conversation between the dark suits was unintelligible, so she moved closer, still looking at the camera and shot angle.

". . . nothing on the tapes . . . damn things were blank . . . call from New York. Oliver's been . . . and cooperate. We can . . . notifications . . . the foundation's name out of it, period!"

The other man nodded, then noticed Leslie, only four feet distant. "As soon as the meetings over, get Oliver and we'll go someplace to talk."

The first man regarded her suspiciously. "Gotcha."

They fell silent, but Leslie had heard the word "foundation," which just *might* have meant the Weyland Foundation was involved, which was one of Mort Yoder's suspicions.

When she went back to the front, some of the reporters were signing up for a helicopter flight to the Cessna crash site. Leslie took the offered government literature, news release, and photographs, then left the room to search for a telephone and phone book.

She started at the top of the list of the hotels near the airport, said she was a secretary calling from New York, and asked to speak to any of the Weyland Foundation representatives. On her second call the reservations clerk paused, then said they couldn't release names or affiliations of guests. Did she have a specific person in mind?

Leslie disconnected. *They were staying at the Hilton.*

She looked at the guidelines the spokesman had handed out. On top was the list of rules to be followed by media representatives. No names were to be used "without the approval of the senior on-scene coordination and control official." They were to use no "documents marked for official use only unless specifically cleared by the . . ." They were to park in the "General Aviation Parking Area" and were restricted to the "immediate area of the RCC" and were not to enter "prohibited areas, restricted areas, or work areas designated for the use of search-and-rescue or airport employee personnel." They were not to interfere with or gain unauthorized interviews with "any person(s) involved in either the air or surface search who might be inhibited in the accomplishment of their duties by such activity."

Next she looked at the photographs—they were the same as those they'd viewed in the briefing room—of the Cessna crash scene. The first, airborne one, showed a light blue, tailless front portion of a fuselage. About it were strewn a number of suitcases and bags.

She went through all the photos and was about to put them away when her eyes narrowed and she went back to the airborne shot. *There was too much baggage for one man.*

Leslie's heart picked up tempo as she hurried out a side door marked RESTRICTED AREA—AIRPORT PERSONNEL ONLY. DISPLAY YOUR RAMP BADGE PROMINENTLY, and spoke to the first persons she encountered, a man and woman in overalls working on a stalled motorized sweeper. They pointed at another group of workers. It took twenty minutes of smiling and delving to learn that wreckage was being flown in and stowed in the hangar adjacent to the RCC building. She went there and slipped through a side door bearing a sign reading AUTHORIZED PERSONNEL ONLY.

They were gathering it all in a corner of the hangar. So far there were two wings, one battered, the other almost pristine. They'd not yet brought the Cessna's fuselage.

"Where do I put this?" called a man in overalls who had entered a door at the front, hefting a large, off-white suitcase.

"On the pallet over in the corner," said the man behind him. He was carrying a matching bag and eyed Leslie as they went past. "That's right, isn't it?" he asked her.

"Yes," she said, and followed them as if she belonged there. There were five bags already deposited on the pallet. She found and opened a leather identification tag, and read the name.

"There's more to come," the first man told her. "All of 'em go in here?"

She nodded. "Handle them carefully, would you?"

"That's what they told us outside. Damned things are heavy as hell." The two men left for the front door.

Leslie looked around, found another tag, and examined

it. Then a third and fourth. The off-white suitcases belonged to Paula Meredith-Dubois, a charcoal-colored one to F. S. Dubois, a pink one to Katy Dubois. All gave the same New York address. She picked up a badly bent number three golf iron. Gold-stamped letters read: Franklin S. Dubois.

She took a deep breath, wondering who they were. She had names, and none were Dr. Samuel Aarons. If she could somehow correlate them to the Gulfstream, that would mean both the Cessna and the Gulfstream had been involved at the light airplane's crash site.

She removed a small Pentax camera from her purse, switched the F-stop to low-light-auto, and took photos of the wings, the bags, and the identification tags, careful to hold the camera steady due to the long exposure time.

The first man in overalls came back inside, carrying a battered, half-opened suitcase in his arms. "You want to look it over before I put it on the pallet?"

"Please."

He placed the load beside her and started out, then turned back. "Better put on your ID badge. The security guards arrived and they're outside checking everyone."

"Thanks," Leslie said as she knelt for a closer look at the bag that had burst open. The tag read J. A. Chang, the name the CNN stringer had given for the flight attendant. *The luggage had come from the Gulfstream!* She had names. Leslie was still numbed by the enormity of her discovery, examining a sun dress, size six-tall, when she heard footsteps and turned to see the fat man named Tom Oliver approaching, speaking to a craggy, dark-haired man.

After an initial jolt of panic, Leslie rose to her feet, forced herself to cast a final look around, then walked directly toward them. The second man was solemn, with large ears and deep lines creasing his face, and wore a blue jacket with W. R. BOWES embroidered in gold script on one side of his chest, EXECUTIVE CONNECTIONS on the other.

A distant memory jogged then, and she wanted to stare but did not.

". . . want any interference from your people," the fat man was saying. "Understood?"

Neither man examined her closely as she passed, then went out through the side door. She saw uniformed guards, but since she was walking away from the building they took no heed.

Leslie felt heady with excitement as she returned to the RCC building, waited until her heartbeat slowed, then hurried to the operation desk and read down the list of aircraft and personnel involved in the aerial search.

She found the name, William R. Bowes, and grimaced hard to recall.

It came to her in a rush, but it was hard to resolve the middle-aged man she'd just seen with the memory from more than twenty years ago. He'd been an Air Force major, and she'd been a fifteen-year-old girl with an *awful* case of puppy love who thought she would never, *ever* forget him or her broken heart.

The list showed that he was flying a Beech Baron, and his call sign was Rescue Three-One. The company that owned the Gulfstream was in trouble for breaking some kind of rules. It made sense that they'd send a representative to the search.

So much was coming so quickly that it left her breathless.

The Weyland Foundation was somehow involved, just as Mort believed. The Dubois family, whoever they were, had been aboard the Gulfstream, which had been involved with the crash of the light airplane flown by Dr. Aarons, which the FAA officers were denying.

Numbed by the avalanche of details, and new mysteries, she felt compelled to get the information out quickly. But first she needed more, like the identity of the Dubois family.

She found an empty room, and this time used her cellular phone. She punched in Mort Yoder's office number and was switched to his voice-mail recorder. She spoke in a sort of code, saying she had confirmation of the matter in question. She hesitated, looked around, and almost whispered as she asked for information about Franklin S., Paula, and Katy Dubois, and gave their New York address. She also asked for background on Thomas Oliver of the FAA, who seemed to be the man in charge here, and about the charter airline, Executive Connections.

When she punched the End button, terminating the message, Leslie was more than a little pleased. She hefted her shoulder bag and headed for the snack bar, where she'd make sure her notes were entered in the electronic memo maker. Then she'd have the photographs developed at a local one-hour service, and find a computer shop that would scan the photos and change them to digital computer format—so she could send them over a telephone line. Tonight, when she had the information she'd requested from Mort Yoder, she'd get out the laptop computer and write the best damned story of her career.

She wondered again about William Bowes and smiled.

Billy looked at the last of the luggage from the Gulfstream's baggage compartment, then went back to the Cessna's crumpled left wing, which had likely been torn off by the impact.

There were traces of Executive Connections' vivid, royal blue color near the tip. He looked over at Tom Oliver. "The wing impacted the Gulfstream."

"I don't want you announcing any of your wild speculations."

"That's your department," Billy said.

Oliver pursed his lips, considering the double entendre.

"Why all the secrecy about the fact that it was a mid-air?"

When Oliver didn't answer, Billy felt there was nothing more to be learned here. He started for the door, deciding it was time to take the Baron up for a look.

Two of the dark-suited lawyer-investigators from the Weyland Foundation came into the hangar, looked about, then one walked toward Billy. "Anything yet?"

Billy motioned at Oliver. "Ask him. He knows everything."

Tom Oliver smiled. "That's the Duboises' luggage."

"We'll want to look through it. Anything on the air search?"

"We expect to find something shortly." Oliver pointed at the wing with the smudge of paint. "I've confirmed there was impact, so we're concentrating on the area around the Cessna crash site. Next we'll look farther along the Gulfstream's flight path."

"Anything new from the flight center's radar video-tapes?"

"Both are blank. The recorder obviously malfunctioned."

"Still no ELT transmissions?"

"No. We're querying the Air Force. They've got a very sensitive satellite that—"

"That's rather odd, isn't it?" The lawyer was looking at Billy.

"Very odd," Billy agreed, drawing a glare from Oliver.

"Could the ELTs have been destroyed?" the lawyer asked. "Or maybe burned?"

Billy shook his head. "It's unlikely. They're designed to withstand fire and impact."

Oliver quickly broke in. "We're considering the possibility that the ELT on the Cessna was somehow buried, and the one on the Gulfstream was faulty."

"You heard Henry," said Billy, working to suppress his anger. "It was just inspected."

"You're flying alone in the search?" asked the foundation lawyer.

Billy nodded.

"Mind if one of us tags along on some of your flights?" he asked.

"Not at all. The more eyes looking, the better."

Oliver butted in again. "I'm not sure that's wise," he said. He looked pointedly at Billy. "If you'd excuse us for a moment . . ."

Billy set his face into a non-expression and walked out of the hangar. He'd overheard Oliver speaking over the telephone with the Weyland people in New York, talking very much as if they, and not the American people, were his bosses. Oliver was overbearing and annoying, yet Billy was trying to cooperate with both him and the foundation people. Unless the wreckage of the Gulfstream showed proof that another pilot aboard couldn't have helped avoid the accident, the future of E.C. could be decided by litigation brought by the Weyland Foundation.

The general had been right. They shouldn't have taken the contract.

"Mr. Bowes?" The second lawyer-investigator had followed him out of the hangar.

Billy slowed until he caught up, then continued toward the coordination center.

"Could I ask a couple of questions?"

He stopped and glanced at the time. "Make it quick. I'd like to get in a couple of flights."

"When you met him at La Guardia, was Frank Dubois carrying anything?"

"He had something in his hand." He frowned, trying to recall.

The lawyer was no help. He just stared.

Billy brightened. "A leather folder . . . the zippered kind. Maybe an inch and a half thick. It was that distressed brown color, like a flying jacket I've got."

"We'd appreciate it if you didn't mention it when you speak to others, Mr. Bowes."

Billy started to ask why, then remembered that the people the man worked for could destroy Executive Connections. "Sure," he said, and continued toward the coordination center.

A few minutes later, he was speaking with Henry Hoblit on the telephone. "No news from this end," he said, "except I found paint from the Gulfstream on the Cessna. The FAA's going to hold off releasing names for another day. What's happening in Washington?"

Henry sounded weary. "We've got FAA people and Weyland lawyers swarming all over the place, looking for someone to blame. CNN picked up Jackie's name, and they're trying to get an interview with her parents. It'll be worse when the press learns who the passengers were."

"I don't think they're going to release the names until the wreckage is found. Any instructions from the general?"

"Nothing new. He talks about Link a lot. This isn't doing his heart any good, Billy."

The thought was depressing. After hanging up, he went to the operations desk and took a long look at the search matrix. The military had flown all night with IR scanners and reported nothing. Already the daylight searchers had examined the terrain for a fifty-mile circumference of the Cessna wreckage. It was as if the Gulfstream had vanished without a clue.

He filled a paper cup with black coffee and went out to the Baron to join the hunt.

Airport Hilton, Salt Lake City

Jaeger and Charbonneau watched closely as Webb fast-forwarded the videotape, then as he paused the picture.

"There it is," Webb said in a hushed voice.

The screen showed dozens of bright radar returns, but Webb pointed out the one flagged: EC992, 7035, 509. He explained that the first designator was the aircraft's identification, the second the height in meters, the third the airspeed in knots. A second, dimmer, and smaller return, marked: ???, 7020, 64, converged on the screen.

"A collision course," said Webb. He ran the tape forward until it showed the next sweep. There was nothing. Both returns had vanished. "Bang. A midair collision," said Webb. "Both blips disappeared over the area where they found the Cessna."

"Then why haven't they found the Gulfstream?" Charbonneau asked in his falsetto voice.

"That's what we'll try to determine," said Webb, ejecting the first tape. He picked another from the stack at his side and inserted it into the VCR. "This morning while the tapes were being converted, I monitored the military frequencies. The Air Force had two airplanes with IR scanners working all night, and they didn't find anything within a hundred miles."

The big man, who was also called the Hunter, stared intently, wondering.

Webb ran the second tape forward, then paused it. "What we see here is a possibility."

On the second tape, of a radar scope covering a lower-altitude regime, where there'd previously been nothing a blip appeared. The flag on the new return read: ???, 4290, 141.

"It may be the Gulfstream," said Webb. "Forty seconds passed between the disappearance at the higher altitude, and the unknown appearing at the lower one. It would take that long to drop nine thousand feet."

"It looks like all the others," rumbled Jaeger.

Webb pointed at three other returns on the screen, one of which showed similar question marks, meaning its identity too was unknown. "Those were already on the screen. But the one here"—he pointed at the question mark at 4290 meters—"popped up out of nowhere. No IFF squawk, just the skin paint at the lower altitude. It's very likely the Gulfstream."

The Hunter was pleased. They were the only ones who knew.

"Let's see where it goes from there." Webb let the tape run. The blip moved much more slowly than the Gulfstream had at the higher altitude, in a steady arc to its right.

"It's definitely an aircraft in trouble," said Webb. "It's flying three hundred knots slower—slower even than a Gulfstream's single-engine airspeed. He's got obvious engine problems, and something's either hanging down or the controls were damaged, making him fly in an arc."

Webb ran the tape on fast-forward for a while, then slowed it back to normal. "Now it's just west of Boise, Idaho, heading north and still in the constant turn."

At 1,500 meters altitude, on a heading of north-northwest, the blip disappeared.

"He just dropped under the radar coverage," Webb said. "He's been in a constant right turn, steadily losing altitude. They crashed." His voice was confident.

Jaeger slowly nodded. "Where would we find it?"

Webb pulled out a chart and traced the course the blip had flown. "Constant right turn," he iterated, "and down to five thousand feet here, where it disappeared." He tapped the map. "They either impacted on this ridge or somewhere in the valley beyond. Once they got in, it would have been impossible to fly out of. The mountains are too high, and they couldn't climb."

The Hunter pulled the map over and let his finger move about the valley. A single dirt road entered from the northwest. There was a large lake, two smaller ones, and several creeks. No towns were shown. "A wilderness area," he said.

Simon Charbonneau edged closer, hardly breathing. "Do you think it burned?"

"Probably not," said Webb. "Most don't."

"Survivors?"

"It's unlikely. The crash would have been violent. If it hit a mountain, the wreckage may all be in one hole. If it went down in the trees, it's likely all over hell and gone. They may have tried to put down in one of the lakes."

"What next?" Charbonneau asked Jaeger, who was still staring intently at the map.

The Hunter looked up at Webb, who nodded. "The airplane's either in the valley or very close by."

Jaeger released a pent-up breath. "Prepare the airplane. We'll fly to Boise."

Webb grinned happily. "Before we land, I'll make a pass over the valley and we can look for wreckage."

"No," Jaeger said sharply. "I want no attention drawn there."

"I'd feel better if you took more people," said Charbonneau.

The Hunter shook his head resolutely. "If it's there, we'll find it."

Webb ejected the tape. "It's there."

"When will we leave?" asked Charbonneau.

"As soon as we've packed," said the Hunter. "We'll rent a vehicle in Boise, pick up some things, and leave first thing in the morning."

Jaeger stared at the map, at the desolate valley where the airplane might be down. He had another reason for hurrying. For the past day he'd been increasingly restless, as if balanced on a razor's edge. He'd felt such powerful emotions before, and this time knew he must be careful and not lose control. Charbonneau was watching him, judging, and there was much at stake for the Hunter.

It was best that he be away from civilization until the emotions subsided. It was doubtful he could get into trouble in the isolated Idaho valley.

9

12:30 P.M.—The Lake

Katy broke the surface and held up a plastic container. Link took it and peered through the plastic top. "Potato chips," he announced. It was the second such container; the first had contained chicken salad. There were others, but water had seeped in and they contained mush.

She'd already brought up a bag containing six apples and eight oranges, a serrated-bladed knife, two six-packs of canned soda, articles of clothing for Paula and herself from on-board luggage, her day pack, Link's gym bag, and her small cassette player/radio. She'd ventured into the cockpit to get maps from a pouch the pilot said was there, but chickened out when she'd seen Jackie's body. He hadn't questioned when she'd come up without them.

"Come on in." He'd tried to encourage her into the raft on her previous trip, and this time Katy was sorely tempted. The water was frigid, and as he'd warned her, the air trapped in the airplane had grown a sickly sweet odor from the gases released by the dead bodies.

"One more," she huffed, and went back to retrieve the thing she'd left at the opened hatch. When she surfaced, she hefted it with effort. It was painted dark red, had a three-foot hard-nylon handle and a metal head with an edge on one side and a spike on the other.

Link took it from her. "It's a crash ax," he said happily. "We'll use it to chop wood. That's enough for today, sport." He reached down and hoisted her aboard.

Katy had stripped to panties and bra for the swim. As she huddled and shuddered, the pilot gathered her close and smothered her in his grasp, unmindful that he was getting wet. The icy chill slowly left her, replaced by his warmth.

"Back into your clothes," he finally said, and Katy pulled on jeans and canvas tennis shoes, then her father's shirt. Since the sun was bright, she was warm enough to turn down Link's offer of his jacket.

They headed for shore, the pilot rowing with his good hand on one side, she on the other.

The camp was clearly visible on the distant shore. When they'd risen, they'd all pitched in to construct a shelter, using the orange tarpaulin anchored to the saplings, propped in front by branches he'd cut with the survival knife. Heat from the continuously burning fire was reflected into the covered area, inside which they'd built mattresses of branches and leaves, overlaid with survival blankets. Frank had been placed on the rearmost one. Link hadn't prepared a bed for himself, saying he'd continue to curl up in a blanket on the opposite side of the fire.

When they'd finished and everyone was sipping hot chocolate for breakfast, Katy had hung Frank's remaining polo shirt, bright red in color, from the top of the lean-to, and solemnly proclaimed it the Dubois family flag. She'd saluted and even her mother had smiled. A few minutes later Paula had spoiled it by balking when Link tried to get her to fish, using a hook and line suspended from a willow branch.

From the middle of the lake the orange shelter and red shirt acted as a beacon.

Frank was aware that his body was shattered and that his moments of lucidity were fogged, but when he drew into the numb sanctity of his subconscious, memories of past events became crystalline clear. His thoughts were organized in an orderly process that simplified and reduced matters to the essential—and produced answers that had eluded him before.

Whenever he wafted toward consciousness he became aware of excruciating pain, so he minimized his time near the surface and drifted in the abyss—the deep, slumber-like condition that veiled him from the agony. As he lingered, reliving events of the recent past, the mysteries of Scarlet 277, the Argentine project, were steadily unraveling.

An image grew in his mind, like an old black-and-white movie.

When he'd returned to Buenos Aires to set up the investigation of El Soleil, Vern Calico and his State Department entourage had arrived for a weeklong diplomatic session with the ministers of foreign affairs of the Central and South American countries. The secretary of state had entertained and been entertained nightly, and Frank had been invited to the social gatherings.

At the first one he'd met Salvator DiPalma, the man he'd come to view as a threat to the Western Hemisphere. He'd first studied the man from across the crowded floor of the reception hall. Although more than eighty years of age, DiPalma maintained the paunch noted in the 1944 photograph of the youthful colonel who had conspired with Juan Perón. Nor had age softened the ice-cold eyes that stared haughtily about the room. Others about him toadied, for the wealthiest man in South America bought respect from the powerful and fawning from officials.

At his side were a young man and two women, one of whom was beautiful, youthful, and meticulously correct. DiPalma was a widower, and the mistress was one of a succession he showed off at such functions. He kept them for window-dressing and to act as hostesses, but maintained them at a distance. Those who pleased him were established in sumptuous retirement at an early age. Rumor held that one had been argumentative, and had been placed in the lowest bordello in a remote mining camp in the Brazilian Amazon basin.

The other woman was raw-boned and dowdy, a daughter married to the president of Venezuela. The young man was blond, with delicate features and feminine gestures, and hung on to the old man's words. In the eighties the grandnephew, Diego DiPalma, had graduated from Harvard, and two years ago had been placed in El Soleil's New York offices, just ten blocks from the Weyland Foundation building. Diego was simpering, fragile, and unpredictable, but sources within El Soleil said he was in New York to prove himself as heir apparent, destined to take over the second-largest privately held banking institution in the world.

There were other relatives. The DiPalmas gathered annually in Buenos Aires for the colonel's birthday, and all had been invited to this, the biggest diplomatic event of the year for Argentinean officialdom.

When Frank was introduced by Vernon Calico, he found DiPalma abrupt and unpleasant. Yet there was a split second during which the hard eyes lingered, and as he stared back a cold wash crept over Frank. In that tiny moment he knew—and had the feeling that Colonel Salvatore DiPalma also knew—that their destinies were inexorably linked.

He'd also attended a second diplomatic reception that week, and a discussion at that one had appeared promising. The memory moved forward in time, to his return to New York. He was at the podium, debriefing the handful about the events of that evening.

"An Argentine air force general I'd previously met found me, and after a few moments he whispered about a conspiracy to take political control of his country. When I pursued it, he said I must be careful, for his intelligence people had learned that a high-ranking official from the United States had been bought by DiPalma. He said millions of dollars were involved, and was about to give me the official's name when we were interrupted by his aide. There'd been an emergency—an airplane had crashed at one of his air bases—and he was called away."

The handful waited expectantly, but Frank shook his head.

"There'd been no crash. The following morning the general and his aide were found beside a country road. Both had been sexually assaulted and methodically beaten to death."

"My God!" exclaimed the woman.

"Colonel Salvator DiPalma is both determined and ruthless."

"He was at the second diplomatic function?" asked Cyril Weyland.

"No, but it was his work. So far we haven't learned the identity of the American official. I'd like permission to look into the financial records of several government officials."

"Our rules are clear," Cyril Weyland replied. "We do not interfere in domestic issues, and that includes investigating American politicians and officials."

"I believe you should make an exception," Frank told him.

"The reason would have to be compelling," said Cyril.

"I think it is," said the grandson. "We've learned more about *trueno*. The word means thunder in Spanish, and keeps popping up in their plans. One of our El Soleil sources said the target individuals are selected and all elements planned, and when the word *trueno* is received, meaning the American media is preoccupied, the plan is executed. We don't know who sends the signals, but we have an idea how they plan to take over the country.

"In September there'll be a general election, and El Soleil is funding the campaigns of a presidential candidate and some eighty legislators, all promising stronger government and strict law and order. Shortly before the election a final *trueno* will be called, and their president and leading candidates for the legislature will be assassinated. The next morning the El Soleil candidates will offer themselves as the only ones who can end the violence."

The woman spoke again. "From what you've said, there've already been several prominent people killed, all strong supporters of the current government. Isn't it obvious to *our* government—and to the international press—what's happening?"

"So far there's been no outcry," said Frank, "and there's little time to act. If they succeed, Salvator DiPalma will become the de facto ruler of Argentina. Our analysts believe he'll continue his military buildup, including nukes as soon as possible, and no country in South America will dare complain when he suggests major policy changes."

Still, the handful had denied his request to search the records of U.S. officials.

The word *trueno* echoed in Frank's subconscious. *Thunder* was loud, to mask the fury of the nights of terror. There was also another sound, the whispering of a traitor. An American.

The general had said the official was from the United States. Not *in* the US, but *from* there, so Frank believed he'd been at the diplomatic function. Vern Calico had attended with a dozen of his Washington staff, and an equal number from the U.S. embassy. Some had been women, and the general had said the traitor was a man. Frank was left with fifteen-odd males.

He believed not only that the official had been present, but that he'd been responsible for the general's death—that he'd seen the general approach Frank and contacted someone within El Soleil who could arrange for the official telephone call to the aide.

Another memory flashed, and another answer emerged.

The wild-goose chase in Russia had been engineered to pull him off the Argentina project. The traitorous official obviously worked for Calico ... was influential in the State Department hierarchy ... and had told Vern Calico about the Weyland Foundation investigation in an effort to have it stopped. The same man had convinced Calico to suggest to the President that the French vessel be boarded ... to discredit the Weyland Foundation. He would surely take other measures to neutralize and destroy them. It all seemed so clear, so obvious.

Frank fought again to emerge from the abyss, for someone must warn the secretary of state that he had a paid traitor among his staff. A moment later he began to speak aloud, rushing his words, pausing only when he was overcome by the agony of his terrible injuries.

Paula was stroking his face, trying to soothe and calm him.

"Tell Vern Calico ... find the turncoat ... a man on his staff," he pleaded.

"I will," she whispered, "as soon as we get out."

Then Paula tried to tell him something about a fish, and that Link and Katy were out in a raft, but Frank was already slipping away, plunging back into that deep chasm where there was no pain, no present. Only the past, and more memories brought into razor-sharp focus. As he entered the bottomless abyss, another answer came to him.

The general had died horribly, and it was likely he'd told his tormentor about the conversation. Frank was the only one who might be able to determine the identity of the official. His life was in jeopardy, and more important, so were the lives of those close to him.

As Katy and Link drew near the shore, they heard Paula calling to them as if something momentous had happened. When they reached the beach and were hauling the raft onto the beach, Paula breathlessly explained that she'd caught a fish, and held up a brownish-colored minnow that still dangled from the line.

Link acted impressed. "A trout," he proclaimed, removing it from the hook. "That's great," he said. "Now we'll need more."

"Yeah," Katy joked sarcastically. "Half an ounce of fish isn't quite enough."

Link cast a glare that made Katy wince. "Take the things from the raft," he said coldly, "while I work on something with your mother."

As soon as Katy had stowed the food, then flapped each article of clothing vigorously and hung them to dry, she hurried to see what he and Paula were up to.

The pilot was helping her fashion a fish line. They'd suspended hooks from driftwood floats, connected at eight-feet intervals. He told them what he wanted, and they began an all-out search for an assortment of worms and grasshoppers. The best ones were placed on hooks.

Link gave the rig a final inspection. "It should work."

Paula was also examining it. "Let me give it a try."

He nodded, not showing surprise at her abrupt change of heart as she gathered the floats carefully, waded in thigh-deep, and tossed the fish line out as far as she could throw it.

"Now bring in the end of the line," Link called.

They all stood on the shore together, staring with keen eyes, Paula holding firmly to the line. Then Paula drew a sharp breath as a piece of driftwood momentarily disappeared. A short while later another wooden bobber was dancing.

"There are fish in there," Link said happily. Paula was grinning, but Katy found her own mouth set in a firm line. She left them and went to the lean-to shelter, where she tried the radio she'd brought from the plane. It didn't work. She found the batteries were fouled, oozing green matter, and felt her depression intensify as she tossed the radio aside and sighed.

Paula hailed her from the beach. "We've caught four so far," she yelled happily.

Katy's mood darkened as she stalked into the woods to use the latrine trench they'd dug that morning. Link said they'd fill it in every couple of days and make a new one.

As Katy squatted over the trench to urinate, she grumbled inwardly. She was being treated unfairly. After her bone-chilling dive, neither adult had given her the slightest thank-you, as if they *expected* her to swim around in ice water to get them things. Then her mother had caught a stupid minnow and it was an instant big deal.

A loud whirring noise came from behind, but she ignored it, thinking it was an insect.

Katy finished, deciding to gather an armful of wood as Link had said to do whenever they went into the forest, then go back and try to present a stupid happy-face. As she stood and hiked up her jeans, she heard the whirring again, and had half turned when something thumped against her leg.

Katy squealed and kicked out. She'd been pulled off balance and almost fell—when she realized that a writhing snake was firmly attached to the denim above her ankle. She shrieked louder and began to run, feeling the heavy weight of the snake as she dragged it along, then almost fell again as her jeans drooped and she had to grip them so she could continue.

The pilot was hurrying toward her as she emerged from the thicket. As she neared him he made a grab for the snake, missed, then grasped it near the tail and pulled hard.

The snake came loose from the denim and writhed back, but he continued his fluid motion and flung it sailing into the trees.

Paula hurried up, mouth agape.

"Lie down!" Link ordered.

Katy sat heavily on the bed, whimpering and watching as he felt and examined her ankle.

"I don't see a puncture mark. Did it bite anywhere else?"

She shook her head, unable to make a sound other than the whimper.

"Are you okay?" Paula asked.

"Ye-e-es," she managed.

Link Anderson found part of a fang, half an inch long and still wet with venom, where it had caught in the fabric. He removed it carefully with tweezers from the first-aid kit, then told her to get out of the jeans and to wash them thoroughly.

Paula began to cry in relief.

The pilot got to his feet and went after the snake with the crash ax. He returned a few minutes later, wearing a hard look. "It got away," he said.

They sat on a log, sipping hot bouillon from cups and munching on apples, as they discussed the latest adventure.

"Snaggle-tooth," Katy said, naming the reptile she'd identified in the survival manual as a Western diamondback rattlesnake. This time no one laughed.

"Is it still dangerous, with only one fang?" Paula asked.

"As long as it's got venom, it's dangerous," the pilot told them.

"He tried to warn me," said Katy. "He rattled twice."

"Rattlers are generally honest. Not like some others. The good news is the only poisonous snakes here are rattlesnakes. The bad news is there are a lot of them. Learn to keep an eye out."

Katy nodded vigorously.

"We caught a few big fish that time," Paula told her, proudly pointing at the collection laid out near the fire. "I wish Frank was awake so I could show him."

"Mom," Katy gushed, "you're a *great* fisherman." The session with the snake had taught her a lesson about pettiness.

After they'd finished the modest lunch, Link said he wanted them to learn to clean their catch. "Fishing is only part of the game. You've got to know how to prepare them." He explained how they'd have to strip out guts, cut off the head and tail, then slice off the filets.

Paula grew wrinkle-nosed, but watched closely as Link used the serrated knife on two fish. Finally he handed Paula the knife. "You first," he said, and went to check on the fish line.

Paula was so nervous about it that Katy thought she might cut herself. After a moment of watching, Katy asked if she could help, even though she wasn't sure about wanting to do it.

Paula frowned and looked at the fish in her delicate grasp. "No," she finally said. She took a deep breath, eyeing the dead trout as if it might bite, then jabbed so tentatively that Katy worried that she might lop off a finger.

She decided to go to the beach to help bring in the next batch. After walking a few yards she noted a dark splash of blood, likely from a rabbit or other small animal killed by a predator. Katy continued to stare at the blood on the flattened grass and then at the nearby forest, wondering what else was out there. The woods were thick and dark, and her nerves were still jangling from the episode with the snake. She had a lot to learn about the wilderness, and did not feel sure of herself at all.

"Katy?" Paula called from across the clearing. "I just cut myself. Would you get a Band-Aid from the first-aid kit?"

10

2:00 P.M.—Weyland Foundation Building, Manhattan

The handful were in session, seated about the small conference table with grave expressions. There had been no new revelations about the missing Gulfstream; however, there were other developments from Salt Lake City.

The briefing officer spoke distinctly. "Both the tapes before and after the ones in question were in good condition, and only those two were destroyed. Our people concluded that they were magnetically erased."

"Intentionally?" asked the woman in the group.

"We don't know. The FAA officer in charge immediately blamed the air traffic control contractor, and they've backed into a damage-control mode, denying everything."

Cyril Weyland considered. "And the problems with the media?"

"A *Washington Post* reporter named Yoder has been making inquiries about the foundation for the past day. General information mostly, about holdings and such, but late this morning he called asking about the location of Frank and his family."

"Someone leaked the names?"

"He's been in contact with a reporter from the *Boise Times-Journal*. One of our people saw her leaving the restricted hangar where they'd taken the luggage, and placed her under surveillance. Half an hour ago she came out of a one-hour photo shop in Salt Lake. We believe she photographed the Dubois family's luggage, but still doesn't know what she has. When she talks with Yoder again, they'll figure the rest of it out."

"What's the worst scenario?" the woman asked.

"A thousand searchers descending on Salt Lake City, including treasure hunters looking for rewards."

"Wouldn't that give us a better probability of finding the Gulfstream?"

Cyril Weyland interrupted, speaking softly. "And if they get to it first, before our people? We can't have a stranger going through the contents of the folder," he reminded her.

"We also can't discount that Frank and his family may have survived," said another member of the handful. "If the wrong person was to discover them, knowing they were extremely wealthy . . ." He did not complete the statement.

Cyril regarded the briefing officer. "Can the reporter's information be contained?"

"We'd have to move quickly, but yes."

"No violence."

"No, sir. Of course not."

The handful approved. As distasteful as it seemed, the media must be further stalled, the names of the Dubois family withheld longer. No one liked the subterfuge, but the alternative could prove disastrous. They also decided that the search effort should be further deemphasized by moving it to a smaller airport, away from a metropolitan area.

"Will the FAA agree?" the woman asked.

"All government agencies have been told to cooperate in the search," Cyril told her. He did not add that the President was otherwise distancing himself from the foundation.

Downtown Salt Lake City

Leslie had returned to her hotel room and added to her incomplete story, which would remain that way until she learned who belonged to the names on the luggage tags. She'd found a photo lab and had the film developed, and then a small computer shop that would scan the prints and change them to digital format so they could be transmitted over a telephone line.

She was sipping cappuccino at a corner coffee house across the street from the computer shop, wondering what she really had, when Mort called on her cellular phone.

He'd gotten her message and learned some about the Dubois family.

"So who are they?" she asked, opening her memo maker to take notes.

"Do you have positive proof they were on the airplane?"

"Maybe," she countered. "Who are they?"

"Come on, Les. We're sharing, remember?"

A neatly groomed man in a dark suit and club tie walked from the counter with his coffee and sat next to the door. Leslie tried to place him, knowing she'd seen him before.

"Were they aboard?" Mort asked again.

"It looks that way," she said. She told him about the luggage from the Cessna crash site, and seeing the flight attendant's suitcase, confirming they'd come from the Gulfstream.

When she explained how she'd traipsed into the forbidden hangar, he chuckled. "You've got balls, Les." He paused. "How about transmitting the photographs so I can have a look?"

"I didn't bring an electronic camera, and it's taken me three hours to get the film processed and find a damned computer shop. They'll be ready in a few minutes. Now who are these Duboises? Start with Franklin S."

As she spoke the name, the familiar man in the suit looked her way.

"I need those photos, Les. When I called the Weyland Foundation, they insisted Frank Dubois was still in New York."

"What does the foundation have to do with him?"

"Dubois is one of their senior vice-presidents."

Leslie deflated. "I thought he might be someone famous . . . or important."

Mort chuckled. "You really *don't* know, do you?"

"That's why I called you. Clue me in."

"Frank Dubois is heir to both the Cyril Weyland—like in Weyland *Foundation*—and Dubois oil fortunes. More money and power than Trump's dreamed of. When we go to print, the women readers will tinkle in their panties."

Leslie felt her mouth curl into a smile.

Mort continued: "Paula Dubois is his wife, so beautiful the guys will take her picture to the john. Katy's the fourteen-year-old daughter for the little old ladies to get misty-eyed over. Something for everyone, and so far we've got an *exclusive*."

Her spirits continued to soar—then an inexplicable feeling

of dread tempered her elation. She looked suspiciously at
the man in the suit. "Have you told anyone about this?"

"Only the one call to the foundation, and my boss here.
If you've got confirmation it's the Dubois family, he'll turn
me loose for two columns of page one and half of eighteen,
which just happen to be tomorrow morning's prime space."

Leslie felt her knees weaken. "I'd have to clear it with
my editor."

"My boss is talking with your publisher right now, in
case this works out. *He* can talk with your editor."

"*Damn* it, Mort. I should speak with my people first."

"Les, just get those photos to me and send me what
you've got for background and color. You get all the credit
in Boise, and we name you as our source here in the *Post*.
How does that sound? If it works out, you've got your big
story, Les."

It was all coming too quickly.

Mort's voice turned jubilant. "My boss just came by and
gave me the thumbs-up. That means everyone here and in
Boise's in agreement."

"I'll still have to check with my editor before I can send
you anything, Mort."

"Sure, but *hurry*, okay?"

"Bye, Mort." As she switched off, her heart was racing.
The photographs she'd left across the street had just turned
to solid gold. She rose and started for the door, but the man
in the suit blocked her way.

He formed a friendly smile. "Miss Rocklin?"

"Yes?" She placed him. One of the "big city lawyers"
she'd seen in the back of the room, whom she now knew
was from the Weyland Foundation.

"I saw you at the press conference this morning and
heard you were from Boise. I've got a friend from there."
He glanced out the window, then looked back at her and
nodded courteously. "Just thought I'd say hello."

She scrambled past him and out the door, was lucky
enough to catch a walk signal, and ran across the intersec-
tion. A moment later she was inside the computer shop.

The female clerk who had waited on her was gone,
replaced by an older man who looked up with a good inter-
pretation of a nervous expression. "May I help you?"

Leslie looked back for a sign of the man in the suit, saw
that he'd not followed her, and shoved the claim ticket

across the counter. "I left photographs to be processed. Standard PCX format on a floppy disk. They should be ready."

He searched through a bin and withdrew an envelope with her name scrawled on top. "Here you are."

She released a heavy sigh of relief, then prudently opened the envelope and pulled out the photographs, strip of negatives, and a single diskette. Then Leslie's heart stalled, and her voice came out in falsetto. "These aren't the ones I left!"

"Are you sure?" He peered anxiously.

"These are of *horses,* for God's sake. Mine were taken in a hangar."

"I'll take another look," he said, and began to go through the bin, shaking his head.

Leslie looked outside. The man in the suit was getting into a sedan with two others.

"I'm sorry, ma'am," the clerk was saying. "Those are the only ones here."

"You *bastard!*" she exploded, then ran out as the sedan pulled away.

Leslie stood on the curb, watching helplessly as the vehicle disappeared into the traffic, feeling her stomach crawl into her throat. She had to wait for a full minute before the queasiness subsided enough to telephone Mort. His extension was busy.

She went back inside the computer shop and pleaded, but the man tried to tell her she'd gotten her own film mixed up. When she threatened to call the police, he didn't budge.

"How much did they pay you?" she stormed, but the man set his expression and shook his head.

Her telephone buzzed.

"We got a development," Mort said.

"Jesus, do we, Mort. They just stole my goddam film."

"They *what?*" he asked incredulously, and she explained, describing the Weyland Foundation by using the majority of curse words in her vocabulary.

Mort Yoder released a sigh. "It doesn't really matter, Les."

"The luggage tags were real, Mort. I'm not making it up, for God's sake."

"I know. Frank Dubois just called my editor from the

foundation building in New York, saying he wanted to clear up a potential misunderstanding. His family sent their luggage ahead to California and *it's* missing. Even if you had the tags in your hand, there'd be no story."

"So who was on the airplane?"

"I don't know, but it obviously wasn't the Dubois family."

"Then why would the foundation people steal my photographs? One of their guys stalled me while his buddies paid off the people in the computer shop. I recognized him."

Mort was silent for a long moment, considering.

She tried another tack. "Your editor didn't actually see Frank Dubois, did he? How does he know it was him?"

"What would they gain by faking it?"

"Something's fishy about all this, and I'm going to keep digging, Mort." She felt another flash of anger. "Who the *hell* do they think they're fooling with?"

"Les, I'm putting together an article using the information I dug up on the Weyland Foundation. They're a lot bigger and richer than anyone realizes. If you learn anything new about them . . ." He went on, but Leslie hardly heard what he was saying.

When she called her editor at the *Times-Journal* and explained the thefts, she received no consolation. She was told to return to Boise. She switched off the telephone, for she'd decided to go back to the search-and-rescue center for another look.

At the airport Leslie was met with yet another surprise. The guards at the hangar where the debris from the Cessna had been collected were allowing reporters inside. There were a few more pieces of the light airplane, but the pallet with the luggage had been removed. When she asked about it, no one knew what she was talking about.

The Lake

It had been a long and busy day, and Lincoln Anderson was appropriately weary, yet he was also pleased. The camp was becoming efficient, and the family in his care were as comfortable as he could make them.

The clothing from the airplane had already dried in the

light breeze and bright sun; Paula was in tennis shoes, tan slacks, and blue cotton blouse, Katy in fresh jeans and T-shirt, and both wore summer jackets. Link wore sweat pants. His athletic shoes were still damp.

He'd shown them how to assist in their rescue. Together they'd prepared the makings of a signal fire, first gathering samples from various saplings and plants, and experimenting with burning them. Branches and leaves from a bush with small red berries billowed awful-smelling, oily smoke, so they'd cut and gathered a pile of them near the fire. Then they'd gone to the beach and carefully trampled the word HELP in the sand, and outlined it with stones.

They'd been hungry throughout the day, for he'd allowed only a can of soda pop and single apple apiece as they'd continued to prepare their new world. He'd fashioned a crude smoker by weaving a latticework frame from thin branches, then stuffing the holes with leaves. They'd draped fish fillets over a rack inside, built a small fire in the bottom, then carefully added dampened alder wood chips. The smoke that issued smelled acrid, but he'd explained that the fish would be tasty, and would be cured so it would last. They should add new fillets every eight hours, and place the smoked ones in a plastic bag suspended from a high branch.

He was now showing them something the Plains Indians had used to prepare their meals. They searched until Katy found precisely the kind of large, flat-topped lava rock he'd wanted, and together they dragged it across the clearing and placed it—porous side down, and finer-grained, flat side on top—into one side of the firepit.

He raked hot coals into place on three sides of the "cooking stone."

"You've got to pick the rock carefully," Link explained as they waited. "They'll crack or explode if they're made of the wrong stuff, and if they've got much coal in them, they'll burn. The Blackfeet preferred lava like this, and once they found a good cooking stone, they'd even take it with them when they traveled."

"It's like a kitchen grill," Paula observed.

"That's the idea." He sent Katy to the lake to bring in four mid-sized trout. When she returned, he tested the lava stone.

"It's hot enough." He looked at Katy. "Hungry?"

She grinned. "Yeah. I was about to eat the bait."

Link kept a straight face. "Grasshoppers aren't bad, but worms taste musty, like dirt."

"Ugh!" Katy exclaimed. "I'll wait."

He had Paula heat the skillet for a full thirty seconds over the open flame, then popped in two fresh fillets, and showed her what to do as they sizzled.

"Keep them in there no more than five seconds on each side before placing them on the stone. The idea's to scorch them to keep in the juice, then let them cook."

Paula continued working intently—for as the fisherman she had a proprietary interest. Link was pleased with the way she and Katy were beginning to cooperate, both with him and each other. He'd tried to make them feel useful and a part of things.

When all the fillets were on the cooking stone, he put them to work moving their pieces around with forks so they'd heat evenly, then pulling them to the outside so they'd remain warm. Both women swallowed often, and their nostrils flared at the pleasant odors.

"It's ready," he finally said, and they all immediately speared a morsel.

After an initial frantic onset, they ate more slowly, and everyone had a share of chicken salad, potato chips, more fish, and finished with an apple. The feast filled them to contentment.

They sat back lethargically, drinking sweetened hot tea from Sierra cups, staring out where the evening sun hovered over the western mountains, painting clouds with bold hues of gold, streaking the sky with reds and violets.

"Sailor's delight. Should be another nice day tomorrow," he observed.

Paula told them how Frank had been awake for a short while. He'd rambled, telling her there was a traitor within the State Department, and to alert Vern Calico. Since Link didn't move in those circles, it made little sense to him.

"Keep water and cooked fish handy," he told her, "and next time, get him to eat."

"I doubt he can chew," Paula said dubiously.

"Chew it for him and wash it down with water. We're going to have to use every trick available to keep him alive."

"I'll try," said Paula. Even when she was fishing, she

kept a watchful eye on Frank, and her love was obvious. The relationship between mother and daughter seemed confrontational, although Katy seemed more amenable since the episode with the snake.

"Do you really think someone's looking for us?" Paula asked. "We haven't seen any helicopters and hardly any airplanes."

"They're having to search a large area. We flew a long way after the collision." He looked at Frank for a long moment, then made up his mind. "I'm going for help in the morning."

Paula gave him a startled look.

"He's having trouble breathing. He needs medical attention."

"Can I go?" Katy asked.

"I'd feel better with both of you here."

She started to retort, then glanced darkly at her mother and held her tongue.

"How long will you be gone?" Paula asked, growing a troubled expression.

"No more than four or five days." Link believed it would take three at the most, but didn't want them concerned if something held him up. He pointed. "I'll go up the far side of the lake where the traveling's easiest, then strike out toward the low ridge to our northwest. If there's a road leading out of here, that's where it will likely be. The mountains are too steep in the other directions."

"And if you don't find anything?" Paula asked.

"I'll keep going until I do. Keep the smoker going. Dried fish will keep, and if it rains or you take a day off, you'll still have a source of food."

"What if something happens while you're gone?"

"Something *will* happen. Just keep your head and do the best with what you have. You can handle it. I wouldn't leave if I didn't think you were prepared."

"How long should we wait?" Katy asked.

"Don't even think about leaving. Stay here until I return or you're rescued. That's the rule of thumb for survival— make yourself comfortable and as conspicuous as possible, and wait until they come for you."

When everyone had gone to the lakeside and scoured their utensils using sand, liquid soap, and water, they sat back on the log, with the shelter reflecting heat and light on them, and talked about the wonderful meal. Paula tried to participate, but she was withdrawing again.

He didn't want to leave them, but another examination of Frank Dubois told him he must. His friend was breathing shallowly, and did not have long to live.

Link had no choice. He had promised.

Ramada Inn Hotel, Salt Lake City

The day continued to be frustrating, for when Leslie went down to the hotel dining room, she arrived at the peak of the dinner traffic. The maitre d' said there'd be a thirty-minute wait.

"It figures," Leslie said caustically, and was about to return to her room when she paused. The pilot from Executive Connections, William Bowes, was being seated alone. She marched over, utterly fearless, for nothing more disastrous could possibly happen in a single day.

"It's crowded and I despise waiting," she said. "Do you have someone coming?"

He scrambled to his feet. "Please join me."

She sat opposite him.

"I'm Billy Bowes," he said.

"I know," she said, raising an eyebrow. "Leslie Rocklin. Ring a bell?"

The answer came slowly, then pleasant surprise flooded onto his face. "Old Gerald Rocklin's daughter?"

"The last time I saw you, you were an Air Force major stationed at Mountain Home Air Force Base."

"Your father invited me to your home in Boise."

"After you took him up in a jet fighter, which he never forgot. He told everyone he'd flown with a died-in-the-wool war hero." And fifteen-year-old Leslie had suffered an extreme case of infatuation, and cried when she'd thought she'd never see the dashing major again.

Funny. She didn't remember his ears being that large. Did ears grow?

"How's Old Gerald?" he asked.

She told him about her father's death the previous month. When they'd gotten past the condolences, they both reflected silently.

"Still living in Idaho?" he asked.

"I left for a few years, but went back."

She guessed at his age. *Fifty?*

"In town on business?" Leslie asked innocently, wondering if there was a way of getting him to reveal the identity of the Gulfstream's passengers.

"Sort of. You?"

"Sort of."

A waiter arrived and recited the specials. Neither waited for the menu; both picked the prime rib house specialty, his blackened, hers with sage. He ordered wine, a forty-dollar bottle of French Chateauneuf du Papé.

"I'm celebrating," Billy explained. "Seeing you is the first glimmer of pleasantness I've had for the past two days. What are you doing in Salt Lake?" he asked.

Leslie started to tell him how she'd just missed filing the greatest story of her life, but hesitated. He would probably clam up, like everyone else in the search had been doing. "Visiting," she finally answered, remaining innocuous.

He smiled nicely, and she had a flickering memory of the young man who had unknowingly broken her heart.

"Do you miss the Air Force?"

"Not as much as I'd thought. I'm still flying ... with a charter service now."

"You said you're here on business?"

The nice smile faded and he hesitated. "I'm here to help find a missing airplane."

She leaned forward, knowing she must tread cautiously. "That must be exciting."

"It's the most boring kind of flying imaginable. We spend our time executing grid patterns and staring at the ground." His brow furrowed. "Didn't I see you at the airport?"

Leslie hadn't thought he'd noticed her.

"Probably not," he muttered, making it easier. She was uneasy with the subterfuge, but she had to learn the identity of the passengers. Leslie was still not convinced it wasn't the Dubois family, regardless of the telephone call to Mort Yoder's editor.

The wine arrived, and after a sip he pronounced it good. They made small talk over the first glass, and she learned he was living in a bachelor's apartment near Washington, D.C.

"Were you ever married?" she asked.

"Once," he said. "Just long enough to find out I wasn't good at it."

"I tried it too. Wrong guy for me. Dad tried to tell me, but it took a long time to figure it out for myself." She grew quiet as she thought of Old Gerald and how she'd ignored his wishes.

He nodded, as if he'd gotten a sudden jog of memory. "I saw you in the hangar."

She started to level with him, but was saved by the arrival of their salads and the fact that he didn't press for a response. She decided not to delve about the passengers, just enjoy the meal and make small talk.

He was a nice guy—honest and vulnerable, she found herself thinking as they made small talk and ate spinach salads with warmed honey and bacon dressing. When they nibbled on hot, yeasty breadsticks and the prime ribs arrived, she thought he was almost handsome, and maybe not *really* too old for her. As they finished the bottle of wine, he became sexually attractive, at ease with her but not pushy. After their bills arrived and he asked if she'd join him in the lounge for a drink, in the same casual way that warmed her, she thought he just might be the kind of man who could talk Leslie Ann Rocklin into squirming out of her L'Eggs and shucking off her Bali. That feat had not been done since the divorce.

Leslie was tipsy, but the fact did not bother her. She felt a thousand percent better than when she'd entered the room, all because of this man who had unwittingly been her first love.

Halfway to the bar, when she was enjoying the way he'd taken over without being pushy and was guiding her with a nice, firm touch on her arm, she felt suddenly remorseful. "I'm a reporter now," she said in a conversational tone, trying to pass it off lightly.

He stopped suddenly, and the nice pressure was removed.

She forced a smile. "I didn't say I was *rabid*. Just that I'm a journalist."

"A reporter?" he repeated, as if it was a momentous thing. He turned suspicious. "What were you doing in the hangar?"

"My job. Let's talk about it in the bar. After today I could use a stiff drink."

He still looked shaken. "I can't. I, uh, my company's in trouble."

"I heard." She wagged her head sympathetically.

"You should have *told* me you were a reporter," he blurted.

"If you don't want me to, I won't mention newspaper work."

He was backing off, shaggy eyebrows furrowed. "Like I told your friends today, I've got no comment. Call my office in Washington." He turned and hurried toward the elevators.

She stood there dumbly, feeling like a jilted bride, then sighed and mentally shrugged. Leslie Rocklin knew how to take such things in stride. Why should she be troubled about this particular man's leaving? His ears were too big and he was too old for her anyway.

She considered going into the lounge by herself. Instead she went to her room, feeling miserable about the lousy day again and wishing she'd been more truthful with Billy Bowes.

11

DAY THREE— MONDAY, JUNE 10

5:50 A.M.—The Lake

Katy crawled out of the makeshift bed when the sun was still below the mountains, casting silver-orange streaks across the sky. She stoked the dwindling fire, moving quietly so she wouldn't disturb the others, then paused to warm herself against the early morning chill.

Finally she went to the lakeside, where she laboriously untangled and laid out the six hooked lines and wooden floats. By the time she'd finished, the eastern sky glow was brighter.

A hundred yards up the shoreline a doe moved cautiously from the trees and stood perfectly still, surveying for danger. Finally she stepped forward and began to drink, and was joined by an ungainly spotted fawn. Katy watched, not moving until they'd taken their fill.

"Nice morning," a quiet voice said from beside her, and Katy started. The pilot stared out at the water for a moment, then nodded pleasantly and walked toward the forest. She wondered how he'd approached so quietly, and if it wasn't because of his Indian heritage.

She used the pick side of the ax to penetrate the dewy grass, then knelt over the soil and dug with her fingers for worms. As she baited the hooks, she thought about Link Anderson—he'd said to call him by his first name. He was good in the forest, a real outdoorsman, but he offered something even more important. He'd drawn them together, and taught them.

A prohibited thought had been growing within Katy Dubois.

The pilot was always correct with her. Even when he'd

hugged her for warmth after she'd crawled out of the frigid water, there'd been no hint of impropriety, yet Katy's face flushed as she remembered his solid, muscular body. He'd told them he was engaged to a woman in Montana—that they were just waiting for the right time. Katy wondered, for if they were really in love, nothing would keep them apart. His fiancée would be with him, not living elsewhere while he was in Washington.

A tingling sensation ran through her. Was there a way to get him to wait? Katy knew she was pretty. The boys at her school let her know by the ways they cast secretive looks. Perhaps Link could see it too. He'd not do anything about it, of course, being a gentleman and her being so much younger, and even the idea of mentioning anything about it embarrassed her.

She was unaccustomed to such feelings of indecision, and wondered if a true modern woman shouldn't be bolder about stating her emotions.

The incomplete thoughts both frightened and thrilled her.

By the time her mother was up and had tended to her father, Katy had caught and cautiously filleted four fish. She'd also cleaned and prepared the lava cooking stone as Link had shown them, and was warming water in the pot for their beverages.

"Since Katy was such an early bird, I can start sooner," Link said pleasantly.

Paula remained silent. She'd awakened moody.

"What does everyone want to drink?" Katy asked pleasantly, and took orders. She mixed coffee for the adults, hot chocolate for herself.

It took only three of the fish to fill them. After the utensils were washed and set out to dry, and Dad had been checked again—there was no change—the pilot gathered them at the fire.

"While I'm gone, don't forget people are trying to find us. If an airplane flies anywhere near, try to get the pilot's attention so he'll come down for a look."

"The signal fire," Katy said.

"That's right. Get the fire smoking, and if the airplane gets close, set off a smoke flare." He held one up. "Remove the cap from both ends, hold it up at arm's length, and pull the lanyard on the bottom. Then wave it around until the orange smoke's going."

He said the flare, the dark smoke from the fire, the word HELP outlined on the beach, and the brightly colored raft and tarp should identify them.

"What if *you* see an airplane?" Katy asked.

"I'll take the signal mirror, but the important thing's to draw them here."

Throughout the discussion Paula seemed increasingly withdrawn.

"I'll get ready now," he told them.

"Your shoes are dry." Katy brought his running shoes from his gym bag, retrieved from the airplane. They had Velcro straps that he could fasten with one hand.

When he was ready, clad in jeans, knit shirt, and his one-armed flying jacket, he picked out survival items and stuffed them into various pockets. He left the Swiss Army knife with Paula, and reminded them both where the match container and tinder were, in the event the fire went out. He took the signal mirror, brass compass, cigarette lighter, one of the small cans of liquid heat, and the tiny fold-up stove. Katy helped him strap the sheathed survival knife onto his belt. Finally he put an apple in either jacket pocket, making them bulge like cheeks on a chipmunk.

"You'll need more to eat," Katy said.

"I'll find food along the way. I want to travel as light as possible."

Paula watched his preparation with narrowed eyes. "Stay here, Katy. I'd like to speak with Mr. Anderson in private."

As the two walked toward the forest, Katy wondered. A moment later she heard Paula's voice raised in emotion, and was unable to stand it. She went quietly, then peeked around a tree.

They were no more than ten feet distant.

"I don't want you to leave," Paula was saying. "Who knows what might happen? That awful bear might return. What if another snake attacks Katy? We're helpless here alone."

"Only if you want to be." The words were softly spoken. "Unless something's done, Frank will die. That is a fact. I know about survival and basic first aid, but I can't provide the level of medical treatment he requires."

"I love my husband more than you could possibly understand. I would die for Frank if I knew that would make him well." She drew a resolute breath. "But I must also think of Katy."

"You're underestimating both her and yourself. Even if you get a little cold or hungry, which you shouldn't, you'll survive until I return. I've got to think of Frank now. Without medical attention he's certain to die."

Her voice caught. "I'm about to lose my husband. If something happened to Katy—"

"She's a capable young lady, Paula, and Frank isn't dead yet. The longer I delay leaving, the longer it will take him to get proper treatment."

"Help may come today. You said so yourself. I'm *pleading* for you not to go."

"I've got to." He stared, then turned and started toward the camp.

Katy scrambled to get back before the others arrived.

Link emerged first. "You shouldn't have overheard that."

"You knew I was there?"

"Your mother's frightened and needs your strength. She's much wiser than you realize, Katy. Listen to her. Forget your differences and cooperate."

Katy remembered her father asking for the same thing. "I will," she said.

Paula came out of the forest, chalky-faced and solemn.

Link knelt at Frank's side. "I'm doing my damnedest, Pig-foot. Hang in until I get back."

There was no response.

Link rose and walked toward the grassy expanse he'd follow around most of the lakeshore. After two hundred yards he entered a thicket of trees and was lost from view.

Paula watched from Katy's side until he reappeared and continued up the shoreline.

"He'll be back soon," Katy said in a cheerful tone.

Her mother remained silent.

"We'd better refill the smoker, Mom."

The Valley Rim

Jaeger was driving, with Charbonneau at his side and Webb in the rear with the supplies. He stopped as they crested the ridge, and they all carefully scanned the wild valley below.

"It's larger than I'd thought," said Charbonneau.

"Yes," Jaeger said in his low, rumbling voice. He'd been plagued by restlessness since they'd arrived at the Boise airport the previous evening.

After renting the Suburban—one with two-wheel drive and a small engine so they'd save on gasoline—they'd transferred weapons and Webb's medical kit and radios from the airplane. Then Jaeger had found an outfitter's store and bought camouflage bush clothing, tents, provisions, and a current, detailed chart of the valley put out by the Idaho Bureau of Mines.

Regardless of how he'd tried to convince Charbonneau that he should remain in Boise, that the valley would be rugged and inhospitable, Simon had insisted that he accompany them.

They'd spent the night in an unmemorable motel on the northern side of the city, where Webb had plugged his computer into a telephone line and scoured the Internet until convinced there was no news about the missing Gulfstream. Charbonneau had made two calls, one to New York to let his contact at El Soleil know where they'd be, the other to San Rafael, where he confirmed that preparations on the trailer were continuing on schedule.

This morning Jaeger had stopped at a service station, topped off the Suburban's tank, and filled two jerry cans. After driving north for an hour, Jaeger had turned east, then, after a similar period, south on the rough dirt road that would take them to the valley. As they'd approached the ridge, they'd searched with binoculars for signs of wreckage, looking for disturbances in the thick stands of trees. Seeing none, they'd proceeded up the steep road. Now they visually searched again from the crest.

"When we find the crash, where should we look for the folder?" Charbonneau asked.

Jaeger quelled a flash of irritation, increasingly intolerant as the restless mood continued to grow. "It's likely with the guard," he finally said.

An airplane etched a white trail of vapor high in the sky above, and Charbonneau stared. "How long before they search here?"

Webb leaned forward from the rear seat. "Without the tape they'll probably *never* get here. It's too far from the Gulfstream's flight path. If we see them getting close, I brought a VHF scanner along so we can listen to the pilots' conversation."

Charbonneau was determined not to listen. "Our man in Washington's concerned that Dubois might be able to identify him. He mustn't be allowed to live."

Webb pointed. "It's doubtful anyone could survive a crash in dense trees like that."

"But not impossible?"

"Nothing's impossible," said Webb, "but it's unlikely."

"Frank Dubois cannot be left alive," Charbonneau repeated.

"You said that," Jaeger snapped, then took a composing breath. "If anyone survived, we'll deal with them. There'll be no one left to talk."

Jaeger the hunter swept his eyes down the wild, tangled valley, trying to suppress the restlessness, wondering if it was a weakness.

He despised any slightest sign of weakness, in others and in himself.

The Hunter remembered the final words spoken by his father. Jaeger—his name had been Johann then—had been eight when Papa had called him in for their last talk. His father had been tall and splendid in his black and silver SS uniform, and he'd been proud of him.

"You look nice, Papa."

"Be quiet and listen, Johann." His father had spoken sternly to his only son, without displaying the slightest emotion.

"I will, Papa." He'd wanted very much to please him, for they'd seldom talked before.

"I was once a man of considerable power, and took whatever I wished from weaker men. They cried with fear when I came near, and I used their daughters and took their gold. Then we came here and our treasures were taken. We had nowhere to go, and there seemed to be no other way. Today I asked for help and was laughed at." He'd named his oppressor.

"He's a bad man, Papa!" young Johann had exclaimed.

"No. Just more powerful. He's taken my gold and now this land and our home, and if he wished he could use my wife and daughters or have me killed, and there is nothing I can do. He has power, Johann. People are neither bad nor good. They are beasts like any other, except they are given cunning. Use your gift, and never allow yourself to become weak. Always be powerful. Trust no one. Kill before they kill you. Devour before they devour you."

Johann had stared at him with wide, trusting eyes.

"Always revere power and despise weakness. Promise me!"

"I will, Papa."

His father had shown him the immaculate, well-oiled officer's sidearm with its silver double lightning bolt inlaid in the grip, and had told him what he would do.

"Don't, Papa," young Johann had pleaded.

"Do you never listen? Pity is *weakness*. Now go."

Johann had waited outside with his terrified mother until the shot was fired. His father's thrashing had bloodied and ruined the uniform, and he'd been buried in a cheap suit.

He had listened well, and never allowed himself to become vulnerable.

Jaeger had now killed thirty-eight times, and remembered each with exceptional clarity. When he was bored he would recall one and feel the pleasure, as if he were doing it again.

The first had been a schoolteacher in Añatuya, the Argentine town where he'd been reared by his useless mother and two older, whining sisters. He had been thirteen, and had smoldered under the teacher's relentless jibes about his slowness and ungainliness. The last time she'd mocked him before the class, joking about his mental and physical resemblances to a skinny ape, his face had burned with shame—and when he'd recalled his father's words an intense restlessness had grown inside him.

Three nights later he'd stolen into her bedroom in the teachers' quarters in back of the school, stunned her with a blow from a club, and dragged her into the fields where she could not be heard by others. There he'd raped and beaten her at his leisure . . . made her beg for forgiveness . . . then raped and hurt her again and again . . . until she'd made no more sounds . . . and then again. When he'd crept back to his mother's shanty, the restlessness was gone. He'd lain in his bed of dried grass covered by rough burlap, pleased with what he'd done, knowing his father would have approved.

As he'd matured the restlessness had periodically resurfaced, and there'd been other victims. Yet of them all the time with the schoolteacher had been the best. Jaeger remembered that she'd worn metal-framed eyeglasses—and everything else about her. He also remembered the power he'd felt as he'd conquered, humiliated, then killed her.

He'd worked at odd jobs at *rancheros* near Añatuya, hired by others of German descent who had known his father. Then he'd become a stalker of predators, the big cats and wild dogs that preyed on calves and lambs, a period when he had been happy with his life. But without family connections or education—and he was not academically inclined—he knew he had no future, so he'd gone to Brazil, and for a few years worked for a lumber company in the Amazon basin—until a rough and tumble American work-crew boss had begun to ride him. When the blood lust came, he'd beaten the man, then raped and killed his wife and young daughter in front of him as he'd died. He had fled then, westward through dense jungles where no lawmen dared to follow, to the vague Brazilian–Colombian border.

For a while he'd worked in gold mines, then for a Dutch oil exploration company. The times of restlessness had come and gone, but even the bloodiest deaths on the primitive frontier had not been investigated. He'd moved westward again and joined a private army charged with protecting coca plantations. Few cared that his periods of restlessness came more frequently. The men who died under his boots or fists were easily replaced.

He'd gained the name of the Hunter when he'd begun to operate alone—and earned a reputation for his ability to stalk government agents in the high mountains and dense, humid forests, and for his brutality when he caught them. There the Hunter had learned something about the restlessness. It was not the sex act he craved, but the heady feeling of domination over those he'd defeated. He'd sometimes preferred females, but he'd raped men as well as he'd beaten them to death. Revere power, his father had told him, and despise weakness.

The *jefes* had noted his effectiveness, and brought him to Cali and Medellín for more sophisticated tasks. He'd assassinated army officers and police chiefs who plagued them, and was even sent to Mexico and Panama, then Florida, Washington, D.C., and New Jersey, to deal with those who cheated them. He'd become known as the hunter who did not fail, who killed so horribly that others trembled, and there were more offers for his services than he could handle.

Finally he'd come to the attention of El Soleil, the organization that financed the largest of the coca operations, and they'd contracted him to protect their Colombian interests. Then he'd been summoned to Argentina to organize the kidnappings and assassinate the government minister. After the third *trueno* he'd met with Salvator DiPalma and been given his current task. His reward would be a high official position in the government envisioned by the aging colonel, redemption for the once poverty-stricken outcast from Añatuya.

Colonel Salvator DiPalma, the man who had taken his father's treasure and then driven him to suicide, but whom he'd been told not to blame. His father had revered DiPalma's strength. Despise weakness, he'd told his son, never power.

Jaeger had flown to New York and met the colonel's nephew, who had called Buenos Aires and uttered the word "thunder" when the times for assassinations were right. And who was now preparing the biggest *trueno* of all—to preoccupy the world with such horror that it would mask the overthrow in Argentina. Jaeger would help him succeed and then claim his prize.

But first they must get the leather folder and ensure that Frank Dubois did not live.

The Hunter carefully scanned the valley for a last time, wondering if the time in the wilderness would preoccupy his mind and make the raw ache of restlessness subside.

An aging Volkswagen bug approached from the rear. As it passed, the occupants waved. There were two of them—a boy driving, a girl peering as they went by. The backseat was piled high with camping gear, and two sturdy bicycles were attached to a rack at the back of the car.

Jaeger was surprised, for he'd believed there would be no one on the untended road, with its deep ruts and potholes. He frowned, staring in the wake of the small vehicle. The girl had worn eyeglasses, and reminded him of someone he recalled vividly.

"I thought it would be deserted here," Charbonneau grumbled.

"We'll follow them at a distance," Jaeger said, and the

others did not argue. As he accelerated on the rough roadway, the Hunter's sense of urgency mounted.

Salt Lake City International Airport

Rumors had floated that the names of the Gulfstream's passengers would be released today, but when Leslie arrived at the RCC nothing had changed. At the abbreviated press meeting she noted that they were down to five reporters.

She sat in the small coffee room, speaking with the occasional pilot or observer who passed through, wondering how she'd handle meeting Billy Bowes in the light of day.

Her cellular phone buzzed, and she was greeted by Mort Yoder's voice.

"Get your article in this morning's paper?" she asked.

"Just ten column inches in the business section, and it didn't turn out like I wanted. I keep running into brick walls when I try to confirm anything about the foundation. Other firms have P.R. people; they hire people to keep themselves *out* of the news."

"They don't like publicity," Leslie confirmed, an understatement when she recalled the events of the previous day.

"I've got the background you wanted on Tom Oliver."

She copied, but there was nothing extraordinary. Oliver was a bureaucrat who had worked his way from middle management to the top of his division, stepping on anyone vulnerable and unlucky enough to get in his path. It was rumored that he'd anonymously blown the whistle on two bosses, then piously replaced them.

"One other thing," Mort said. "We just learned the Gulfstream's captain's name is Abraham Lincoln Anderson. He's thirty-three years old, a veteran of the Gulf War, and the FAA's looking into his credentials. He supposedly replaced Executive Connections' chief pilot, name of William R. Bowes, as captain on the flight."

Leslie stopped writing and frowned. "Is Bowes in trouble?"

"Looks like it, but it's all sketchy and unclear. Except to confirm the names of the crew, neither the charter company nor the FAA are releasing *anything.*"

"Thanks, Mort."

"Let me know if you get anything else on the foundation, would you?"

"You're going to write another article?"

"Maybe. After my piece came out, I got a call from a
guy who said he's connected with the government and has
information about the Weyland Foundation—things I
couldn't possibly know—and he'd send a sample in the
mail."

"Mort, I get all kinds of calls from wackos. You listen to
them much, you'll start believing the whole world's a giant
conspiracy."

"I think this one's real. We've got caller ID on our
phones here, and I checked out the number. It's shown as
U.S. Government *unlisted,* which means it's a classified
line. Only a few of the top bozos over there get those."

"So he's a high-level wacko. I wouldn't get excited until
I saw what he's got. Anyway, I may not be able to get you
anything more. Unless I get *something* pretty quick, I'm
going back to Boise. So far I don't have a story, and I'm
doing this on my own nickel."

"Stay in touch."

Leslie disconnected, thinking about her friend. Mort
dreamed of unearthing a real exposé, something so big it
would shove aside other headlines, as Watergate had done
in the seventies. That one had started as no news—who
cared what political parties did to spy on one another?—
until two *Post* reporters had doggedly fueled the prurient
interests of readers with mysterious tales of deep throats
and skullduggery in the White House. Even then the silent
majority had supported the President they'd elected in a
massive landslide, until they'd realized he was too stupid
to burn the tapes. Then they'd deserted him, and the press
had helped the opposition party turn him into an ogre.

The term *crime wave* had been invented by New York
reporters, to provide something to write about in the news-
less dog days of July and August. *Most* news was boring
until a resourceful journalist made it appear important.
Mort Yoder wanted such a chance, a juicy exposé, and now
he had a subject: the Weyland Foundation.

Leslie wandered out to the operations desk, hoping to
run into Billy Bowes, but when she studied the flight board
she discovered that his airplane was no longer assigned to
its previous parking place. Leslie started to question, then

held her tongue. He was listed separately, under a column labeled ELKO, NEVADA, with four other pilots.

She learned that the RCC was being reestablished there. A wall map revealed that Elko was not only closer to the Cessna crash site, it was near the flight path of the Gulfstream if it had proceeded on course.

Two reporters joined her, angry that the move hadn't been revealed to the press, and discussed the merits of going to Elko. One decided to give up on the effort. The other said he was going to try again to get the FAA to release the names of the passengers. Unless they were newsworthy, there was little reason to hang around.

The Valley

They'd followed the Volkswagen on the rugged back road for most of an hour, and Jaeger had begun to believe the youths would go on through the valley when they finally turned off.

He waited to let them get well ahead, then turned onto the rough trail behind them, driving slowly because the way was difficult. After fifteen minutes, he killed the engine. The bug was parked to their right, nosed up to a clump of bushes. The forest was far too dense for the bicycles, which were still clamped in place on back. The youths had gone ahead on foot.

"Wait here while I see what they're up to," Jaeger instructed, then snapped his fingers at Webb. "The carbine." The weapon was light and stubby, well suited to carry in thick brush.

He dismounted quietly and eased the door closed, the restless feeling becoming pronounced.

Their tracks were distinct in the damp, soft earth, and Jaeger followed them, soundlessly parting the brush with the carbine's barrel. They'd not gone far, and he quickly drew close and listened as they talked. They were walking blindly, first in one direction, then another, and the young man complained that he knew the cabin was *somewhere* nearby.

They paused to rest, and talked, and went on. Jaeger remained close behind, hidden by foliage. They were clumsy and inept, and presented not the slightest challenge. He'd

let the game continue, hoping it would get better, all the
while allowing his restlessness to grow.

Jaeger learned about them during their wandering, which
never took them more than two hundred yards from the
parked vehicles. He followed, often very closely, and they
did not suspect, for the Hunter was good at stalking and remaining unseen.

They were fresh from completing their first year of col-
lege, and both had signed up for summer courses. Although
they were friends, they were cautious about their relationship, as if unsure about what attracted them. Both were
slight and wore glasses, and they talked about computer
languages, throughput, and other things that were of no interest to Jaeger.

Neither their friends nor their parents knew where they'd
gone. The boy had told his old man he'd spend the weekend with a friend in Pocatello.

They were nowhere near Pocatello. They were in the
valley entrusted to Jaeger's care.

She'd telephoned her parents in Spokane and explained
she'd be helping a girlfriend move into an apartment, and
couldn't give a phone number because one hadn't been in-
stalled.

A lie. She was here with the boy. They were perfect for
his purpose.

They emerged from the forest and came upon a large
field with shimmering emerald-colored grass. A deserted,
fallen-in cabin was across the clearing.

The boy pulled a map from a pocket on the side of his
pack, then knelt to spread it.

They examined closely. "The lake's not far," the boy
said.

But she was enchanted with the meadow. "Let's camp
here and go on tomorrow."

He refolded the map and carefully put it away. They
were fastidious about such things. As the two young people
continued to stare out at the clearing, a distant eagle
flapped to altitude, then circled. They watched as it plum-
meted out of sight.

"It's diving for a fish at the lake," the young man explained.

They walked across the clearing, then to the far side of
the cabin. There they shrugged out of packs and lay back

on the grass, staring out at the emerald-colored clearing.
Jaeger circled, remaining hidden in the foliage, then approached, masking himself behind the cabin.

"I like this," she said softly. "Being alone here."

They'd begun their mating ritual, and would soon begin
to touch each other. Jaeger's lower jaw began to tremble,
as it did when the restlessness was unchecked. He crept
into the open, then ever closer until he was within six feet,
still unseen and unheard.

Suddenly he thought about Charbonneau, waiting at the
vehicle. The two were so close and the feeling so intense,
yet . . . might he think Jaeger was too impetuous and unstable for the position he'd been promised?

The girl abruptly rose and stretched, then turned and
gave a yelp of surprise. Her eyes widened, magnified behind the eyeglasses, reminding him of another, and in that
moment Jaeger's restlessness returned in full fury.

An animal's sound issued from his throat as he made a
measured, vicious motion and the carbine's butt crunched
hard into the girl's side. Her eyeglasses fell to the ground
as she grunted sharply and fell to her knees, wheezing.

The boy's mouth drooped as he scrambled to his feet,
but the carbine swung again and the steel barrel made a
*thunk*ing sound as the front sight was embedded in the side
of his skull.

Jaeger wrenched it free, and the boy staggered drunkenly, blood streaming.

The Hunter dropped the carbine and came closer. He
grasped the boy's wrist in a vise-grip, smashed his fist into
the bony chest, then twisted the arm until the joint cracked.
As the boy squealed, Jaeger lifted a boot and kicked hard
into his abdomen. The boy sucked desperately for air as he
crumpled, the arm bent in an unnatural angle. He posed no
threat, so Jaeger returned his attention to the girl, the urgent, roaring sound loud in his head.

He pushed her onto her back, then unzipped and pulled
off her jeans, dragging her across the grass with the effort.
He knelt and grasped, tore away her shirt and underpants.
Her ribs were stove in on the right, and she breathed in
ragged wheezes. Jaeger's lower jaw trembled violently as
he gazed on her slight naked form.

"No!" the boy whispered as he found his wind, but when

he tried to move he shrieked with agony. He examined his arm dumbly, frowning with disbelief, still screaming.

Jaeger rose from the girl, a crooked smile working at his mouth. As he approached, the boy turned away and began to cry, then to plead. Jaeger hit him in the head, stunning him again, then pulled off his jeans as he had the girl's.

Almost an hour passed before Jaeger rose and stared for a moment longer, then exhaled sharply and pulled up his trousers. When they were secured, he scooped and hefted the girl under an arm, then grasped the boy's shirt and dragged him. He deposited them near the forest's edge, then went back to gather the carbine, their packs and clothes and their eyeglasses.

When he returned, the girl was perched on all fours, drooling blood and coughing. Jaeger was surprised, for he'd thought she was dead. She made little sound as he cut her throat with his pocket knife, and her death throes were slight.

He dragged them through the forest, leaving trails of bright blood in their wakes. He'd decided to put the bodies in their vehicle and burn it. *When they were discovered, the police would think . . .* He tried to reason it through, but for the moment could not, the aftereffect of the consuming emotion. As he continued, dragging first one body, then the other, his thought processes slowly returned and began to function. The pent-up fury had been released, and Jaeger worked briskly, pleased with the newly stored memories. There would be others, but until then he could savor the images of the girl and the broken, pleading boy.

He arrived at the Volkswagen and unceremoniously stuffed the bodies inside.

"Jesus!" Webb exclaimed, frowning as he dismounted and stared.

"Get back inside," Jaeger ordered, slamming the Volkswagen's door. He went to the Suburban and swung open the rear hatches. He remembered striking the boy with the carbine's barrel, and checked the front sight. It was bent, so he wiped away bloody hair and attempted to center it with his fingers, then by tapping on it with the pocketknife. He'd have to sight it in, he thought irritably, then tossed it in back and pulled out a can of gasoline.

Once the fire was going, they'd proceed down the trail.

The lake was not far, and they'd look there first, as Webb wanted, then methodically work their way to the other end of the valley.

When he'd set the blaze and climbed into the vehicle, Charbonneau's eyes were wide.

"They were exploring," Jaeger explained gruffly. "They would have been a problem."

Walking the grassy shore had been easy enough, but since Link had left the northern end of the lake he'd encountered difficult tangles of underbrush. He continued relentlessly, alternating between trotting and walking. *Keep going, soft man,* he'd tell himself when he found himself wanting to stop. During the weeks in Washington he'd allowed his physical condition to deteriorate. By the time he walked out, he'd be in shape.

Whenever they were visible, he used the distant mountain peaks for positioning. The last time he'd estimated that he'd come two miles since leaving the lake, six or seven miles total. Several times he'd come across rattlesnakes. The valley—this end at least—was thick with the reptiles, and he trod carefully.

An hour earlier he'd heard distant squeals, unlike those of any animal he could recall. They'd been similar to sounds of a mountain puma in rut, but those didn't seem quite right either.

Bright sunlight filtered through the trees ahead. A clearing meant easier walking. It was about time. He'd seen less dense undergrowth in Panamanian jungles, and thus far there'd been no road, path, or other sign of human presence.

As he emerged into an open field with knee-high, emerald green grass, Link felt a rush of excitement, for a cabin was directly across the clearing. He sobered quickly, for it was obviously abandoned. An old homestead? Beyond were several mounds where someone had dug and deposited earth. Miners, he decided, likely searching for gold or silver.

When he arrived at the center of the clearing, he took another survey of the peaks and estimated that he'd not traveled far since the last sighting. The forest beyond the clearing appeared as dense as that he'd just left.

Link eyed the distant, low ridge. He'd change course and

walk in that direction until there was no light remaining. Then he would rest until morning and go on.

As he continued toward the cabin, he heard the sounds of an engine starting. It came so unexpectedly that he scarcely believed it.

A vehicle was close by!

Link yelled out exuberantly and began to run.

A tendril of black smoke rose from the forest beyond the clearing. Something had been set afire and the vehicle was leaving.

He called out again, and ran faster.

Part II

The Wilderness

12

Link sprinted across the clearing, then slowed very little as he crashed into the dense forest and desperately shoved his way through. He came across two trails of profuse, bright blood—animals dragged out by hunters?—and followed them.

The smoke smells were distinct as he burst from the forest onto a crude path. A car was to his right—a Volkswagen bug, just beginning to burn. The engine sounds came from beyond, farther down the path.

"Hello!" Link shouted. As he passed the Volkswagen he noted that the blood trails led to the passenger door. He slowed to glance inside, then abruptly halted.

A nude human body was sprawled in the front seat, and another, partially clothed, was wedged beneath the first. He could make out their faces, a girl with her head almost severed, and a youthful male wearing a bloody mask with a fixed expression of horror.

He smelled the sharp odor of gasoline. They'd been killed in the meadow, then dragged here and the fire set. The flames inside were becoming intense, licking the bodies. He tried the handle, then hastily pulled back, his hand seared from the heat.

The fire torched, filling the interior with yellow-blue flame, and he drew away.

An explosion blew the rear hood open, crumpling two bicycles attached to a rack.

A feeling of foreboding swept through him as the engine sounds proceeded on the primitive trail, angling in the general direction of the lake. Whoever was in the vehicle had killed and disposed of the two in the Volkswagen. If they found Frank and the women . . .

Link hurried down the path, grimly determined to find out who he was dealing with. He'd not gone far before he caught a glimpse of a halted Suburban van.

He hid in trail-side foliage as the engine was shut off.

He heard voices but was too distant to understand the words. He crept closer, until he could see the man who emerged from the driver's seat. He was extremely tall, and was giving directions to others hidden from view on the opposite side of the vehicle.

The driver pulled a lever-action carbine from the Suburban and peered at the front sight, then tossed it back inside and picked up a large rifle case.

Link continued closer, until he was within fifty feet and could hear them.

The tall man was speaking in an accented voice, saying something about wreckage. If they found it and anyone was around, don't kill them until he'd had a chance to speak with them. They'd leave one—he called him Charbonneau—behind to watch the vehicle while the others searched at the lake. He pointed in the proper direction, at a small trail.

Link's chest tightened. He did not have time to sort it out—not only were they looking for the airplane, they would kill the survivors. It was no idle threat. They'd slain the two in the Volkswagen.

He must draw them away, then elude them and return to the camp.

A stocky, brown-haired man came into sight, carrying an assault rifle and staring in his direction. Link tensed but remained in view.

"See something, Webb?" the tall man asked, stepping up beside him.

The suspicious one pointed at the foliage that partially masked Link. "Something's in the bushes there." A third man joined them, blond and slight, looking frightened.

The stocky man carried a familiar weapon. Link had seen great numbers of Kalishnikovs captured during the Gulf War.

Link crouched lower, then turned and retreated a few feet before purposefully snapping a branch.

"There!" A flurry of shots sounded, coming so fast they blended into one another.

Link ran, angling into the forest toward the clearing. He

heard a shout, then sounds of pursuit, and hurried faster. He crashed through the brush, unmindful of noises he created or the trail he left—wishing only to draw them.

He could not lead them to the family, or give them time to go there.

He veered sharply right, encountered a tangle of thick underbrush and circumvented it until he found a place he could push through, then ran again.

Link burst into the clearing, stumbled, and fell headlong, sending a jolt of pain through the immobilized arm. He pushed to his feet and ran toward the abandoned cabin. As he approached it he heard a yell and dove behind the structure as another staccato of shots rang out. Then he scrambled forward, momentarily hidden from their view by the cabin, and reentered the thicket, clawing and pushing his way past growth that seemed to purposefully reach out to slow him.

He was not cautious, wishing simply to put distance between himself and the pursuers.

An acrid odor rose from the ground as he parted underbrush with his free hand, but there was no time for investigation. He pushed on ... then flailed wildly as the earth beneath his feet shuddered and gave way.

Link clawed vainly for purchase as he fell, then slid on slick, moist clay, tumbling past man-made timbers. His injured arm struck one and he yelped with pain.

He came to rest thirty feet below the surface, lodged precariously against two timbers. It was an abandoned mine shaft and extended even farther, angling downward into inky darkness. The acrid smell was now pronounced, coming from the shaft beneath him.

Link huffed tortured breaths, waiting for the pain in his arm to subside as he stared up at the small cone of light. A weight shifted against his left foot. He moved cautiously, and contact was made again. Something was alive and moving. He wanted to investigate, but knew he mustn't reach down until he knew what was there.

He heard people above, speaking excitedly—one of them the familiar, deep voice of the tall man—as shadows darkened the cone of light.

Link remained perfectly still. A loud, distinct rattling sound came from near his feet, then a second snake joined in. They twisted, writhing about his feet.

"Did you hear that?" asked the stocky man in an awed voice. "Rattlesnakes."

The tall man spoke. "Maybe you should go down for a look, Webb."

The stocky man's voice rose in protest.

"Give me that," the tall man muttered, and Link heard the ratchet sound of a weapon being cocked.

He pressed himself against the wet earth.

The roar of the automatic weapon was loud in the enclosure, and Link was spattered with mud from bullet impacts. The mass surged at his feet, and he fought the urge to panic.

"I heard something moving. I think you hit him."

"We'll wait for a while longer," said the tall man.

Some of the weight on Link's right leg was relieved as a snake slithered down the shaft.

After five minutes the two men relieved themselves, laughing as they pissed into the hole, then grew silent again. Time passed before one of them called out the name Jaeger and the tall man replied. They spoke together, in low voices, wondering if the one named Charbonneau might be getting concerned.

"We'll go back," the tall man finally decided.

Link heard sounds of movement, then nothing.

Although he heard only silence, there was no way of knowing if they'd left, or if one or both remained to see if he'd emerge. He continued to wait. After a while the weight on one, then the other foot moved. For the moment, at least, the roiling mass was gone.

Elko, Nevada, Airport

Billy landed, turned off the runway, and taxied toward his assigned parking spot. Several new aircraft were gathered near the hangar they'd use as the new coordination center. The numbers of searchers had been increased. He'd learned that the move from the much larger Salt Lake International had been made to accommodate the Weyland Foundation in their quest for anonymity, but Billy was pleased. There was less air traffic congestion, and their departure and landing procedures were much simpler.

It was his second flight, and thus far he'd seen nothing

except mountains, farmland, the high, stark desert of Nevada—and other searching airplanes.

He decided to have lunch, give Henry Hoblit a phone call, then fly again, concentrating his efforts in the Ruby Mountains to their southeast.

He shut the engines down and got out, then set chocks under the wheels.

"Hi there."

Billy watched Leslie Rocklin approach, then returned his attention to making sure the airplane wasn't going anywhere if a gust of wind blew up. Finally he stood and flexed his shoulders, still weary from the flight, and wondered how he should handle her.

"I'd like to apologize for last night," she said.

"That's okay. I lied too," Billy said. He started across the parking ramp toward the terminal building. He'd not rented a car or a room yet, and decided to do so before eating.

"I did *not* lie," she said from close behind him. "I just didn't tell you I was a reporter right away." She paused then. "You say you lied to *me*?"

"I'm married and have five kids. Now good-bye and go away."

She laughed. "No, you aren't and no, you don't, Mr. William R. Bowes of Arlington, Virginia. You just had your fifty-third birthday. I'd guessed you were younger."

"You seem to know everything. And just like you heard, my company's in deep shit because of the accident."

She formed a pixie's grin. "May I quote you?"

"No, but I'm sure you will."

He went into the small terminal and headed for the first auto-rental counter. It was closed. So was the next one.

"They're about to hold a cowboy poetry festival," she said, still on his trail. "It's a pretty big thing out here, and they're already out of rental cars."

"I see the signs." He huffed an irritated sound.

"If you don't have one, you'd better call for a room too. I'd suggest the Red Lion. They only had four left when I got mine half an hour ago, and everything else was full."

He went to a nearby phone booth. When he hung up there was only one room remaining.

"Thanks," Billy mumbled as he started for the restaurant.

She was still with him when the hostess led him to his table.

"Mind if I join you?"

"Look, I can't help you. I don't know anything more than I just said."

"Be nice. I got one of the last rental cars. I can give you a ride to the motel later."

He sat and opened the menu.

"Mind if I sit with you?" she asked again.

"I shouldn't be talking to a reporter."

"How about an old friend? Did you know you were the first man I fell in love with?" She continued to chatter as she took a seat across from him. "It really was good seeing you last night, and I really did enjoy dinner."

"Yeah. Too bad about your father. I liked him." *Why was he talking to her?*

The waitress took his order for a hamburger and cup of coffee. Leslie ordered tea.

"See anything when you were flying?" she asked, still trying to be friendly.

"Nothing that shouldn't have been there."

"I'm sorry about last night. Not telling you sooner that I was a reporter, I mean."

Billy softened. "You've got your job to do so. I'm just testy, with all that's going on."

"The FAA's really after your company, aren't they?"

What the hell, Billy decided. He could see no harm in talking, as long as he was careful about what he said. "It's not really my company. It's a four-way limited partnership, but it means a lot to my buddy who owns the majority. The general's an old friend, and he's not well."

"Anything you can tell me about the Gulfstream pilot . . . Lincoln Anderson?"

"He's the general son. He was a fighter pilot in Desert Storm, and he's got more moxie than about anyone I've met."

"The FAA's bringing up questions about his competence."

"They're wrong. Link's a natural pilot, one of the best I've ever flown with, and he's meticulous about anything concerning flight safety."

"A witch hunt?"

"They're questioning our judgment for letting one of our pilots return to Washington."

"That was you, right?"

"Yeah." He still didn't feel good about leaving the flight. "They're not playing fair. Their own rules were met. The client's a qualified pilot."

"Why won't they release the names of passengers?" She arched an inquiring eyebrow.

"I can't talk about them either. The Weyland Foundation's putting pressure on the FAA to . . ." He stared at her, realizing he'd said too much.

"Do you mind if I write that?"

Billy sighed. "No . . . I mean, *yes*. We've got to be careful. The foundation can ruin us and likely will, even without my encouragement. I forgot who I was talking to."

"I'm still a friend. You don't want something included, I won't."

He wanted to believe her.

"Honest," she said. She grinned and poked her glasses into place with a forefinger. He decided she was pretty in a pixyish sort of way, and certainly full of lively energy.

When the hamburger arrived, Billy realized he was hungrier than he'd thought. Halfway through, he glanced up as an idea formed. "What kind of story are you after?"

"More background stuff. Talk to the pilots and find out what they've seen. Get a finger on how they feel about it, and what a search-and-rescue operation smells and tastes like. I almost went back to Boise this morning, then I decided I had to get *something* out of all this."

"You have good eyes?"

"I'm nearsighted. The eyeglasses aren't for show."

"You can't see things at a distance?"

"My glasses correct my vision. I can see fine with them on."

He went back to the hamburger, thinking it was probably a bad idea.

"Why?" she asked, cocking her head inquisitively again. She was cute when she did that.

Why not? "I was going to ask if you wanted to come along as an observer. Four eyes are better than two and all that."

She grinned. "I would *love* to."

"Just don't ask who the clients were or things I can't

talk about ... and don't call me William again. I went
through all the fistfights about Sweet William when I was
a kid, and earned the right to be called Billy. Do you get
airsick?"

"How about Will? I secretly called you that when I was
in love with you."

"Just Billy."

"That's too bad. I liked Will. No, I don't *think* I get airsick."

"Get something to eat if we're going to fly together.
There's no restaurants up there."

A few minutes later, Billy called Henry Hoblit at the
Washington office to tell him there'd been no developments regarding the search-and-rescue effort.

Things were hopping at Executive Connections. The
foundation and FAA people were still around, and after the
Gulfstream crew members had been identified, a number of
news hounds had descended with their noses up and sniffing, trying to get more on Link and Jackie, and the names
of the passengers. Henry had been forced to make innocuous statements.

"Can't refuse 'em all," he said dejectedly. "That might
make it worse."

Billy was noncommittal. Three days earlier Henry would
have gloried in the attention.

"Anything else happening there?" Henry asked. "Like
ideas about why there haven't been transmissions from either bird's ELT?"

"Nothing except speculation," Billy said. "They still
can't find the Cessna's tail, where the ELT's located. One
pilot thinks it may have been torn away in the impact and
somehow got lodged in the Gulfstream. Maybe in the luggage compartment, since their bags were scattered all to
hell and gone."

"I've been thinking something like that. If the Gulfstream's not nearby, it was still flying after the impact, and
maybe it took the Cessna's tail section along for the ride."

"That might not be good news, Henry. It would mean the
Gulfstream could be anywhere along their route of flight."

"Or about anywhere else. Link might have turned back
toward the Salt Lake airport, or gone on to land there at
Elko."

"Who knows, Henry? And even if the Cessna's tail is

buried in its baggage compartment, it doesn't explain why we're not getting an ELT signal from the Gulfstream."

"How about if Link got the Gulfstream turned and went down in the Great Salt Lake? If the antenna's under water, the ELT can't transmit."

"The lake's not that deep. An airplane as big as the Gulfstream would be visible, and we've had a lot of people looking."

"Yeah," Henry said with a sigh. "Guess it's another bad idea."

North of the Lake

A full hour passed before Link decided he couldn't afford to wait longer. He began slowly clawing his way up the incline, trying to do it with the minimum of noise, concerned that the men might have gone on to the lake, yet also wary they might have left someone behind.

The shaft had likely been dug by the same people who'd inhabited the cabin. They'd probably sunk several exploratory shafts in the valley. It was something to remember.

He continued climbing, and the cone of light grew larger and brighter as he approached the surface. Twice he almost slipped, but was able to make purchase with his good hand. He crawled on, digging in with the hand and drawing himself ever upward, and had come within three feet of the top when he stopped and waited, listening for human sounds.

Something moved against his hip.

Link resisted a powerful urge to move quickly, and cautiously looked down. A rattlesnake was working its way up, now gripping to his leg for its task. The flat head drew back and the tongue darted to taste the air.

He eased his good hand downward, moving it ever so slowly. Snakes had poor eyesight, but could detect motion, and Link knew to move cautiously so it wouldn't be aroused.

It took five long minutes to position the hand. The head drew back and the snake hissed nervously, as if it knew something was wrong.

Link grasped in a deft motion, capturing it just behind the head. As he did so a shadow fell over him. He shifted his eyes upward.

"Jesus!" The stocky, brown-haired man stared with a wide-eyed, surprised look, hesitated for a split second, then swung the muzzle of his weapon.

Link grasped the rattlesnake tighter, and in a fluid movement hurled it into his face.

The stocky man released a squeal as he backpedaled out of view with the snake draped about his neck.

Link levered his way up, almost slipping back as he tried to push himself over the lip. He grasped at the base of sapling and pulled . . . and was out. He lay still for no more than two seconds, panting from exertion, free of the horror below but knowing he must flee.

A scream and a shot, then another and another . . . the brown-haired man was a dozen paces distant, his upper body hidden by branches as he fired wildly at the snake that twisted and coiled at his feet.

Link pushed himself to his feet and lurched into the brush, shoved his way past a mass of branches, and stumbled on. More shots came from behind, and the deep voice of the tall man shouted as he approached. Link staggered ever farther from the scene, clawing through undergrowth, continuing westward.

The voices faded as Link began to run, trying to put distance between them—and to continue to draw them away from the lake and the Dubois family.

13

4:15 P.M.—The Valley

Link knew where they were, or at least the general part of the world, for both vehicles he'd seen had carried Idaho plates. There were two vast wilderness areas in that state, one north and the other northeast of Boise. He'd thought of those as he'd scrambled through underbrush and dense stands of spruce trees. In either area, civilization would lie over the tall mountains to the south. As Link continued, each step jarred his broken arm and battered body, but he continued doggedly. He encountered thick brush again and proceeded with difficulty—crawled through an impossible thicket of manzanita and sumac—then rose and kept going.

As his heart continued to pound from exertion, he wondered if he was being pursued. If not, he should immediately return to the camp, but if he was, that would only draw the murderers to the family.

He emerged onto a lakeshore and felt a wave of despair that he'd run in a circle. Then he realized that this lake was smaller than the other, oblong and shaped like a dog bone. He took out the compass and observed the mountains. He'd veered, but was still proceeding generally west.

Link began to walk down the shoreline, then stopped and looked about. *Perhaps they've gone back.* Something inside told him they had not. He must find out, yet carefully.

A fallen tree, some six inches in diameter, was to his immediate left.

He approached it, bent at the knees, grasped with his good arm and stood, grunting with the effort. He staggered for a few feet, put it down, then lifted and tottered for another distance. Link lifted again, this time slogging into the water before releasing it. He went back ashore, carefully eliminated the drag marks and footprints, and slipped out of his flight jacket. The water in the lake was as cold as that in the larger one, and they'd learned how valuable dry clothing could be when you emerged.

Link stripped off the remainder of his clothes, placed them on the jacket, and zippered the front. He waded out to the log and tied the bundle to a branch, pulling the jacket's right arm around it and through the other, pinned one. The task was difficult with one hand, but he persevered. He tugged until the log floated clear of the lake bed, then returned to the beach, where he gathered telltale twigs that had fallen from the dead tree. Except for the depression where the dead tree had lain, there were no signs of disturbance.

He carefully smoothed footprints as he backed into the water, then waded out to the log, held it with his good arm and flutter-kicked, heading for a rocky shore across the lake. He progressed slowly in the ice-cold water, and when he was two hundred yards out, he prayed no one would burst out of the forest while he was so vulnerable.

It was past five o'clock when the water grew shallow enough that he could gain his feet. Link continued to drag the log forward until he was waist deep. Then, with weary, near-frozen fingers, he untied the bundle and gave the log a hearty shove to set it adrift. After wading ashore, then shivering violently for a few seconds, he staggered toward the forest.

When he'd reopened the bundle and pulled on his clothing, he found a suitable bush and lay behind it, trembling from cold and exhaustion. Yet now that the task was done, he was pleased with his effort, for he'd soon learn if anyone was tracking him and, if they were, observe their proficiency. As he waited, Lincoln Anderson took an assessment.

He was hindered by the broken arm, but was fast regaining his forest skills. As a boy his father had taken him on wilderness camping forays, and later the Air Force sent him through several survival training programs. More recently he'd served on a search-and-rescue team in the mountains of Montana, and then studied the ways of the Piegan Blackfeet, who had been masters at concealment and stealth. There was much to remember. *Advantage to Link.*

He thought of his adversaries, remembered the stocky

man who had looked down at him at the lip of the mine shaft. The tall man had called him *Webb,* and from what Link had seen and heard, he was neither a leader nor a good woodsman. The tall man—Webb had referred to him as *Jaeger*—had obviously been in charge, but was otherwise an unknown. He had seen the slight blond man only once, at the vehicle, and he'd appeared frightened. The others had mentioned a name, *Charbonneau.* He'd been left to guard their vehicle, and they'd worried about him. The two, Webb and Charbonneau, did not appear to be overly competent. Perhaps it was the same with the large man. Link was outnumbered three to one, but the fact meant little unless they were capable. That he would have to determine.

They knew about the airplane and weren't reluctant to kill. He did not know their intentions, and must not use deadly force until he knew more. *Advantage pursuers.*

They were armed, at least one of them with an automatic weapon, Jaeger with the firearm from the case. He had only the survival knife. *A huge advantage to the pursuers.*

He stopped, realizing he could become downright despondent if he continued, and decided to eat an apple while he waited. As he pulled it from his jacket, he wondered again if they were indeed still following him. So far there was nothing across the lake. Perhaps . . .

A figure stepped cautiously from the forest. The stocky man appeared weary from the chase, still carrying the assault rifle: an AK-47 or SKS, the Chinese copy. Those used 7.62 by 39 millimeter rounds. Not great for long shots, but good for killing in the forest.

Link took a bite of apple and chewed thoughtfully as the tall man emerged into view, looking wary, appearing not at all tired. He'd sent Webb out first. As bait? He pointed, and Webb walked past the place where Link had launched the tree, searching for tracks. After a dozen paces Webb slowed, walked a bit farther, and stopped. He backtracked and studied the shoreline in the other direction, then stopped and looked about again, baffled.

It was as Link had believed. Webb was not a capable stalker.

Link was pleased with his ruse. He'd sensed that he was being followed, and it had proven true. Intuition would be a good thing if he was to continue evading. He finished the apple as he studied the men across the lake, wishing the third one was with them.

The tall man was carrying a hunting rifle, handling it familiarly. It was quite long, likely an oversized magnum tailored for the big man's frame. The scope was also large, indicating high magnification and that it would be good in low light conditions.

As Webb continued searching, the tall man approached the water and stared at the bottom, then slowly raised his eyes and scanned the opposite shore. He said something to Webb.

Jaeger was good, even better than Link had feared, for it hadn't taken him long at all to reason it out. Link gained his feet, satisfied that he knew more about their capabilities. It was doubtful they knew as much about him. *Advantage to Link.*

It would soon be dark enough that they would have trouble tracking him, but he did not wish to elude them completely. Not yet. He'd continue until he found a suitable place to spend the night, then think it all through and settle on a plan of action.

The Lake

Katy and her mother leaned back against the log, several smoked fish fillets set out before them on a survival blanket. They'd earned the repast. That morning Paula had continued to put out the fish line as Katy refilled the smoker and added smoke-cured fillets to the plastic bag. They had more than five pounds of it suspended from the tree limb.

Paula stared gloomily into the fire. Just after noontime they'd heard faint popping sounds, then others awhile later. Katy had wondered if it wasn't hunters, but her mother had imagined all sorts of terrible alternatives.

"We should eat, Mom." Katy had been working hard to get along, as Link had told her.

"I'm not hungry."

A few minutes earlier, Paula had said she was starved. "Oh, God!"

Katy looked at her mother, then followed her eyes. Something shifted in the shadows. When she looked closer, the shape moved. "It's Fuzz-butt," Katy said in a disgusted voice.

"Go away!" Paula cried out, rising from the log.

The shadow reversed course and moved in the other direction.

Mom stood and stamped her foot. "Go away. Get *out* of here!"

Katy retrieved the orange flashlight. "Bears are afraid of light," she said knowledgeably.

"There he is again," Paula whispered.

Katy switched on the light. A weak glow issued as Fuzz-butt came closer, zigzagging cautiously into view as if the dim light interested him. She uttered a squeaking sound, then grabbed a fillet and tossed it past him into the darkness. The bear ambled off to investigate. They heard a snuffling sound as he ate.

Katy added wood to the fire, increasingly frightened.

"He's coming back!" Paula said in a high voice.

Katy immediately threw another fillet.

They huddled on the log, tossing fillets into the darkness when the bear reappeared, until the last of them was gone. Fuzz-butt was obviously still hungry because he returned and edged closer to the fire. Katy would have given him the rest of the fish, but it was hanging from the limb and she didn't dare venture there in the darkness.

They tried sitting very still, but the bear just came closer, until he was within a few feet, and Katy became so frightened she almost lost the tiny remainder of her cool.

The bear extended its quivering snout toward her and made a snuffing, pig-like sound.

"Get away!" Paula said suddenly, as if she'd come alive, and moved menacingly toward Fuzz-butt, a cup clutched in her hand.

The snout withdrew a few inches.

Paula grabbed the frying pan from beside the fire and brandished it. "Shoo!" When the bear took a backward step, she clapped the cup against the pan, making a loud, tinny noise.

The bear lurched farther away, and drew back its head as if surprised.

"Go *away*!" Paula cried, and clattered the metal harshly.

Fuzz-butt reared, and Katy issued a squeal.

The bear turned and scampered into the darkness.

They were quiet for a long moment, then Paula raised
the cup and pan and clattered them together a few more
times. They heard sounds from farther away in the forest.

"Good work, Mom," Katy said in an awed voice. She'd
almost peed her pants.

Paula sat back down, trembling, and Katy couldn't tell if
it was from anger or fear.

"I wish Link Anderson was here," Paula said in a quiet
tone.

Katy put even more wood on the fire. "He'll be back. He
knows what he's doing, Mom." She sure hoped so, anyway.

Frank was floating near the surface, close enough to feel
the agony of his wounds, for he'd sensed that his family
was endangered. The feeling lessened when he heard his
wife and daughter speaking again, and their tones no
longer sounded fearful. Pleased, he allowed himself to
sink back from the pain into the numbed comfort of the
abyss.

He wafted about, seeing images, searching for answers.
He recalled how important the dates of the *truenos* had
been: April 1995, the date of the Oklahoma City disaster—
October 1995, when the Simpson murder trial had been
decided—November 1996, following the dramatic U.S.
election. Now analysts at the Weyland Foundation examined each important news story, and wondered which might
be tied to the next Argentine atrocity.

Yet other important events had occurred which capti-
vated the media and the public, and there'd been no
truenos since the election. Why?

To find the answer, Frank analyzed the *truenos* of the
past.

The first had come after the Oklahoma City bombing,
and it was unlikely that El Soleil had previous knowledge.
They'd simply picked a time of turmoil, and their assassins
had killed the police officials and reporters who'd been
looking into their Patagonian operation.

But El Soleil had known that the next kidnappings and
murders, in Buenos Aires, would have to be better planned.
The timing of the second *trueno,* following the verdict of
the Simpson murder trial, was to have been more predictable, but that one too must have been somewhat of a surprise since the jury had deliberated such a short while. The

assassins had likely been rushed, and since the murder of the minister of the interior would have to be timed even more precisely, they'd waited for a scheduled news event—the American presidential election.

The minister's assassination had gone off as planned and was hardly reported, but Frank wondered if the people at El Soleil hadn't wondered about that one too, for if the election had not gone as it had, it would have been a ho-hum event and the press might have been looking for other stories.

Why had there been no new *truenos*? The Weyland Foundation analysts waited and culled the news, for there were more opposition leaders El Soleil wanted eliminated. There'd been other spectacular news stories, but no *truenos*. Why?

In his newfound wisdom, Frank came up with the answer.

El Soleil would no longer leave the timing of future *truenos* to chance—it would be too difficult to set up the next, critical assassinations on short notice—so they would make them happen! They would no longer be satisfied to wait for news, they would *create* it. The thought brought new speculation—that El Soleil might send terrorists to America.

The final one must be especially spectacular to mask the killing of the Argentinean president and the actual overthrow of the government.

What did El Soleil possess that could draw the attention of every American?

For a moment Frank's mind became barren. Then came a flash of light, followed by a billowing vertical cloud. Not a nuclear explosion, but something akin and extremely powerful.

That image dissolved and he was back further in time, at a military briefing, listening to a captain explain a weapon. *Unstable* and *implosion* were words used. The briefing officer discussed the phenomenon and showed a video clip. Another mushroom cloud erupted.

Fire and air. The final *trueno*.

The explanation fit. Another puzzle solved, this one with terrible consequence, and Frank grew an overpowering urge to relate it to others. He forced himself from the chasm—toward the surface, where pain and suffering lurked. He came partially awake, crying out in agony, and sensed that Paula was at his side. She soothed him and poured precious water past his lips. Frank drank greedily, and again was overpowered by the awful pain, enduring only because he must.

"Truenos," he gasped. "They ... won't wait. They'll ... make them happen."

His wife murmured gentle words.

"They have ... FAE," he whispered. "Tell Link."

"He's gone to get help, darling."

"Tell him," he repeated, and sank away from her.

Elko, Nevada

They were eating light pasta salads with oil dressings and drinking glasses of chablis. Billy had thought he might gain a moment of respite from Leslie Rocklin's tireless chatter when their dinner arrived, but now she continued between bites, telling him about the theft of the film by the Weyland Foundation people and how she'd believed she was onto a truly big story—not that she wasn't getting good stuff now, observing a search-and-rescue effort from the pilots' and observers' views—but how she wanted something *really* big.

She told him about a *Washington Post* reporter friend named Mort Yoder; how he'd picked the Weyland Foundation for his exposé, and how he'd just gotten information from what he called a *reliable government source*.

Billy interrupted. "We might have reason not to be fond of them, but the foundation's known for their good work with charities and such."

"I'm not saying I *like* what Mort's doing," she said. "Dealing with whistle blowers is one of the less desirable things about our job, but we can't always ignore them. Anyway, Mort's contact says the Weyland Foundation's into some big things they shouldn't be. He says a group there called the *handful* has been pouring investments into poor third world countries for years."

"Is that bad?" Billy asked.

"Maybe not, but it's *news*, especially if they've worked hand in glove with American presidents of both parties. He gave Mort the name of a corporation in the Czech Republic and said to check into their ownership. He also said to watch for two very large companies being formed in Estonia, and that they're being funded by the foundation. It's like they're some kind of private United Nations, helping out countries picked by the President."

"I still don't see what's so awful about it. Anyway, there's something sleazy about government officials leaking secrets."

"True," she admitted. Done with her meal, she began to nibble on crackers.

"There's a dessert tray," Billy said.

"No way. I've gained three pounds since I left Boise." She finished the crackers and pushed her plate away. "Get your call through to Washington?" she asked.

"Yeah. Henry's convinced the Weyland lawyers are going to bring legal action because we failed to provide a second pilot."

"Who were your clients?" She asked it innocently, not for the first time.

"Don't do that, Leslie."

"Were they the Dubois family?" she tried, watching his face for a reaction.

Billy huffed an angry breath. "Damn it, *stop* that." He had a lousy poker face and wondered if he'd given anything away.

"Anything you don't want me to print, I won't, but I'd love to know."

"Let's change the subject."

"Okay. Why did you think you could get away with having only one pilot?"

"What if the client's a fully qualified pilot, both in the Gulfstream and in that model, and he specifically asked to go with only Link and himself at the controls?"

"Is that legal?"

"Sure. Problem is, we've got nothing in writing from the client. There's only my word, and it'll look like I'm trying to protect the company. That's what Henry thinks."

"What's this Henry Hoblit like?"

"He's a good guy, but he's sorta odd." He told her his anecdote about Henry being smooth as baby shit, and she couldn't contain her laughter.

"I'm sorry," she finally managed. "I know your friends are in trouble."

He shrugged. "Link and Jackie both had good senses of humor."

She raised an eyebrow at the *had*.

"I've lost faith that they're alive," he said. Then he shook his head miserably. "That's not true. I never had faith. The Gulfstream's not built to land on anything but a prepared runway."

"They were just names, but now that you've described them, they've become real."

"It's a quick way to go," he said. "I've accepted that they're dead, but I'm concerned about Link's parents and how it's going to impact them. His death, the lawsuit and all."

She reached across and put her hand on his arm. "When the airplane's found, you'll find it wouldn't have mattered if there had been a dozen pilots on board. That way the foundation won't have a leg to stand on, and the litigation will go away."

He liked the feel of her hand. Leslie Rocklin was an attractive bundle of energy, and Billy was increasingly drawn.

"Thanks for letting me fly with you today," she said softly.

"My pleasure." He meant it.

When the waitress came with the bill, he pulled out a company credit card.

"I'll get the next one," Leslie said. When the waitress left to ring it up, she removed a map from her purse, unfolded it, then frowned as she studied it. "Where *could* they be?"

"They had enough fuel to make it anywhere on there," he said. "The Gulfstream has long legs, and after the collision they could have limped off in any direction. I've been hoping some desert rat or rancher would either remember hearing the airplane or come across the wreckage."

Leslie stared at the map. "There's a lot of outback in this part of the West," she said, but she'd grown a thoughtful look.

The waitress returned with his credit card and the form, which he signed. Billy was tired and out of ideas. "I'm going to the lounge for a drink before I head to my room and collapse. Care to join me?"

"Sure," Leslie Rocklin said as he went around to pull out her chair. "Just don't run away this time." They were becoming friends.

14

DAY FOUR—Tuesday, June 11

1:00 A.M.—Elko

Leslie had gone to bed thinking about the conversation with Billy, and had fallen asleep telling herself she'd check something out first thing in the morning.

A woman had phoned her the morning after the Gulfstream was lost, complaining that an aircraft had buzzed low overhead the previous day. Coincidence? Certainly, if it had just been a reader calling from near the airport with a complaint. They got those often. But there was something about the name and the familiar way she'd spoken that niggled and tried to tell Leslie that she'd overlooked a lead.

At midnight she'd half awakened, thinking about the phone call, and almost got up. Instead she'd fallen back to sleep. Now Leslie was awake again and this time turned on the bedside light, for she knew it wouldn't go away until she proved something to herself. It took several seconds to collect herself enough to search through the electronic memo maker.

She selected the "Newstips" category and scanned the entries. She found *Joan Cecil,* and a seven-digit phone number, then looked up the prefix and cursed herself soundly for not doing it previously. It was one of those associated with the 208 area code for southern Idaho, but *not* the one for Boise. The call had not been made from near the airport, as she'd thought.

Leslie remembered the conversation had come over a poor connection, and how the woman had acted as if they knew each other. She'd not been able to place the Joan Cecil name. Not then, anyway. She picked the "Personal" category and the search mode to find data on a friend she'd known since high school.

Joanne's married name was Schull—which she might have mistaken for Cecil over a bad phone connection. *Joan Cecil ... Joanne Schull.* Leslie's excitement mounted as she switched back and forth, staring at the telephone numbers. They were the same!

Dummy, she cried to herself for missing it the first time.

Joanne lived in a godforsaken little town in the mountains, where she and her husband ran the post office in one side of a rustic building and a general store in the other, selling everything from ammunition to flannel underwear to groceries. The last time they'd talked face to face, Joanne had joked about having to send out for sunlight. How they had ten- and fifteen-foot snowdrifts in the winter. How they enjoyed the primitive life.

Leslie started to put the memo maker away and return to sleep, but she was too excited.

She dialed Billy's room number. It took five rings before his gruff and sleepy voice muttered something unintelligible.

"Remember what you said about wishing somebody living in the boonies would call about an airplane going overhead that day?"

He paused for a yawn. "Yeah."

"They called!"

He hesitated again, but when he finally spoke his voice was alert. "*Who* did they call?"

"Me! I'm in room three-twenty-one. Come on up, and bring a map of Idaho."

"Be right there," he said, and Leslie fleetingly wondered what he slept in. Billy might be getting older, but he still had a nice body. It was difficult to dispel her mind's vision.

She pulled on her robe and took time to run a brush through her hair.

Five minutes later, Billy was at the door to her room, carrying a handful of aerial charts. His shirttail was out and he'd not taken time to put on socks.

He yawned and gave his head a violent shake. "What's it all about?"

Leslie filled him in on the telephone call, how she'd disregarded it. "You said the airplane could have ended up about anywhere. How about in Idaho?"

"Maybe, but no one's reported an airplane going down there."

"It's rugged country."

He spread the chart onto the tabletop. "Where does your friend live?"

She hesitated, then pulled in a breath. "How about a deal? Tell me who the passengers were and I'll let you in on everything."

"I can't. Both Tom Oliver and the foundation would crucify Executive Connections."

"I've promised not to print anything you don't want me to. I just want to know if the story's as big as I thought, or if I was all wet about the Dubois family."

She held her breath as Billy hesitated, weighing what she'd said. Finally he looked evenly at her. "You weren't wrong."

The Dubois family had been aboard the Gulfstream. The Weyland Foundation had scammed Mort Yoder with a fake telephone call.

Leslie was still grinning as she leaned over the chart, then searched until she found a location northeast of Boise. "Joanne lives right there."

He held his finger on the five black specks on the map that represented the buildings of the village, speculating. "That's a long way from the Gulfstream's course."

"It was them, Billy. I *know* it. It was a terrible, stormy day, and no other airplanes would have been flying that low, especially *there*."

He gave a small nod, still trying to blink sleep from his eyes, but she could tell his excitement was mounting. "It's sure as hell worth a try," he said gruffly.

She bit her lip in anticipation as she dialed the number of her friend in Idaho.

Joanne's husband answered in a sleepy voice. This time the connection was clear.

The Valley

Simon Charbonneau was sleeping soundly when the interior of the Suburban was filled with static and the sound of a voice. He abruptly sat up, heart pounding unmercifully until he realized it was coming from the hand-held radio.

The hour was early, for the valley was just beginning to fill with light.

"Simon?" Jaeger asked again. "Can you hear me?"

He located the correct button. "Yes?"

"We're moving west again."

"Still no sign of him?" Charbonneau asked.

"Lots of sign. I'm keeping him out ahead of us as we search for the aircraft. If I get a shot, all the better. If not, I'll take him after we find the wreckage."

"I wish you hadn't killed those two," Charbonneau said peevishly. "Then we wouldn't have to worry about a witness."

Jaeger was silent for a moment. "It will all work out," he said.

Simon Charbonneau sighed, depressing the button so Jaeger could hear his displeasure.

"I'd like you to search too," Jaeger said. "The lake's only three miles south of you, and Webb thinks it would have been a natural place for the pilot to want to put down."

Charbonneau looked out of the vehicle suspiciously, wondering what sort of wild creatures were there. He'd heard noises during the night. "I wouldn't want to get lost," he said.

"Just follow the trail to the lake. If you see anything there, give me a call on the radio."

"I'll try," he said, huffing another sigh.

He put the radio aside and would have gone back to sleep if it hadn't been for the importance of finding the Gulfstream. The information in the folder would be used to expose the Weyland Foundation and stop their investigation. And Frank Dubois must be confirmed dead, for only he could identify their man in Washington.

The Lake

Although Katy's eyes were grainy, she was up at first light. Neither she nor Paula had gotten much sleep. Twice more they'd heard Fuzz-butt, or at least sounds they *thought* came from him, and both times Paula had rattled the pan and cup vigorously.

The cantankerous bear had served a good cause, though, for Katy's father had awakened. The first time he'd ranted about *truenos* and someone named Fay, and had not been with them for long. The second time he'd appeared so alert it was hard to believe he hadn't been conscious all along. He'd spoken coherently, asking how they were doing. Paula had talked as Katy trickled water past his parched lips, telling him they were fine and that Link Anderson had gone for help.

"He's my friend," he'd said proudly. They'd been jubilant that he seemed so much better, when he'd stiffened and cried out with pain. A moment later he'd begun to rant and warn about someone named Fay again, and about *trueno* and how the sounds of thunder were deceiving.

Katy thought about the puzzling words as she went to the lake. She'd run out the fish line, caught and filleted six mid-sized trout, and had the smoker going before Paula awakened.

They checked on her father together, hoping he'd come around, but he was breathing in scary, shallow gasps. Paula washed him where he'd released dribbles of urine during the night, and carefully dried him with a cloth. When she stroked his face he made a small sound, and she spoke reassuring words to him, although it was improbable he could hear them.

Katy got out the small beach pack she'd retrieved from the airplane and started putting in things, like the flares, the Swiss army knife, the matches and fire tinder, thinking it was a good place to store them. In a corner of her mind troublesome thoughts loomed. If rescue did not come, and if Dad died—she didn't let herself ponder on the awful thoughts, but they were possibilities—they couldn't stay forever at the lake. If those things happened, regardless of what Link Anderson had said, they'd have to walk out. It would be best to be prepared.

Katy added the small first-aid kit, then scissors and tweezers from the larger kit, and placed the pack in the corner of the shelter where she'd be sure to remember it.

Paula joined her at the fire. "He's not doing well," she said quietly.

"Hungry?" Katy asked, switching to nicer thoughts.

"I suppose I could eat, since Fuzz-butt stole our dinner last night."

"Want to try the stuff from the smoker?"

"It's sacrilege, but I'm tired of fish. Let's gather berries."

As they walked toward the brambles behind the big tree
at the back of the clearing, discovered by Link Anderson
before he'd left, Katy looked around. "If things were different, this wouldn't be such a bad place. Like if Dad was
okay and we had a safe place to sleep."

"You're crazy, Katherine."

"Dad says there's something good about every place,
just like there's good in every human. You just have to
look for it."

"I was up half the night worrying about that stupid bear.
Yesterday I was stung by a wasp. I can't even feel safe going to the bathroom, because I'm afraid of brushing against
poison oak and your silly snake."

"Not *my* snake," Katy said, frowning at the memory of
the most frightening experience of her life. She looked
around more carefully as they selected a section of blackberry brambles.

"Ouch!" Paula cried, and sucked her finger where she'd
been stabbed by a thorn.

They heard a rustling, snuffling sound from the opposite
side of the thicket.

"Fuzz-butt!" Katy cried.

As her daughter began to squeal, Paula grabbed the
spoon from her jacket pocket and clattered it against the
side of the pan. After a full minute she paused and Katy
stopped yelling. When they heard nothing, they exhaled
pent-up breaths of relief.

"You're right about not coming back, Mom. Fuzz-butt
isn't about to leave. We're probably sleeping next to his
den, and this is probably his private berry patch."

Paula returned the badly bent spoon to her pocket, then
stooped and began to pick up the berries that had been
flung from the pan.

Katy observed her. "Mom?"

"Yes."

"You're sure different. When we got here you didn't
know anything about the woods, but now you're catching
fish . . . and you know what to do when Fuzz-butt comes
around."

Coming from Katy, it was a rare compliment.

"I still feel utterly inadequate."

"Dad's always said that doing our best is all that's important."

"That's true. And I suppose we are."

"Think Dad knows?"

Her voice softened. "I'm sure he does." She'd never missed anything nearly as much as she missed Frank; nor had she ever worried so incessantly.

"What's *trueno*?" Katy asked.

"The word is Spanish for thunder, and it has to do with one of your father's projects at the foundation." She knew about the Argentine investigation, but his words made little sense.

"Dad's mind's been full of mysterious things lately." Katy paused, then shook her head sadly. "I'll sure be glad when he's back with us."

Paula wanted to put the pot on the ground, reach out for her daughter, and hug her fiercely. She'd not been able to do that for a long time, since the barrier had descended between them. But if she did so now, Katy would think it was just another sign of her weakness.

When they finished a few minutes later, and were returning to the camp, Paula thought of how they'd come to live so close, yet in such different worlds, and wondered if there would ever be a time when she and Katy could be friends again.

Link's wilderness skills continued to improve as he moved through the valley. He remembered his father's lessons from his youth, and the advice of the instructors during his training at Fairchild, the Air Force's basic survival school. The school commandant had spent four years in the Hanoi Hilton as a prisoner of the North Vietnamese, and he'd been motivated to teach the young fighter pilots and air crew members to evade capture. Yet Link's current task was more difficult, for not only did he have to elude the men, he also had to leave enough of a trail that they'd continue to follow and not return to the lake.

Link was on the move, periodically looking back with squinted eyes to make sure he wasn't leaving too obvious a trail, wanting them to have to work at tracking him.

From a field three hundred yards back he'd spotted an earthen promontory that rose higher than the surrounding forest, and he was going there for another look at the pursuers.

During the night he'd decided that at some time during the day he would turn southward, toward the high mountains. There were rocky areas there, Link reasoned, and the pursuers would have difficulty tracking him. He'd lose them in the high country, return to the lake for Paula and Katy, and hide Frank Dubois until they could return with help.

He wanted another look at the men who were tracking him, to judge how difficult it would be to get around them.

As he approached the barren hillock, he found it wasn't a natural mound, but tailings from an old mine. He'd passed others, but this one was the largest, with dirt and rocks piled to a height of thirty feet. He began to crawl up the slope on his good hand and knees.

As Link flattened himself on the summit and looked back toward the field he'd crossed twenty minutes earlier, he felt something hard against his leg. He shifted, exposing the end of a metal rod. He dug and levered with the survival knife, until he was able to extract a six-foot length of half-inch rod—made of sturdy steel and not pliable iron, and not so badly rusted that he couldn't make out a bolt head at one end and threads at the other.

The miners had discarded the treasure into the refuse pile. He hefted it, decided it wouldn't be too heavy to carry. He now had a weapon . . . of sorts.

Link stared back at the clearing. The men were there now, following his path through the grass. He concentrated, picking out details. Both wore light backpacks and carried the rifles he'd seen the previous day. Except for the fact that they'd changed into green and tan camouflage clothing, there was nothing new about them.

They paused to talk, and a moment later Jaeger separated and went southward, toward the mountains.

"Damn," Link muttered as the man continued, for he'd cut off his intended path.

He observed that Jaeger moved confidently, walking in sure strides, constantly searching with his eyes. He was the better of the two, and also the more aggressive.

Webb continued to follow Link's trail cross the clearing, then stopped and lifted an object to his face. A radio, Link believed. He nodded at something that was said and went on.

Link looked at the tall man again and released a sharp breath as he flattened himself.

Jaeger had the big rifle to his shoulder and was peering through the scope, swinging it slowly until he gazed directly at the tailings mound where Link remained stock still.

The tall man was both wary and capable, and Link reevaluated his plan, wondering if it wasn't impossible to remain undetected in the sparsely forested foothills. Perhaps he should try to waylay Webb, who was the less proficient of the two.

He decided against it. He believed he could take Webb, even though he had the automatic weapon, but if he failed he'd be leading them back in the direction of the lake. He would stick with his plan and find a path around the tall man. Jaeger was clever, but so was Link. If confronted with a choice, he would kill neither of them. Violence bred violence, and he didn't want someone taking vengeance upon the Dubois family because of something he'd done.

Then a more realistic thought arose. Link might be forced to make a life or death decision, but it was more likely the choice would be made by his stalkers.

Jaeger was at the edge of the clearing, and had stopped again to stare in his direction. Did he know he was being observed? The tall man finally turned and jogged resolutely toward the southwest, and was quickly lost from his view.

Link found a fist-sized chunk of lava in the rubble, stuffed it into his pocket, then hefted the steel rod and backed down the mound. Whenever he stopped to rest, he'd use the abrasive stone to sharpen the threaded end of the rod.

As soon as he reached the bottom he turned and broke into a trot, angling slightly away from the tall stalker yet still toward the mountains, gripping the metal rod at its balance point.

Webb was cautious, and he'd be hesitant about approaching the tailings mound. He would find, then lose Link's trail, for he was running lightly and no longer leaving the telltale signs of his path.

Jaeger would be harder to fool.

After thirty minutes, Link slowed to a walk as he turned directly south. Going more cautiously and leaving no sign of passage at all now.

Link slowed even more as he encountered a massive tangle of undergrowth. After making his way around it to the left for a while, he remembered that Jaeger might have turned this way, and he pushed directly forward—into the tangle. It was slow going for the first twenty yards and he knew he was making noise, so he stopped, then proceeded quietly, placing each step carefully, mindful that the rod in his hand did not scrape against branches.

When the thicket thinned, Link paused to rest.

He heard movement and huddled lower, motionless, observing in the direction of the sound. He'd done the same twice earlier, but both times it had been a small animal.

He heard the sound again—this time unmistakably of foliage brushing against cloth.

Jaeger appeared beyond the edge of the thicket directly before Link, the big rifle at the ready, squinting into the shadows and *almost* seeing him. The eyes shifted.

Link hurled himself over a log as the gunshot resonated. He clutched the rod tightly and crawled in an oblique movement, hidden behind the length of the log, then paused, making not the slightest sound. Noises of Jaeger's pursuit would have been apparent—there were none.

He cautiously rose a few inches and observed, and could make out Jaeger's previous firing location. The big man had neither stayed in position, nor had he followed. But *why*? The obvious options were to continue shooting or immediately come after him.

The plausible answer came to him. Jaeger had seen something in his hand—the steel rod—and believed it was a firearm.

What would he do in Jaeger's place, believing his quarry was armed?

Find the place his prey would likely emerge and wait.

Link remained stock still, suppressing even the sounds of his breathing, listening hard.

The noise was very slight, coming from his forward and right. Link waited until he heard another. Jaeger was circling the clutch of undergrowth, as he anticipated.

Link crept back to the log, then continued cautiously past where the big man had been. He used stealth as he passed through the place. Five more minutes passed before Link came upon a less dense area and was able to walk faster.

He did not believe Jaeger had heard him moving in the thicket, yet the man had somehow found him. Link was facing a professional. Intuition was a good thing for both stalker and prey, and in this encounter Jaeger's had proven equal to his own.

He rested and stroked the threaded end of the metal rod with the lava. After a few minutes he replaced the stone in a jacket pocket and went on. Not much farther Link came upon a familiar plant, with tuber roots that tasted like raw sweet potatoes. He dug up two to eat later. For the moment at least, the pursuers had succeeded in blocking his path to the lake.

Gowen Field—Boise

Billy leaned over the map, examining the area beyond the red X Leslie had drawn over the location of the Schulls' general store.

At Elko that morning, Tom Oliver had listened with a dubious ear and caustic comments, but others had appeared interested, so he'd reluctantly agreed to set up a much smaller control center at Gowen Field—located on the far side of Boise International Airport, where the Air National Guard flew aging F-15 Eagles—and to dispatch four fixed-wing aircraft and a single helicopter for the effort.

Billy had once trained in air surveillance, and knew that such a tiny search force was utterly inadequate, for the area was vast. He'd decided to forget about any search grids Oliver established, and instead look in the most likely areas. He wanted to get in two flights before nightfall, when they anticipated a storm. On the first he'd take a general look at what they faced.

Leslie looked on intently as he used a plastic Weems plotter to pencil a line past the Schull store on a heading of 045 degrees. During the last phone call, Joanne Schull had said the airplane had flown past them toward the northeast, which raised new doubts. The Gulfstream's intended flight path had been far to the south, in a westerly direction.

Leslie's telephone buzzed in her purse, and she walked

a few steps away for privacy. The last call had upset her, for her reporter friend in Washington had gained approval for his article about the Weyland Foundation, and it was about to assume blockbuster dimensions. She'd said it was filled with unsubstantiated innuendoes.

Billy examined the map closely, concentrating on the rugged, mountainous terrain to either side of the pencil line. He decided to use a partial fuel load to keep the Baron light and maneuverable at the higher altitudes.

Leslie returned. "I've got to visit the lawyers," she said. "They're trying to convince me to sell Dad's house so they can pay off the last of his debts." She shook her head sadly. "A lot of history and family memories are buried in that old house. I hate to sell it, but Dad left too many bills for me to handle on my salary."

Billy sympathized, then looked at the map. "I'm going up for a look at the countryside."

"Fly carefully." Leslie's voice was sincere.

15

Billy Bowes had examined the route beyond the Schull general store, and found one high mountain and wild valley after another. If the Gulfstream had veered left of the path, the airplane could have headed toward the distant Banff, Lake Louise area of the Canadian Rockies—to the immediate right were the high Sawtooth Mountains.

He landed on Boise International's main runway, let the Baron make a long run to bleed down speed, slowed with a tap of the brakes, and turned off on the military side— Gowen Field, where the RCC was set up. A tower operator told him to return to the same parking spot.

Two other search airplanes and a rescue helicopter were parked together only a hundred yards from the line of military fighters. He taxied in beside them, shut down engines, and stuffed the charts back into his small, many-pocketed canvas flight bag. Lucky Anderson had given it to him when they'd flown together in Thailand thirty years before. Billy had had it patched several times, but it was still functional and he refused to fly without it.

Bring my son home, Lucky had told him, and Billy was determined to do so, although he felt no closer to finding the Gulfstream than he had the first day of the search.

Leslie Rocklin had walked out from the small hangar on loan from the military. When he swung the airplane's door open, she was putting the chocks in place.

"See," she called up cheerfully. "I'm learning."

Billy stepped down onto the concrete, hefting the flight bag.

"Tom Oliver's inside, letting everyone know how he thinks coming here's a mistake, and how you in particular are a fool."

"That's fair," Billy said. "My feelings about him are the same."

"He's about to move the entire effort to Reno."

Billy's first stop inside was the operations desk, where he told the attendant to have the Baron refilled to half tanks. When he entered the flight-planning room, Leslie was speaking with a neatly dressed, smallish man in shiny boots and Western-cut suit.

"This is the pilot I told you about," she told him. "When I was fifteen years old, I fell madly in love with him. Billy, I'd like you to meet Joe Rodriguez, our U.S. marshal here in Boise."

They shook hands. Rodriguez had policeman's eyes, as if he categorized the things about him into neat niches while missing very little, but he regarded Leslie with a softer look.

Her voice grew sad. "I was telling Joe about selling my father's place. After I talked to the lawyers, I drove by there and got all nostalgic."

Rodriguez regarded Billy. "It doesn't seem right, somehow. There've been Rocklins in Idaho since long before we were a state. The house she's talking about has been declared a historical site."

"I visited there once as a guest of Old Gerald."

Leslie whispered theatrically to Billy. "Don't tell anyone, but Joe was sent here twenty years ago to investigate my father."

The marshal smiled. "I was a deputy, still wet behind the ears. If they'd been serious, they'd have sent someone with clout."

"The Secret Service said Dad threatened the President," Leslie said. "All he did was write a letter saying President Carter should stop interfering out here."

"Not exactly in those words. Old Gerald said he'd personally string up Carter and his cronies, and display them from the Capitol dome if they didn't keep their greedy hands off range and water rights. *That's* what he wrote."

"Joe let Dad off."

"He didn't try to string up the President."

"The law wasn't changed."

Rodriguez chuckled. "He was quite a guy, your father." He excused himself, saying he wanted to locate Tom Oliver and offer him any support the Marshal's Office could provide.

"Joe became a friend of Dad's," Leslie said, looking after him. "He's a good man to turn to. All of my father's friends are." She spoke as if she was just realizing that to be true.

Billy almost commented that Rodriguez was obviously fond of her, but held his tongue. The marshal was a few years closer to her age, and the fact was somehow irritating.

"Joe's wife is very nice too," Leslie added, and Billy felt more charitable.

"Coming along this time?" he asked.

"That's why I hurried."

Billy opened his map and pointed out where he'd flown. "It's difficult terrain, mostly forest and high mountains."

"Where are they setting up the search matrix?" She was getting the lingo down.

"Oliver doesn't think the airplane could have deviated this far, so he wants to start down near the Nevada state line."

"That's silly. Joanne said it proceeded northeast from their store."

"Something's been bothering me." Billy placed a finger over the Schulls' store. "If they deviated all the way up there from the original flight path, and were on that heading, there had to be a reason. Also, how do we explain the difference in flying time?"

"Damage from the collision?"

"Sure. So if the airplane was so badly damaged that they were forced to fly slower, and in a right-hand arc?" He moved his finger along an eastward path.

There were two valleys, one small and a larger one beyond.

"We'll try the closest one first. If we still have fuel, we'll pop over the mountains to the big one. We'll have to hurry, though. A storm front's moving in from the west."

The Valley

Jaeger lay in the high rocks, alternately looking out over the valley for sign of aircraft wreckage and down at the forested area where he believed the man would emerge. He was warier now that he knew the man was armed—he'd seen a rifle in his hands in the thicket—yet he remained confident that he could take him. While the quarry was good at moving without leaving a trail, he'd met others who had made the mistake of believing they could escape the Hunter.

He had decided to shoot to wound, for Jaeger wanted to know who the man was and what he was doing in the valley. He had no vehicle here, or at least he'd made no attempt to reach one. Webb believed there would be no survivors of the Gulfstream crash, yet Jaeger could not ignore the possibility. And even if he wasn't from the airplane, the man might have seen the crash or come across the wreckage before they'd arrived.

During that first brief glimpse Jaeger had noted that he was tall and lean, with neatly shorn raven black hair, and that he was extremely agile.

Jaeger waited, motionless and silent, peering out over the valley through the rifle scope. He shifted slightly, saw Webb at the edge of a clearing about a mile distant, then scanned slowly down to his previous view.

He believed the quarry was moving toward the mountains again, as he'd previously done. Twice he'd had snapshot glimpses of him through the rifle scope, a shadow moving in a fluid, trotting pace, head up and alert. Both times he'd waited patiently, rifle poised and ready, and had been disappointed. The man was not predictable.

He would wound him, question him, and then kill him.

A subtle shadow flickered, and Jaeger adjusted the scope slightly and waited. He saw him then, angling ghost-like toward him, still several hundred yard distant. Jaeger moved the ring on the scope and slowly zoomed in, looking at where he should be. *Nothing* now. He looked harder, then realized the man had been in view all of that time, immobile and blending with shadows about him, slightly crouched so only his chest and part of head were visible.

Jaeger judged the bullet drop at the distance to be about four feet, and as he compensated the man shifted very slightly and looked up the hillside toward him. The hunter partially exhaled, held the breath, and took up the minute amount of trigger slack.

He felt a wave of exasperation, for the man had

disappeared—melted from view. It was the third time it had happened. Another shadow moved a few feet from where he'd just seen the man. Jaeger shifted and quickly fired, then cursed himself as the thunderous sound echoed across the valley. He'd been lured by a dark branch that swayed in the wind.

"Jaeger, this is Simon."

"Go ahead," the Hunter said wearily into his radio.

"I heard a shot."

"Disregard it. We're a long way from you."

"I'm halfway down the side of the lake, and there's nothing here."

"Perhaps you should walk all the way around it."

"I can see the other side. There's nothing here, I tell you."

"Return to the vehicle, then," Jaeger finally said, and masked his disgust as he released the transmit button. The lake was too large to give only a cursory examination. Charbonneau was lazy and easily frightened, but Jaeger did not dare to openly criticize him.

Webb radioed. *"Did you get a shot at him, Jaeger."*

"He may be coming your way now. Keep your eyes open."

Jaeger surveyed the valley again. There was no sign of wreckage or disturbances in the stands of trees, and he wondered if they'd been right in coming here.

He decided to join Webb. They'd finish searching this end of the valley, deal with the man who believed he could elude the Hunter, then return to the other end and look the lake over.

An hour had passed since the encounter. Link's intuition had not deserted him, for he'd sensed the big man's presence high above in the rocks. He'd seen him then and moved slowly out of his view. The shot had come seconds later, the impact shattering a branch that had moved with a gust of breeze. Any pleasure that the bullet had missed was tempered by the fact that Jaeger had hit his mark from more than five hundred yards. He was a superb shot. And Jaeger had again correctly anticipated him, a fact just as unsettling.

Link anchored the rod spear by scissoring it between his legs, and began to stroke the tip with a new stone. It was becoming very sharp, and its presence was somehow reassuring.

He thought of the ancient Piegan warriors—who had visited these same mountains in search of game, enemies, and likely adventure—and wondered how they would have coped with the situation. He felt kinship with those ancestors.

Since the shooting he'd been shadowing Jaeger, but it was difficult. He couldn't follow the tall man's tracks closely, for he doubled back often to set up ambushes. Link believed he was moving toward Webb, but he wasn't sure and it would be foolhardy to get too close. The spear would offer little comfort in a shoot-out.

With the big man moving away from the foothills, Link decided to try for the mountains again. He gained his feet and was moving out cautiously—for he was now close to both Jaeger and Webb—when he heard the angry mosquito buzz of airplane engines.

Lincoln Anderson stopped and stared intently at the sky.

Katy had taken in the fish line for the third time, and came up with a whopper that had to weigh six or seven pounds. She knelt and deftly gutted it, and as she rose to her feet, she heard a distant buzzing sound. She stood perfectly still as realization swept over her, and for a moment even denied it, wondering if it wasn't her imagination. Then she uttered a squeal and ran to the fire, where Paula was depositing an armload of firewood.

"An airplane!" Katy yelled, and began to pick branches and leaves from the green pile and place them on the fire.

Paula looked at the sky, frowning.

"It's an *airplane!*" The fire smoldered, then began to billow dark smoke. As Katy piled on more green brush the smoke grew heavier, issuing its nauseous smell.

"I think I can see it." Paula's voice was hesitant.

Katy exulted as the speck in the sky became distinct. She ran to the lean-to, pulled out one of the smoke flares, and as she hurried back she felt her legs turn to Jell-O. She took a few more wobbly steps toward the beach, pulled the cap off the end of the flare, and waved it about.

Nothing was happening.

"Here," Paula said excitedly, and took it from her. She

pursed her lips as she pulled the lanyard at the bottom end. Bright orange smoke puffed, then began to spew forth.

Katy laughed and danced up and down, waving her arms. The airplane was close enough to tell it was sleek, painted royal blue, and had two engines. It made a swooping turn and flew directly down the lake toward them.

"Yeah!" Katy squealed.

The aircraft approached, made a lazy circle across the water, and came back. Katy grabbed another flare from the pack, ignited it, then joined Paula, dancing and waving billowing smoke.

The twin-engine airplane flew directly over them, then turned, and they could see the people inside staring back.

"It's them!" Leslie Rocklin shouted, grinning out the side window as he banked.

Billy noted the international orange tarp and life raft, and the orange smoke. The word HELP was outlined in large letters on the beach.

"Yeah," he finally said, cautiously ebullient. After another turn, he was even more sure. He thought he recognized Paula Dubois, waving a smoke flare and dancing around on the sandy beach. The other woman wasn't tall enough to be Jackie Chang. The Dubois daughter?

He tried to radio Boise to tell them they'd found survivors, but the call went unanswered.

"What's wrong?" Leslie asked.

"We're too low," he said. "I'll try again when we climb up within line-of-sight." He nodded at the west, where a roiling cloud bank masked the waning sun. "Can't wait much longer, or they won't be able to land a helicopter. This place likely gets as dark as the back side of the moon when the sun goes down, and the storm's getting close."

Billy pulled out his pencil and drew an X on the map at the southern shore of the lake. It was difficult to stop smiling, so he quit trying and let it spread across his face.

"Fly over them again," Leslie said, breathless with excitement.

"One last time." He swung the bird around and flew down the lake very low and slow, offset only slightly from the campfire. As they approached Leslie waved enthusiastically.

He pulled the nose up and waggled the wings, then set full power and began the climb.

"How many did you see?" he asked, hoping he'd been wrong.

"Two on their feet, and one under the tarp lean-to," she answered.

"Me too, but I wasn't sure if the one under the shelter was a person or a pile of clothes."

"Billy, I just saw a light blink on and off from the other end of the valley."

He looked there but saw nothing.

"It flashed twice."

"Could be a signal mirror. There's one in the survival kit."

"Shouldn't we look?"

"We're low on fuel, and I want to call in the sighting. When we get back to Boise, we'll bring a chopper back out—quickly, so we'll beat the storm."

"Billy, I was so excited I forgot to take photographs."

"You can get one when we return. Hell, you can even ask them to pose."

She clapped her hands exuberantly. "It's really them." Her happiness filled the cockpit.

Billy tried the radio again, calling on one of the airport-tower frequencies, and this time he got through. He said they'd spotted survivors from downed airplane echo charlie nine-nine-two, and requested that they prepare a helicopter for the rescue.

He was given another frequency and told to contact the rescue coordinator.

A moment later Tom Oliver's voice came over the radio. "You're positive?" he asked, using the arrogant tone he reserved for Bowes.

"Roger that," Billy said, determined not to let the man irritate him. "We saw an international orange raft and two women waving smoke flares. Notify the helicopter crew."

"Give me the coordinates."

Billy read them off the chart, then added: "They're at the south end of a lake. We're only twenty minutes out. If the chopper hasn't taken off when we get there, we'd like to go along."

"The helicopter won't be available for another half

hour." Oliver's voice grew sarcastic. "They're checking
another sure thing, a hundred miles south of yours."

"Then for God's sake get another chopper—from a television station, the local cops, *anyone*. We've got to get
back there. There are likely injuries." As he continued the
climb-out, they entered clouds, and the world beneath them
disappeared.

"I'll talk to you when you get here," said Tom Oliver.

Billy turned to Leslie and gritted his teeth. "*Dammit!* but
that asshole is obnoxious."

"At least two of them are alive," she said, her happiness
undampened.

He pulled out his terminal let-down booklet. It would be
an instrument approach in the weather. Billy wanted to get
on the ground quickly, then head back so they could find
out what had happened to the others in the Gulfstream. He
wondered about the still form they'd seen under the shelter,
and remembered his promise to Lucky Anderson.

It would be wonderful if Link was alive.

Quit doubting, Billy told himself. He *is* alive. Although
he'd not seen Link, for the first time since the ordeal began
he felt hope.

Water streaked the windscreen as it began to rain.

The Valley

Jaeger had seen the airplane and then the column of smoke.

Webb was crouching nearby, listening intently to the pilot on the radio scanner. "He said he saw two women," he
repeated, then shook his head. "It's hard to believe they
could be alive. They had to have put down in the lake."

Jaeger contacted Charbonneau, who was back at the vehicle.

"*Did you see the airplane?*" Charbonneau asked anxiously.

"Webb just listened in on the pilot's report. He saw two
women survivors at the south end of the lake. You're closest, Simon. Go there and question them. Find out about the
folder."

"*There may be more of them, and they may be armed, I
won't go alone.*"

"The pilot said there are only two women. You can handle them."

"I'll wait for you, so we can all go together."

"That would take too long," Webb told Jaeger. "We're thirty miles away." They'd been studying the map when the airplane had arrived.

The Hunter huffed an angry sigh, then forced a reasonable tone to his voice. "Simon, I want you to drive to the road and then proceed west for precisely twenty-seven miles. There's a small bridge there. We'll meet you and return to the lake together."

"That's better," Charbonneau said.

"We're seven miles from the road," Webb said as Jaeger put his radio away. "It'll take us too long if they send a helicopter right away."

They set out quickly, Jaeger establishing a relentless pace as they hurried northward.

Killing the students had been a mistake. If he'd not allowed the restless feeling to take over his reason, they would have the folder and be gone. Jaeger's self-reproach mounted as he felt the lucrative position in Argentina begin to slip from his grasp.

The colonel in Buenos Aires had told him to please Charbonneau, or he would not continue to work for them.

"Faster," he growled to Webb.

16

_____

5:40 P.M.—The Valley

Link watched as the airplane ascended into the clouds. He'd tried the signal mirror, but the occupants of the familiar-looking twin-engine Beech Baron hadn't seemed to notice. While it would be nice to have someone know he was still in the valley, that was of less importance than other things that raced through his mind.

The Beech had been the same royal blue color that Executive Connections painted their birds. If it was a company airplane, who would be at the controls? Billy Bowes, he hoped, for the aging combat pilot would be his best bet in an emergency.

The pilot had flown the length of the lake three times, so low and slow that he'd obviously sighted the camp. If he'd known what he was looking at, he'd send a helicopter to check it out. Thus part of Link wanted to celebrate, for the smoke proved the women were still alive and might soon be rescued. But his elation was tempered. Jaeger missed very little, and had surely seen the distant sky smudge from the signal fire.

He shifted his eyes to the peaks. Clouds cloaked the highest ones, and a storm was boiling in from the west, but he could see enough. The camp was some thirty miles distant.

Link could not allow the murderers to reach the family before the rescue helicopters arrived. If help was sent immediately, the helicopter might appear within the hour, but with the storm coming he couldn't be sure.

He set out. While it would be impossible to reach the lake quickly, he would reposition himself closer, then try to block Jaeger and Webb. He'd remain obscured in the thick forest until the storm arrived, then move up to the sparsely treed foothills where traveling would be easier.

They'd been found! They'd be rescued! Katy was at the beach, still gawking toward the dark clouds where the airplane had disappeared.

She looked at the boiling sky for another moment, then began to pull in the fish line in preparation of stowing it. If rescue came quickly they'd not need it. But the sky was continuing to darken and if a storm came, as it seemed was about to happen, they might be delayed. The pilot had told them to use their heads, and she was doing so.

"I wonder if Link Anderson sent them," Paula called from beside the fire.

"I don't think so. He'd have sent more airplanes and maybe a helicopter."

As Katy continued rolling up the fish line, a gust of wind brought a sprinkle.

"It's going to rain, Mom. We'd better be prepared."

Gowen Field, Boise

Billy and Leslie were as excited as birthday kids as they ran from the parked airplane toward the hangar, ignoring the light drizzle. Inside, Billy hurried toward Tom Oliver, who stood at the makeshift operations desk studying a wall map.

"You're sure of the coordinates?" The voice had an edge of irritation.

Billy found the lake on the map, then poised his forefinger at its bottom. "Right there."

"You were outside the search matrix," Tom Oliver said in disapproval. "It's too far from the Gulfstream's flight path."

"It was them." Billy's voice held no slightest doubt.

Oliver picked up a sighting form and pushed it across the desk. "Fill that out."

Billy pulled out a pen and hastily began to complete the blocks.

Oliver observed the map. "Did you see the airplane?"

"No, but there's a lot of dense forest and a big lake for

it to hide in." Billy looked up from the form. "What we *did* see were two of the passengers—alive!"

Joe Rodriguez, Leslie's friend from the U.S. Marshal's Office, entered the room. "I hear you found survivors," he said pleasantly as he approached.

"It was them!" Leslie exulted.

"We had another sighting a bit ago," Oliver said archly, "and the pilot was just as sure. He claimed there was wreckage and survivors. Turned out to be a rusted-out 1940 Buick and a bunch of kids fishing on the Snake River. Everyone's calling in bullshit."

Billy refused to be baited. "This one's real. We saw the Gulfstream's life raft and two people waving smoke flares. The letters H-E-L-P were outlined on the beach." Billy stopped filling blocks and printed in large letters: SIGHTED CAMP AND 2 FEMALE SURVIVORS OF EC-992 CRASH, then pushed the form toward Oliver.

"Go over it for me again. What do you *think* you saw?"

"Let's get back to the lake so you can see for yourself. We need a rescue chopper out there *ASAP*."

"The helicopter won't be back for another five minutes," Oliver said, looking at this watch. "By the time we turn it around, it'll be too dark to operate in mountainous terrain. There's a storm front coming through, if you haven't heard."

"Dammit, lives are at stake, Oliver."

The pudgy bureaucrat glowered. "I'd prefer you called me deputy director, Mr. Oliver, or even Tom. I'm not a private in the Army."

"For Christ's sake!"

"Whatever you saw will still be there after the storm's past."

"If we go now, we can beat the worst of the storm."

"I make the decisions when it comes to flight safety, and I say we wait. Now I'll ask again, what do you *think* you saw?"

"Survivors from nine-nine-two," Billy said doggedly.

"It's not just Mr. Bowes' word," Leslie said. "I saw them too."

Oliver put on his "correct for the press" expression. "I didn't say I didn't believe him. I simply said we'll have to wait to check it out. Now ... precisely *what* did you see?"

Billy told him, Leslie nodding along for emphasis.

"Did you take photographs?" Oliver asked.

"I didn't want to make another pass," said Billy. "We were low on fuel."

"But you saw no wreckage?"

"We saw an orange shelter, a life raft, and two females waving orange smoke flares. The word help was drawn on the beach."

Leslie spoke up. "There was a third person under the shelter."

"Could they have been campers?" Oliver asked.

Leslie wagged her head vigorously. "Why would they have a life raft?"

"Precisely like the one carried in the Gulfstream," Billy added.

Oliver sighed, as if he were dealing with children. "You can buy inflatable rafts on the open market. Did you check to see if a vehicle was parked nearby?"

"It's a wilderness area," Billy said. "There's no access."

Oliver smiled thinly. "There's an unimproved road shown on the map a few miles north of there, and these days campers use all-terrain vehicles."

"Damn it, we've got to get back to help the survivors."

"We'll check it out tomorrow, weather permitting," Oliver repeated.

"I'm going to file a story, Mr. Oliver," Leslie told him angrily. "You may not like what I have to say about your attitude and lack of cooperation."

"I wouldn't be hasty, Ms. Rocklin. In this business you learn that sightings can be deceiving, and you can't trust your own eyes." He cast an expression of disgust at Billy, that he'd take a member of the press along. "When the storm's past, we'll gather here to check it out."

"I'd like a couple of my deputies to tag along," said Marshal Rodriguez.

Oliver gave a terse shake of his head. "Not enough room."

"We can supply our own helicopter."

Tom Oliver turned his gaze on him. "This is a search-and-rescue operation, and has nothing to do with the Department of Justice. If you want something to investigate, look at Bowes' company."

Billy exploded. "I'm *tired* of your damned insinuations."

"Insinuations?" Oliver smiled thinly, his dislike obvious.

Billy stalked from the room, Leslie close behind. As soon as they were outside, she glared back at the building. "The man is detestable."

"They raise them that way in Washington. They call them civil servants as a joke. They don't serve anyone but themselves, and it's impossible to get one fired."

"They're not all like that. Joe Rodriguez works for the government."

Billy's anger subsided. "Most of the FAA people are good too. It just seems the worst rise to the top too often. Something in the Washington water, I suppose."

"I know what we saw, Billy."

"Yeah, and by tomorrow the survivors will be safe." He nodded at the rain and huffed a defeated breath. "Oliver's right. You can't fly a helicopter in a dark valley in bad weather."

"You're being charitable. He's an ass."

"I'll get my bags from the airplane. Can I get a lift to a motel?"

"Sure." She walked beside him, huddling in her coat as the rain intensified.

He was frowning. "We saw two women, but where were the others?"

"Someone was under the orange shelter, Billy. I'm sure of it."

"That means at least one of 'em's injured."

"That's better than we thought was possible just a couple of hours ago. And what about the flashes of light? Maybe those were from the others."

"We'll see in the morning." He opened the airplane's baggage compartment and hauled out his bags. When he'd buttoned back up, she led the way toward the parking lot.

"I'm going to release the news of our sighting. I'm that sure."

"Can you do that without photographs?"

"I'll go to the publisher. He was a friend of my father's, and my word will be enough for him. I just wish I could tell him who the passengers were."

"I believe I recognized Paula Dubois, and the other one was the size of the daughter."

"Come with me to the newspaper office, Billy."

"Don't be too long." He was tired. "Someone phoned

my room damned early this morning, and it's been a busy day."

She laughed merrily. "Glad I did?"

"Yeah. The Duboises will thank you even more in the morning." Link Anderson too, he thought as they walked faster in the downpour. The more he thought of it, the more sure he was that Link had survived. He was rock tough, and damned capable.

When they reached her car and he'd deposited his bags in the trunk, they crawled inside, out of the rain. Leslie punched numbers into her cellular telephone and spoke with the owner-publisher at the newspaper. She told him she had a zinger on its way, that she'd been on the airplane with the pilot who had just discovered the survivors of the crash—alive.

"Go ahead and give him the names," Billy suddenly said, thinking to hell with Oliver.

Leslie covered the mouthpiece. "Are you sure?"

"Yeah. You might as well get credit for the scoop. Everyone else will know when they're picked up tomorrow."

Her voice trilled as she added the identities of the Gulfstream passengers. She covered the mouthpiece again. "He wants verification. The last time I identified them, the Weyland Foundation called and advised that the Dubois family was definitely not on board."

"You've got your confirmation. I'll back you up."

She told the publisher her source, and said they'd be there in fifteen minutes. Billy had the thought that she was a dynamo that refused to wind down. She was also cute as a baby's grin, and probably had a few dozen guys on the line.

As she started the engine, Leslie regarded him with an appraising expression. "Thanks for taking me along, Billy."

"Good thing I did. You saw the smoke first."

"How about when we're done at the paper, we grab something to eat and take it to my place? I'll open a bottle of wine to celebrate."

"I'm awfully tired." Billy's energy reserve was dwindling.

"I won't keep you up too late," Leslie murmured as she drove toward the parking lot exit.

The Valley

The rain was falling in earnest as the two hurried through
the dark forest, guided only by Jaeger's sense of direction.
Several times he'd had to slow for Webb, and each time
he'd prodded relentlessly.

It was as good as Jaeger had dared hope for. No helicopter had appeared over the lake, and now it was too late, for
none would fly in the weather and darkness.

"Jesus," he heard from behind, followed by sounds of
Webb slipping and falling.

"Hurry," Jaeger barked angrily. They should be getting
close to the road. Charbonneau had called from the bridge,
saying he was waiting for them with parking lights turned
on.

Webb was panting in wheezes as he regained his feet,
then slipped again. The Hunter harshly dragged him upright, then led out.

Another half hour passed before they came to the dirt
road, which was becoming a sea of mud. Although they
were only three hundred meters from the small bridge,
there was no sign of the Suburban.

"Where is he?" Webb wondered.

Jaeger radioed Charbonneau and told him to turn on the
headlights, then observed carefully in both directions. Still
nothing.

"Hold down the horn," he said into the radio.

A faint noise sounded from west of them.

"You've gone too far," Jaeger told him.

"I'm at a bridge," Simon said stubbornly.

Jaeger released a sigh of exasperation. "It's the wrong
one. Turn around and come back."

As they waited in the downpour, Webb huddled in his
rain poncho. "One thing's in our favor. The helicopters will
be hangared for the duration of the storm."

Jaeger's mind was working on another problem. "The
man we've been following was probably from the airplane,
but he wasn't Frank Dubois."

"Then he's either the guard or the pilot."

"He was wearing a blue jacket."

"Probably the Gulfstream pilot, Lincoln Anderson."

Jaeger was concerned that the man might escape while

they dealt with the women, but did not dare spend more time searching for him.

"You were listening to the radio. When will the storm be past?"

"They're guessing noon tomorrow," Webb said. "The weather people say it's going to dump a lot of rain, and they have wind advisories out."

"That should give us enough time," Jaeger muttered. They'd find the wreckage and the folder, then eliminate Frank Dubois and all sign of the survivors.

He heard sounds of an engine revving in the distance. A moment later Charbonneau's plaintive voice came over the radio. *"I'm stuck in the mud."*

Boise

On their way from the newspaper office, Leslie had picked up an eight-piece chicken dinner from Kentucky Fried, and they entered her apartment talking about the eventful day, feeling *good*. Then she put the chicken on the table, asked if he preferred red or white wine, and forgot that too as she put her arms around him as if she'd been doing it for years.

It was the excitement of the discovery, she told herself later, but as it happened she did not question. The kiss was the kind she'd wanted from the first time she'd seen him so many years before. Long . . . and hungry. When he tried to change it to something more innocent, Leslie made a sound from deep down and clutched closer, and the kiss grew wetter and better.

They pulled back and looked at each other as if observing rare treasures, and a tingling sensation started somewhere around Leslie's neck and zinged down to her toes, slowing along the way to make her aware that she was oh-so-ready.

Then he formed an embarrassed look and drew away. Billy Bowes could have pressed his advantage, and Leslie would not have stopped him—she was attracted, and her sexual hunger surprised even herself—but it was too soon and he had not, and she felt another kind of warmth she hadn't experienced for a long time. This one was even more disturbing than the first, creating an unsettled feeling in the pit of her stomach.

Leslie made a fuss over the chicken, following an incomprehensible urge to show how domestic she could be, but her mind was busy.

She'd learned something about the guy she was falling in love with for a second time. If she'd left it to him, the kiss would not have happened. He might be a great pilot, but Billy wasn't nearly as sure as she was, which meant she'd sometimes have to take the lead. That was no problem. She was a Rocklin, and it was seldom that she didn't know what she wanted.

Leslie shooed him to the table to wait as she got out dishes and transferred chicken and salad from the boxes. "Red or white wine?" she asked again.

"You name it."

"White." She'd already taken a chardonnay from the cabinet.

He was nodding with sleepiness, and Leslie Rocklin had decided he would spend the night on her couch. The thought that he would remain so close was pleasing.

17

DAY FIVE—
WEDNESDAY, JUNE 12

3:50 A.M.—The Valley

The rain was coming down in bucketfuls, and they were thoroughly soaked. Jaeger and Webb were both outside, grunting and straining, trying to push the heavy Suburban from the muck. Jaeger could no longer fault Charbonneau for getting stuck that first time, for after they'd freed him Webb had not driven far before they'd been mired again and, after a few more miles, yet again. This time the wallow had appeared suddenly in the middle of the road, and they'd bogged down as soon as they'd entered it. When they'd dismounted, the mud had been shin-high, and they'd only pushed the vehicle in deeper, until the thing was now mired to the axles.

Charbonneau was in the driver's seat, looking back as the others labored in the downpour, muttering unkind words about their predicament. "You should have gotten a four-wheel drive," he announced.

"Get ready," Jaeger huffed, then turned, grasped the bumper with both hands as he pulled in a deep breath, and lifted and strained. "Now!"

When Charbonneau placed the lever into drive, the Suburban slid toward the ditch for a few feet, then straightened as the wheels caught. The two outside were caught in a shower of mud as he drove out of the wallow. Jaeger slipped and cursed, and would have fallen if Webb hadn't grasped his arm. They slogged on until clear of the bog.

"How much farther?" Simon asked as they got in.

"We're still four miles from the turnoff."

Charbonneau sighed. "I thought we were closer."

Webb approached the driver's side.

"I'll drive," Charbonneau said irritably. "You got us stuck last time."

Webb began to argue, but Jaeger silenced him. "Simon drives," he said, determined to recapture Charbonneau's goodwill. He crawled in back, Webb into the front passenger's seat, where he huddled over the heater duct for warmth. Charbonneau placed the vehicle in gear and leaned forward to observe the road through the heavy downpour.

"There are only two hours of darkness remaining," Jaeger said, "and we still have to walk to the lake."

"I'm doing my best." Simon's voice was petulant as he drove faster.

"Of course," Jaeger said quietly. "We all are."

"Are all of your operations this confusing?" Charbonneau asked.

"No," Jaeger said.

They'd gone only a mile when Charbonneau slid to a stop. They stared out at a new sea of mud illuminated by the headlights.

Jaeger eyed the wallow, knowing they would become stuck again. "Webb?"

"Yeah?" The smaller man turned to him.

"Walk to the end of the lake where the women have their camp, then just stay out of sight and wait for us. I don't want them going anywhere."

Jaeger reached into the back, where they'd stored their weapons, and gave him a scoped rifle, chambered and bored for 7.62×39 millimeter rounds. The rifle and AK-47 used common cartridges, a tactical consideration. He also handed forward Webb's pack containing medical and electronic equipment.

"Tell us what you find," Charbonneau said as Webb wearily shouldered the pack and cinched the poncho's hood about his face.

Webb gave him a dismal nod, dismounted, then slogged through the muck in the glare of the headlights and quickly disappeared in the thick, swirling ground fog.

"I don't like him," Simon said.

"He's useful," Jaeger answered.

"You should have brought more men," Charbonneau complained, then placed the vehicle in gear and pulled straight ahead.

"To your left some," Jaeger tried, but Simon Charbonneau was already firmly stuck.

Webb found the turnoff and followed the path past the burned-out Volkswagen, which looked eerie in the rain and dense fog and set him to thinking about Jaeger. When they'd met in Colombia, he hadn't known about the man's predilection for blood and violence.

Webb had built his own reputation there, flying people and dope from every cruddy kind of air strip imaginable, and he'd been in demand because good luck meant everything to the Stone Age mentalities of the Colombian *jefes* who ran the cartels. But then he'd worked for a boss who'd been set up by a rival and thrown into jail, and the others associated him with *bad* luck—which meant no work and a bleak future, for he'd still owed big money on the Piper Navajo, which had needed a fifteen-thousand-dollar overhaul, and didn't even have the cash for a ticket home to the States.

Then he'd heard about a man called the Hunter, who was looking for a pilot with a bird like his, but whom others were avoiding as if he had an advanced dose of AIDS. No one would even *talk* about him. But Webb, which hadn't been his name then, had been desperate.

Jaeger had listened quietly to his spiel about his qualifications and his predicament, and then looked the airplane over. There'd been no haggling. Jaeger told him he would be expected to do precisely as told. If not, the alternative would be something more permanent.

Webb hadn't listened hard enough to that part of the deal.

They'd flown to Buenos Aires in mid-1995, and for a month Webb had lived well and got the work done on the Navajo. Then the Hunter had dropped by his apartment one afternoon and said it was time to seal their relationship, and Webb had known it wouldn't be anything good.

"It is time for the second thunder," Jaeger had told him in Spanish.

That night he'd had Webb wait with him in a deserted old warehouse until three people—including a woman Webb had just watched on television—were herded in and bound hand and foot by people in military uniforms. Then the soldiers had left, and Webb watched in horror as Jaeger went into a blood frenzy, beating a hostage with fists, boots, and a baseball bat until there was no life left in him. Then he'd sexually assaulted and killed the woman.

Webb had been cringing in a dark corner when Jaeger rose, chest heaving, his clothing saturated with her blood, and eyed him dispassionately.

"Oh, God, don't," Webb had moaned in fear for his life.

"The last one is yours," the Hunter had said quietly. Jaeger had not spoken more, just handed Webb the bloody bat and nodded at the hostage who remained alive, an overweight newspaper publisher with bulging, frightened eyes.

Webb had protested vociferously, until the Hunter turned and stared with an even look that said he didn't care one way or the other, as if Webb was nothing in his eyes and he wouldn't mind if he joined the others. He'd trembled as he'd raised the bat, meaning to be merciful and kill with the first swing, but the bound man had writhed, and he'd struck a glancing blow. He'd begun to cry then, and slammed the bat down again and again as blood splattered.

"Enough," Jaeger had finally said, and their bond was sealed. Webb could never escape, for he'd killed for the Hunter. His employment would continue until he was no longer needed, a fact that made him try to please the big man even at things he was not good at.

Like now. He felt confident at the controls of most aircraft, had worked in the high-tech world for a few years, even as a medical technician in a hospital O.R. room. He felt okay with all of those, but he certainly wasn't prepared to have rattlesnakes thrown in his face, or chase around backwoods with a rifle as he'd been doing for the past few days.

He'd walked for two hours, the last one down the length of the lakeshore, when the gloomy light of false dawn began to brighten things some, and the ground fog wafted enough that he spotted a bright orange rectangle in the distance. Webb slowed and proceeded carefully, then stopped and waited for another glimpse.

The fog slowly lifted, forming into a roiling ceiling not far overhead, and Webb could make out a raft, a tarp configured into a lean-to shelter, and a woodpile. There was no fire smoke, but that was understandable with the previous night's drenching.

He stood near the treeline three hundred yards distant and stared, then called Jaeger on the radio, speaking in a low voice. "I've found their camp."

Jaeger said they'd left the vehicle and were at the northern end of the lake.

"I don't see any airplane wreckage, and no one's moving in the camp."

"Keep looking," Jaeger said.

Webb took a dozen tentative paces closer, then halted as a new concern surfaced. Jaeger said the man he'd pursued was armed. *Were there other weapons in the camp?* A chill ran through him, and he decided to remain at the present distance. He raised the rifle and sighted through the scope, as he'd seen Jaeger do, lowered it and wiped moisture from the lens with a finger, and tried again. He found the orange shelter, the raft on the beach, then swung back to the camp and saw movement within the shelter.

Webb tensed, and did not notice that his finger had curled quite naturally into the trigger guard. He waited and watched.

Katy stretched as she got to her feet, then walked over to see how much work it would take to rekindle the fire. Neither she nor Paula had gotten much sleep as they'd huddled beneath the wind- and water-swept shelter, trying to stay warm under the survival blankets . . . talking about the airplane and wondering how long it would be before they were rescued.

"At least it's stopped raining," Paula called out. She was busying herself with tending to Katy's father, who had been restless throughout the night.

Katy leaned over the pit and removed the thoroughly soaked firewood, then retrieved drier wood she'd stacked around the sides of the shelter to help keep out the driving rain.

"I think he's breathing easier," Paula said. Her voice grew tender whenever she spoke about her husband.

Katy made a tepee of kindling, got the fire starter from the day pack in the shelter, and had the flame going with her third try. "Make sure it doesn't go out, Mom," Katy said as she walked toward the lakeside. During the night she'd worried that the water might rise, yet even with all the precipitation it seemed no higher.

As she glanced down the lakeshore, she thought she saw a human figure in the distance. She looked harder, staring at the foliage there, and was even more sure.

"Hey!" she yelled loudly, waving her arms.

Paula walked from the campfire. "Did you see someone?"

"I think so." Katy cupped her hands to her mouth. "Hey!"

"Perhaps it's Link."

When there was no response, Katy began to wonder if she wasn't imagining things. Then she saw movement as the tiny figure slowly edged back toward the forest.

Paula was at her side now, so Katy pointed. "There." She had phenomenal eyes. "He's just standing there."

A gust of blowing fog obscured their vision as Paula stared. "I don't see anything."

"I don't either, now."

Paula started back toward the camp, but Katy continued peering across the lakeshore.

The fog cleared and she squinted. The figure had something raised to its shoulder. Katy's jaw dropped as she realized that he was aiming a rifle—at her! She was dumbfounded and just stood there and gawked, then sprang to her feet.

"Mom!" she cried. Then her legs were stung by a spray of sand, and a loud *crack* rolled across the lake.

Katy screamed and ran toward the camp. "A man's over there shooting at us!"

Paula was riveted into place, her eyes as wide and unbelieving as Katy's had been.

They heard a distant shrill shout. "Stop!"

Her mother came to life, grabbed Katy's hand, and pulled her toward the forest.

Another shot rang out.

"Dad!" Katy exclaimed, looking back.

"Hurry!" Paula said desperately, and continued pulling her along.

"We can't leave Dad!"

"We've got to."

After a few steps Katy turned and fled with her.

They entered the forest together, then Katy stopped, heart pounding but knowing she had to go back. "The pack," she said in a trembling voice.

"Forget it!" her mother exclaimed, tugging her hand, but Katy wrenched free and hurried to the clearing, trying to remain out of the intruder's sight.

He was walking hesitantly toward the camp, still two hundred yards distant.

Katy bent low behind the orange tarp shelter, then cautiously reached inside and retrieved the day pack.

"Bye, Dad," she said in a choked voice, then saw his eyelids flutter.

"Danger," he whispered. He'd heard the shots and was lucid.

"Dad?" She wondered if there was a way to take him with them.

"Take Paula . . . go. You're . . . in *danger*."

Katy backed away, then turned and hurried to the nearby tree where the bag of dried fish was suspended. Her hands were shaking as she fumbled to untie it.

"Go *now!*" her father rasped urgently.

The man was nearer, walking in his slow, cautious gait. He raised the rifle. "Stop!"

Katy abandoned the food, turned, and began to run.

Her mother had returned to the treeline and was waiting anxiously. "This way," Paula said in a trembling voice, and led the way into the forest, then past the big tree and the blackberry brambles.

They heard a distant rumble, and a wind gust carried a final light spatter of rain. Remnants of the diminishing thunderstorm. As they hurried, Katy wanted to tell her about her father's whispered warning, but choked up and couldn't. She was trembling, holding fast to the pack, and they ran ever deeper into the forest as the wind whistled eerily through the trees.

When the rain had begun, Link had climbed the sparsely treed mountainside, then walked doggedly throughout the night, making as good time as he dared, pausing only to negotiate particularly treacherous or steep areas in the darkness. When first light had come, it had been no easier, for he'd found himself in heavy fog.

For the first time he rested. He believed he was approaching the lake, and did not want to go beyond the camp. As the fog began to thin, he found a rocky promontory and waited for a glimpse of the lake to regain his bearings, for the mountains were obscured.

Wisps of moist air blew through his vision as he stared intently, and finally got a single wafting vision of the water. He'd gone too far by a mile. He continued staring as the fog lifted more, and discerned the small clearing and then a small streamer of smoke from the fire. The women were up and about, and he felt giddy with relief.

He'd started to descend the stony promontory when the first rifle shot sounded, and a few seconds later another. With each he felt a jolt, as if the bullets had struck him. A wave of foreboding descended, and it took effort for him to push it aside. He could not allow himself to despair, not yet. He stared intently again. A distant shout sounded as a tiny figure moved on the lakeshore east of the camp, then became obscured in the blowing vapor. Webb, he believed. The fog lifted once more. The man was walking cautiously, waving his arms and shouting words Link could not discern, but he recognized the urgency of a plea.

The visibility improved more, and Link's eyes narrowed as distant movements from farther up the lakeshore caught his eye. Two tiny figures, also making their way toward the camp, one taller than the other.

"Get away from them," he whispered to the women, hoping that was what had just happened, wondering why Webb had not just walked into camp.

A rescue helicopter was sure to come when the weather improved, but Link did not know when that would be, and Paula and Katy might still be in danger. He drew a mental line west from the camp, for that was where the women would likely flee. They were not good in the forest, and he doubted they'd go far.

He descended the promontory and began to walk briskly toward them.

Webb waited, mentally kicking himself and cursing in self-deprecation for what he'd done, until Jaeger and Charbonneau arrived.

Jaeger stared about, then pinned him with a look. "The women were here," he said in a low voice, "and you *shot* at them?"

"It was an accident," Webb tried. He'd prepared his

explanation, but with Jaeger looking at him with cold eyes, the hedging words only made him feel more foolish.

Jaeger continued the even stare.

"I was looking at them through the scope, and . . ." Webb swallowed. "An accident," he repeated. He didn't even remember having his finger on the trigger.

"And your second shot?" The words were scarcely audible.

"You said you didn't want them to get away," Webb explained, trying a reasonable tone. He'd panicked when he'd seen the women fleeing.

"Another *accident,* and I will kill you," Jaeger said softly.

"Jesus, Jaeger," Webb said, believing him.

"How many were there?" Charbonneau lisped, huddling in his rain gear for warmth and huffing from the long walk.

"Three," said Webb. The two women, and the man under the shelter there."

Simon Charbonneau walked over and smiled. "Frank Dubois," he exulted.

"We can't kill him yet," said Jaeger. "Because of this idiot, he's the only one left to tell us where to find the brief."

"I examined him," said Webb, wanting to exhibit his value. "Both legs are broken and his skull's fractured."

"Just get him well enough to talk," Jaeger said.

Webb cast a dubious look. "I can set his legs, but his head . . . I don't think he'll ever wake up."

"What about the leather folder?" Jaeger asked, staring about.

"The women didn't have it when they ran, and I've looked everywhere. It's not here."

"The airplane?" Jaeger wondered.

"I think they landed in the lake and used the raft to get ashore."

"It's a large lake," Charbonneau said, staring. He looked at Webb. "What about the women? What did they look like?"

Webb described them as best he could.

"Paula and Katherine Dubois," Charbonneau said.

Jaeger nodded at the forest. "If Dubois can't talk, we'll need them to tell us where to find the folder."

Webb desperately wanted to be helpful. "The ground's

soft and they left a clear trail. You want me to go after them?"

"Later." Jaeger gave him a stare as if observing a cockroach, then turned away. "First we must gain time." He explained, and they went to work.

After an hour Webb prepared Frank Dubois to be moved, then followed with an armload of camp gear as Jaeger hefted the severely injured man and carried him through the forest. They'd walked for no more than a quarter mile when Jaeger found an appropriate place.

"Hide everything," he said, and carefully deposited Frank Dubois behind a large bush.

"This is too close." Charbonneau came huffing up from behind and looked about. "Won't they search the area?" he asked.

"Perhaps not, if we do our job well. If they do, we'll kill Dubois and hide his body."

"And leave without the Weyland files?"

"Of course not. But it will be much easier if the searchers don't stay."

They returned to the camp previously inhabited by the Dubois family.

Frank Dubois had heard gunshots and the panic in his family's voices, and struggled to the surface in time to tell Katy to flee. Then he'd dropped deep into the abyss, waiting and biding his time, praying his women would escape. When he'd ventured to the surface again, he'd been alarmed, for he'd recognized the blond man with the feminine gestures. He'd seen him in photographs, and at the diplomatic party in Buenos Aires, but had believed he was in New York.

Another called him Charbonneau, but that was not his name. Then Frank recognized the much larger man, who he'd believed was in Argentina carrying out the assassinations. He was said to be a vicious killer, and was called the Hunter. The two were his worst nightmares, and they'd come for him . . . and for the folder. His family were in mortal peril, for they'd leave no witnesses.

Frank remained utterly quiet, stifling the urge to groan in his agony as he sank back into the sanctity of the abyss. He would remain there, free from the worst of the pain, and continue to search his subconscious for answers. If he did not die, he would periodically reemerge to learn their secrets. But he must be careful, for if they suspected he was aware, they would force his knowledge from him.

Before his mind became numbed he remembered that Link had gone for help, and prayed that his friend would return in time to save Paula and Katy.

After an hour Jaeger was finally satisfied that they'd eliminated every possible sign of the survivors, and led Webb and Charbonneau back to the hiding place where Frank Dubois, the raft, and other items from their camp had been deposited.

As they settled, Jaeger pointed at Webb's pack. "The radio," he said with a growling sound. "It's time for a newscast."

Webb tuned to the Boise talk-radio station, and they waited expectantly.

It was the first thing covered. A Boise newspaper reporter had been aboard an airplane searching for a lost Gulfstream executive jet, and claimed they'd sighted two female survivors in a remote and isolated area. The pilot of the search aircraft had confirmed that the passengers were the Dubois family of New York. A rescue helicopter would be dispatched as soon as weather permitted, which should be shortly.

The announcer explained that Frank Dubois, a senior vice-president at the Weyland Foundation, was heir to two of America's richest fortunes. His wife and daughter were reported also to have been aboard, and were believed to be the two seen from the air. There was no knowledge of the survivors' physical condition.

Spokesmen for the FAA would not comment on either the validity of the sighting or the names, but they'd previously dispelled a similar rumor about the passengers' identity. The Weyland Foundation had flatly denied that any of the Dubois family members were missing.

"Interesting," said Jaeger as the newscaster turned to a new subject. There'd been an undercurrent of disbelief about the sighting and the identity of the people.

Charbonneau gazed apprehensively at the sky. "When will they arrive?"

"The announcer said soon." He motioned to Webb. "Go after the women."

"Shouldn't we wait until the helicopter's gone?"

"That's when I want the women preoccupied, so they won't be signaling anyone."

Webb reached for the hunting rifle, but the Hunter pulled it harshly from his grasp and tossed him the stubby carbine. They'd carried all the weapons from the Suburban in the event Anderson somehow reached it, and of them the Winchester was most unlikely to be misfired.

Jaeger stared coldly. "Don't shoot *anyone*. Just hold them until the helicopter's gone, then bring them here."

Webb swallowed hard, then hurried toward the lakeside camp, where he would pick up the women's trail. The Hunter followed, to eliminate his tracks.

The Valley

They fled through the forest, only trying to put distance between themselves and the man who had invaded the camp. When one way became impassable, they'd pick an alternate route, hoping it was away from the lake.

Paula stopped, panting. "Let's rest." They were tired, and she knew they should be traveling with more purpose to their direction. When they'd settled for a moment, the insects set up their familiar whirring and clicking noises, as if cheerful after the rain.

"I thought he'd come to rescue us," Katy complained. "Then he started shooting. It wasn't a mistake. He could *see* me."

Paula cast a tender look and almost recanted the decision she'd arrived at as they'd run through the forest. Her voice was quiet. "You shouldn't have ignored me and gone back."

"We needed the pack. I wish I'd gotten the food too."

"This isn't a game, Katy. From this moment until we get to safety, I want you to promise to do as I say."

Katy eyed her and sighed.

"Will you do that for me?"

"I don't know." The words emerged in a low voice, and Paula knew she was being truthful.

"Then I'll have to conclude that you'll continue to defy me, as you did back there and when I told you to stay in your seat on the airplane."

"Aw, Mom, this isn't the time for a lecture."

"You're right." Paula gained her feet, feeling a new wave of fatigue. "I suggest you continue straight ahead. The sky seemed brightest behind us, so I believe we've been going west. Link thought there might be a road there."

Katy looked confused.

"I'm going back to your father."

"But the man back there . . ." Katy began.

"I left your father at the camp because your well-being is very important to me. But if you don't trust my judgment and won't listen, there's no reason for me to be here." She looked at her daughter. "If that's the case, my place is with Frank."

"You can't go back." Katy's voice quavered.

Paula pointed. "As I said, that way is west." She turned abruptly, not wanting her daughter to see her expression, and started.

"Mom? The man back there will shoot you!"

"I'll try to talk with him and, if he's following, to slow him down. You'd best hurry." She continued, wondering if she'd ever know if she'd made the proper decision.

"Mom!" Katy's voice broke, and Paula heard the sounds of her running.

She turned back and her daughter fell into her arms, sobbing.

"I'll do what you say, Mom." Her daughter's voice was a plaintive cry.

Paula held her tightly, as she'd not done for a long while. Finally she said, in the same soft and even voice: "Then we'll go on together."

"That's what Dad wanted. He was upset when I went back, like you were." Katy rattled on then, telling her about Frank's lucidity.

"We've got to be strong," Paula said solemnly. "I suspect we can be as long as we're working together."

Paula turned her mind back to their dilemma, and then to the people in the blue airplane, wondering if they hadn't told the man back there where they were. *Kidnappers?* They'd lived with the specter of abduction for years.

Who could they trust?

Now the popping sounds they'd previously heard from the forest became even more ominous. She decided that Link Anderson had likely been killed.

"We'd better be going." She tried to make her voice sure.

18

10:25 A.M.—The Lake

Billy opened the helicopter's side door and was outside
within seconds of their settling onto the grassy area. As he
looked about, his heart felt increasingly heavy.

Tom Oliver was behind him, wheezing as he waddled.
"Show me these *survivors*," he shouted over the noisy din
of the blades. He'd been especially irritable since reading
Leslie's front-page story in the morning *Times-Journal,*
which had not only named the passengers, but also described Oliver's reluctance to believe and his caution to
act.

Bowes pointed at the sandy area. "There was an international orange life raft pulled up on the beach." He turned.
"On the other side of that log, an orange tarp was tied to
the saplings so it made sort of a lean-to shelter, and there
was a red cloth on top."

Oliver's eyes glittered maliciously as he looked about.

A para-medic trailed behind them, then went to the edge
of the forest and peered into the thicket. Billy was shaking
his head, as if what they were seeing could not be. Oliver
was also wagging his head, but his look was pure disgust.

Billy pointed. "They'd written the letters H-E-L-P on the
beach. Over there they had a fire going, between the log
and a shelter where those saplings are. They'd piled on
green wood because it was billowing dark smoke."

"Funny. I don't see any of those things, Bowes."

"It was there. We'll find sign of the fire."

Oliver shrugged. "Whoever they were, they were responsible campers. They smothered their fire and cleaned
up before they left."

Billy could contain neither his disappointment nor be-
wilderment. He walked about the grassy area confused, as

if his senses were playing tricks. There was no tarp or life raft—no fire—no word stamped and outlined in the sand—no women in distress. He would have sworn it was the wrong location, except this was the only lake of any consequence near the eastern end of the valley.

Was it the right valley?

It had to be. His navigation couldn't have been that bad.

He went where the fire had been, now neatly covered with dirt, and in exasperation he dropped to his knees and dug with his hands. He quickly found charred wood.

"It's still warm," he announced and held up a piece. "They were here this morning."

"Campers," Oliver repeated. "They probably left early."

Leslie was looking around with the same shocked expression Billy wore.

Oliver came close to Billy, and his voice dropped to a whisper. "You told her the names of the passengers."

Billy did not answer.

"You betrayed our trust, Bowes. Your company will be crushed like a pissant on a sidewalk."

Leslie came closer, as if she wanted to hear what they were saying.

"Satisfied?" Oliver asked her, unable to mask the smugness of his tone.

"They were here," she said stubbornly, but her voice was unsure.

"Do you still stand by your story, Ms. Rocklin?" The *Times-Journal* had run the article despite a dozen pleading telephone calls from Weyland Foundation lawyers.

Billy rose to his feet. "We were *not* wrong. I recognized Paula Dubois."

"I don't know who you're talking about," Oliver said for Leslie's benefit.

"We saw them," Leslie protested.

"Another wild-goose chase," Oliver grumbled and waved his hand in a circle at the helicopter pilot so he'd know not to shut down.

"We should at least take a look around," Billy said. "*Someone* was here, and *something* happened to them."

"Sure did," Oliver said. "They crawled back in their Jeep and went home."

The para-medic returned from the forest. "Nothing but a

couple of slit trenches. They were neat about it. Filled them in so you can hardly tell they were there."

"Dig them up," Billy said.

The para-medic gave him an incredulous look.

"They'd be just full of bodily excrement, like some other things around here." Tom Oliver smiled at his own humor.

Billy started to retort, then sighed in disappointment and continued to look about.

Oliver motioned to the para-medic. "Let's go."

Leslie Rocklin pointed down the valley. "I saw flashes from that direction."

"You're sure of that too?" Oliver asked and gave a mocking shake of his head. "Oh, yes, you wrote something about them in your newspaper article."

Leslie flushed. "I saw them yesterday, then again a few minutes ago when we were about to land. This time they appeared dimmer, but I was looking for them and they were there."

"Odd. Did anyone else see anything?" Oliver looked about in exaggerated expectancy. "Bowes, did you see any—what was it again Ms. Rocklin—hot flashes?"

Billy didn't answer, and Leslie was too distraught and confused to respond in kind.

"Tell you what. Since we've already wasted taxpayer dollars on this boondoggle, I guess we can add a final swing around the valley in the helicopter to check out your *flashes*." He paused with a thought and looked at Billy. "Your company willing to pay for all this, Bowes?"

The Valley

Link had watched the helicopter from the moment it entered the valley, and had tried to capture their attention with the signal mirror. Since the day remained overcast, he wasn't hopeful.

He'd walked until he'd reached the mental line he'd drawn west from the camp, and not much farther he had come across the women's trail. They'd made no attempt to hide their tracks—in fact, did not know how to—but were wandering generally away from the lake. He saw no signs of pursuit by Jaeger and crew, but the forest was too thick to see more than a few feet and it would be difficult to hear them after the rain had rendered the ground soft and spongy.

Link prayed the people in the helicopter had rescued Frank Dubois, but knew it was unlikely. When he'd overheard them, Jaeger had talked about killing the survivors. Yet he also remembered that the big man had said to question them, and the fact gave him faint hope.

As he followed the women's trail he kept his mind busy. When the helicopter was airborne he would signal again. The sky grew brighter with each passing minute, and he had more hope for success. Once he was aboard, they'd find Paula and Katy quickly enough.

Link pushed the last branches out of his path with the rod spear, observing a clearing just large enough for the helicopter to land, and walked the dozen steps to its back side, where he'd have the best viewing angle. He stuck the spear upright in the grassy earth and withdrew the metal mirror from his jacket pocket. A small hole was at its center. He knew to peer through it, capture the spot of light, and steer it to the target.

Link held up the mirror, and this time when he peered through the hole, he detected a much brighter glare spot against the diminishing overcast.

"That's better," he muttered, and practiced steering the spot about the clouds.

The helicopter's rotor blade noises became audible as the engine revved. Link held the mirror and waited for the craft to rise into view—and became aware that someone was close, moving toward him so noisily that the sounds were barely masked by the distant helicopter.

He'd wrenched the spear free and turned to run when Webb burst into the clearing and stared, chest heaving and open-mouthed from exertion, eyes wide with surprise. He raised a stubby carbine and stared over the sights.

"Don't move," Webb ordered in a high falsetto. He was trembling with trepidation as he slowly circled, and Link knew he was deadly in the nervous state.

The helicopter was coming their way, blades clacking loudly.

Webb gave a glance skyward, chewed on his lower lip as if wondering what to do, then motioned with the carbine's stubby muzzle toward the forest, his finger curling dangerously against the trigger. The barrel was pointed at Link's chest; it was obvious the frightened man would shoot at the slightest provocation.

Link slowly retreated into the brush. Webb followed, mouthing something that was lost in the noise of the approaching helicopter.

The pilots hadn't seen him, Link lamented as the helicopter flew directly overhead. *Find the women!* he silently urged them.

As the din of the blades receded, Link heard new sounds—whispers of movement in the forest from behind Webb—and wondered. *Jaeger?* It seemed unlikely, for the noises were from the wrong direction.

He had to move soon if he was to escape, yet Webb continued to act nervously and the finger was still poised on the trigger.

Webb studied his bound arm, then the thin rod in Link's hand, and his look became confused. "Where's your rifle?" he asked suspiciously.

Link waited as the sounds came closer. "I'm unarmed," he finally said. As he'd crept through the forest, the knife and metal spear had provided a sense of security. Now, with Webb here and Jaeger closing, both carrying firearms, the spear seemed a desperate contrivance.

Webb was frowning. "Jaeger was fooled by a pipe?"

Link had practiced with it, had even tried throwing it, but the metal rod was neither balanced nor aerodynamic. For accuracy's sake he'd decided to hold onto the knobby handle as he jabbed, which severely limited its range. He also remembered the other thing—that he should not kill, for he couldn't risk their reprisal upon Frank and the women.

Webb backed into the clearing, the muzzle still trained, close enough that he could not miss yet remaining out of the spear's reach, and Link felt like a hunter confronting a tiger with a fly swatter.

He heard another sound from directly behind Webb, as if a branch had been pushed aside, and glanced that way, half expecting Jaeger. His heart fell as Paula and Katy emerged from the dense forest.

They saw Webb and abruptly halted.

Go back! his mind screamed out to them.

As if she'd heard him, Paula motioned Katy back into

the thicket. Then, as her daughter slipped into the foliage, Paula advanced cautiously—fearful eyes glued on Webb.

Link was unable to contain his warning. "Run!" he yelled to her.

Webb smiled, gaining a seed of confidence that he hadn't been decoyed so easily.

"Link?" Paula's unsure voice wavered.

Webb spun about, mouth drooping with surprise. At the same moment he fired, Link lunged desperately with the spear.

Gowen Field

Leslie's face burned with humiliation as she walked from the helicopter.

"Rocklin?" she heard, and she blew out a heavy sigh as the news editor from the *Times-Journal* stalked toward her. Billy Bowes, the one person she wanted to stay—so she could find a place to hide with him—continued toward the Beech Baron.

The news editor cocked her head. "Was what I heard true?"

Tom Oliver had radioed ahead about the false alarm, so the other pilots would continue to concentrate their search elsewhere.

"What's that?" Leslie asked with a lame expression.

"That every word of the article we printed was a lie."

"We saw them," Leslie said stubbornly.

"Campers," snorted Tom Oliver from nearby, unable to keep amusement from his expression. "I told Ms. Rocklin she should wait on any news releases until this morning."

The news editor glanced skyward. "I wish to God she'd listened," she said.

"We were *not* mistaken about what we saw," Leslie cried.

"I'll see you at the office," her boss snapped, "and we'll try to recover from your grandstanding."

Leslie tried to glare back, but her effort was weak.

The news editor turned to Oliver with a mellower tone. "I apologize about the article. You told us it might be a false alarm."

The FAA executive shrugged. "This sort of thing happens. Alarmists and glory seekers are part of the game, and we have to rely on the good judgment of the media."

"I assure you that you'll have our full cooperation in the future."

Oliver's expression became sly. "We, ah, still haven't released names."

"We'll make a full retraction, including the fact that we went to print prematurely and have no idea about the identity of the passengers. I'll let the wire services know immediately."

Oliver smiled in his victory. "I believe that's both prudent and appropriate."

The news editor offered a smile. "Is there anything new with your search?"

"Not much," he said grimly. "I'll fly to Reno this afternoon. We've had some new sightings near there. Probably pie-in-the-sky stuff like this, but we've got to follow leads when we get them."

"I certainly understand. It must be very frustrating." They walked together toward the hangar, the news editor continuing to fawn, Tom Oliver pontificating.

Leslie glanced to where Billy stood beside the Baron, giving instructions to a man in overalls.

She went closer and watched him check a fuel trap on an engine. He'd told her that the slightest presence of alien moisture could shut down an engine without warning in flight.

"I'm a pariah," she lamented, wishing he'd stop puttering and hold her.

He grunted in response and began buttoning up the cowling.

"No one believes us," she said, feeling increasingly distraught.

He nodded as he waved to a fuel truck lumbering down the ramp toward them.

"I feel awful," she tried, but he still didn't respond. The truck arrived and he gave instructions. As the refueling began, he stepped back beside her.

"What do we do now, Billy?" she asked miserably.

"Not feel sorry for ourselves. There are more important things, like finding Link, Jackie, and the Dubois family."

"Yeah," she tried, but couldn't erase her frown. "We saw them, Billy."

"We saw *someone* and it looked real. I reported the sighting, like I had to. You wrote about what we'd seen. We both did our jobs. I just shouldn't have confirmed the names. The foundation people are concerned about fortune hunters."

"But wasn't it really them? You said you recognized Paul Dubois."

"I thought I did." Billy shook his head. "Now I don't know *what* to believe."

They'd watched the refueling operation for fifteen minutes when Leslie's telephone buzzed from her purse, and she answered as Billy went closer to the airplane. It was Mort Yoder, calling from Washington.

"They weren't there," she said miserably.

"CNN got the word out fifteen minutes ago." Mort was abrupt, as if he was in a hurry. "How about the Dubois family being aboard the airplane, Les. Was that part accurate?"

She remembered Billy's regret, and how opportunists might become involved. "Probably not," she lied.

"Well, if you find out it's true, or get anything at all on the Weyland Foundation, let me know. I've gotten more from my government source. This is going to be damned big, Les, especially if he can provide what he says about the involvement of past administrations. We're talking FDR, Truman, Ike, JFK, Reagan, Bush—all of those guys, I guess they didn't trust Nixon or Clinton, but who would?" His voice was excited.

"That's great, Mort."

"Let me know if there's anything new. Too bad about the screw-up." He hung up.

Credibility was the lifeline for a journalist, and Leslie's lurked somewhere below zero. She wondered if she'd be able to get a job with the Podunk Weekly News when the dust settled.

She folded the telephone and put it away, wondering how anyone could go from a wonderful evening to such an awful day in such a short period of time.

The Valley

Simon Charbonneau was pleased with what he'd just heard on the radio broadcast. The announcer said the newspaper had erred. The rescue helicopter had found no sign of survivors from *any* airplane, and the focus of the search was being moved farther south. The Boise newspaper would print a full apology and correction in tomorrow's edition.

"Did you hear that?" he called out to Jaeger.

"Yes," the big man said. Just after the helicopter had left they'd heard a shot, and he'd been preparing to go out to investigate.

Jaeger frowned, then cautiously stood and waited, his rifle up and ready. A moment later Webb hurried into the makeshift camp—his teeth were clenched, and dried blood streaked his shirt front.

"The women did that to you?" Jaeger asked incredulously.

Webb knelt on a survival blanket laid out beside the still figure of Frank Dubois, then stripped off his shirt to examine his wound.

"The carbine?" Jaeger asked.

"They got it," Webb said angrily. He pulled over his pack, where he kept the medical kit.

"There's a lot of blood," Charbonneau observed uneasily.

"A pinprick," Jaeger said with scorn. "I suppose they got away?"

"Yeah." Webb pulled out a syringe, which he filled from a rubber-stoppered bottle.

"Will that make you sleepy?" Jaeger asked in his rumbling voice. "We need to talk."

"Tetanus. Anderson stabbed me with a damned spear." Webb trembled slightly as he administered the needle into his arm. "It was a spear, Jaeger, not a rifle."

"Anderson?" The Hunter was surprised. "He's here?"

"I was following the women's trail when I came across him trying to signal the helicopter. I was holding him when the woman came up behind me."

"We heard the shot. Did you get one of them?"

"You told me not to harm them so I—I missed on purpose. Then Anderson jabbed me and I dropped the gun.

There wasn't anything left to do but run or let him kill me with the damned spear."

Charbonneau watched as Webb washed the wound. Jaeger had been right. It was shallow and did not appear serious.

"Was the girl with them too?"

"I don't know. I took off when Anderson got me with the spear." Webb finished cleaning and peered at the wound. "Anderson's left arm's in a sling," he added, as if in afterthought.

Jaeger turned and stared into the distance. "And now he has the women to worry about."

Webb grunted at the sting as he poured antiseptic into the puckered wound.

"We can't let them get away," Jaeger said, still staring southward, as if visualizing Anderson trying to get over the mountains.

"Will you send Webb again?" Simon Charbonneau asked.

"I'll go this time."

Webb pursed his lips as he taped a pad of gauze over the puncture.

Jaeger slung his rucksack onto his back and looked at him. "Bring the tents and food from the Suburban. We'll probably be here for another day or two."

"Be careful. Anderson's got the carbine," Webb reminded him.

"I'll call you on the radio when I take him, or did he take that from you too?"

"Of course not."

"Bring the supplies from the Suburban," Jaeger repeated.

Webb recognized something dangerous in the tone and scrambled to his feet. He pulled on his blood-streaked shirt, picked up the assault rifle, and departed.

Charbonneau cast a cautious glance at the forest, then looked back at Jaeger. "You're leaving me alone again?" He wanted to make his displeasure apparent.

"Webb will be back soon. You heard the radio. The rescue crew found nothing. Now time's on our side, but I can't allow Anderson and the women to get away. We need them to tell us about the folder."

Simon noted the look growing in the Hunter's eyes, the

same as he'd seen before the killing of the secretary. "We need them alive," he said reproachfully.

"Of course. I'll bring them in."

"You didn't catch Anderson before."

"I was looking for the airplane. Now we know it's here in the lake, and he has to worry about two very helpless women. It shouldn't be difficult." Jaeger picked up his rifle, nodded brusquely, then departed southward, toward the high mountains.

Simon exhaled a sigh. Although he felt vulnerable with both of them gone, he was pleased with the new twists of fate. With the rescue effort stopped, they'd have time to search for the Weyland file. Jaeger was good in the forest. They had Frank Dubois and would soon have the women—and the folder.

When Salvatore DiPalma was done in South America, the order of things would be changed forever. Even his great riches were paltry when measured beside the power he'd assume. But first Simon must have the files from the folder, so their man in Washington could destroy the foundation. Getting it would be worth the discomforts he faced.

Salvatore DiPalma's genius was profound, thought Charbonneau, but the idea of the *truenos* was his own contribution. The world disregarded the news from South America because of the thunderous noise of the *truenos*. Much progress had already been made, masked by the first rumblings, and more would be accomplished with the next one.

But none would compare to the fifth one. The final *trueno* would be his personal triumph. His team of technicians in San Rafael were preparing the trailer. Charbonneau had observed a demonstration when another such device had been ignited in Patagonia. The fiery implosion had left a hundred-foot-diameter crater.

When the great peal crashed in California, no one would notice events in a land far away, only the tragedies that splashed across their television screens. The final *trueno* would happen, and with it his great-uncle would succeed.

It was a brilliant plan. But first they needed the folder, to use its contents to ruin the Weyland Foundation and stop their investigation.

19

3:20 P.M.—The Valley

Link desperately hoped the people in the helicopter would return, but had no faith that they would. With the women to look after, he had to be much more careful, and while he was thankful that they were together, the responsibility was heavy.

After putting distance between themselves and the lake, they were resting as Link decided on a specific route of escape. He was forced to travel more slowly than he'd done alone, and the women had to stop more often. They traveled noisily and left a clear trail and, worse, alarmed animals, large and small, as they passed.

Webb had fired, narrowly missing Paula, before Link had lunged with the rod spear. The point had hardly penetrated Webb's chest, yet he'd squealed as if he'd been skewered and fled, leaving behind the short-barrel .30-30, with three rounds of ammunition loaded in the magazine.

The weapon's presence was reassuring, although Jaeger carried his oversize magnum and his men had access to rifles, all with much longer effective range. That fact had made Link pause as he considered the open terrain of the foothills and mountains, but that way remained the only direct route out of the valley, and if they were where he believed, civilization lay not far beyond.

"We'll change directions and go south now," he told them.

"It's awfully thick that way," Katy said, with a wrinkle of her nose.

"Not for very far. We'll continue over the mountains."

"I think we should—"

"Listen to him, Katy," Paula said softly, then nodded to Link. "Just tell us what to do."

Link regarded Katy. "Remember when I told you I was part Indian?"

Katy nodded eagerly.

"Piegan Blackfeet moved across the plains like ghosts, hardly leaving a trace of their passage. They could sneak into an enemy camp and walk away with their best horses. I've been thinking of them a lot recently, because that's the way we have to be. Each of us has to learn to be stealthy, and to work together as a team."

The women leaned forward, listening intently as he instructed them.

Katy led the way through the dense forest, parting the foliage with the spear, carefully lifting her feet and placing each step, periodically turning back to him for direction.

Link had shown them how to leave the least sign. He'd told them to think of a cat as they walked, and mimic the way they lifted and positioned their feet when they were stalking and wished to remain unnoticed. Katy had picked it up quickly, and since she had good vision, he'd told her she'd be in front for the present. He went last, listening for pursuers.

As they entered the sparser forest near the base of the foothills, Katy stopped and pointed, their signal that she'd seen or heard an alien presence.

Link quietly moved forward. He too had heard the faint sound of rocks sliding.

"Wait here," he whispered, and handed the carbine to Paula.

Katy was immediately upset. "Let me look. I'm the scout, remember?"

Paula placed a hand on her daughter's arm and gave her a harsh look. Katy sighed and nodded as Link went on, dropping low and disappearing into the undergrowth. There were fewer trees, so he went cautiously, finally wriggling on his belly to the perimeter. He remained still there, squinting cautiously and moving only his eyes. It took a moment before he spotted the big man, although he was only two hundred yards above.

Jaeger too was immobile, wearing a fresh camouflage tiger suit, looking out from the hillside through the magnification of his rifle scope. He swept the area slowly, then paused as he observed the area where Link had left the women. It was impossible that he could see them, yet Link understood that the man knew something was there. It was a sixth sense, possessed only by a true stalker, picking up on tiny movements and variations in the environment. Yet Link also knew that Jaeger could not be certain that his attention was drawn by humans—it might be a bear or deer, or other large animal. After a moment's observation, Jaeger moved the rifle's aim point and observed another area of suspicion and, after a minute, moved to yet another.

Link took in the terrain to either side of Jaeger until the images were stored, then eased back slowly and soundlessly returned to the women.

"Jaeger's up there," he told them. He'd told them about the big man, and that he was the most capable of those they faced.

"Can we get around him?" Paula asked.

"Maybe, but not here. We'll continue farther west."

Katy gained her feet and grinned. "I'm getting stealthy."

"Yes, but don't make sudden moves like you just did. When you stood, the birds above us stirred. Jaeger notices things like that. He already knows something's here, and we don't want to keep drawing his attention."

Katy's face fell, and her mother touched her arm. "We'll learn together."

"I'll lead for a while," Link said. "Watch me, and try to remain very quiet."

He hefted the carbine and silently walked westward.

After an hour they stopped again, so the women could rest and he could make another observation.

"Why don't I climb a tree?" Katy asked. "I could see him from up there."

"He'd see you first, and Jaeger is a very good shot," he said.

This time he returned after only fifteen minutes, and again he did not bear good news.

"He's up above, paralleling us on the hillside."

"Does he still know where we are?" Paula asked.

"He's got a good idea. We're not far from a place I call Dogbone Lake, and he's watching a disturbance in the forest there, too."

"He's spooky," Katy said.

"We just have to be careful. Now let's all have a bite to eat."

"I wish I'd brought the smoked fish," Katy complained as she eyed the tubers he drew from his pocket.

"Eat slowly," he said. "Your system isn't used to them yet."

She wrinkled her nose at the twisted root. "I brought bouillon cubes and tea bags."

"There'll be no fires. You can try them with cold water from a stream."

Katy sighed. "Maybe we can find blackberries."

"We can't afford to stop."

Paula bit into the root and ate very carefully. "It's not that bad," she said.

A moment later Katy was trying her own, making faces but continuing until it was gone. "What other wonderful delicacies do you have for us?"

"I've been living on wild sweet potatoes and insects."

"Bugs?" Katy shuddered, so he did not further enlighten her.

"Is your arm any better?" Paula asked him.

"Every now and then I start thinking I'd like to remove the splint so I can have the use of both hands. Then I hit it against something, get nauseous, and chicken out."

"Better keep it like that," Katy counseled. "The survival book says four weeks minimum for a broken arm."

"Why are those people chasing us, Link?" Paula asked.

"I stumbled onto an atrocity. They'd killed two kids and burned their bodies."

Paula's face paled, and Katy looked about uneasily.

"I thought they were trying to get rid of me because I saw the bodies," Link said, "but that doesn't explain why they shot at you, or why Webb didn't kill me when he had me."

"Can we get away?" Paula asked.

"We've got to." He smiled. "It was pretty bleak this morning when I heard the rifle fire. You ladies look awfully good to these eyes."

"You sure took care of that guy," Katy said.

"I wouldn't have been able to if your mother hadn't called out."

"Yeah," Katy affirmed, looking at her mother with respect.

"Will he live?" Paula asked.

"He wasn't badly hurt," Link said. "Just frightened."

"And now we've got his rifle," Katy said.

"Carbine," Link corrected. "Winchester manufactures Model 94's in long- and medium- and short-barrel versions. This guy's got a stubby sixteen and a half-inch barrel, and they call it the Trapper model. It's not good for long shots."

Paula shook her head resolutely. "I don't want anyone else hurt. Let's just get away and bring help for Frank."

"Yeah." Link got to his feet. "It's time."

"Listen," Katy said. She stopped and cocked her head inquisitively.

Then he heard it too—the distant sounds of airplane engines—and withdrew the signal mirror from his jacket pocket.

Airborne Northeast of Boise

As Billy descended, he reset the altimeter to the 30.05 pressure setting forecast for the area.

Back in Boise, a TV reporter had collared him in the rescue center, jabbed a microphone in his face, and tried to get him to admit that the previous day's report had been a scam so that, one, Leslie could file a "big" story, or two, it might somehow help him with Executive Connections' problems. After telling him to get lost for the third time, Billy had told him to leave him alone or he'd not take his boot off the arch of his foot, which he was casually stomping down upon with all of his weight. By then the reporter had been squealing and pleading. Then Billy told him to lay off Leslie too, or he'd find him and massage his other foot. When he'd finally walked down the hall toward the operations desk, the reporter had been hopping up and down.

Before takeoff he'd called the office. Henry said the FAA had been successful in subpoenaing all aircraft records, indicating a full-blown investigation was now under way. The media was coming down hard after the erroneous report carried in the *Times-Journal,* somehow laying the blame upon Executive Connections. And finally, Weyland Foundation lawyers were asking tough questions about the

safety aspect of having a single company pilot aboard, regardless of the qualifications of a passenger. The day had
not begun well.

Billy flew high around the valley's circumference, taking
careful looks at its features, determined to learn its baffling
secrets. Then he skimmed past a peak on the eastern side
and descended. He flew directly to the lake, throttled back,
and observed carefully as he flew up and down its length.
The camp area was the same as they'd seen that
afternoon—no shelter and no raft. He saw nothing else of
interest there.

Billy flew a few miles to the north and circled a
meadow, with a small, seemingly deserted cabin at one
side. He'd not noticed it on his flight with Leslie, but
wasn't surprised. It had been late, and they'd been exuber-
ant about the discovery of survivors. A mile southeast of
the cabin, a dark-colored vehicle was parked at the end of
a primitive path. It was hidden under trees, and he
wouldn't have seen it if he hadn't been low and trained in
visual reconnaissance. He wondered if that wasn't how the
campers had brought in their camping gear. If that was the
case, they'd have had to carry it for several miles, but
he supposed it made as much sense as the other puzzling
things about the camp's disappearance.

He climbed to two thousand feet, followed the crude
path north, and came upon the dirt road that climbed the
side of the ridge. He flew back south, then over the lake
once more. As he was about to cut power to descend again,
he saw a vague flash of light in a corner of his vision. He
held his altitude as he turned west, wishing Leslie Rocklin
was along to observe.

He missed her presence. She was a dynamo of energy,
and unlike any woman he'd known. Leslie evoked latent
emotions in him. Contentment when she was happy, an
urge to laugh when she did, protectiveness when she was
confronted or seemed troubled—all of those caveman in-
stincts came snorting out of Billy when she was near.

There was another glint, but again he'd been looking
elsewhere. He banked, staring at the source, thinking it had
likely been a reflection from a stream or one of the several
smaller lakes.

He saw it again—a lingering, medium-bright flash of
light—and flew toward it.

Billy rolled the airplane onto its side and spotted three figures in a small clearing. Were they waving? It was hard to tell, but that was definitely where the flashes had come from. He felt a tremor of excitement, then quelled it as he remembered the phantom survivors of the previous day. He had to get lower so he could see better.

He entered a long, descending arc, leveled at three hundred feet above the ground, and headed toward the small clearing in the mass of trees with flaps lowered, flying very slowly.

Billy saw another human—this one on a barren hillside—and slowed even more, then banked to fly closer. He was dressed in camouflage. He frowned, wondering . . .

The figure had a rifle poised, and he saw a bright wink of light.

He was being fired on! "Damn!" Billy yelled as he jammed the throttle forward and twisted the yoke, diving to his right and away from the man, at the same time raising the flaps.

The aging fighter pilot cursed again as he leveled, but he was flying fast and low, and it was improbable he could be hit. After a couple of miles he climbed some, over the lake now, and looked ahead. There was another tiny figure on the eastern shore, and this time there was a staccato of light blinks. He wrenched the column left and turned sharply away.

As he rapidly ascended then, Billy felt his anger grow. *They'd shot at him!* So much for seeing "flashes." Now he was happy Leslie *wasn't* along. As he continued the climb-out, he periodically banked and stared, and saw another glint from up the valley. Why were they shooting when he was so far out of range? There was something different about the last flashes, but he wasn't about to investigate.

He monitored the gauges to ensure both engines were running properly and everything was under control, then looked down on the valley again. Billy stared hard, trying to fix the area in his mind, then set power and turned toward Boise. As his pulse calmed, he pondered whether to report the firings—some of the flashes had obviously come from an automatic weapon—and decided that unless there was damage to the airplane, he would not. Oliver wouldn't believe him, and it was doubtful anyone else would listen after the morning's humiliation.

He tried to think of a logical next step. Perhaps it was time to get on with the search, to rid himself of the fixation that the Gulfstream's survivors were in the valley.

But who the hell had been shooting at him, and what were they doing there?

The Valley

Jaeger was on the hillside when he heard the airplane, and then heard Charbonneau calling excitedly about it flying overhead.

"Don't be concerned," he muttered into the radio as he watched.

The airplane made a circuit of the northern part of the valley, which did not concern him, but then turned and came directly toward him. Had the pilot seen something?

It came to him that Anderson might be below, signaling, so he stepped into the clear and raised his weapon. If the pilot was aware, he would surely see the muzzle blast from the big rifle.

He fired twice when the airplane was still two miles distant, not to hit it, but to warn the pilot off. A third shot was unnecessary, for the airplane dove away. Jaeger watched with satisfaction. If Anderson was using a signal mirror, as he suspected, the flashes would be similar.

The airplane was near the lake when Jaeger heard the staccato sound of an automatic weapon's burst—the muzzle report from the AK-47 Webb had taken.

"Stop firing, you fool!" he radioed as the airplane turned sharply and climbed.

"I heard you shooting." Webb responded. *"You didn't want me to?"*

Jaeger did not answer, but he followed the aircraft's path carefully.

"It doesn't matter," he finally said into the radio. The airplane appeared unharmed. Perhaps seeing the second muzzle blasts had convinced the pilot to leave, for it was now much higher and headed westward. "Monitor the scanner and see if he reports the incident."

After ten minutes Webb called back. There'd been no emergency calls.

Jaeger pulled a map from his rucksack and was studying

it when Charbonneau radioed, wanting to know the situation.

Jaeger looked out over the valley. "I'll have them by morning."

"That long?"

"Don't be impatient," Jaeger snapped, then immediately softened his voice. "We're all tired. I'll get them in the morning."

"Don't let them escape."

"I won't. This is what I'm best at." He stared at the valley. There were disturbances from several places, and one he believed was being made by Anderson and the women.

The Hunter had mastered other challenges. The roads he'd traveled had been difficult, from poverty to become the most feared assassin in South America, promised a coveted post as head of the Argentine secret police. Trusted to assist Simon Charbonneau, who would create the final, great thunder. But first they must have the leather folder—and for the past week it had beckoned like a distant, elusive light, always just out of his grasp.

He would already have it, if not for the killing of the students. He would have gone to the lake as he'd originally planned and simply walked into the women's camp. Now the familiar restlessness was rising again, but this time it must be subdued—lest it destroy him. The survivors must live until he knew the location of the folder.

The valley was vast, and to catch them they either must be contained or tracked down. He thought of bringing Webb in to help, then rejected the idea. Charbonneau would be frightened of being left alone through the night, and Jaeger could ill afford to anger him. Perhaps tomorrow.

When darkness fell he wanted to be in a good vantage so Anderson—now hindered by the women—could not slip past. Then he would rest, for he'd not slept for thirty-six hours and wasn't thinking as clearly as he must to find and take them. No man was better at tracking a quarry than the Hunter, but he was weary and prone to make mistakes.

He walked on, traversing the hillside, paralleling the survivors, watching for minor disturbances. He thought of his foe—tomorrow his prey. Webb had said Anderson's left arm was bound to his side, and that he'd gotten in a lucky jab with his spear. Perhaps he was right, but Anderson must be at least marginally capable to have eluded them for so long.

Jaeger would have them all tomorrow morning. He looked forward to the challenge, and to the victory. He wanted to watch the life leave Anderson's eyes as he died.

Katy waited restlessly as Link Anderson came back into the small copse of trees he'd left them in. It was growing dark.

"He's directly above our position."

"Does he know where we are?" Paula asked.

"Not precisely. I got near enough to hear him talking on the radio. He's going to rest, then come for us in the morning."

"You've got the carbine," Katy said.

"He's got a long-range rifle, and his men have better weapons than this. We'll have to get away tonight."

"It's getting late," Paula said dubiously. "We won't be able to travel in the darkness."

"We'll have to," he said. "While I'm thinking about it, let's eat."

"There's not much left," Katy said, reaching into the day pack for the plastic bag.

Despite his morning lecture they'd stopped once to eat blackberries, then in a swampy area where he'd shown them how to recognize and dig up wild tubers. Roots and tender shoots were often good eating, he'd explained.

"Use up everything. This time we'll be walking a long way."

As they each ate a handful of mushy berries, two tubers, and dandelion shoots, Katy thought of the smoked fish left at the camp. They hadn't known how good they'd had it.

Throughout the meal Link looked out at the dwindling light and remained thoughtful.

As Katy started to discard the empty bag, he stopped her.

"Watch." He rearranged a small mound of spruce needles until he had a trough, placed the bag inside, then covered it. As he finished, he repositioned the topmost needles with care, so the surface appeared undisturbed.

"Pretty neat," Katy said. It was unlikely anyone would be able to pick out the small mound, which looked identical to others around.

"When you go to the bathroom, cover it with dirt," Link

told her. "Human feces smells different than wild animals'. Also, wipe mud and dirt on your clothes and skin. That'll make it harder for him to see or smell you."

So much for the hygiene lessons she'd learned at camp, where they'd been cautioned to stay as clean as possible so they wouldn't catch all manner of diseases.

"You're starting to get good in the forest, Katy. I've just been to all the right survival schools, courtesy of the U.S. government."

"And you're part Indian."

"That won't help us. It's knowledge that will get us through, and you're learning."

"I still get scared sometimes."

"Try to think differently. Use darkness and the forest to your advantage, and let the other guy worry about what's out there."

"I missed you when you were gone," Katy blurted, and immediately kicked herself. *Why had she said that!* she wondered, and was happy it was too dark to see her red face.

They were quiet for a while.

"Here's the plan," he finally said, and drew them close. "Jaeger keeps trying to head us away from the mountains, because he knows that's our quickest way out. Let's play his game." He detailed what he wanted to do.

"Won't he know we didn't get past when he can't find us?" Paula asked.

"He knows we've got the carbine, so he'll move cautiously," Link said, sounding increasingly pleased. "By the time he's on to us, we should be far away."

"What about the others at the lake?"

"Jaeger's the key. If we can keep him searching the mountain long enough, we'll succeed. Now, let's take inventory."

Link had the lighter, snare wire, compass, signal mirror, the can of liquid heat and fold-up stove, and several impregnated wads of tinder. He also had the carbine.

Paula had a battered spoon in one jacket pocket, the cup in the other.

Katy's pack contained the Swiss army knife, the small first-aid kit, the remaining smoke flare, matches and more tinder, four bouillon cubes, and a few other items like soap, that now seemed useless. She also carried the spear.

"Time to begin," Link said, rising to his feet. "You ladies can help with the first part."

A half hour later, when they'd prepared the beginning of an obvious trail leading south toward the mountains, Link Anderson gathered Katy and Paula back in the dark copse of trees.

"Now it's my turn," he said. He would continue the trail up the mountain, past Jaeger.

"Why don't we all go there, then just keep on going?" Katy asked.

"There'd be too much noise."

"You said we were getting better. If *you* can do it—" Katy started.

Paula touched her arm. "It's time to listen again."

Boise

Leslie Rocklin's world had turned so dismal that morning that she'd not considered eating all day. Instead she'd commiserated as she'd borne the brunt of the news editor's scorn and wrote a statement for the morning edition disclaiming everything she'd written the previous night.

She stalked about her apartment, still feeling rock bottom. Billy had called, saying he'd drop by for his bag. Leslie was anticipating him, hoping his presence could make some of the hurt go away. After all, just the night before she'd realized she was falling for him again, middle-aged, big ears, and all.

Crazy, she told herself. Certainly she was more sensible than that.

The doorbell's sound brought a new feeling, though, and she found herself hurrying.

"Come on in," she said, and when he brushed by she tingled from the contact.

"You okay?" he asked quietly as she closed the door.

"I was depressed and utterly miserable all day."

"Yeah." He stood very still and stared back.

She went closer, and what followed surpassed all the childhood dreaming of a fifteen-year-old girl. It began with another kiss started by Leslie, and she clung to him as it continued.

When they finally drew apart, Leslie swallowed only once and then did not look back.

"In here," she thought she whispered, but wasn't sure anything came out. She pulled his hand to lead the way, then closed the bedroom door behind them. He started to say something, but she was scared he was going to mess it up, so she made a *shh*'ing sound as she slipped her sweater over her head. There was just enough light to know he was undressing too.

When she was down to bra and panties, she reached out once to make sure it was truly happening. She brushed his hand and his ... My *God,* but it was real.

When she was unclothed, she hurried to the bed and pulled back the covers. She'd left it unmade and fleetingly hoped he hadn't noticed. Then he came up behind her, and it didn't matter because she turned and they kissed again as they lay down together.

Hours and days passed then as he was considerate and nuzzled, kissed and stroked her. The books said women needed a period of foreplay. *Not after three years of abstinence.*

Not when the sex act might erase the terrible day.

"Now," Leslie breathed, but he only became more attentive, and she writhed as he traced light fingers over breasts and belly. "Now!" she wailed louder. As soon as she felt him positioning at her slippery gate, she arched, released a ragged breath, and arched again—then crooned aloud as he penetrated.

Leslie wasn't quiet about it, as she remembered always being with her ex-husband. Not that she was *trying* to be loud—the noises just seemed to want to come out, as though she wasn't in control of them. He was stroking slowly, ever deeper, playing her like a delicate violin. She loved his gentleness, and the trust she felt allowed her to be bold and deliciously wicked.

She moaned and he paused, holding himself up so she could move freely—arching, pushing, shoving him deeper yet. A wave of heat blushed over her, and she knew she was making noises again and didn't care. Then Billy released a small cry of his own and could no longer be still. He ground down and began to move in earnest—the male making his conquest. They moved together and made the noises again, but they emerged in jerks and wheezes.

"Oh, God, Billy!" she cried as he arched and groaned, pressing so she felt utterly filled. He shuddered and heat spread into her. "I *feel* it!" she exulted.

He stayed that way forever, then exhaled a ragged breath and slowly relaxed.

After a moment she brushed his face lightly with her hand, feeling very womanly. Another century passed before he moved off her.

His voice was low. "Guess I wasn't as tired as I thought."

She stroked his face more, wondering at her depth of emotion when she'd really known him for such a short time. She remembered her mother telling her she'd known that Gerald Rocklin was the right one the first time she'd met him. Maybe it had been the same with Billy Bowes. She'd been smitten very young, and was angry that it had taken him so long to return.

You are finally mine, she thought and felt giddy with a rush of emotion. Then she had a horrible thought, wondering what he thought of how she'd almost dragged him into the bedroom. What *could* he think of her? She searched for words, wanting to say anything to dispel her worry.

"Do you have a boyfriend?" His voice was hoarse.

"No," she blurted. *Hadn't she told him?* "I'm not into promiscuity, Billy."

She felt suddenly languorous, as if her muscles had turned to mush. "It was wonderful," she whispered, and cuddled close.

"I, ah, didn't come here to . . . take advantage."

She put her arms tightly around him. "Mmmm," she said. "Some advantage. I first saw you when I was a young girl, but I knew you were special even then."

"I'd better find a hotel." His voice was uncertain.

"No!" She turned on the bedside lamp and looked solemnly. "I want you to stay."

"Then I will."

"I am not promiscuous. I don't normally go running around chasing men." She was repeating herself, but desperately wanted him to know.

He looked surprised. "I thought I was the one chasing."

"Great!" she said and bounced out of bed. "That means my mama taught me properly. Now let's eat. I'm starved."

"I could have a bite," he said as he swung his feet onto the floor.

They ate leftover cold chicken from the previous night— barefoot in the kitchen, she wearing his shirt, he his trousers. "What do you usually sleep in?" she asked coyly.

"Nothing."

"That's what I thought." When he looked puzzled, she grinned.

"It's been quite a day," he observed.

Leslie finished off a drumstick, nibbling away every tiny, edible morsel, and pointed the bone at him. "Might as well enjoy the night," she said happily.

They returned to bed after she put the refuse away and tidied up, following yet another urge to exhibit how domestic she could be.

"God, but I'm beat," he said as she turned off the light. "Billy?"

This time the loving was tender, slow, and quite different, but Leslie liked it just as much. Then, after he'd held her for a few minutes, she nestled close and they relaxed together.

She kissed his arm and smelled him, and a delicious thrill shuddered through her.

"I love you," she whispered hesitantly, hoping he wouldn't move away.

When he responded with a snore, she wriggled a little until she was comfortable, and smiled in the darkness as she listened to his sleeping sounds. Leslie had learned something. Misery wasn't nearly as bad when it was shared.

20

DAY SIX—THURSDAY, JUNE 13

5:12 A.M.—The Valley

They'd set out at two heading north, directly away from the foothills. They'd done so slowly, silently, and with caution, using the stealthy ways Link had taught them so they wouldn't alarm animals or leave sign of their passage. After an hour he'd left them and gone back to further erase their trail.

Now it was growing lighter in the glow of false dawn and they were moving faster, with Katy in the lead, Link trailing, to ensure they left no obvious prints.

Link observed the women. Katy moved with sureness, the same way she approached life. Paula was slowest but was continuing doggedly. They were doing as he'd told them, drawing their feet up from the ground and placing them surely, with even weight distribution so they'd make the least impression in the damp earth. Still, they were leaving too much sign. If Jaeger wasn't fooled by what he'd left for him on the mountain, he would be able to follow.

When he estimated they'd traveled two miles, he clucked with his tongue, a low sound to draw their attention, then motioned with his hand so they'd stop while he took an observation.

Link went quietly into the brush, then on for a hundred more yards, until he arrived at the tailings mound where he'd found the steel rod. He climbed carefully, and when on top, he stood immobile as he surveyed. Finally satisfied, he crawled down and returned to the women.

Katy hiked up her jeans, wearing an embarrassed expression. Paula was looking about keenly, and Link saw more determination than fear.

"There's still no sign of him," Link told them, "so we'll set up a new routine. First we'll be stealthy, then we'll walk, then we'll trot, then rest. Fifteen minutes for each, in hourly cycles."

"How long will we keep going?" Paula asked.

"Until we're out of this damned valley and find civilization."

Jaeger had awakened as glimmers of dawn traced the sky. Refreshed by sleep, he'd aroused Webb over the radio and told him to prepare to go to the vehicle.

Before he'd slept he'd thought more about Lincoln Anderson, and decided to enjoy the chase. It was too bad the man had only one good arm, for Jaeger wanted a savory victory.

They must be taken alive, and only Jaeger was so skilled that he could make sure of it without being harmed himself. There would be no blood violence this time, no loss of control as he'd done before.

He began to descend the hillside toward the last position he'd believed they'd been the previous night. He went quickly, for there were no longer signs of disturbance, then smiled as he drew close, for they'd left obvious tracks.

Jaeger hurried faster, backtracking easily until he approached a tangle of underbrush. He slowed and entered a tiny area within a copse of trees with a matted area in its midst—they'd slept less than a quarter mile from where he'd spent the night.

He knelt carefully, not wanting to disturb the earth, digesting what he saw. Then the Hunter leaned low to examine closer. He drew a breath through his nostrils and defined the odors, then repeated the act as he knelt lower.

Jaeger held a hand over the mat of pine needles and peered suspiciously at a mound that looked like others until he brushed matter aside, exposing a plastic bag. He lifted and smelled it, then picked out a small particle. He tasted. *A dried remnant of wild sweet potato.*

He was interrupted when Webb radioed from the camp. "I'm ready," he said. "Do you want me to go to the Suburban now?"

"Wait there. I'll call back in a few minutes."

Jaeger stood, his eyes narrowed as he followed the survivors' trail out of the copse. Then he wondered, for the footprints angled toward the hillside. The Hunter followed the tracks silently, growing angrier with himself as the trail continued upward.

He'd studied the mountain behind him when he'd arisen from the crevasse in which he'd slept, but had seen nothing. Had he missed something? It seemed unlikely, for there were few places to hide in the elevations, but Jaeger followed the tracks farther, noting a displaced rock here and there. They'd been sloppy, leaving obvious signs.

He felt self-reproach. They'd traveled in darkness, which explained the overturned stones. But even if he'd slept harder than usual, he should have heard them. His mind was more alert during a hunt, especially when a quarry was known to be dangerous.

He came to the edge of the forest and set his mouth firmly. There was only barren rock and earth before him, and a meager trail leading past his previous night's hillside camp. The survivors had obviously made their way around and beyond him. Yet if they'd been that good, why was he continuing to find overturned stones and places where they'd obviously slipped?

And he hadn't heard them?

He cocked his head, trying to unravel the puzzle. Would anyone good enough to get past him—and they'd passed very close—make the errors shown by their trail?

Jaeger examined an overturned stone, then again looked up the mountainside.

"They're not there," Jaeger muttered to himself, then turned to stare northward over the wild valley and slowly nodded. Anderson was better than he'd expected.

He unfolded his map, then radioed the camp. When Webb responded, Jaeger told him to hurry to the vehicle.

"Simon too?"

The Hunter considered for a moment, then rejected the idea, even though he could use more bodies for the task he envisioned. "Just you. Take the vehicle to the road, then drive exactly twelve miles west."

"I understand. What then?"

"Walk south for a hundred yards, then hide and wait. I'll drive them to you."

"Jesus, Jaeger. Anderson's got the gun."

Jaeger put the map away. "Just do as I say, Webb."

Webb was silent for a long moment. "Okay."

"Don't fuck up again. There won't be another chance this time."

Charbonneau's shrill voice came on the air. "I'll be left alone again."

"They won't come anywhere near you, Simon. The next time I see you, I'll have them with me." He switched the radio off before Charbonneau could argue, then slung his rifle.

Not just any rifle, and not at all like the rifles the others carried. The stock, hand-crafted to fit the large frame, was well oiled. The barrel measured twenty-eight inches in length—four inches longer than the norm—and was bored and chambered for .338 Winchester magnum cartridges. He loaded his ammunition to precise specifications, and when he practiced, he could fire a four-inch group of big 230-grain soft-point bullets at three hundred meters' distance. A single round could take down a charging water buffalo.

To test his skill he'd once killed a fleeing Indian, an agent paid by the DEA who had been viewing activity at a cocaine factory in Peru. Jaeger had tracked him for a day, then used a single shot from eight hundred yards, which he'd paced off after the kill. It was a heavy and remarkable weapon, suitable for the hands of a skilled hunter.

Jaeger preferred the weapon in most places and conditions. Others could carry their puny, inaccurate assault weapons. Jaeger would use his big rifle and take them out with a single shot.

He strode confidently back toward the copse where the survivors had spent the night.

Anderson was good, like a cagey leopard trying to throw him off the scent. He liked that. It would make the hunt as enjoyable as he'd hoped.

As Jaeger approached, he slowed and squinted carefully, then continued past, looking for subtle signs. They were there. He walked faster, setting a relentless pace through the dense forest, eyes alert and nostrils flared, slowing only where the quarry had tried to throw him off the trail or there was a difficult decision between paths.

An hour passed before Jaeger stopped, lowered his head warily, and sniffed, detecting a new odor. He smelled again, then squatted and patted his hand over the earth.

There was moisture, as he'd known there'd be. He lifted a finger and sniffed the human urine.

"The girl," he muttered to himself.

How fresh?

It had begun to evaporate. He judged the humidity in the air and made up his mind. Two hours, no more.

Jaeger resumed the pace, moving in the relentless fast walk. The survivors were ever closer, and with each step they were becoming more firmly enmeshed in his trap.

Boise

Billy came awake slowly, thinking about the men who'd shot at the airplane, and the others he'd seen in the valley, and his mind offered the only plausible answer.

"Poachers," he announced in his sleepy fog.

Leslie muttered something and nestled closer, but then the clock sounded with a raucous squeal that made him bolt upright.

"Jesus!" Billy exclaimed.

Leslie slapped a bar on top of the device to bring silence.

"Sounds like a Chinese fire truck," he grumbled as he staggered out of the bed.

"It's cheerful," Leslie said brightly. She slipped on a T-shirt and began her limbering-up exercises.

"What sort of masochist wants to be cheerful in the morning?" Billy groused. He'd awakened earlier that morning, more than pleased that his dream was real, but then he'd turned over and dropped back asleep. Now he was learning the dark side of Leslie Ann Rocklin. She was one of those obnoxious people who awoke energetic and pleasant.

"How about a bagel and juice?" she asked between stretches.

Billy was headed for the bathroom, groggy and bumping into things. He made some sort of intelligible response and continued.

He shaved, nicking himself, then stepped into the shower. The pulsing water was tonic, and he slowly came to life. Billy thought about the previous day and glowered as he scrubbed.

Bad day.

Then he remembered the night and his grumpiness dwindled.

Great night.

Billy grinned at all they'd packed into the dark hours. Then his awakening thoughts resurfaced—that the men he'd seen were off-season poachers out for deer or elk, taking potshots as a warning for him to keep his distance. It was the only thing he could think of that made sense. While it might be weak reasoning, Billy's mind was such that he felt better if he could place everything into a reasonable semblance of order. He was not an imaginative man, and the valley had already presented too many unsolved riddles.

"You about done in there?" Leslie called from outside the curtain.

"Almost."

"Darn. I was going to join you." She handed in a glass of orange juice, which he drained as she peeked. "You have a great body, William Bowes."

"Dammit, I've been Billy all my life."

She took the empty glass and leered again. "How about we do it standing up in the shower."

"I'm too old for that sort of thing."

"Is it good standing up?"

"If you can prop me up in a few days, we'll find out."

"You're supposed to know."

"Good thing you're not jealous." He started to turn off the water, then paused. "Want me to leave it running?"

"Might as well." She handed him a towel as he came out, and stepped in behind him. Her voice dropped to a malicious tone. "Don't even *think* about having another woman in your life."

He began to towel off. "Then you *are* jealous."

"Not of the women before me. You can mark those up to on-the-job training. If you ever touch *another* woman, I'll cut it off and you can mount it over the mantel."

"Ouch. I don't remember entering a bargain like that."

"That happened when you seduced me last night." She made sloshing sounds as she washed. "You sure you don't want to try it in the shower?"

He finished drying himself. "I'm going to the airport and give it another try, see if there's anything in the valley I

missed the other times." He hadn't told her about the riflemen.

"I'll be at the newspaper trying to salvage my career."

He splashed on aftershave. "How *are* things at the newspaper?"

"Shitty. My boss is smiling a lot now that little miss
snippy bitch—that's me—has got her comeuppance. If the
owner wasn't a family friend I'd be out on my ear. By the
way, I just checked on the computer and found my old
buddy Mort's filed the big story he wanted. It seems the
Weyland Foundation gave the President some bad information, and he had the navy board a French ship looking for
some stolen nukes. The President won't comment, which
makes it look more like the truth. Now that they've got
problems of their own, maybe the foundation will back off
on your company."

"When I was in the Air Force, we hated reporters. Especially the kind who would find a file clerk somewhere and
call him a reliable source."

"Mort's still listening to the government official who's
trying to destroy the foundation, and this is only the first
shot. He's been promised a zinger that can ruin them and
make the government look bad as well."

Billy looked about the bathroom where she'd laid out his
toilet utensils. "You want me to leave my stuff in here?"

"I'm holding you hostage until we try it standing up. Get
a lot of rest so you can seduce me again tonight. I think
I'm addicted."

He smiled. "I'm going," he said as he departed the room.

Billy drove his rental car to the airport, thinking about his
idea that the men wielding the rifles were poachers. It
made a degree of sense, which he could build into more of
a case by the liberal use of imagination, but he remained
troubled about what he'd seen—beyond the fact that they'd
shot at him. The winks of light from the rifle muzzles
hadn't been the same as the other flashes. When he flew
there this morning he'd take a better look—from a safer altitude.

As he entered the rescue-coordination center, he found
the place deserted. As he looked about, a man walked toward him, high-gloss western boots ticking on the hallway
tiles.

"Joe Rodriguez," said the wiry man in introduction.

"I remember," Billy said. He also remembered that he was the local U.S. marshal. Since Tom Oliver didn't like him, Rodriguez couldn't be all bad.

The marshal motioned at the deserted operations desk. "They've moved on to Reno."

"I'll continue looking here for a couple more days," said Billy. "Since they're shut down here, I'll head over to general aviation on the other side of the field to do my flight planning."

"Mind if I ask a few more questions about what you saw in the valley?"

"Not at all."

Rodriguez led the way down the hall. "We've been waiting since eight-thirty."

We? Billy wondered.

The marshal opened the door on a small room with a table and chairs. Three men were inside. One was young and pleasant-appearing, and wore a western-cut suit like Rodriguez's. The second was a Weyland Foundation lawyer-investigator he'd met at Salt Lake. The last was a reed-thin elderly man who sat ramrod stiff and examined him with watery blue eyes.

"Please have a chair, Mr. Bowes," Rodriguez said, switching to a more formal tone.

Billy frowned. "Is this an official questioning?"

Joe shrugged, then nodded at the pleasant man and introduced him as his deputy from the U.S. Marshal's Office. The Weyland lawyer lifted a hand in greeting as he was introduced, but seemed more nervous than before. Rodriguez didn't name the elderly man.

Billy took his seat.

"Let's get started," Rodriguez said, and the deputy marshal reached forward and switched on a tape recorder.

For the benefit of the tape, Rodriguez reintroduced himself and the deputy, and asked Billy to state his name, company and position, and tell how he came to be involved in the search.

"William R. Bowes, chief pilot for Executive Connections, a charter airline registered in the state of Virginia. I was one of the original crew for flight EC-992. Due to a reported automobile accident involving a family member, I was taken off the flight. The following day, after the aircraft was confirmed missing, the company sent me to assist in the search."

He looked at Rodriguez.

"More detail, please. Tell us what happened from the time you met your clients in New York until the present."

Billy explained the radio call from Henry Hoblit about his sister, then about meeting the Dubois family at the airplane at Teterboro. For the lawyer's benefit he emphasized that Frank Dubois had *insisted* they not send another copilot.

No one objected or interrupted.

He told about the early morning at the Executive Connections office, Henry digging out and copying records for Tom Oliver, then the later decision to send Billy to Salt Lake to join the search. Billy told them about the initial flights, then moving to Elko and asking Leslie Rocklin to fly as his observer.

He explained how Leslie had remembered getting the telephone call from a high school friend, complaining about the airplane passing low overhead, and how they'd thought it might be a lead in the absence of all others.

"Did you speak with the woman who heard the airplane?" Rodriguez asked.

"I've spoken with both Joanne Schull and her husband on the telephone, not in person."

"And you believed it could have been the Gulfstream?"

Billy nodded. "Except for the direction of flight, everything seemed to fit. From their descriptions, it sounded like a jet aircraft in distress."

"But the time was much later than you might have expected, right?"

"I felt the Gulfstream may have been badly damaged by the impact, and Link—"

"That's the pilot?"

"Yes. Lincoln Anderson." He looked at the Weyland Foundation lawyer, emphasizing his next words. "Mr. Anderson is a *highly* qualified pilot, with cockpit time in a variety of aircraft, and he's extremely capable under stress."

"Go on."

"I wondered if the damage hadn't somehow restricted him to flying much slower and turning only to the right, which would explain the timing and heading."

"What could do that?"

"During the midair impact, about anything could have happened, and if they were flying around with part of the Cessna attached, that alone would have slowed them down and made control difficult."

"What makes you feel that could have happened?"

"The absence of the tail section of the Cessna that impacted the Gulfstream makes me think it *likely* happened."

"That possibility was brought up by your office, but the FAA investigators said the probability was remote."

"Only one FAA official said it was improbable. Tom Oliver is an ass—" He caught himself, but noted a smile on Rodriguez's face. "Excuse me, but I disagree with a lot of things that have come out during this search, including the way it's being managed. If you spoke to them privately, you'd find most of the FAA's investigators feel the same way. The search is not being properly pursued—even the terminology is non-standard—and there's too much interference from Washington. Finally, regardless of his position, Oliver's not qualified to run a search, yet he's appointed himself as the search-and-rescue coordinator."

"Let's go on to what you saw at the lake."

"We saw . . ." He hesitated, and as he did the picture returned very clearly in his mind's eye. "We saw two women, and either a person or a mound of clothing under a tarpaulin shelter. The tarp was the same international orange color as the one carried in the Gulfstream's survival kit. Same with the life raft on the beach. The letters H-E-L-P were outlined on the beach." He brightened, hesitated, then blurted, "I saw something else."

Rodriguez and the others waited.

"There was a crash ax, like the ones we carry aboard our aircraft. It was painted bright red, and was lying beside a pile of wood near the fire."

"Not your standard camp ax."

"Not at all. I also think I recognized Mrs. Dubois."

The old man spoke for the first time. "You knew her?"

"I'd only seen her the one time at the airplane at Teterboro, but she was striking, not the kind of person you'd easily forget."

"How *sure* are you that it was her?" asked the Weyland lawyer with a hint of skepticism.

"At the time I was positive."

"Even from that altitude and speed?" The lawyer was trying to make a point. It was obvious he did not believe him.

"I'd throttled back and we were flying down low, just above the water. We could see the camp very clearly."

"How slow is slow?"

"We were just above the Baron's flaps-down stall speed. I'd say eighty-five to ninety miles an hour."

"That's not slow, Mr. Bowes."

"In an airplane, it's slow." Billy snapped.

"I'm only saying that with the inducement of a large reward, perhaps you may have been tempted to see things that weren't there."

"That's enough," Billy said brusquely, and stood.

The elderly man brushed his hand on the questioner's sleeve, and the lawyer immediately gushed an apology.

Amusement flickered across Joe Rodriguez's face as he watched the exchange.

Billy accepted the apology and sat down.

Rodriguez cocked his head. "But *none* of those things you'd seen at the lake were there when you returned yesterday morning after the storm?"

"It was like an altogether different place. That was what went through my mind at first—that we were at the wrong place. But we weren't. We didn't look that closely, because Oliver's mind was made up. I dug with my hands and found warm embers from the fire, but he wouldn't take time to look around more. A crew member found latrine trenches that had been covered over, but Oliver wouldn't allow us to dig and see if there was anything that might identify them."

"What did you expect to find?"

"Something to confirm what we'd seen the previous evening. Maybe the tarp, or the spent flares, or *something* we could say was from the Gulfstream . . . or not."

The Weyland Foundation lawyer's face crunched into a frown. "You found nothing at the site indicating the survivors might have been there, rather than a group of recreational campers?"

"It seemed like an altogether different place from what we'd seen Tuesday evening."

A long, awkward silence followed, and Billy knew they

doubted, just as everyone else had, for if he'd been listening he would have felt the same.

"Anything else?" Rodriguez finally asked.

Why not? "My observer, Miss Rocklin, saw reflections from the western side of the valley. We thought they may have been made by a signal mirror. She saw them again when we returned in the helicopter."

"Did *you* see them?"

"I was looking the other way both times."

"Did you investigate?"

"Oliver let us take a single quick pass down the valley in the helicopter, but we didn't find anything. I flew back there yesterday afternoon in the Baron for another look."

"Did you see anything that time?" Rodriguez prodded.

"I saw what I thought were reflections from a clearing in the trees, then a small group of people, so I circled around and flew lower. That time I saw a man on the hillside take a shot at me. A couple of minutes later another guy fired from the lakeshore with an automatic rifle."

"So *that's* it," said the deputy marshal.

Billy was puzzled by his outburst. "What do you mean?"

The deputy looked at his boss.

"Go out and take a close look at your airplane," said Joe Rodriguez. "You'll find a bullet hole in the aft fuselage. The refueling truck operator noticed it last night when he tried to fill your aircraft and fuel poured out. That's part of the reason we wanted to talk with you."

"I was hit?" Billy asked incredulously. During the return flight he'd not checked the fuel status because he'd known there was plenty. He'd looked the airplane over after he'd landed and found nothing amiss. Which meant the tank had drained dry and also explained why the airplane had felt squirrely and out of trim. He felt like a rank amateur pilot.

"You're very lucky," said Rodriguez.

"Lucky and dumb. I should have noticed it," he confided.

"Why didn't you report the shooting to the police?" Rodriguez's voice was not unfriendly. Billy remembered that Leslie said he was a good man.

"If I'd known I'd been hit, I would have. But I didn't, and since no one believed what we'd seen at the lake, I didn't want to give them something else not to believe."

Billy shook his head, still angry with himself. "I should have checked the airplane closer."

"The hole's not apparent, but the tank won't hold fuel. Do you mind if we retrieve the bullet? We think it's still lodged in there."

"Just don't tear up the airplane." *A fuel tank?* He wondered how close he'd come to disaster. The thought was hard to dispel as the conversation continued.

They had him go over the previous day's flight and what he'd seen again. When he told them his thought that the riflemen were poachers, Rodriguez became thoughtful.

"There's a lot of that going on," the marshal said. "There are also a lot of illegal weapons around. The Citizen's Militia, that sort of thing."

Billy wondered if anyone in the room believed the rest of his story. "Is that all you wanted?" he finally asked.

Rodriguez looked around at the others, then nodded. "I think so. Thank you for your—"

The Weyland lawyer interrupted. "If you don't mind, we'd like to speak with Mr. Bowes in private."

"Certainly." Rodriguez and his deputy left, taking the tape recorder and closing the door quietly behind themselves.

The elderly man cleared his throat and examined Billy for a short moment.

"My name is Cyril Weyland," he finally said.

Billy wasn't surprised. He'd identified him from the way the lawyer had responded.

"As soon as I heard survivors might have been sighted, I prepared to fly out here. My grandson and his family are dear to me, Mr. Bowes, as I'm sure you'll understand."

"Of course."

Weyland's hands rested before him on the tabletop, and he used them expressively as he spoke. The skin covering the knuckles was transparent and as thin as onion skin, and fragile blue veins showed through clearly. Yet while they were old, the hands were steady.

He leaned forward. "Do you believe any of them could still be alive?"

Billy considered for a long pause, then sighed. "I really don't know, Mr. Weyland. I've thought about it a lot. Sometimes I think we were just seeing what we wanted to so badly. I've also wondered why there's no signal from

the locator transmitter. It's very sturdy, and to destroy it
would take a tremendous impact."

Weyland's head dropped some.

Billy wished he had more positive news for the distraught man. "I really can't tell you more. The Gulfstream
pilot's father is a close friend, and I wish I had more for
him too."

Weyland cleared his throat once more, as if something
was sticking there. "In Salt Lake you told my people that
you remembered seeing my grandson with a brown leather
folder when he boarded the airplane."

"Yes, sir." Again the interest in the folder. Billy wondered, as he had in Salt Lake City.

"When we locate the wreckage, what part of the airplane
would we find it in?"

"When I first saw it, Mr. Dubois had it—then he gave it
to the bodyguard. It's probably in the rear cabin."

Cyril Weyland looked at him evenly. "It's extremely important that we recover the folder, Mr. Bowes. I can't explain more, but if it was to fall into the wrong hands a
number of innocent lives could be lost. If you remember
anything that might help us find it, or my grandson and his
family, please contact us."

"I will."

After another pause Weyland thanked him. Billy left the
small room without looking back, not unhappy to be away
from them.

21

10:10 A.M.—The Valley

They crouched on their haunches to rest, as Link had taught them. It was the Blackfoot way to stretch tired leg muscles, and had the added benefit of leaving the least sign. At first it had seemed awkward, but as they grew accustomed to it the pauses became delicious respite for their bodies. Still, Katy wished they had more food to fuel them at the rapid pace the pilot was setting. She'd seen berry brambles, but he'd not allowed them to stop even though Jaeger should be far behind, preoccupied with the false trail he'd made up the mountainside.

Katy heard a faint guttural sound and happily announced, "It's a car!"

Link Anderson nodded, as if he'd been listening to it for some time. "Their vehicle was parked in that direction."

"There may be a highway?" Katy asked, wanting very badly to be optimistic.

"It's starting and stopping too often—probably a trail or bad road."

"Perhaps they're leaving."

The pilot did not respond.

"He's bringing more people to look for us," Paula said quietly.

"Maybe." The distant engine sound stopped, and Link stared there, as if he could see it.

"I wish we knew why they're after us," Katy grumbled.

"Ransom likely," said Paula.

A bird squawked raucously in the distance. Katy's heart began to beat faster, for only minutes before she'd led them around a blue jay guarding a high tree branch, as Link had said to do. Now, as the bird continued to chatter, Anderson's mouth became taut.

"What is it?" Paula asked, the tremor returning to her voice.

"It's likely we're being followed again. I've got to find out what's back there." He looked evenly at her. "I'm about to take us in a circle, so our direction will seem confusing. Be very quiet, and if anyone sees or hears anything, make the low clucking sound I taught you."

Jaeger ignored the jay that jumped angrily about branches, squealing at the man below. If Anderson was as capable as he now believed, he'd been alerted, but there was nothing to do about it except proceed until the bird no longer felt its nest was threatened.

The Hunter reproached himself. He'd been out of the bush too long and had allowed his skills to deteriorate. If he'd been using his wits rather than concentrating so intently on the survivors' meager trail, he would have noticed the bird in time to avoid it.

As he disappeared from its view, the blue jay's sounds subsided.

He'd followed Anderson and the women for more than five miles. His quarry was now alternating between running and walking, and Jaeger had found the places where they'd stopped to rest—crouching on their feet, not sprawling as they'd done the previous day. While Anderson was hindered by the woman's slower pace, it was not by much. Jaeger usually found prints of only the woman, Anderson went almost unseen, as did the one leading—who he knew was the girl. When they went slowly there was little sign left by any of them, and if he'd not been diligent, he would have been unable to follow the clues of passage.

The women were learning. His admiration was building for all of their abilities.

Would they alter course after realizing they were being followed? Jaeger decided it was probable. He'd have to remain observant.

Webb radioed from the road. He was in position.

"Walk a half mile farther west, where you'll find a sharp curve in the road, then position yourself as I told you. I don't want them to get past you, Webb."

"Shouldn't I bring the Suburban?"

"That would give your position away. If there's no other

way, take out Anderson when they arrive, but not the women, understand?"

"I can shoot him?"

"Only if you have to. I do *not* want the women harmed, though."

Jaeger continued walking and searching, and soon came upon another resting place. There he squatted to examine their spoor. He wanted to get to know them, and to do so the Hunter did not need to wait until he had them face to face,

He detected a subtle odor that hadn't been prevalent before. Animals' bodies secreted differently when they experienced emotions. He did not know the chemistry of it, but he could discriminate the smell of fear when he drew close to a stag or boar—or human prey. This one was pronounced. The woman? The girl? The man, now that he knew his ruse had not worked?

Yes, he decided, they knew they were being followed. It was a good game.

As Jaeger rose to go on, he did not see the shadow figure that observed him, then slipped soundlessly into the forest.

Gowen Field

The mechanic had removed the fuel tank and was creating a cantaloupe-sized hole with metal shears, wielding them like a dressmaker cutting a pattern from a swatch of material.

Billy leaned closer, then glanced up at the partially gutted airplane. The rifle bullet had passed through the aircraft's metal skin and then a reinforced bulkhead. By the time it entered the tank, a considerable amount of impetus had been lost. The fuel had obviously slowed it even more, for the spent round was still inside.

The mechanic stopped snipping and put the shears aside. He punched the hole open with his fist, peered with a flashlight, and reached in. He grinned as he pulled out the bullet.

Rodriguez's deputy took it from him and held it up for examination. "Good thing it didn't spark when it went in."

The mechanic shook his head. "'Long as there's enough

fuel in a tank, it usually won't torch. It's the fumes you worry about."

"Where did you learn that?" Billy asked.

"I'm in the air guard here, and until last year we flew old F-4G Phantoms and would deploy every six months to Saudi Arabia. We were the SAM hunters, the only ones still flying routine combat patrols over Iraq, and we took a few hits."

"I've flown my share of combat," said Billy. "Another war, but the basics were the same. You're right. I'm fortunate the tank had gas in it."

"Sometimes they'll burn no matter what—but not with that kind of round." The mechanic nodded at the bullet. "It's unjacketed alloy, cheapest kind of Chinese military crap available, so it remained intact and didn't spark. You want to knock down airplanes, you use incendiary rounds."

"How would it be for deer or elk hunting?"

The mechanic peered closer. "Mediocre to poor. That's a seven-six-two or something damned close. Too light for an American .308, so it's probably from an AK-47 or Chinese military rifle. There's a large number of them around. Fair guns, crummy ammo."

The deputy marshal placed the misshapen bullet into a small plastic bag.

Billy nodded at the Baron. "How long will it take to repair?"

The mechanic examined the damaged bulkhead, then the fuel tank. "Might be a couple weeks before I can get a tank shipped in from Beechcraft. You in a hurry?"

"Please."

"Then I'll weld the tank and patch the bulkhead. Give me four days for repairs, and a day for the inspectors. Five days total if I can get right on the inspection schedule."

Billy sighed. It would be expensive. "Okay, do it." He thanked the mechanic, then joined the deputy marshal, who had begun walking toward the parking lot.

"I'll send this to the FBI lab in Washington," the deputy said.

"You heard him. It's a common bullet. An out-of-season hunter took a shot, and the airplane forgot to duck."

"Joe Rodriguez wants it analyzed. He's thorough."

"He seems to be a nice guy."

"Joe's a tough boss, though."

Billy turned back and saw two men boarding a small, Hughes-built, bubble-canopied helicopter across the ramp.

"Speaking of Rodriguez, that looked like him getting in the chopper."

"Oh?" The deputy was not a chatterbox.

"Think anyone believed what I said in there this morning?"

The deputy gave a sideward look as if he was considering it. "Got me," he finally said, and nodded amiably as he left.

Damn! Billy thought as he walked toward the small rental car. He had five days to kill, stuck here on the ground, before the Baron would be ready.

He slid into the driver's side and pondered what he should do next. He'd concluded that no one in the room had believed anything he'd said except that he'd been shot at, which was undeniable since they had the bullet. Whatever he did would have to be on his own.

There weren't many options.

Billy dug into the glove compartment, searching for the paperwork from the rental agency. He remembered seeing a four-wheel-drive vehicle in their lineup.

The Valley

Link pulled a small can from his jacket pocket and nestled it into place in the pine needles at the base of two trees. Next he placed the several remaining wads of fire-starter tinder atop of and around the sealed can, and finally added a collection of hastily gathered kindling.

Jaeger was getting too close, and Link needed to slow him down. A wildfire offered a viable option. The idea had come to him the previous evening as they'd taken inventory.

Link could not spare much time, but he wanted an intense fire, such as might be started by the can of liquid heat should it explode and spray its burning contents about the area. The warning label read that the mixture was extremely flammable. Whether it would actually explode was unknown, but he had to try something, and few alternatives readily came to mind.

The big man was less than twenty minutes behind, and

Link had already spent too long with his task. He picked
up the lighter and produced a flame, then ignited the cube
of cotton tinder. That one flared and immediately spread to
the others. The kindling would catch quickly.

He rose to his feet, gave a final look about, and hurried
in the new direction they were taking. As he disappeared
the blaze flickered brighter in the midst of the dense stand
of trees.

Jaeger was moving in his steady gait but stopping more often. His quarry was no longer walking in a straight line,
and had become difficult to track. But of course that meant
they were going slower.

It would not be long.

As he drew ever closer he went over his plan. He'd radioed Webb and repositioned him even farther west, so he
would intercept Anderson and the women on their newest
course. He'd directed him to remain as quiet as possible,
for they would detect his noises if he did otherwise. His respect for Anderson was continuing to increase. It was a
good hunt.

He stopped suddenly, and lifted his head. *Wood smoke.*

What was Anderson up to? *Starting a fire to divert his
attention?* He decided that was the case and hurried. The
direction was no longer in question, for he trotted toward
the smell.

Jaeger slowed as another thought emerged. *Anderson
might be drawing him, waiting in ambush with the carbine.*

Of course. It was something he would do, and his admiration grew again. He could avoid it, but the fire must be
extinguished. If allowed to get out of control, firefighters
would be sent to check it out, and he could not have that.

Jaeger continued forward, wary and looking for a sign of
a trap. He would approach unseen, then come around and
kill Anderson from behind. There were no more thoughts
of taking the man prisoner. Anderson was dangerous and
must be eliminated. They'd have to get the information
from the women.

Jaeger arrived at the edge of a pine thicket, remaining
hidden as he observed from the foliage. The small fire
seemed innocuous, like one a camper might build. His
mind confirmed that it was an ambush; otherwise it made
no sense. He stood silently, looking for visual clues to be-

tray the man's hiding place, since the fire-smoke odors made it impossible to smell him.

The Hunter began his circuit about the periphery, creeping soundlessly through the brush, searching for Anderson and wondering why he hadn't found him. Then he came full circle and paused, puzzled. Perhaps the small fire was only to draw the attention of outsiders.

Jaeger took a tentative step into the thicket, then stopped as he slowly swept his eyes about. *Nothing.* He went forward quickly, intending to kick at the fire and spread it, then leaned closer to examine, wondering why . . .

There was a bright flash, and Jaeger was stunned with surprise, immobilized for a moment until the terrible realization came that he was *burning.* He immediately lost his composure and began to dance about, then to scream involuntarily, pawing at his face and the clothing that blazed brightly from knee to collar.

And not only clothing blazed. His face was covered by orange flames . . . his hair torched in a single, audible whoosh. Eyes! *Guard the eyes!* Jaeger closed them tightly and dropped to the ground, still squealing shrilly as he rolled, trying to extinguish the flames. He stopped, reduced to whimpering as he frantically dug up handfuls of dirt and held them to his face.

He dared to open his eyes—found the flames were gone. A camouflage pants leg still smouldered, so he rubbed dirt there until it too was out.

The Hunter held his hands up, willed them to stop trembling, and observed. They were bright red, as if scalded, and the fine, dark body hairs had been singed away. His face felt hot, as it might under a tropical sun, but there was no intense pain. Not yet.

He was ashamed that he'd screamed, even though the sounds had not been voluntary.

Jaeger regained his feet, then methodically began to put out the fire that had spread onto limbs and branches.

Anderson. The name rolled through his mind as his anger grew.

He heard the distant, throbbing noises of a helicopter, and he turned his head sharply.

Charbonneau's voice sounded on the radio, but he ignored it as he continued to put out the fire. *Anderson!* his mind screamed as his rage continued to build.

When they heard the shrill screams, Link set his mouth thoughtfully. The can of liquid heat had obviously exploded as he'd hoped, but instead of being turned back by burning trees and brush, Jaeger had been caught in the inferno.

The screaming subsided.

"Link?" Paula whispered in a tone filled with fright.

"Keep going," he said grimly, hoping Jaeger was so badly burned he could not continue. He'd not wanted to kill any of them, lest it endanger Frank Dubois—but if the big man wasn't forcibly stopped, he would continue to dog their trail.

"Faster," he encouraged Katy, just loud enough for her to hear.

Jaeger was proud. It was evident in the way he moved and spoke, the haughty way he stood. He was also brutal, a fact made evident by the terrible memory of the burning bodies. There'd be no quarter now. If Jaeger lived, the lines had been drawn. One of them would die.

Airborne, Northeast of Boise

Joe Rodriguez hated flying in helicopters, especially ones like this with the almost transparent canopy that gave the impression you were magically suspended in the sky— which God had intended for only birds and clouds—and could at any moment fall earthward.

He was not a real cop, as he'd once been, and his job description mentioned nothing about going out in a bubble-canopied helicopter to look for a lost airplane.

The primary job of a U.S. marshal was to open and monitor proceedings of the U.S. district court. He did that just fine, just as he administered to the needs of the deputies who worked under him as they transported prisoners and looked into transgressions of citizens and officials who might be interfering with or corrupting federal courts.

The helicopter pilot grinned and leaned toward him. "Nice day for flying."

Joe nodded and stared past his lizard-skin boots at the earth passing below. He immediately grew queasy.

The pilot noticed. "Keep looking out ahead and you won't get sick."

He tried it, examining clouds and distant mountains, quelling the urge to tell the pilot to return to Boise. But there would be no turning back until he knew there was nothing to find.

The previous day he'd gotten an interesting telephone call from his boss's boss's boss on the scrambled "hello" telephone, the number of which was listed in the name of some obscure and nonexistent citizen, and over which you never stated your name.

"Hello."

It had been the attorney general of the United States of A. The A.G. had started by telling him that some of what he was about to say had been cleared with Joe's boss and his boss's boss. Enough so they'd know he'd spoken to him.

The A.G. assumed the line was secure.

"Yes, sir."

Marshal Jose Rodriguez was empowered to form and lead a joint task force of local and Department of Justice law enforcement assets, including those of the district FBI director, *if and when* it became necessary to do so. They were to assist in locating and securing a leather folder—brown in color, to be further described by a man presently on his way to Boise.

"I understand, sir."

The man was Cyril Weyland, executive director of the Weyland Foundation. The folder was believed to be in the Gulfstream IV that had been lost, possibly in Idaho. *If and when* the aircraft, its passengers, or the leather folder were located, or if he *suspected* any of those to be in his area of responsibility, he was to form the task force.

If and when found, the leather folder was to be provided to Mr. Weyland—whom he was to meet in an hour when he landed at the airport—without opening or examining it, or *allowing* it to be opened or examined.

He was to provide Mr. Weyland with all possible information regarding the lost airplane, the passengers, and the leather folder.

"I understand."

He was to accept the requests of Mr. Weyland as if they came from the attorney general himself. If required, the

A.G. would notify the governor and attorney general of the
state of Idaho to ensure their assistance and cooperation.

"That shouldn't be necessary." Joe was a personal friend
of both men.

The matter was to be maintained in secrecy and pursued
with the highest priority. The folder contained information
that could directly impact the interests of the United States
government. If the aircraft was discovered in other than his
area of responsibility, he was to assist Mr. Weyland with
transportation, then forget about this conversation. All
costs incurred would be charged to the A.G.'s operational
accounting code, which he gave him.

"Understood." Now he *knew* it was important.

There'd been a slight pause before the voice told him the
order did not come from himself, but from a higher authority.
Thank you, he'd said.

Click.

"I'll be damned," Joe had muttered to himself, staring at
the telephone with reverence. There was only one authority
higher than the attorney general of the United States of
America.

Five minutes after the A.G. had left the line, he'd gotten
a call from the district FBI director over the hello telephone, telling him he'd just received a phone call of his
own. He was aboard and promised full cooperation. When
did he want to meet?

"If and when, just like the man said. At the present, that
seems unlikely."

"Too bad. I'd love to get some of that free money from
Washington. Stay in touch."

Click.

The FBI district director was normally extremely reluctant to share any sort of investigation or operation, and especially the taking of credit for cracking a case.

Joe had met Cyril Weyland the previous evening as he'd
disembarked from a private executive jet, and they'd
talked. He'd told him about the bullet hole just found in
Bowes' airplane. This morning he'd called William R.
Bowes in for a short question-and-answer period to see if
there was anything to his and Leslie Rocklin's story.

Likely not, he'd concluded, but there was enough to create suspicion that something was going on at the wilderness lake. So Joe Rodriguez had not sent a deputy in the

bubble-canopied helicopter to examine the lake, as he would have done if he'd not been called. Even more likely, he would have written the sighting off as embellishments in Billy Bowes' and Leslie Rocklin's overeager minds, and passed the details of the shooting on to the Idaho state police.

Now he was going himself and enduring the waves of nausea that rose in his gut.

As they flew over the long ridge north of the valley, Joe stared to his right.

"Big valley," the chopper pilot said.

"Yeah." Joe pointed at a distant glitter. "That's the lake, I believe."

The pilot examined a chart and looked again. "That's it," he said happily.

They tilted sharply to their right, and Joe knew he was about to be sick.

It was several more minutes before they hovered over the grassy area at the south end of the lake Bowes had pointed out on the detailed map. The pilot settled the helicopter onto the grass none too soon. As soon as he gave the signal that it was okay to dismount, Joe popped the door and staggered out on the grass to heave up his breakfast. He scarcely heard the helicopter's engine shut down as he tasted his wife's bacon and pancakes for a second time that morning.

"See the smoke on the other side of the valley when we were coming in?" the pilot asked as he walked up, ignoring the fact that Joe was bent over, huffing and blowing as strings of puke drooled from his mouth.

"No," he finally managed, wiping his mouth with a handkerchief.

"I think it was out before we landed, but we ought to take a look on our way back. The forestry guys like to hear about any fires we see before they get a chance to take off on 'em."

"Okay." Then Joe remembered Billy Bowes' experience with the trigger-happy poachers. "Just don't get too low. There's a bunch of rednecks with guns in the area."

The pilot was smiling as he looked around. "Sure is pretty. Every summer I take the wife and kids over to the Lost River, just across the mountains here, but it's darn

near fished out by all the tourists and California trans-
plants. Wonder if there's anything in the lake here?"

Joe Rodriguez scanned about the clearing, trying to decide where he should start.

"What are we looking for?"

"Get the shovel and a couple of plastic bags, would
you?" While the pilot returned to the helicopter, Joe
walked to the saplings where Bowes said he'd seen a shelter fashioned out of an orange tarp. He looked until he
found marks where a cord had been tied.

Proving nothing. Just as asshole Tom Oliver—he agreed
with Bowes' description—had said, whoever had been here
had been responsible campers. It was almost *too* tidy.

So what?

Joe went to the bare spot near the log, where Bowes said
he'd found the remnants of a firepit. The dirt over the fire
site had been smoothed. Bowes had told them he'd dug
there with his fingers to expose the warm embers. Had
someone come back and covered it *again*?

That was another "so what?" There was no crime in returning. Still . . .

The pilot arrived with the shovel and plastic sacks.

"This way," Joe said, and walked into the forest where
Bowes said he'd wanted to dig up the waste trenches, feeling it was reasonable to believe that the campers might
have left something to identify them.

Joe found the first trench, covered as neatly as the firepit
had been, and pointed. The pilot crinkled his nose, knowing what to expect, but he pitched to. The earth was soft,
and he quickly unearthed apple cores and orange peels.

"Want those?" he asked.

"No," Joe said. "Keep digging."

The pilot grimaced. "That's what I thought."

There was human feces and an empty tin.

"Get that," Joe said.

"Jesus," the pilot said, but he reached for the tin.

"Just a minute." Rodriguez bent closer to examine. Instant chocolate, the tin's label read. On the outside chance
they'd be able to get prints, he used his handkerchief and
placed it in the plastic trash bag without smearing possible
latents.

"Want me to fill it back up?"

"Leave it." Joe gestured. "There's the other trench."

The pilot raised the shovel high and took a swipe at something on the ground. "Damn thing got away," he muttered. "I hate snakes. Better watch your step."

The second trench produced another tin—that label reading it had contained instant coffee—as well as several tea bags, a cassette player with batteries removed, the batteries, a profusion of fish heads and guts, and a larger and smellier collection of human waste.

"How much of this stuff do you want?" asked the pilot, frowning again.

"Everything but the fish and shit."

"Wasn't much there," the pilot said a few minutes later as they headed back to the clearing. There had been no tarp, spent flares, or crash ax. It indeed looked as though there'd been no one here except responsible campers.

Joe went to the sandy beach, and looked up and down the lakeshore for sign of the raft Bowes said they'd seen. He'd found nothing and was about to walk back when he noted something odd at the water's edge. He picked up a collection of sticks attached to a mat of fish line and several partially rusted hooks.

The pilot deposited the shovel and bag behind the seats and came over. "Looks like something a kid made up as some kind of fishing rig," he offered.

Rodriguez turned the contraption over in his had. "Or maybe someone stranded in a survival situation without a rod and reel." Finally he sighed. He was grasping.

"This would be a nice place to bring my family," the pilot remarked.

"Let's fly up the valley to where you saw the fire, then get on back to the city," Joe said as he eyed the damnable helicopter and wondered if he'd get sick again.

Probably, he decided. What was worse, it looked like he'd come on a fool's errand. There was no proof that survivors of an airplane disaster had been here.

22

Link had become adept at determining Jaeger's presence—it was not only the varied sounds of the birds and insects, but also an inner, sixth sense that something dangerous and evil was near. The ruse with the fire had bought a few minutes, but only that, and the big man was drawing ever closer, although the women were hurrying as fast as they could possibly go.

Paula and Katy sensed Jaeger too, Link knew, for they looked to their rear more often.

They came to the edge of a field more than a hundred yards across, bisected by a small creek. The grass was knee-high and emerald green, like that in the meadow surrounding the abandoned cabin where the confrontation had begun. Link held them up for a moment of observation, then made a hand signal, and Katy led the way across. Paula, then Link, followed.

Halfway across Paula stumbled and fell. She pushed herself up and continued, crossing the stream where there was no exposed earth as Katy had done, so they'd leave the least trail. On the other side she teetered again. As they approached the forest on the opposite side, Link knew she could not go much farther without resting. It was time. When they reached the trees he gave a double cluck of his tongue, and they stopped and gathered.

Paula leaned forward, propping herself with hands on knees to catch her breath. "Are we ... stopping to ... rest?" she asked hopefully.

"I'm sending the two of you ahead."

"I don't want us ... separated again, Link."

"This will be the last time." His voice was calm.

"Which way?" Katy asked, eyeing the forest.

"Angle to the left. Keep going for two hundred yards, then stop and rest."

Katy hesitated, then slowly nodded as if she'd realized what it was about.

He looked at the carbine in his hand, which had three rounds loaded. "If you hear a shot, it'll be me slowing Jaeger down. If you hear more than one shot, don't wait. Continue north until you find the road, but be damned cautious. Jaeger may have brought in the other two men in the vehicle we heard. The engine sounds stopped east of us, but they could have moved this way on foot. If you don't see anything on the road, forget about stealth and just go as fast as you can toward the low ridge." He lifted the carbine and pointed. "That way."

"How far?"

"Until you're out of the valley and find help. If you hear their vehicle, hide until it's past, then keep going."

"What about you?" Paula was observing him closely.

"I'll catch up."

"Be careful," Paula told him. She stared for another second, took a bolstering breath, and followed her daughter.

Link went to the edge of the clearing and scanned about for a suitable firing position. He found one—not perfect, but usable. A mass of low bushes was set in front of a sapling that had a branched V some two feet off the ground. He wished he'd removed the splint, for what he was about to do would be easier with two hands. Now there was not enough time.

He knelt and placed the carbine's stubby muzzle into the V—balancing it just in front of the forestock, then moved the lever until the chamber was partially exposed. A bullet was loaded, as he'd known it would be, yet he could leave nothing to chance.

He closed the chamber, careful to do it quietly, then settled into a comfortable position and cocked the hammer with his thumb. There were no other safeties on the .30-30.

He was ready. His view included the entire field.

Jaeger was following at a fast pace, but would slow some as he encountered the field, and again as he approached the creek. That would be the best time to fire, he decided.

He recalled the way he'd mentally prepared for shooting competitions as a youngster. Lucky Anderson had encouraged him, saying he should learn to shoot safely but accurately. Link remembered the feeling of responsibility that had grown in him, the pride his stepfather had displayed when he'd done well. He waited, immobile, as minutes passed.

"Hi," he heard just behind him, and whipped his head around.

Katy crouched six feet away, smiling unsurely, careful with the spear.

She'd disobeyed him. "Why aren't you with your mother?"

"I told her to catch her breath, and I'd come back with you. She's upset at me again, but I told her you might need help."

"Go back."

"I listened real good. There wasn't anyone near us, so—" Her voice dropped to a lower whisper. "Watch it!"

Link had seen the big man emerge on the opposite side of the field. Now his balding pate was utterly devoid of hair, and Jaeger's face and head were bright pink in color, covered here and there with gnarled patches of black skin. But he was still lean and strong-looking, and moved warily as he carried the huge hunting rifle.

"Go back to Paula," Link repeated.

Katy eyed the caricature across the field.

"Right *now*." He'd whispered, but the man across the field stared their way.

Katy sighed. "Yes, *sir*." It was a sulking tone, which she'd rarely displayed to him.

She left, but Link could not watch her departure. The tall man had hardly moved since emerging from the forest. He raised his head, as if sniffing for a scent, then stared again. Did he sense Link's presence? Surely he'd not heard Katy, for she'd gone soundlessly, but it was possible that she'd created some slight disturbance.

Link judged him to be at least six-five, and to weigh two hundred forty or more, and from the way he moved, Link could tell he was powerful. He strode a few feet farther into the field—head and upper body constantly moving, like a predator, master of his environment.

Jaeger looked up as the *clop-clopping* noises of a helicopter sounded in the distance, but Link kept his own eyes fixed on his target. The big man edged back to the treeline and stared skyward until the engine and blade sounds receded, then lowered his vision and cautiously started across the grassy expanse.

Link breathed normally, aiming through the buckhorn rear sight, using the white mark on one side, thinking that was likely the zero for a hundred yards. Which meant the bullet would fly—or rise—an inch at the present range to target.

Jaeger approached the creek and paused to look again.

Link held his breath at the middle of an inhalation, as he'd learned so long ago, the front sight centered on the middle of the big man's chest.

Jaeger was searching for something, then found where they'd crossed the small creek.

Link began the trigger squeeze. Lightly, with only the meaty ball of the fingertip contacting the metal of the trigger.

He hardly heard the carbine's report. It bucked only slightly against his shoulder.

The sight was off. The bullet had flown wild, missing to the left.

Link moved his hand smoothly downward and worked the lever, ejecting the shell and ratcheting a new round into the chamber, then moved the sight picture back onto the target. The big man had turned and begun to run toward the trees, but it seemed he did so in slow motion.

Breath normally.

Time warped, and milliseconds became snapshots.

Hold the breath.

Sight picture on target. Shift right to compensate for the error. *Squeeze lightly.*

The big man twisted as he fired, but Link knew he'd hit—and prayed it would be enough to at least slow Jaeger down.

Link backed slowly into the anonymity of the forest, and began to rise.

A wasp stung his right thigh, followed by a tremendous boom that reverberated across the field as Link was spun by the force of the impact. He gasped as he fell, momentarily wondered how badly he'd been wounded, then quickly rose, for there was no time to worry about it.

Lincoln Anderson desperately hobbled into the forest, leaving a bright trail of blood. He had to lead Jaeger away from the women, then evade the big man, find their trail, and shield them as they fled to safety. His mind was numbed with shock, and he did not yet realize that he was bleeding so profusely that the loss would soon drain him of energy and life.

Jaeger lay stone still, the sound of his shot still echoing loudly in his ears. He'd fired blind, at a place behind the bushes where a moment before he'd noticed a slight disturbance that he'd foolishly ignored. Since there'd been no outcry or thrashing, he had no idea if he'd hit him.

His right biceps were bloodied where Anderson's bullet had pierced him, but the wound was slight, little more than a graze as the round had passed between torso and arm. Jaeger worked the bolt, withstanding an ache from his burned and tortured body, and methodically moved his eyes about the opposite treeline.

The radio crackled. "I heard gunfire," Webb exclaimed.

"Stay where you are and be quiet," Jaeger answered. "They're coming you're way."

"Did you kill Anderson?"

Jaeger did not respond.

Katy led the way north as Link had told them, trying to cast the sounds of gunfire from her mind. The first two shots had come so rapidly they'd almost seemed one. Seconds later there'd been another, more like a dynamite explosion than a rifle report. The deafening boom—the same as they'd heard when he'd fired at the airplane—meant Jaeger had not been stopped.

When they'd heard it, they'd begun their flight. Katy hoped Anderson was okay, but doubted it was so. Tears flooded her eyes as she bit her lip and continued, raising her feet higher than normal as she'd learned during the chase.

Her father was likely dead, and now Link . . . the dread that ran through her was powerful and might have consumed her had it not been for the fact that she might lose her mother as well if she didn't remain alert. Again she had ignored Paula, breaking the promise she'd made, and Katy prayed that her mother wouldn't turn back and leave her as she'd threatened.

Katy slowed as she entered a small, grassy glade, sensing that something was before them. She sniffed back a tear and looked cautiously back at her mother, wishing she'd observed more closely before stepping into the clearing.

Paula had halted at the edge of the trees, her chest rising and falling dramatically as she watched Katy and tried to catch her breath.

There was a slight rustling sound. Katy frantically motioned her mother back into the forest, then turned and cocked her head as she regarded the thick brush just ahead.

There was only silence.

Had she really heard an alien noise? She crouched and slowly crept forward, frightened and hardly breathing. Then Katy heard another subtle sound. An animal? She stopped cold, gripping the spear, listening. She'd begun to back away, had turned toward Paula to motion again, when she heard the noise of rushing feet.

Katy spun about and desperately hurled the spear, but it fell far short of the man who ran toward her, a rifle clutched in his hand.

"Stay right there and don't move!" the man shouted, in the same frantic voice she'd heard at the lake.

"Run, Mom!" she shouted desperately, praying that at least Paula would escape.

The stocky, brown-haired man stopped before her, looking as frightened as Katy felt, the rifle trained squarely at her chest.

"Don't hurt her," Paula called out, and Katy despaired, for her mother was walking toward them, face blanched pale and wearing a pleading expression.

Jaeger waited. There was still no movement across the field. After another full minute, the Hunter decided he could delay no longer. He had to determine if Anderson was there or chance them all getting away.

He wondered if Anderson wasn't a poor marksman, for the first shot had been wide and the other had almost missed. Then he remembered that the front sight had been bent during the killing of the boy at the cabin, and felt a flash of elation at his good fortune. According to his count, there was only one bullet remaining in the carbine, and if he could get him to use it . . .

The Hunter took a resolute breath, then pitched forward

and rolled into the open field—a visible but difficult target—ready to react as soon as Anderson fired or presented himself. The effort made him want to cry out, for the contact of earth upon his burned skin brought agony.

There was no response. Jaeger scanned carefully and sensed the absence of life in the opposite trees. He stood slowly, prudently wary but knowing the man was gone.

His radio crackled with Webb's excited voice. The Hunter reached for it and winced as a sharp pain emanated from his upper arm. "Jaeger," he answered evenly.

"I've taken the women." Webb said.

Jaeger felt a rush of adrenaline. "Are they harmed?"

"They're awfully dirty, but I don't see anything wrong with either one."

Jaeger estimated he was not far from the road. "I'll be there in a few minutes. If you see Anderson, shoot him."

The Hunter stopped at the thicket from which Anderson had fired and saw a gout of blood, then a trail of it leading into the forest. He had not missed. With so much bleeding it was doubtful the man would survive for long.

Simon Charbonneau's voice sounded on the radio. "You've got the women?"

"Both of them," Webb responded.

Charbonneau laughed with delight. "When will I get to see them?"

Jaeger keyed his radio, told Webb to turn his volume down momentarily so the prisoners couldn't overhear, then spoke to Charbonneau. "I have a suggestion." He explained what he wanted him to do when he arrived with the hostages.

"Certainly." Simon's voice was jubilant. "Have you got the pilot?"

"Not yet," Jaeger responded. He put the radio away, followed Anderson's sign for a hundred yards, and stopped where the profuse red trail abruptly diminished. A bloody pants leg had been discarded. The Gulfstream pilot had finally noticed that he was bleeding to death, and had cut away his trousers and somehow stopped the flow.

The Hunter looked about for a moment, then turned toward the road. There was no time for the reckoning now. While he wanted to go after Anderson and finish things, he knew he must first tend to business. When they'd retrieved the leather folder and disposed of the Dubois family, he would return and track him down. Anderson had lost too much blood to act or think effectively. The pilot could not go far, and would grow weaker with each passing hour.

As Jaeger continued northward, the intensity of his hatred grew. He regarded the trickle of blood that ran down his right arm and onto the rifle in his burned, aching hand. He shuddered with raw emotion and walked faster.

When he arrived at the road, Webb waited a hundred yards distant, the rifle trained on the two women. As he approached them, Webb made a frown.

"Jesus," he said in an awed voice, for the Hunter had never been harmed in the past. Other men thought him to be too canny to be wounded or killed. The burned face and clothing, and the blood drenching the sleeve of his shirt, were the first signs of his vulnerability.

"Let's go to the vehicle," Jaeger snapped. He led the way, stalking purposefully in long strides on the road. Webb following with his rifle trained on the females.

"I've got burn salve back at the camp," Webb called out, but Jaeger ignored him and continued walking.

When they arrived at the Suburban, Jaeger noted a weathered, once yellow square of cardboard tacked to a nearby tree. He went to the vehicle, found the felt-tip marker he'd left on the console, then walked back and scrawled a message.

When he returned, Webb had deposited the women in the rearmost seats. He handed Jaeger a towel. "For the bleeding."

Jaeger pressed the towel firmly to the wound as he crawled in. "Let's go."

Webb looked back at the square of faded cardboard. "Think he'll see it?"

"Probably not. The bastard's bleeding to death."

Link was moving cautiously, painfully, grasping the tourniquet as he followed the women's trail through an area where the earth was imprinted by other footprints he'd seen before.

He stopped and formed a stone-hard gaze. Webb had taken them.

The end of the spear protruded from a nearby bush, where Katy had tried to defend herself. He went on, creeping soundlessly through the forest, following the tracks until he arrived at the road he'd known was there. Then he reeled and almost fell. He steadied himself, panting as myriad bright dots fluttered in his vision.

Too much blood had drained away before he'd been able to fashion a tourniquet from the remains of the splint and sling that had protected his broken arm. He'd applied the gauze and material directly onto the entry and exit wounds, and pulled it tight by twisting it with one of the pieces of driftwood. Then he'd strapped the carbine with snare wire and carried it slung over his shoulder, so his right hand would remain free to apply pressure to the wound.

He'd expected Jaeger to pursue him, for his blood loss was made obvious by the bright trail from the shooting scene, and he was so vulnerable. But Jaeger had not, and now his reason was apparent. He had his hostages, and Link was too badly wounded to interfere.

Link examined the footprints on the road, found those of Jaeger, Webb, and the women, and followed. There were bright droplets of blood at the right side of the big man's tracks. Jaeger was also wounded, but not as severely as he'd hoped.

He continued down the road, walking as rapidly as he dared, staggering periodically, feeling raw pain course through the leg with each step. As he rounded a sharp bend, still reeling and giddy, he paused to study the road's surface where the vehicle had been parked. Link examined the dirt road for other sign. There'd been only the two men and the women.

A cardboard square nailed to a nearby tree bore fresh letters. Jaeger's large boot prints led there, and words had been hastily scrawled.

A.
It is not over I do not forget. I will be back. Run.
J.

A smear of blood, yet undried, had been swiped across the bottom of the cardboard.

Were the words intended to frighten him . . . or to draw him?

Link turned and stared westward, wondering where the road terminated. If he went there he would likely find civilization, but would he have time?

He went on, following the vehicle tracks on the mud-slick, badly pocked road. The course would take him far-ther from safety, but it was the quickest route to wherever the women were being taken. As he went, he prayed that Jaeger would continue to focus his rage upon him and not transfer it to the women.

He'd walked for less than an hour when he staggered, and fell for the first time. Link lay immobile a moment, then attempted to regain his feet, but found himself devoid of energy. He must wait longer, somehow replenish him-self.

As Link rested, and his weary muscles relaxed, he couldn't stop thinking about Paula and Katy, and how he'd failed in his vow to Frank Dubois.

The leg was becoming numb, so he relaxed the tourni-quet slightly. There was less seepage, and he wondered if it was because the wound was healing or there was simply no more blood. Regardless, the leg felt better with the les-sening of pressure.

Link did not know how much time passed, lying there in the road, but he came slowly alert and realized that he'd slept. Since there'd been little new bleeding, he relaxed the tourniquet more and rolled it aside. The bullet had pene-trated muscle, thankfully missing the thigh bone, and both entry and exit wounds were of similar diameter. The bullet had not mushroomed. He examined the front wound first, since it was most accessible, and used spittle to wash it. Blood immediately began to seep, so he stopped his clean-ing effort, removed the small roll of gauze from the pocket of his jacket, and wrapped it about the leg, again directly on the wounds, until it was expended. Next he reapplied the blood-soaked elastic bandage from the splint, and ob-served. He decided it would suffice, and that he would not need the tourniquet, but he kept the cloth sling and piece of driftwood in case the wound reopened.

Katy had carried the disinfectant in her day pack, so he'd have to wash it to avoid infection. For that purpose he would need clean water. Link painfully rose to his feet, staggered precariously as he shouldered the carbine, and began to walk again.

Images of Paula, whose good life had been so abruptly shattered, then Katy—rebellious yet ever optimistic—loomed distinctly, and he was unsuccessful in pushing them away. They'd been sheltered and were unaware of the nature of evil men, and Jaeger would know that and show them not the slightest mercy.

By road and trail, Link decided he was still some ten miles from the camp, if it was located near the former one as he believed. That distance would not take long if he were well, but now it seemed formidable and impossible.

He continued on.

23

When Webb had set up the camp, he'd laid the tents out in a row, first Jaeger's, then Simon's larger one, then his own, with Frank Dubois on a survival blanket beside it. After Jaeger's radio call Simon had prepared things there, then gone to the lakeshore to await them.

When the four were still in the distance, Jaeger turned and went into the forest, directly toward the tents, and Webb prodded the women on toward Charbonneau. As the dirt-encrusted females were brought before him, Simon grew a smile he did not have to feign. Jaeger had said to lull them, and suggested what should be said. It was a task Simon could do well. He enjoyed role playing, and was a liar of uncommon ability.

"Mrs. Dubois, my name is Charbonneau. I'm pleased to see that you're unharmed." He tried to control his lisp, made more pronounced by his excitement.

Paula Dubois regarded him warily, her eyes periodically darting to her daughter.

Simon shook his head sadly. "When I learned that Webb had accidentally fired his rifle at you, I chastised him severely. I apologize sincerely, Mrs. Dubois. I'm a business man, and I abhor violence in all its forms."

"My husband?" she whispered in an unsure voice.

"We found him at the brink of death. I briefed our medical person—Webb there—to make him as comfortable as possible, and do everything in his power to hasten his recovery."

"Frank's alive?" Her voice held a trill, and she dared to smile.

"I mustn't raise your hopes falsely. We've cared for him

to the best of our ability, but he requires medical treatment far beyond our means in this primitive hell."

"Where is he?"

"There's a matter we must discuss first, Mrs. Dubois. As I said, I'm a man of business, sent here to recover something taken aboard your airplane in New York."

She appeared surprised. "You're not after ransom?"

He rolled his eyes. "What a repulsive thought, although I'm sure you and your family have to worry about such things. No, Mrs. Dubois, I assure you we had nothing to do with the airplane crash or your husband's tragic condition. We sincerely wish to help you and your family, but first I must obtain the brief that was prepared for your husband to read on your vacation. I believe it was carried in a brown leather folder."

She shook her head. "I don't recall anything like that."

Simon's heart almost fell, but then he wondered if she too wasn't a good actress.

"Please think about it and try to remember. As soon as I obtain the folder, I'll have your family driven into Boise and left within walking distance of a medical facility. I would have you taken to the hospital door, but I'm sure you can understand my reluctance to be confronted by authorities who might misunderstand what's transpired here."

She'd seemed to calm somewhat, which was his intent. That, and to plant the idea that all would be well as soon as he obtained the folder.

He nodded at the lake. "Perhaps you could tell me where the Gulfstream's located?"

She became thoughtful, as if trying to remember. "Somewhere near the other end. We had to row a long way, and were pushed here by the wind. Could I see my husband now, Mr. Charbonneau?"

He stared for another moment, then nodded. "Follow me."

Simon led the way, Webb at the rear with the rifle. The camp was not far, only two hundred yards from the lake, in a hidden forest glen. Frank Dubois lay on a rubber pad beside Webb's tent, covered by a blanket. When Paula saw him, she released a small cry of happiness.

"Go ahead," Charbonneau encouraged her.

As Paula Dubois knelt by her husband, Charbonneau wasn't concerned that words might pass between them.

Dubois had seemed to regain a spark of lucidity on one occasion, but when Simon had examined closely there'd been not the slightest flicker of eyes or change of expression. Dubois was hopelessly unaware, but Simon was pleased that they'd kept him alive.

"Frank?" she asked, but of course there was no response. The daughter was standing beside her, observing the camp with a suspicious glare.

Webb ducked into his tent and emerged with his medical bag.

Charbonneau frowned. "Was someone injured?"

"Jaeger," said Webb.

Simon formed a look of surprise as he followed him, then took a step back and gasped. The Hunter stood near his own tent, staring impassively at the women. His exposed skin had been charred and was peeling, his face become a terrible mask. Much of the Hunter's shirt had been cut away, but the right sleeve was blood-drenched and stuck fast to his arm.

Webb cautiously began to apply salve to Jaeger's neck, slowly working his way upward.

"My God!" Simon cried, and couldn't help wrinkling his nose at the distasteful sight.

"It's not as bad as it looks." Jaeger regarded the prisoners. "You put them at ease?"

"Just as you said to do. Paula says she knows nothing about the brief."

"Did you ask about the airplane?"

Charbonneau avoided looking at Jaeger's awful face. "She says it's somewhere at the other end of the lake."

"She knows where it is. All we need to do is apply appropriate persuasion."

Simon's curiosity betrayed him. "You're burned. What happened?"

"Anderson planted something in a fire. When I tried to put it out, it exploded." Webb continued daubing. When he'd finished with his head, he began on the Hunter's hands.

"That's good," Jaeger said impatiently. "Now the arm."

Webb poured water from a jug and soaked the shirt sleeve, then cautiously began pulling the cloth free.

Charbonneau's eyes remained on Webb's efforts. Then

he felt a jolt of apprehension and looked out at the forest. "Where's Anderson?"

"I shot him and left him to crawl away to die. He lost too much blood to still be alive. When we're done here, I'll go back and dispose of him."

Charbonneau calmed, then beamed as he remembered the other thing. "I've been listening to the radio. It happened, Jaeger. The fourth *trueno*. The news is full of revelations about the Weyland Foundation's conspiracies. Members of Congress are in an uproar, demanding an inquiry. This evening more of our opponents will disappear in Buenos Aires."

Jaeger forced a smile. "It's almost complete. Next it will be your turn."

Simon giggled almost childishly. "It's my favorite bridge, you know. I look forward to visiting it next week for the last time." Then he turned anxiously toward the women. "I spoke too loudly."

"It no longer matters what they hear."

Charbonneau lowered his voice nonetheless. "When will we have the folder?"

"In the morning." Jaeger explained how he would get Paula Dubois to cooperate. Charbonneau frowned with repugnance, but knew it must be done.

Webb pulled the last of the fabric from Jaeger's arm and cautiously scrubbed the wound with liquid disinfectant soap. The exposed hole was puckered. "It's not bad," he observed.

Charbonneau regarded the bullet wound with distaste, then turned and walked back to Webb's tent, where Paula Dubois still knelt at her husband's side. The daughter was watching Jaeger with a sullen expression.

Simon thought he saw a flicker of Frank Dubois' eyes, but when he looked closer he decided he'd imagined it. The man was comatose. It was fortunate they had the women to tell them about the folder.

He observed the daughter. Jaeger was right, Charbonneau decided. It shouldn't take long to get the information. He smiled as he thought of another way to build complacency.

"Mrs. Dubois, why don't you and your daughter freshen yourselves in the privacy of my tent? You'll find soap, a basin of water, and some of the commodities of civilization inside."

"I'm concerned about my husband just now."

Simon discerned a gentle grace about her, and even through the layers of dirt he found her more exquisite than her photographs suggested. It was a waste for such a person to have to die. His great-uncle, whom Charbonneau revered, felt he should take a wife. Although he was seldom attracted to women, he wondered if he'd be able to find one like Paula.

"I'll have a meal prepared," he said. "We only have freeze-dried food and such, but if you're sufficiently hungry I've found it marginally palatable."

Paula Dubois succeeded in forming a smile. Breeding was of ultimate importance in humans, Charbonneau thought, as it was in thoroughbred horses or fine dogs. He came from proven stock. If he could find such a woman ...

As Webb finished bandaging his arm, Jaeger nodded toward the lake. "Return to the vehicle and drive up to the ridge, then back again. Take food and blankets, because you'll spend the night. I don't want Anderson escaping on the road."

Webb looked surprised. "You just said he was dead."

"That was to stop Charbonneau's worrying. Men like Anderson don't die easily. He'll try to get away, or come here. Either way, he's likely to use the road. In his condition it's faster then going through the bush. If you see him, chase him off the road and call me."

"Jesus, Jaeger."

"He has a broken arm, and he's lost so much blood he may not even be able to walk."

"But he's *armed*."

"The carbine's front sight is bent, and he's only got one bullet left. He'll want to use it to free the women, so I doubt very much that he'd shoot at you. I've grown to know him."

"It's going to be dark soon." Webb was unenthused about his task.

"Don't let him get away," Jaeger repeated softly, feeling the hatred welling inside. "Just try to find out where he is, and I'll deal with him when we're done here."

* * *

Link lay in the growing darkness, sprawled on the crude path near the burned Volkswagen, where he'd collapsed for the fourth time since he'd begun his impossible and endless trek. It was over, he knew. There was no more energy left in him, and even if he found their camp, the man he faced was formidable. Yet he had to continue until there was no more life remaining, for he'd promised his friend that he would not fail him. The vow had echoed relentlessly each time he'd wanted to stop to tend to his battered and empty shell of a body.

He knew he must sleep, rest, recuperate, if only for a short while. There was no other way for his body and mind to continue functioning.

That's a craven excuse, a voice inside told him. *The Dubois family, all of them now, need you. You promised!*

First rest, cried the more reasonable voice. *Then go on.*

Rest, he decided. But not here, where the air was permeated with acrid odors of the burned vehicle mixed with the sweeter ones of the deteriorating bodies.

He would continue just a little farther.

Lincoln Anderson painfully drew himself onto all fours, and even that effort was Herculean. When he tried to rise he was unable, so he began to crawl, dragging the carbine and tossing it ahead, crawling to it. Tossing it again. Making involuntary noises each time he put weight on his wounded leg, where the damaged thigh muscles contracted and quivered from the continued abuse.

Get up, the voice said, but he tried and was still unable.

He heard a noise of an engine starting farther down the trail and paused, head drooped and chest heaving as he tried to make sense of it. *Danger!* something inside told him, but his mind was not functioning well and he grew confused.

Move off the path. They'll see you!

He tossed the carbine into the brush at his side of the trail, then crawled there, and struggled to sit up. Finally he drew the weapon into his good hand . . . and waited.

They're taking the Dubois family. Stop them!

The vehicle engine sounds became louder as it was placed into motion. Then Link saw headlights as the vehicle jockeyed back and forth, turning around in the meager space. The Suburban was backed for a last time, and began to come toward him.

Link pulled the rifle up, then held it awkwardly with the one hand, trembling with the effort as the headlights swept over the small bush that masked him.

See who's in the vehicle.

The vehicle came closer, then was abeam—but Link couldn't tell how many were inside.

Can't fire into the vehicle. The Duboises may be inside.

He'd raised the muzzle, wondering if he should shoot at a rear tire, when the Suburban came to a halt not fifteen feet down the path.

He waited, hardly breathing, then heard the sound of someone talking.

"I'm on the path now," came Webb's voice.

Jaeger's voice responded on the radio, but Link couldn't make out the words.

"I'll give you another call from the ridge," said Webb.

Shoot Webb! the inner being urged. *Then use the vehicle to get help.*

Link took aim, but the barrel wavered badly. He pulled in a breath and steadied it on the shape in the driver's seat.

The sight is off. Compensate.

Before he could make the correction, the Suburban began to move.

Link lowered the weapon and exhaled the breath. If he fired, it was unlikely he could hit either the driver or the tire, and if he shot out the tire Webb would simply kill him and fix the thing. He heard the vehicle sounds diminish, angry at himself for delaying the attack. With the opportunity lost, his odds of success were diminished again.

Jaeger knew he was alive. He'd sent Webb to stop him from escaping.

I'm not escaping, Jaeger. I'm coming for you. It was frivolous bravado, but it was better than despairing. He felt with his good hand and found that the pressure bandage was working, for the seepage had not begun anew.

Stop and rest.

Did the big man know he had only one bullet left? It was likely. Jaeger could subtract.

Keep going. Stop only when you can go no farther.

He placed the butt of the carbine on the ground and used it to lever himself ever so slowly to his feet. He almost fell, but steadied himself. The first steps were hell and his leg throbbed mercilessly, but the next ones were easier.

Link went on. When his mind rambled, he'd try to pull it into focus, thinking of Marie, his fiancée in Montana, and how he missed her, of his childhood, and then of the thrill of flying fast airplanes, but he would always come back to the Dubois family. He hobbled past the Suburban's parking place and found the much smaller trail that extended toward the lake.

He set his next goal. He would continue to the lake, where he would stop and cleanse the wound. Then he would rest for a while.

Frank Dubois and his family had been placed under his care by Providence—and the vow he'd once made. Now they were taken. A wave of self-reproach swept over Link, and he gritted his teeth and continued. One step at a time, then one goal at a time. Slowly. Stubbornly.

Boise

Billy was late showing up at Leslie's apartment. He'd called twice earlier, but she'd not been home, so he'd eaten at a restaurant before trying again. That time she'd answered and demanded that he come immediately.

When she opened the door, Leslie glared, then hauled off and socked him in the arm.

"Ouch!"

"I went to the airport to meet you for lunch. Someone took a shot at you, and you didn't even *tell* me!"

"I didn't know they'd hit anything."

"I have to know when you're threatened, Billy Bowes. That way I can worry sufficiently and rattle enough beads." Suddenly she looked horrified. "I left soup on the stove!" she exclaimed, and ran for the kitchen.

He followed, and watched her pull a sauce pan from the burner. "You haven't eaten?"

"Not since this morning, thanks to you. My stomach couldn't take it."

Orange liquid bubbled in the pan. "Tomato soup?" he asked dubiously.

"Yes." She pulled a bowl from the cabinet. "I still can't believe someone was actually *shooting* at you. It was when you were flying over the valley, wasn't it?"

"Yeah."

"They wouldn't tell me. No one wants to talk to me anymore." She poured streaming soup into the bowl, sat at the table, and pointed the spoon at him. "Something awfully odd is going on in that damned valley."

"Poachers," Billy said. "Rodriguez said there's a lot of those around. That's probably who we saw in the camp."

"I don't believe that for a minute. Even if it wasn't the women from the airplane, it was *someone* in trouble." She studied the matter rising from the bottom of her bowl. "How badly was the airplane damaged?"

"I'll be out of the search for a few days."

"Oliver ordered the operation here terminated. They've moved on to Reno."

"I heard." Billy stared. "There's black things in your soup."

"Gives it character," she said. She swallowed a spoonful and maintained a straight face. "I had to get back to the newspaper because of all the front-page stuff. Mort's latest story made it *really* big time, even better than he'd imagined. He wrote that modern Japanese industrialization was financed by the Weyland Foundation after the Second World War, and they're still funding businesses in countries that will end up in competition with the U.S."

"That doesn't sound earthshaking."

"It's the way he's writing the articles, like the Weyland Foundation is a huge, subversive creature out to destroy the country. People are up in arms, and the foundation's making it worse by refusing to confirm or deny. Members of both houses of Congress are howling for blood. Mort got top coverage and reprints in a lot of newspapers."

"And you're writing about it here in Boise?"

"No way. I'm down to handling second-rate stuff. Like some kidnapping in Buenos Aires. Five people are missing there, and two are American businessmen."

"Now, that *does* seem important."

"You've gotta understand this dumb business, Billy. It's all timing. People like to think about one thing at a time. Mort's zinger about the Weyland Foundation hit like a bombshell, both here and abroad, and everything else is no news."

Billy almost told her about meeting Cyril Weyland but held his tongue.

She pushed the bowl away. "The newspaper owner's a

family friend, so I don't think he'll let them fire me, but I've certainly been put in my place."

"We've got two major newspapers in Washington."

Leslie tried to give him a coy look, then sighed. "My name's mud there too. Aw, hell, Billy, my name's mud everywhere. I blew it when I went ahead with the story before checking it out. Maybe if I bring in something good, they'll trust me again. It'll have to be convincing, though, because I'm on everyone's crud list."

She began to nibble on crackers, then gave him a tender look. "I'm glad you're stuck here with me. I like you around to share my misery."

"I exchanged the rental car for a Jeep. I'm going to drive to the valley tomorrow."

"It's going to be a rough drive. It's an old, unimproved forestry road."

"I'll make it. I saw another vehicle there yesterday."

Leslie shook her head. "Now and then I start wondering if Oliver and the others aren't right. Maybe it was a sort of mirage, like we wanted to see survivors so badly we fabricated it in our minds. Not all of it, but enough to get us excited. Then I remember it again, and it was so damned *real*. I keep bouncing back and forth, thinking one way, then the other."

"I'm going to find out," said Billy. "It won't go away otherwise."

She got out peanut butter and began swabbing it onto crackers, then stopped and became excited. "I want to come along."

"Not this time, Leslie. I plan to stop at a cabin north of the lake and see if anyone's there, then walk all the way to the campsite. I'll have to get an early start and won't be back until late."

She didn't appear deterred.

"A *very* early start," he tried. "Maybe get up at four-thirty or five?"

She snorted. "I'm a better morning person than you'll ever be. I'll pack a lunch and we can eat at the lake."

"It might be dangerous if the poachers are still around."

"Then I *know* I'm going. Even the worst men around here wouldn't think of mistreating a woman. They've got old-Idaho beliefs in western chivalry too ingrained in them."

He couldn't think of a response that might change her mind. When Leslie got something in her head, she stuck to it. "Do you have a rifle or shotgun? Regardless of how noble your rednecks are, I don't like the idea of being shot at, then going back unarmed."

"I'll get something from Dad's house. We can swing by there in the morning."

Later, as Leslie prepared the picnic basket, she told him stories about her father that he hadn't known. Old Gerald Rocklin had been a colorful person with a different type of wisdom.

24

DAY SEVEN—Friday, June 14

3:15 A.M.—The Camp

"It's time," said a deep voice, and Charbonneau felt Jaeger's hand on his shoulder.

"I listened to the radio," Jaeger told him as he came awake. "The *trueno* was effective. All they talked about was the Weyland Foundation. There was no mention of kidnappings in Buenos Aires, and nothing about Argentina."

Simon dressed for their task. It was an awful hour, but Jaeger said it was the best time, when the women's mental defenses were most vulnerable.

As Charbonneau emerged from his tent, he noted that although the night was chilly, Jaeger wore only trousers and the bandage that swathed his right biceps.

Jaeger handed him the propane lantern. As they approached Webb's empty tent, Jaeger stopped and regarded the women, huddled asleep beside the comatose Frank Dubois. Charbonneau saw that the Hunter's eyes were narrow and fixed, as they'd been when he'd seen him regarding the secretary in Wisconsin. He started to warn him not to go too far, but Jaeger crept closer, like a feral animal examining its prey.

The Hunter moved abruptly, and dragged Paula to her feet. She reeled, bewildered and drunken from the lack of sleep.

"Where is the airplane?" Jaeger demanded in his abrasive tone.

Paula Dubois blinked with confusion, then tried to look past him at Charbonneau.

"We must have the folder," Simon said, trying to make his own voice stern.

The Hunter grasped and harshly ripped her blouse down

the front, and Charbonneau couldn't help drawing a breath at the perfection of Paula Dubois' freed breasts.

The daughter screamed and tried to push away her mother's tormentor, but Jaeger turned and lashed out, his hand a blur in the night as he struck her in the stomach with his huge fist. She doubled up and wheezed, and fell helplessly to the ground.

"Where is it?" The Hunter held Paula from behind and grasped abundant breasts, one in each hand. The flesh bulged as he squeezed—the nipples extending sharply outward—then he displayed her to Charbonneau. "Do you want her?" Jaeger rasped.

Her helplessness struck a primitive chord in Charbonneau, and made him instantly hard. While he knew it was only part of Jaeger's game to terrify her, he did indeed want Paula Dubois.

"The folder," he said weakly.

"Stop." It was a whispered plea, but Charbonneau turned in amazement, for Frank Dubois had risen onto an elbow. "Don't . . . hurt them," he croaked.

Webb had believed Dubois would remain in his coma until he slipped into death, but Jaeger regarded him with no surprise, as if he'd anticipated the miraculous recovery.

"The folder you carried onto the airplane. Where is it?"

"Please . . . don't . . ." Frank Dubois sank back, as if the burst of energy had depleted his meager reserve, yet his burning eyes remained fixed on his wife and her tormentor.

Jaeger was squeezing Paula's breasts in such powerful grasps that they seemed about to burst. Her body strained, and a shrill note emanated from her throat, growing louder as her agony became more intense.

The Hunter spoke harshly into Paula's ear. "Where is the folder?" He squeezed her breasts harder yet, evoking another long scream. Finally Jaeger relaxed his grip, then picked up a rope he'd brought and fixed the noose about her neck.

"Where?"

She stared, mouth open and breathing harshly, but did not respond.

"She knows," Jaeger said in his quiet voice. He shoved her against a tree trunk, then wrapped the rope about it and her neck several times, securing her.

Charbonneau stepped close to the husband, still holding

the lantern. "You're a civilized man, Dubois, a business-man like myself. Tell us where it is so I can stop him and have you all taken to a hospital."

Dubois' agonized eyes remained fixed on his wife, but he didn't speak.

"At least tell us where the airplane went down. This is a business matter. Your family shouldn't be involved." He nodded at Jaeger. "It is about to get much worse, Mr. Dubois."

When there was no response, Simon turned to the Hunter and sighed helplessly.

Then Dubois desperately clutched Simon's legs, and Charbonneau shrieked.

Jaeger formed a look of disgust and kicked out. His boot struck Dubois' face, driving his already shattered head to one side, and as Simon scrambled free, Frank Dubois re-leased a high, inhuman sound that echoed, then faded. He shuddered once, then became silent.

Paula's voice crooned as she was racked with more sobs, beyond despair, oblivious of the rope cutting into her neck.

Jaeger went to the daughter, still gasping for air and now struggling to her feet. He reached down and grasped an ankle, pulled and toppled her, then dragged her thrashing body toward Paula, ignoring her squeals. When they were close he released her, placed a heavy boot on her stomach, and stepped down. Katy Dubois exhaled sharply and her shrieking was stifled.

"Oh, dear God," Paula cried. "Leave her alone."

The Hunter made a ragged snorting sound as he unbuck-led his pants, and Charbonneau saw that his lower jaw had begun to tremble, as it did when he approached his blood frenzy.

"Don't forget what we're after!" Charbonneau whis-pered, but Jaeger did not respond.

Paula Dubois' voice was imploring. "She's a child," she cried.

Jaeger grinned crookedly as he lowered his trousers. His penis bobbed free and swayed obscenely. The Hunter knelt then, regarding the daughter coldly, as if examining a bitch about to be bred. Simon Charbonneau relaxed some, for the big man's lust was obviously feigned.

Jaeger grasped the girl's shirt, grunted as if he felt a

twinge from the wound, then deftly ripped it away. Katy Dubois was well formed, lithe and small-breasted.

Charbonneau's own breath was coming ever faster, yet he remembered their objective and leaned close to Paula Dubois. "Where's the folder?" he asked in a thick voice.

Jaeger was upon the girl, his muscular buttocks quivering as he reached down to loosen her jeans.

"I'll tell you!" Paula screamed.

"Where is the folder?" Charbonneau asked eagerly.

"In the lake, in the back of the airplane. I know where it is. I'll tell you."

Charbonneau laughed, then grinned victoriously.

The girl cried out. Jaeger grunted, and Simon saw that the Hunter had freed the buttons and was pulling at the girl's waistband.

"*Stop* him!" Paula screamed. "I'll tell you everything."

"You heard her, Jaeger," Charbonneau said, his voice a whisper as he watched the spectacle. The Hunter's eyes were burning with intensity, his salve-coated face taut and glistening in the lantern light as he continued to work the girl's jeans downward. Charbonneau had never been so disgusted—yet so aroused. His eyes shifted from the writhing girl to the mother, then back.

"Please," Paula Dubois cried out between racking sobs.

Charbonneau pulled himself from the trance. "Get off her," he said hoarsely.

The Hunter ignored him, pulling the girl's jeans lower, now past her knees, and Simon knew he'd lost control.

"Get off her," he screamed. "You'll ruin everything!"

Jaeger reared slightly and struck the girl in the temple with his fist. It was a glancing, uneven blow, but her head rocked back sharply and she fell limp. Blood trickled from her nose as Jaeger huffed a tortured breath, and drew the fist back again.

"He'll kill her!" Paula Dubois screamed.

Charbonneau desperately kicked, and his boot struck Jaeger's injured arm. The Hunter grunted with anger, then shifted his eyes to his tormentor.

"You've got to stop." But Simon stepped back out of reach, for Jaeger's expression was deadly.

The Hunter rolled off the girl, advanced a single menacing step toward Charbonneau, then blinked and looked back at the woman bound to the tree.

"She said she'll tell us," Charbonneau whispered desperately.

Jaeger took in a deep breath, and his eyes slowly regained focus as his fury slipped away.

Charbonneau's attention became fixed on the girl again. She lay still, bared and vulnerable, blue jeans bunched at her ankles. Her eyes were rolled so far back they showed only white, and blood trickled in delicate rivulets from her ears and nose.

Jaeger turned and spoke calmly to Paula, as if his madness had not happened. "She's alive. If you lie to us, I'll finish with her. Now, where is the airplane?"

Lincoln Anderson had made it to the lake, where he'd cleansed his wounds in its frigid clear water. He had lain on the shore then, panting deep breaths and trying to summon the strength to go on, but when he'd tried to rise he had collapsed . . . and entered a deep, dreamless state, for both his body and mind had shut down.

At first he sensed rather than heard them—the distant sounds of animal agony—and although he tried, he could not ignore them. They welled ever higher in pitch, seemed constant at first, then to come intermittently.

Link tried to shut them out, for he did not want to know what was happening.

But he knew. As the faint sounds continued, he painfully lifted the flying watch to his face, then squinted and was able to focus on the luminous dial. Four hours had passed since he'd arrived at the lake. Time wasted while the family in his care suffered at Jaeger's hands.

He felt his leg and found that there'd been no more bleeding, but he reapplied the pressure tourniquet directly over both wounds.

How long did it take to regenerate lost blood? He'd heard the answer once, but it eluded him, and he decided it did not matter. He could wait no longer.

The cries grew silent. They would not have been audible at all had it not been for the lake, across which sound carried so easily. They'd come from the southern end of the lake, and when he stared he saw a light flickering through the trees not far north of their old campsite.

He tried to estimate the distance remaining. While it was more difficult, the route would be shortest around the western side of the lake, so he decided to go that way. With difficulty he struggled upright in the pitch dark of the night, then pushed to his feet, using the carbine for leverage.

There were no more sounds from across the lake. *They're likely sleeping,* he tried to tell himself, and would not allow the thought that the Dubois family had been killed.

He began to hobble, and suppressed an outcry from the intense pain as the muscles in the leg rebelled. As he continued, he tried to play out the rest of it. They had weapons. Jaeger was good in the forest and was a good shot. He had only the inaccurate carbine and a single round.

"Stay alive," he whispered to the Dubois family. "I'm coming."

6:20 A.M.

Simon trailed behind, bringing the plastic oars as the Hunter and Paula Dubois carried the raft to the beach, then deposited it at the water's edge.

Jaeger tossed her the looped rope, and she dutifully replaced it about her neck. She'd spent the hours until daybreak with her hands bound, the noose cinched securely about her throat. The other end had been tied to a tree branch, so she'd be unable to sit or lie down.

The Hunter had wanted her so weary she could not rebel.

"Now tell us again," Jaeger demanded. "First the airplane."

She pointed toward the center of the lake. "There's a small island. The airplane's just beyond. When you get close you'll see the top of the tail above the water." Her voice was mechanical, as if the words were spoken by a robot. In the camp her husband continued to cling miraculously to life, her daughter curled beside him in a unresponsive, fetal ball.

Jaeger's eyes were fixed in the direction she pointed. "The folder?"

"The security guard had it," Paula recited, using the same words she'd uttered a dozen times. "His body's in the rear-most seat in the passenger cabin."

He shoved her to the opposite side of the raft, and they

pulled it farther into the water. When it was afloat he motioned her inside.

"You'll help row." His voice was as hard as the look he gave her. "If it's not there, you know what will happen to your daughter."

"It's there." Her voice contained no hint of defiance as she crawled into the life raft. She'd tied her torn blouse together, but it had come open, and her once lovely breasts, now swollen and discolored, were exposed.

"Has Webb found the pilot's body?" Charbonneau asked Jaeger, his eyes lingering on Paula Dubois, wondering how she could endure the pain so stoically.

"Not yet. I'll track him down and dispose of the body later."

As if summoned, Jaeger's radio crackled with the sound of Webb's voice. *"A car just passed me on the road."*

"Where are you?"

"At the ridge."

Jaeger eyed the distant mountain. "Authorities?" he asked, and Charbonneau tensed.

"I don't think so. A man and a woman in a Jeep Cherokee."

"Follow them. When you find out where they're going, call me again." He put the radio away and turned to Charbonneau. "We shouldn't be long."

Simon Charbonneau watched as they rowed away from the shore, then turned back toward the camp. After he'd returned to his tent the previous night, the images of the daughter and mother—helpless to prevent anything that befell them—had been relentless. He'd masturbated, yet still had been aroused and it had been difficult to sleep.

Now Simon was even more giddy about the prize waiting in the airplane. They were close. Jaeger's plan was working.

The Valley

Billy listened to Leslie talk on about the man in the muddy Suburban parked at the crest of the ridge. "What's he doing there?" she wondered.

They hit a particularly deep pothole, and Leslie grabbed and held on.

He glanced in his rearview mirror. A vehicle was following in the distance.

Leslie fished in her purse and dug out her cellular telephone. "I'm going to give Joe Rodriguez a call. He's probably awake by now, and someone should know we're here." She punched numbers into the telephone, then grumbled, "It's showing there's no service here."

As the road descended the ridge, the vehicle behind drew near enough that Billy could tell it was the Suburban, which was the only vehicle they'd seen since leaving the state highway.

"Billy, could the man back there be one of them who shot at you?"

"No way to tell. He's behind us, by the way." The Suburban had drawn closer yet.

Leslie swiveled her head. "He's got a rifle propped on the seat beside him."

Billy had seen it as they'd passed by. "There are probably guns in every second vehicle in Idaho."

"He's making me nervous."

"Then we'll let him by." He pulled to the side of the road and slowed.

The Suburban slowed with them and crept along fifty yards behind.

"I don't think he's going to pass," she said. "Try stopping."

He did. The vehicle behind them stopped too.

After a moment Billy started the Jeep rolling again. The Suburban followed.

As they'd passed, he'd noted it was a cheap, stripped-down version. "Load the shotgun," he told Leslie.

"While we're moving?"

"Yeah. I don't like being followed like this." He pulled the lever beside the console until a light on the dash indicated FULL TIME, showing they were in four-wheel drive, high-range. He continued to drive slowly as she bent over the shotgun, pressing 12-gauge shells into the tube magazine. It was a twenty-year-old, well-used Remington Wingmaster. Leslie's father had removed the magazine block so it would accept five shells rather than the standard three. It was a common practice in the states that allowed it.

The most potent shells they'd found had been number

two goose shot. He'd wanted double-ought buck, shotgun shells filled with deadly .32-caliber pellets, but there'd been no stores open at the early hour.

She finished her task and looked up. He observed. She was strapped in.

"Hold on."

Leslie grasped the handhold. "I'm ready," she said, wearing a determined look.

Billy negotiated a sharp, climbing switchback and, as he was pulling out of it, shoved the accelerator to the floor. The V-8 gave a throaty roar and the Grand Cherokee leapt forward.

"Hang on!" he said as they bounced over a series of potholes, still accelerating. When they entered the next turn the Suburban was falling far behind. Halfway through he jammed the accelerator pedal back down and kept it there until they entered another hairpin curve. He let off and they skidded only slightly—then all four tires grabbed at the dirt, and they rocketed into another straightaway.

"I can't see him," Leslie said as he negotiated another high-speed turn. They flew over a small rise and began the descent into the valley again. Still Billy did not let up, although there was no sign of the vehicle behind them.

After five more minutes the road leveled and they clattered over a decrepit log bridge.

"I saw that from the air," Billy said. "Up ahead's a big turn in the road. We're still a long way from the trail at the other end of the valley." He glanced at her. "Who owns all of this?"

"Forestry and the Bureau of Lands and Mines. There are probably a few old abandoned homesteads and mining claims scattered around, but it's all government property now."

Each mile they continued the road became worse, and Billy began to wonder if even the Jeep could stand up under the abuse. Finally he saw what he'd been searching for and slowed. Leslie gave a startled squeak as he whipped the wheel to the right. They bounced over an embankment and into the trees. He continued until the Jeep was hidden, then shut off the engine.

Billy lowered his window. "Try your telephone again."

Leslie examined the read-out. "Still no service."

After several minutes they heard the sounds of the Suburban approaching, then the rumble as it hurtled by.

"He didn't see us," Leslie said happily.

Billy nodded, thinking hard and wishing he hadn't let her talk him into coming along. "I saw him lifting something, like he was talking into a radio. There may be another vehicle."

"Why are they doing this?" Leslie cried.

"Got me." Billy took the shotgun and walked down to the embankment, where he examined the Jeep tracks and kicked at the dirt until he'd smoothed out the ruts. He went back nearer the Jeep and knelt behind a bush. Twenty minutes passed before the Suburban returned, going slower, a brown-haired man peering anxiously. He passed on by and didn't notice the different shades of soil where Billy had smoothed the tire tracks.

When the vehicle's sounds were no longer audible, Billy returned to the Jeep and handed the shotgun, butt-first, through the window.

"He's gone for the moment." He crawled in and started the engine.

"*Now* what do we do?" she asked.

"Go on while he's back there." Billy drove toward the road.

"Think he'll come back?" she asked.

"Yeah. He's looking for us."

"Why, Billy?"

"Why did someone shoot at the airplane? Who's he talking to on the radio? I've got a lot of questions, and not many answers."

"We saw the survivors. They were there, and they did something with them."

"They also may be poachers trying to run us off so they can protect their turf."

Her voice was determined. "We saw the women, Billy. We're not crazy like everyone tried to tell us. That guy and his friends did something with them."

"Maybe." As he pulled onto the road he noticed a faded-yellow square of cardboard nailed to a tree, and stopped. "What's that?" he asked.

"Forest rangers put them up to identify different blocks of timber."

"Someone left a message."

A.

It is not over. I do not forget. I will be back. Run.

J.

Leslie shuddered. "It sounds ominous."

Billy didn't answer. It was definitely not a love note. He put the Jeep into gear and they went on, bouncing over potholes and small chasms from a dozen untended years.

Paula rowed doggedly, matching Jaeger's strokes as he'd told her to do, ignoring the weariness and terrible ache from her injured breasts. As they drew within a few hundred yards of the island, she got a glimpse of the Gulfstream's tail. It was lower, hardly protruding from the water.

As she'd labored, she had devised a desperate plan. When he dove into the airplane she would somehow free herself—she felt he would tie her—and row away. It was two miles to shore, and she doubted he'd be able to swim that far after the dive. Even if he was a good swimmer, he was more likely to go to the rock island to rest, and she'd return to the camp. Charbonneau was much less dangerous than Jaeger, and she was no longer the helpless woman who had left New York.

The radio sounded at Jaeger's side. Webb had found new tracks from the Jeep, where it had turned off onto the trail.

"They'll see the bodies," Jaeger told him. "Capture them and find out who they are."

"Jesus, Jaeger. They may be armed."

Jaeger's voice turned dangerous. "Call me when you have them."

The turnoff onto the trail had been obvious, for it had been in use since the last rain and deep ruts showed the way.

"The cabin's a couple more miles," Billy told her. "Halfway between here and the lake."

Leslie was hanging on, looking out at the trees and thick foliage.

A few minutes later they approached the shell of a burned-out VW.

"The cabin's not far." He pulled in beside the Volkswagen and killed the engine.

"It's pretty here," she said as he got out.

Billy reached inside and took the loaded Wingmaster, then pulled out the ammo box and methodically began to stuff his pockets with shells.

She opened her door and emerged, then stared about. "Where are we going?"

"Not we. *I'm* going to take a look at the cabin."

"Then *I'm* tagging along. No way I'm staying here." She hung her purse from her shoulder. "It's not pretty anymore. It's damned creepy, and there's a terrible odor."

"Dammit, Leslie, there may be trouble."

She gave a single derisive snort.

Billy sighed helplessly. "At least keep quiet and stay behind me."

"Okay," she said, pushing her glasses firmly into place with a forefinger.

As they passed the VW, the acrid smell grew worse—one he'd not sensed in a long time. When he peered inside and his brain registered what was there, his face drooped.

"My God," she whispered at the sight of the charred corpses.

"Let's get out of here," he said firmly.

She didn't argue. "We've got to get back and contact the police."

Then he heard the familiar sounds of the Suburban's engine as it labored down the trail.

"Here!" Billy said. He handed her the shotgun and bolted for the Jeep. As quickly as he was inside, he started up and rammed forward, past the Volkswagen into a bank of foliage, not caring that he ran over a few bushes in his path. He wedged the vehicle in a thicket, out of plain view, then shut off the ignition and scrambled out.

"Come on!" He took the shotgun and pulled her along, hurrying faster as she gained her balance and ran behind him. When they were well out of sight, he slowed, then listened as the Suburban's engine stopped and idled.

"He's found the Jeep," he said in a low voice.

The Suburban's engine shut off and he heard a voice, then the whisper of a radio response.

A single shot rang out, and Leslie grasped his arm. "What's he shooting at?"

"I think he just killed Mr. Hertz's Jeep. We're going to have to evade him. If you'll listen and do everything I say, we can do it."

She nodded, breathless.

"Step where I do, and don't look at anything but my feet."

Billy continued in the direction of the cabin, scanning the foliage, which was so thick they could not see more than a few feet in any direction.

"I don't hear him," Leslie whispered.

He continued until they came to the edge of the clearing. The cabin was deserted and fallen in. So much for finding someone living there.

"Wait here," he said. "After I've checked it out I'll wave, and you come running."

He took a deep breath and walked slowly forward, wishing he knew what the hell was going on. The sight of the bodies had shaken him.

Leslie sneezed, and when he looked back she gave him an apologetic look.

Billy heard a rustle in the brush from another direction, then a rabbit jumped up and darted past. He went on, nerves a-tingle, wishing he was as alert and woodwise as he'd been as a younger man. He heard a slight noise and looked back once more.

Leslie held her hand over her face, turning red as she suppressed another sneeze.

"Don't move!" The voice came from beyond Leslie. The brown-haired man from the Suburban appeared nervous, and aimed his Kalishnikov assault rifle directly at Leslie's chest.

Jaeger had docked his oars as they passed the aircraft's tail. Now they waited for word from Webb after he'd disabled the Jeep he'd found on the trail.

The radio sounded: *"I've got them."* Webb voice was nervous. *"They went to the clearing."*

"There are just the two?"

"Yeah."

"Armed?"

"He was carrying a shotgun."

"Bring it and them to the camp. If they resist, shoot them."

He stowed the radio, looking thoughtful, then glanced at Paula. "Get in the water."

She felt a moment of panic. "I'm not a good swimmer."

"Except to help row back to shore, I no longer need you. If you give the slightest trouble, I'll kill you and go on alone."

Paula stared back for a moment's hesitation, then rose and slipped over the side, and shuddered violently at the shock of the ice-cold water.

Jaeger stripped off his clothing, stowed it, then eased in beside her. He held up the rope tether so she could see he had it, then took a breath and went under.

Paula quickly followed, lest she be strangled. Under the surface Jaeger was frog-kicking downward, and she awkwardly mimicked him. He paused at the open hatch for the few seconds required to loop the rope about the hinge, gave it a tug, and disappeared inside.

She waited, sculling water, knowing it could not be long, for her endurance had never been memorable. And waited longer yet, now praying he would find the folder quickly. It seemed forever and her lungs had begun to ache, but he still did not reappear.

Hurry! Paula's mind cried desperately, but there was no sign of him.

She began to claw at the noose then, for she would soon drown . . . and then stupidly tried to scream. Water rushed into her mouth, and she fought the urge to swallow, thrashing wildly, knowing she was dying, not noticing the naked form that passed by.

Her mind was becoming foggy when the noose became taut, and it was no longer a matter of drowning but one of being strangled as she was yanked harshly upward. She clasped her hands about the rope—and was drawn violently again, like a fish being landed.

Paula burst to the surface, gagging for air, still unable to breathe, for she was strangled by the noose. Hands grasped her roughly and pulled her into the raft, then loosened the rope. She desperately sucked in air, but after only a partial breath bitter bilge rose inside her stomach.

As she began to vomit into the floor of the raft, Jaeger cursed her, then grasped her hair and dragged her to the side. She poised there and heaved in great spasms, gushing volumes of water through her mouth and nose. After a single long breath, the outpour of liquid began anew.

He ignored her as he sat nearby, observing something in his hand.

"Thank you," Paula finally gasped, for he'd saved her life.

He roughly dragged her forward and shoved her into position. "Row," he said tersely, and she realized that was the only reason she'd been spared.

25

11:00 A.M.—The Camp

Charbonneau stood by his tent, observing the unhappy man and woman brought into the camp. Webb carried two weapons, his own and a slide-action shotgun.

"No problems?" Simon asked, observing the two new hostages.

"Not this time," said Webb, but he released a breath of relief as he propped the shotgun against a nearby tree.

"Who are they?"

"I just brought 'em in. We didn't stop for coffee," Webb said insolently, then grinned at his humor and called Jaeger over the radio.

"I'll be there shortly," Jaeger's voice rasped.

Simon grabbed the radio from Webb. "Did you find the brief?"

"I have a leather folder that matches the description. You can open it when I get there."

Charbonneau laughed exuberantly. "He's got it," he announced to Webb.

"Good. I'm ready to get out of this damned place."

The woman who had just arrived was looking about inquisitively, then frowned as she observed Frank and Katy Dubois. "Billy?" she asked. "Is that them?"

"Frank Dubois and his daughter."

Charbonneau didn't like the outrage in the man's eyes as he observed the battered girl. "Tie them," he said to Webb.

"Be my guest," Webb said. "I'm tired."

"Tie them!" Simon demanded, his voice rising.

Webb sighed, then searched around until he found a rope. Charbonneau held the rifle as Webb bound the man to the same tree Paula had been tethered to the previous night.

"The woman too," Simon said.

Webb gave him an exasperated grimace, then marched over and removed her glasses and tossed them into the forest.

"I can't see," she said, and blinked about blindly.

"That's the idea." Webb shoved her toward Dubois and his daughter. "I don't think Jaeger's got long-range plans for them anyway," he told Charbonneau.

"Find out who they are."

"Jesus, you're bossy," Webb said, but he went through the bound man's wallet. "William R. Bowes," he muttered, and Charbonneau remembered it was the name of the pilot who had sighted the survivors. Then Webb went through the woman's purse and identified her as Leslie A. Rocklin.

Jaeger entered the camp with Paula, who collapsed, exhausted, beside her husband and daughter.

Simon's heart beat faster as the Hunter approached him—faster yet as the Hunter smiled and thrust a zippered folder into his hands. Charbonneau hardly breathed as he examined it. The exterior leather had dried during the voyage from the middle of the lake. He slowly turned it and found it to be of good quality.

Simon's fingers trembled as he repositioned, then carefully began to unzip it.

Two folds of overlapping soft plastic—yellow in color—protected the interior. If moisture had seeped in during the week it had been submerged, the document would be soaked, perhaps rendered unreadable. He carefully parted the plastic and stared.

A feeling of numbness crept over him.

Jaeger was standing beside Webb, lips pursed and blue eyes brooding as he looked on.

"It's here," Simon said, hardly trusting his voice.

The first pages were a list of contents, showing color-number codes—with the country and major industry each stood for in parentheses. Charbonneau slowly leafed through the brief. Together, the papers in his grasp revealed the Weyland Foundation's worldwide covert operations. Key officers were listed by name and position, of individual firms and entire industries. Some were national treasures such as airlines and railroads. Most were massive corporations that provided the fabric and lifebloods of countries. Numbers were shown: production levels at onset and milestones achieved. When they were passed to their man in Washington, and from him to the press, the foundation would be emasculated.

There was a second section of the brief, with codes assigned to investigations of the leaders of nations. Simon found the one he searched for and paused.

El Soleil. Colonel Salvator DiPalma. The brief listed the men on the board of governors of El Banco del Soleil Eterne who worked for his great-uncle, and Simon felt a flood of outrage. Two of the eight were providing information to the Weyland Foundation, as were a number of Argentinean politicians who'd been believed to be trusted friends.

The investigation had been in progress for the past seven months and was approaching culmination. There were six pages describing El Soleil's most secret programs. The disposition of the Bolivar missiles and details of the weapons programs were known. The master plan to gain control of Argentina was detailed, but they did not understand the last two *truenos*. Most important, they knew nothing about the final peal of thunder, the trailer in San Rafael.

The fact that a high American official had been paid off by El Soleil was suspected, but they did not know the identify or high position of their man in Washington.

A tentative plan of action to stop the colonel, and El Soleil, was attached. The president of Argentina, as well as key officials of the World Bank and finance ministers of the major industrialized nations, would be provided documented proof. The colonel would be exposed, as would the activities of El Soleil. Governments would seize their assets.

All of that was to happen in two weeks, when the Weyland Foundation investigation was completed—but *none* of it would occur. Tomorrow the American president and the foundation would be reeling when selected contents of the folder in his hand were reprinted in the *Washington Post*. The fifth *trueno* would quickly follow, and their warnings would be lost in the thunder of the worst man-made tragedy in American history.

The president of Argentina and the leading candidates would be killed. At the same time the agents of the Weyland Foundation and the turncoats within El Soleil would be eliminated, for they were shown by name, position, and location. The list was extensive and complete.

No one would be left in their way. By the time anyone suspected, it would be over.

"Is it what you wanted?" Jaeger asked.

"Even more than I'd hoped." Charbonneau looked up, smiling, for his future within El Soleil was assured. "They don't know about the final *trueno,* Jaeger."

"Then it's time to finish here."

A chord stirred within Simon Charbonneau. He looked at the pallet where Frank Dubois lay unconscious, and at the woman who crouched beside him.

Jaeger followed his eyes, then smiled. "When you're done with her, I'll dispose of them."

Did he dare to try? Simon carefully rezippered the folder, then leaned back and laughed aloud, letting his exuberance bubble. A celebration was indeed in order.

He walked jauntily toward the dying man's pallet, where the women were gathered, then stared down at Paula Dubois. She was a lovely woman, of obvious refinement. When the crisis was over, he decided to turn his attention to finding one. Buying one, more accurately, for that was how men of wealth acquired such toys. Perhaps he would discover one as loyal as Paula Dubois had been to her husband. His doubts that he would be able to perform sexually had melted away. Even now he felt himself growing hard.

The new woman, Leslie Rocklin, cringed, and the daughter remained curled in her fetal ball. All were his for the taking, but he wanted only one of them.

"You got the folder," Paula said, her expression and eyes neutral.

"Yes, thank you." He knelt and removed the noose from her neck, then cast it aside.

Her eyes shifted to Jaeger, and she gave a tiny nod of confirmation. "You're not going to release us." It was a statement, not a question, but her voice remained calm.

"Of course you'll be released." Simon wanted Paula Dubois' cooperation in what he was about to prove, both to her and to himself. "There's just one more condition. A tiny sacrifice for the safety of your husband and daughter. Please join me in my tent, Mrs. Dubois." Charbonneau felt himself stirring even more. It had *never* been like this.

Paula Dubois looked at her husband, whose breathing had diminished to tiny quivers of his chest, and reached out to touch his cheek. "No, Mr. Charbonneau. I've done a treacherous thing by telling you about the folder. Anything more will be taken by force."

Simon was surprised. "Do you want me to give your daughter to Jaeger?"

"I despise you and him equally. No, you even more, for you're the cause of our suffering and he's only a tool. You were aroused when my daughter was attacked. The look on your face was apparent. You are no man. You're a despicable coward, and you'll never be anything more."

It was not going at all as he'd intended. Simon cautiously reached for her hand.

Paula Dubois' voice remained low and purposeful. "I'll scratch and fight you, Mr. Charbonneau. You'll have to force yourself upon me, and perhaps you'll succeed. But that is the only way you will have me."

Simon withdrew his hand, the damage to his fragile ego done. "We'll see," he told her, his high voice quavering with shame and anger. "After you've been subdued by Jaeger, you'll be *begging* for me to take you."

"Never," she whispered, and began to stroke her husband's face with the gentle hand. "It won't be long," she told the immobile man beside her.

Paula Dubois' daughter looked up then, staring at the men as if she'd just realized they were there.

Simon turned to Jaeger. "Finish them," he hissed angrily, and stepped back. He no longer wanted Paula. She'd become common in his eyes.

The Hunter picked up the shotgun that had been taken from the man named Bowes. He stepped forward, and grasped and examined the bound man's jacket.

"The same company," he said. "Do you know a man named Anderson?"

Bowes did not respond, just stared back evenly.

"I killed him," he gloated, "like I'm about to kill you."

"Untie me," Bowes said evenly. "Then we'll see how tough you are."

"You wouldn't last a minute, old man." Jaeger stepped back, grasped the shotgun by its barrel, and swung hard. There was a meaty thump as the stock struck Bowes' chest. The older man released a groan, and a tortured expression grew on his face as he slowly sagged in the ropes.

The woman captured with Bowes could not see clearly,

but well enough to know what had happened. She screamed in horror.

Jaeger laughed lightly, then grasped Bowes roughly by the hair and lifted his head. "How does it feel to die, old man?" he asked, but Bowes only gasped, desperately trying to draw air into his broken chest.

The Hunter smirked as he stepped back, lifted the shotgun into a batter's stance, and drew back to swing again. The weapon was in motion when a shot rang out from the forest, and the shotgun was torn from the Hunter's hands. He turned, mouth opened with surprise.

Charbonneau cried out in terror, then recovered his wits sufficiently to turn and scramble into the forest. Jaeger and Webb dove in different directions.

Link hobbled toward the camp, the now empty carbine clutched in his hand, praying they'd be too shaken to remember that he was out of bullets. The men had scattered, two diving behind tents while the third fled into the forest.

He'd been surprised when he'd hobbled close enough to observe the camp—and watched the effeminate man handling the brown folder he'd last noticed in the airplane—because he had seen Billy Bowes bound to a tree.

Then he'd seen Paula, brutalized, and Katy huddling in shock, and if he had allowed it, rage would have consumed him. Yet he'd also noticed that while Frank Dubois lay very still, the side of his face puffed and blue, his friend still lived—and although Paula and Katy might be beaten and subdued, they were also alive. For those blessings, Link had been grateful as he'd painfully crept closer, determined to kill Jaeger, who posed the greatest threat.

He'd still been too distant for a sure shot when Jaeger gripped the shotgun and swung the stock violently into Billy's chest. No man could withstand a second blow, so he'd aimed and fired hastily, and missed Jaeger for a second time.

Link limped toward the Kalishnikov rifle thirty feet distant, abandoned by Webb as he'd fled. *Hurry!* his mind cried, but he'd sapped his reserve of energy and could not go faster.

"Get down!" Link yelled hoarsely to the others as he neared the rifle, for he intended to spray bullets wildly into the surrounding brush. A woman he didn't know stood, then hurried toward Billy. "Down!" he repeated.

"Kill Dubois!" squealed a high voice from the forest.

He reached the weapon and dropped to a knee to retrieve it, then sensed movement—and chanced a glance. Jaeger was only a dozen feet away, observing calmly, his oversized rifle raised to his shoulder. The big man walked forward, expressionless.

Link's hand was poised over the AK-47, frozen there.

"Forget it, Anderson," Jaeger said. He was closer, the muzzle of his big magnum trained squarely. "Stand up," Jaeger ordered.

Lincoln Anderson staggered wearily as he regained his feet, and Webb and the effeminate man cautiously filtered out of the trees.

A low chuckle sounded. The big man called Jaeger, whose abilities he'd grown to respect the most, stepped closer. The muzzle of the huge rifle was inches from Link's face.

"Couldn't resist coming back, could you?" said Jaeger. His accent was pronounced.

Link looked past him. The woman had loosened Billy Bowes' ropes, and he'd collapsed at the base of the tree. He dully wondered if the chief pilot was alive.

The effeminate man called Charbonneau was at Jaeger's heels. "Kill Dubois," he squealed in a high tone.

"We'll kill all of them," Jaeger responded.

Link's mind raced, searching for any weakness—*anything* to delay the inevitable—for when he died, so did the chances of the others. He remembered the words the big man had left on the tree poster.

"I read your message, Jaeger," he said. "You're afraid of me."

The big man smiled. "I pulled you in, Anderson. I placed the bait and you came."

"You look like you've been in a fire," Link taunted as the man's finger moved within the trigger guard. "I'm better than you, Jaeger.

"You had the women, and I took them. Now we've got what we came for. You're better? I don't think so." Jaeger's voice lowered. "When their throats are cut, the women will thrash around. They'll be alive, and feel the energy drain away as their muscles convulse. I've seen it before ... when I defeated other men and killed their women."

The finger began to curl.

The sound was loud in Link's ears, and an involuntary, violent shudder trembled through his torso. Then he stared in deafened amazement, hardly believing as Jaeger grasped at a bloody hip, his burned face distorted as he bellowed with pain.

Sound and comprehension were slow in returning.

Another shotgun blast boomed, that one barely missing the big man, who clutched his rifle desperately and dragged it behind as he lurched toward the safety of the forest.

Billy Bowes had reached the shotgun, or the woman had brought it to him. Now he painfully swung the shotgun's barrel.

Link grabbed blindly for the AK-47 at his feet, and—as his senses returned sufficiently to allow it—began to look for Jaeger and Charbonneau. All the while Billy covered him, swinging the shotgun's muzzle as the woman clung to him.

Clopping sounds filled the air. Faint at first but growing even louder.

Helicopters!

Hurry! Link prayed. He saw movement in the corner of an eye, whirled, and blindly fired three rounds into the forest.

Billy followed his lead and blasted with the shotgun. "Out of shells," he gasped after the third one, and the shotgun fell from his hands. He leaned onto the woman at his side, groaned, and slipped to the earth.

Link moved to the edge of the forest, scanning carefully and trying to take everything in. When he'd reasoned that no one was there, he turned back—wondering if Charbonneau or Webb might be closer, perhaps crouching behind the tents.

"They all went the same way," Paula said in a wooden voice that displayed no fear. "Away from the lake."

He'd settled his eyes upon Frank when an explosion sounded, and a hole appeared in the tent not two inches over his friend's head. Link spun about, looking hard, knowing only Jaeger's gun could have made the tremendous roar, yet he could see no sign of him.

Link lifted and fired into the brush where Jaeger had

gone, and when he heard the rustling of someone retreating, he fired again.

A helicopter passed overhead, then another and yet another, so low they blew loose debris around the camp, and Link could no longer hear the subtle sounds such as Jaeger, Webb, and Charbonneau might make in the forest.

Watch my six o'clock, he and Frank had once solemnly agreed in the room they'd shared, sealing the vow with a shot of whiskey, *and I'll watch yours.*

The Dubois family had survived, yet it was obvious that Jaeger still wanted Frank dead. Link continued to scan the foliage, the rifle to his shoulder, moving the muzzle as he searched.

Jaeger was still a threat. He must find and kill him.

The helicopters began to circle, then to land in the clearing, which was not far.

"Jaeger!" Link bellowed to the forest over the noisy din.

A loudspeaker sounded from an unseen location, telling everyone to put down their weapons. A moment later men began to scurry into the camp with FBI, U.S. MARSHAL and STATE POLICE stenciled on bulletproof vests and olive drab jackets. One aimed his weapon and shouted for Link to drop his rifle.

He did as told.

Paula Dubois stood protectively over Frank, looking about with wary eyes. Her blouse was ripped and her bruised breasts were exposed, but she seemed not to care. Katy clutched fast to her mother's hand—a shell of the vivacious girl Link remembered.

Where was Jaeger!

A lean Hispanic man approached him warily, his face taut, pistol held with the muzzle raised but ready. He looked at a photograph, then peered at him. "Anderson?"

"Yeah." Link observed Billy, who appeared to be unconscious. He looked again at Frank Dubois, and at Paula who was still crouched protectively over him, glaring fiercely about.

"I'm Marshal Rodriguez." The lean man was regarding Link. "We heard gunfire."

"There are three of them. Jaeger, Webb, and Charbonneau. They got away." He remembered something. "They've got a vehicle parked north of the lake. They'll probably try to reach it."

Rodriguez spoke on his radio and dispatched a helicopter. Then he stared in amazement at the woman beside Billy Bowes. "Leslie?"

"He needs help!" she cried.

"Get the medics over here," Rodriguez yelled in a rough voice.

"He's not the only one," Link said in a voice drained of passion and energy. "That's the Dubois family by the tent there. Frank's badly injured, and the women have been harmed."

A team member wearing a red cross band on his arm knelt over Billy. "He's having trouble breathing. We'd better get him out."

"Check out the family," Rodriguez told other medics.

Link watched as they positioned Billy Bowes onto a litter. The woman beside him turned to Rodriguez. "I can't see without my glasses, Joe. They took them." She looked about, squinting. "I've got another pair in my purse. It's here somewhere." She went to search.

Medics carefully loaded Frank Dubois onto a second litter and carried him toward the helicopters. Katy followed, stumbling and unsure as a corpsman led her with a firm grasp on her arm. Paula went last, still hovering protectively and looking about with alert eyes.

Lincoln Anderson watched, not allowing himself to lower his guard.

Rodriguez motioned. "There were supposed to be two more from the airplane."

"The guard and flight attendant died in the collision. Frank and I set the Gulfstream down in the lake next to a small island. Their bodies are inside." He knelt and picked up the AK-47, but the marshal pried it from his grasp and passed it to a nearby agent.

"I've got to find Jaeger," Link said in a low, strained voice. "He's dangerous."

"We'll deal with him." He observed the swollen arm and bloody bandage on his leg. "We'd better get you into town."

Link shook his head. "I'll stay until you've caught them."

Joe Rodriguez answered a radio call. They'd found vehicles. A Suburban—also a Jeep Cherokee and a burned-out Volkswagen farther north on the path.

"Have them look in the VW," Link said, and Rodriguez

relayed the order. A moment later he was told about the charred bodies.

Rodriguez eyed Link questioningly.

"A couple of kids. I saw them after the fire was set. I think Jaeger did it."

"He's one of the kidnappers?"

"Yeah." Link looked at him. "They were after something." His voice failed him. He took a breath and continued with difficulty. "The big guy . . . Jaeger . . . still wants to kill Frank Dubois. You can't . . . let him escape."

"We'll find him."

An FBI agent came over. "The chopper pilots still haven't found anyone out there."

"They can't be far. Tell 'em to keep looking," said Rodriguez, and the message was relayed.

A state trooper walked out of the trees. "We've found a blood trail. One of 'em's hit."

"That's Jaeger," Link said. "Billy shot him." Link grew giddy, as if none of it was real. Dark spots danced gaily before his eyes.

The woman called Leslie had found her glasses. "Where's Billy?" she asked Rodriguez.

"He went out on the helicopter, Les. They're flying him to the hospital with the family."

She huffed a sad breath, then looked around before heading for a group of agents.

"Leslie's a reporter," Joe told Link. "There are things I don't want you to mention around her. One of those is a brown leather folder. Do you know where it is?"

"It was in the airplane. Now Charbonneau has it."

"You mentioned him."

"I think he was the reason they were here. He wanted the leather folder, and the others were along to help him get it."

"What does he look like?"

"Slight, blond hair, light complexion. Flutters his hands like a woman."

Rodriguez broadcast for everyone to be on the lookout for the man and to retrieve whatever he was carrying.

"How about the others?" Rodriguez asked.

Link described them, then added: "Jaeger's good in the forest. He's ruthless and dangerous." He knew he was babbling, but did not care.

Joe Rodriguez hailed a medic. "Check him over," he said.

"We've got to find Jaeger," Link said impatiently as the medic helped him out of the dirt-laden jacket, then put a cuff about his upper arm to take a reading.

Another man joined them. Rodriguez introduced him as a regional FBI director, and asked Link to go over everything he knew about the situation.

"You can't let them get away," Link said doggedly.

The regional director nodded toward the valley. "There's more than fifty men out there in helicopters, looking for them. We'll get more if necessary."

Rodriguez agreed. "No one's going to get away, even if we have to bring in the National Guard."

"Damn," whispered the medic, as if he'd made an error. He checked the cuff's placement, reinflated it, and took another reading.

The woman reporter came over. "Did you say the Guard will be coming, Joe?"

"Whatever it takes," said Rodriguez. "We've alerted them and they're standing by."

She regarded Link. "I'm Leslie Rocklin, a close friend of Billy's. He talked a lot about you, like you're special. Now I understand why."

Leslie swayed in his vision, and Link leaned against the medic for support.

She looked at Rodriguez. "Is there any word on Billy's condition?"

"It'll be awhile, Les." His voice was gentle. "You'd best take the next helicopter."

"I'm not *about* to leave. There's a story here and I've gone through hell to get it." She motioned toward the FBI agents and state troopers. "They won't talk to me, Joe."

"They're not supposed to."

Another helicopter landed at the clearing, drowning out their conversation. When the din subsided, Rodriguez yelled to one of his men. "Anything yet?"

"The chopper pilots say there's still no sign of them," the agent called back.

The medic taking his second reading suddenly yelled for a stretcher, then grasped Link to support him better and shook his head at Joe Rodriguez. "Back off, Marshal."

"I've only got a couple more questions."

"Damn it, back off! If I don't get him to Boise right away, he's dead. There's no blood left in him."

Part III

The Fifth Trueno

26

WEDNESDAY, JUNE 19

11:00 A.M.—Boise

Five days had passed since the confrontation in the valley, and Leslie was still trying to put the picture together. While the pieces didn't fit smoothly, it all went *something* like this:

After questioning Billy, Joe Rodriguez had taken a helicopter to the lake for a look. Finding nothing obvious at the camp, they'd flown across the valley to investigate a fire and spotted a vehicle, and two men in the forest wearing camouflage and carrying rifles.

Joe had reasoned that they were members of the Idaho Citizen's Militia, a group of generally harmless military-gun addicts who gathered in the mountains to play soldier and complain about the government, although a call to their self-proclaimed colonel had brought angry denial. After talking it over with his bosses at the Justice Department, Joe had gathered a small team of federal and state law enforcement personnel, including a couple of FBI negotiating specialists, to go out and investigate.

He'd planned the operation at the same time Leslie and Billy were commiserating that no one believed them, and deciding to drive to the lake.

Before they'd launched the following morning, a startling report had arrived from the National Crime Information Center. A fingerprint lifted from an empty tin of chocolate found at the lake had been identified as that of Paula Dubois. The nature of the operation had immediately changed. Joe had hastily added helicopters and lawmen, and the task force had gone out like a military airborne assault. The pilots had gone in low and fast, using terrain-masking and noise-suppression techniques so they'd not be discovered prematurely.

Joe's concern had been warranted; they'd landed just in time.

Leslie had put all that together, *but none of it had been printed*.

When Link Anderson had been flown to the Boise hospital, Leslie had also been taken out, despite her loud objections. After checking on Billy, she'd hurried to the newspaper and marched into the owner's office. When she'd explained what had happened, he'd been appalled.

"*Now* can I write it?" she'd demanded.

He'd grinned at the display of Rocklin tenacity. "Les, you can banner it with I WAS RIGHT in hundred-point type. Just don't go chasing off like that again without telling someone."

An hour later, as she'd been finishing the lead-in to her story, four "big city lawyers" trooped into the owner's office. When they'd left he'd called her back in and displayed an embarrassed smile.

Leslie had guessed what was coming and pointed angrily. "Two of those characters stole my damned film in Salt Lake."

"They've, ah, admitted the Dubois family was on the Gulfstream."

"That's charitable of them. The whole world knows now. Did they tell you about the men who wanted to kill us all?"

The owner looked uneasy, like a child who'd just been visited by the toughest kids on the block. "The foundation people are asking us not to mention the kidnappers and show it as a normal rescue effort."

"The men out there weren't kidnappers. They were going to *kill* us, not hold us for ransom. Damn it, there's a big story here."

"They asked for our cooperation and I agreed. No speculation until it's over."

Leslie had argued, but in the end had no choice but to either go along or quit. She was promised the story when it broke, which should not be long. Joe Rodriguez had sealed off the valley and was calling in two hundred members of the Idaho National Guard, who would call it a "joint exercise." He felt the kidnappers would be quickly found and brought to justice.

She'd ended up with six column inches of lead-in on page one, and twenty more on page ten: a story about the

Gulfstream and Cessna midair collision, followed by a crash landing in the wilderness lake and hardships faced by the family. There was no mention of the Dubois' terror, the hostage-takers, or even of the bodies she'd seen in the burned Volkswagen bug, and Leslie chafed under the restraints.

Her story about the family's survival, incomplete though it was, was picked up by most of the national media. When Mort Yoder had gotten through to congratulate her, he'd said her article was informative and concise. She'd wanted to tell him there was something much bigger at work, but did not.

Since the family's return, several high-ranking government officials had visited Boise, and Leslie had been granted an interview with the secretary of state, who was a personal friend of the badly injured Frank Dubois. She'd found Vernon Calico easy to talk with, as long as she listened a lot. He'd been raised on a small ranch near Abilene, in west Texas, and tried to come off as a colorful, down-home Westerner. But Leslie had lived most of her life around the real thing, and Calico couldn't shake what he'd become, which was a grandstanding Washington politician. She'd run into those before too, and felt it was like Billy had told her—there must be something in the Washington water to make them obnoxious.

That day she'd returned to the valley in a government helicopter with an FBI agent on Joe Rodriguez's task force. He'd had her retrace the route she and Billy had driven, and show where Webb had captured them. He'd then asked if she'd heard them mention hiding places, but of course she had not. Leslie had been amazed by the numbers of agents, police, and National Guardsmen in the valley. Bulldozers and graders were busily improving old roads and putting in new ones, and there'd been an armada of HUM-V's and armored personnel carriers. Swarms of Idaho National Guard helicopters patrolled overhead.

The evening after Link Anderson had been brought out, his pretty fiancée had joined him from Montana, overjoyed that he'd been found alive. After he'd rested for a few twelve-hour stretches and a gallon or so of whole blood had been transfused, they'd been flown to Washington in an Executive Connections jet.

Immediately after the Dubois family had been examined,

a staff of surgeons, internists, psychologists, nurses, medical technicians, and physical therapists—Leslie had learned there were more than two dozen of them—were flown in from various medical centers and set up shop in a professional medical building two blocks from the hospital. An army of construction workers had worked night and day to reconfigure the building with living facilities and a state-of-the-art operating theater.

The family had remained in the hospital for three days, until Paula and Cyril Weyland had made short statements to the media, with Marshal José "Joe" Rodriguez and the district director of the FBI in attendance. Tom Oliver of the FAA had tried to be part of it, but the U.S. Marshal's Office controlled the list. Paula had generalized the details of their ordeal. Afterward, she'd refused to take questions and had withdrawn into the hospital. Cyril Weyland had added nothing except how pleased he was that his grandson and his family had been found alive.

Immediately afterward they'd been relocated and all contact with the outside world severed.

During a phone call the previous day, Link had told her the Weyland Foundation had called off their litigation, and he'd reasoned that Paula Dubois might also be able to help with the government inquiry, since she'd overheard her husband authorize the change in the contract. Yet when Link tried to phone her, he'd been told she wasn't taking calls.

Leslie had said she was faring no better. She'd crouched beside Paula and Katy and shared their terror, but that short period of contact had been her last. Now a host of security guards ensured that the medical building was as impenetrable as Fort Knox, and they were refusing all calls.

As she started to leave her desk, Link phoned again. "Billy just called Henry and said he'll be ready to go to work in a couple of days."

"That's ridiculous," Leslie snorted. Billy had suffered several broken ribs, and most of the organs in his chest were bruised.

"How's he really doing?" Link asked.

"He's walking some, but only a few steps at a time. There's a chance he'll be released from the hospital in the morning, but I want him right here where I can keep an eye on him."

"I agree. Tell him to stay in Boise and relax for a while."

"You bet," she said happily.

Leslie was in Billy's hospital room, telling him about the conversation with Link. She dropped by several times a day.

"I ought to be with them," he complained.

"No, you ought to do what Link said. When you're released, I'll take you home so you can be my sex slave."

As he began to grin, Leslie glanced at her watch. "I've gotta go." She'd told him she intended to have lunch with a police lieutenant who had provided good leads in the past.

"Love you," she said happily, gave him a smooch, and left. She hadn't dared tell Billy the policeman friend was still conniving to get into her L'Eggs, using the excuse that he had something she'd want to hear. The Boise Police disdained the way the FBI agents—they called them "fucking fibs"—and other feds interfered with local matters, and she hoped she might benefit from the squabble.

When she met him at the restaurant, the lieutenant was nervous, and as soon as they took their seats, he wanted her promise not to reveal her source.

"I won't." She doubted he had anything she didn't already know.

He started by telling her there was a large-scale manhunt underway in the same valley where the Dubois family had been found, and she feigned ignorance.

"Who are they looking for?" she asked.

"Three men. The fibs have computer composite drawings. No photographs, so I don't think they have positive ID yet. There's a big guy, a stocky one, and a wimpy character."

He remained brooding as they ordered, then as they waited.

"I thought you'd be more interested, Les. They've got troopers, fibs, government spooks, and National Guardsmen scouring the whole valley for those guys."

By the time the waitress delivered their sandwiches, she'd grown impatient, for there seemed to be nothing new.

"There's something else." He gave her an uneasy look. "They're searching for a brown leather folder. If they find it, no one's supposed to open it, just bring it in without looking."

Leslie remembered that Charbonneau had been handling something like that, but she hadn't been able to see clearly without her eyeglasses.

"If all of this is so secret, how did you learn about it?"

"I've been getting all the briefings. Twenty of us on the Boise P.D. have been named as augmentees. I'll be going out there in the next couple of days to replace one of their shift supervisors."

Leslie finished her sandwich, fended off his invitation to drop by his place for a drink, and returned to her desk at the newspaper, wondering if anything he'd told her was relevant.

She phoned Joe Rodriguez's office, hoping he wasn't at the manhunt, and found him in.

"I read your story this morning, Les. Another good one."

More half-truths, she thought angrily. "Remember when you said to call you if I remembered anything? Well, I just did. The blond guy out there had something in his hand."

He hesitated too long. "Oh, yeah?"

"One of those zip-up leather folders. He seemed pleased by whatever was inside."

"I see."

"Tell me something, Joe. Was it his, or did he get it from the Duboises?"

He'd had time to recover. "Got me, Les."

"I think maybe it was what they were really after." She changed her tone then, as if she was thinking something over. "Perhaps I should include something about it in tomorrow's article. One of our readers might come up with an answer."

Joe's tone was abrupt. "I've got to go, Les. Call again if you think of anything more."

Leslie hung up and then waited. It was only twenty minutes before two "big city lawyers" appeared down the hall at the owner's door, wearing concerned expressions.

She was on to *something.* Both the Weyland Foundation and the authorities were hiding the real motive of the three fugitives, and it had something to do with the folder. But regardless of what she learned, there was no way they'd let her print it, and the fact was frustrating.

* * *

Cyril Weyland walked slowly down the hall, his aide on one side and Paula on the other, taking their time on the way to the conference room, where Marshal Joe Rodriguez would brief them on the latest news from the manhunt. They stopped to look in on Katy, found her sleeping peacefully, then went to Frank's room, where Paula rested her hand lightly on her husband's arm.

"I'm back," she said, keeping her voice light and cheerful. Frank was unresponsive, as he'd been since he'd been brought from the valley. Paula spoke to him often, repeating words of devotion, praying he could somehow hear, and Cyril believed that he might; he'd heard of such things, and she'd told him how his grandson had periodically regained consciousness in the valley.

Sequestered in the converted medical building, Cyril Weyland spent much of his time reviewing the developments in the outside world. The revelations about the Weyland Foundation were dwindling, but there were still loud voices calling for congressional inquiries.

Fortunately, nothing had been written about the abuses Paula and Katy had suffered. Katy's physical condition was healing, but her mental scars ran deep. Her recollections of the valley remained dim, as if part of a dream, and she remembered nothing about the assault. The psychologists called the block an obstacle to treatment, but Paula refused to allow them to delve.

Paula's injuries—mostly abrasions and livid bruises on her breasts—were now more bothersome than serious, yet she too was scarred. Although she'd watched Frank slipping ever deeper into the coma, she was unable to accept the possibility of his imminent death. She and Frank had shared life so utterly that it seemed impossible that he'd not emerge safely with them. Yet while the surgeons had relieved the pressure on his brain, they were not hopeful.

"It's almost time," Cyril told Paula. "If you wish, we'll talk to the marshal and fill you in when you're done here."

She shook her head. "I'd like to attend." She leaned close and whispered words, and Cyril's heart ached as he heard the last ones: ". . . Don't leave me alone, darling." Paula cast a long look at the man she cherished, then turned and joined them in the hall.

The building was said to be secure, yet Cyril could not repress concern about his grandson's family. He too was endangered, but after ninety-two years of life, most of it productive and enjoyable, it would be presumptuous to ask for more.

During his visit, the attorney general had warned them that an informant who'd infiltrated an outcast, splinter group of the Idaho Citizen's Militia had overheard a plan to assassinate Cyril while he was visiting his grandson at the hospital. The attorney general felt the plot was due to the *Post*'s exposé.

The secretary of state had also visited, offering congratulations from the President that the Dubois family had been found, and his own condolences, for Frank was a personal friend. He'd been outraged at the actions of the kidnappers, and was adding the technical services of the State Department's Intelligence Bureau to the effort to find them.

Paula had told Vern Calico what Frank had revealed during lucid moments in the valley: that an official in his department had been bribed to help destroy the Weyland Foundation. The secretary had been dubious, but said he'd look into it. Then he'd turned to Cyril and asked for other particulars about the Argentinean investigation, but Weyland had not responded.

After he'd left, Cyril had called in the project leader for Scarlet 277. "No one mentioned the investigation," he said, "yet Vern Calico knew about it. Could Frank have told him?"

"It's unlikely. I'm sure he would have told us."

So Cyril was concerned about that too. He'd had the project officer brief Paula about Salvator DiPalma and the investigation in Argentina. From photographs she'd identified DiPalma's grand-nephew as the man she'd heard called Charbonneau, and Jaeger, the assassin who worked for El Soleil. That was when they'd realized that the family was in jeopardy not only from local rednecks, but also from Salvator DiPalma and his professional killers.

Weyland Foundation security people had already leased the medical building, but they'd moved the family much sooner than planned. Then they'd blocked all approaches so vehicles could not come too near, and limited their communications and visitors. The attorney general had told them Joe Rodriguez was trustworthy and would be their window into what was happening in the valley, so he became the only outsider with free access to the building.

When they entered the conference room, the project leader already was waiting. A moment after they'd taken their seats, a security guard escorted Marshal Rodriguez inside. It was unlikely that he could fathom the Weyland Foundation's status. All he knew was that he'd been told to cooperate by the attorney general, that there was executive branch involvement, and his requests for military support had been filled immediately.

Cyril greeted the marshal, then asked: "Is there anything new?"

"Only the telephone call from Leslie Rocklin that I called your people about."

"We spoke with the newspaper owner," said Cyril's aide. "He's cooperating."

Cyril cleared his throat. "Since Miss Rocklin was one of those who helped save my grandson and his family, I'd like to ensure that she's rewarded."

"That would be nice," said Rodriguez. "Her father left a lot of debts, and she's about to lose the Rocklin home, which is one of our local historical landmarks."

Paula spoke. "She's been discreet about Katy's and my privacy."

Cyril nodded. "She'll be given information before other journalists. Not yet, though."

"How about the search?" the project leader asked Rodriguez.

"So far we've found no sign of either the men or the folder."

"You've told the searchers to be careful?"

Rodriguez nodded. "From what Anderson told us, Jaeger's the dangerous one. We've cautioned our men that he's armed and good in the forest."

"Exceptionally good," said Paula. She did not betray her bitterness, although Jaeger had savaged her husband and brutally assaulted her daughter.

Cyril asked the question he had a dozen times. "Do you have any idea where they went?"

"Absolutely none. We used dogs, but they just led us down the valley. We've had aircraft with infrared scanners flying over the area from night one, and they've got a fix on every large animal in the valley. There are seven elk and a grizzly at the western end, and twenty-two sheep on the surrounding mountains, but we've detected no humans other than our own people. Although I don't understand how it could be, some very knowledgeable experts insist they got away that first day."

Cyril had learned that the search had begun efficiently, then had deteriorated as infighting broke out and misinformation had been bandied about—as if someone was purposefully interfering. "Which experts are insisting they got away?" he asked.

"State Department Intelligence."

"And what do you believe?" Cyril asked.

Rodriguez mused for a moment. "They're probably right. They have observation equipment and resources that aren't available to the rest of us."

"How much longer will you continue looking?"

"The expenses are mounting. We'll pull out of the valley by the weekend, unless you feel we should stay longer."

Cyril tried not to reveal his discouragement. "That will be left up to you."

"Then Friday I'm going to assume they've escaped and begin pulling out. We'll provide their composites to the media, so the networks can show the drawings on prime time. I still have faith that we'll find them."

"Anything else?"

"No, sir." Rodriguez rose to leave. "I'll let you know if we learn anything more."

"Thank you."

As the marshal flashed a smile and departed, the project leader for Scarlet 277 was called to the door and handed a covered paper. He returned to the table, reading the fax he'd been given, then looked up at Cyril with a grave expression.

"More troubling news from Argentina," he said. "Two informants in Buenos Aires confirm that there's about to be another *trueno*. The *final* thunder, they call it. They're saying it's imminent, and it's going to occur in California."

"How will this one be different from the others?" asked Paula.

"They're talking about a disaster of immense proportions."

"How could they know something terrible is about to happen?"

"Because they'll create it." As the project leader told Paula about other revelations from their investigation,

Cyril regarded the tabletop solemnly, feeling the weight of his years.

He turned to the aide. "Get the President on the telephone."

Five minutes later he was told that the President was indisposed.

"Tell them it's a matter of life and death," Cyril said.

He was asked to call back in an hour.

The White House

The President nodded to the man he'd summoned from his home, and picked up the receiver. "Hello, Cyril. I believe this is the first time we've spoken together."

"Yes, and I wouldn't do so now if the subject wasn't time-critical and important."

"My receptionist said it involved life and death." He paused. "Is this line secure?"

"My technicians have checked this end." Weyland took a breath. "Mr. President, I'm in receipt of information regarding a potential act of terrorism."

The President leaned forward. "Where?"

"All we've learned is it will occur in the near future, and that the location will be somewhere in the state of California."

The President frowned. "That's an awfully large area, Cyril. Ahh, what sort of terrorist act are you concerned about?"

"We're not sure. All we know is that it will be disastrous."

"I see. And just who do you believe's involved?"

Cyril Weyland proceeded more carefully. "A dissident group in Argentina has been working to overthrow the government. We'll tell you more in a few days, but since lives are at stake, as soon as I learned about this development I felt it was my duty to inform you."

"Certainly. You say they're from ... Argentina?" The President smiled.

"Yes."

"So ... what's your suggestion, Cyril?"

"Alert the FBI regional offices in California that something's about to happen. Perhaps they've heard something through their sources."

"But you don't know what it might be that's about to occur?"

"Only that it will be cataclysmic and newsworthy, and will happen very soon."

"I see." The President paused thoughtfully. "Thanks for your input, Cyril. I'll take the matter under advisement."

"The threat is real, Mr. President." Weyland's tone was an attempt at persuasion.

"Yes, I'm sure. If you learn something more definitive, please pass it along."

"I shall."

The President remembered something. "Is there any change in your grandson's condition?"

"No." Cyril Weyland's voice was sad.

The President hung up and regarded his visitor. "He's passing on more alarmist information. This time it's a disaster in California."

Vern Calico nodded. "The old coot's flipped his bucket. He mentioned Argentina?"

"Something about a group of dissidents there."

The secretary of state snorted. "My people in Buenos Aires say everything's going just fine with the election. If I was you, I'd distance myself from the Weyland Foundation 'bout as far as I could."

Boise

Cyril stared at the telephone for another moment, then at the group still gathered about the table. "He didn't believe me."

"Perhaps if we knew more answers," said the project leader.

"Frank had some of them," Paula said. "There at the last, when they captured us and took us to their camp, he mentioned the final *trueno,* then the person named Fay again, and said to tell Link."

"What did Link Anderson have to say?"

"I didn't have a chance to speak with him before he returned to Washington."

"Perhaps he'd be willing to help," Cyril said. They'd talked about bringing Link aboard.

"We've kept track of him," said the project leader, who referred to a notepad. "This morning he walked the perimeter of his parents' property, which is some twenty-five acres, and other than a pronounced limp, he showed no signs of his injuries. Tonight his fiancée will fly back to Montana, and in the morning he'll attend the flight attendant's funeral at Arlington."

"You've had him under observation?"

"The Hunter's the most dangerous assassin on El Soleil's payroll. With the possibility that he's escaped, we're concerned about the safety of everyone who was involved. That includes Mr. Bowes and Miss Rocklin as well as Lincoln Anderson."

The Valley

Webb despised the poorly ventilated, cold, and dark tunnel, which had begun as a natural cave in the first high rise of foothills of the Sawtooth Mountains. Miners searching for some mineral or other had extended and shored the cave, and the timbers inside were still sturdy.

Jaeger had found it when he'd traversed the hills, trying to block the survivors from reaching the mountains. The Hunter had discovered other mines in the valley, but this one was different. Foremost, it was not shown on the detailed map Jaeger had brought, and the mouth appeared like just another pile of rubble on the hillside. It was also well situated, high enough to observe the length and breadth of the valley, as well as the large lake a few miles northeast where the searchers were camped. Not even Charbonneau, the eternal pessimist, believed they could be discovered here.

The Hunter was crafty about such things, always looking for ways to escape should the worst occur. Like leaving the camp in the direction of the vehicles, then circling around on a confusing network of trails, staying in dense foliage while the authorities chased the bait.

The feeble sunlight that filtered from three small ventilation ports cast a constant gloom into the enclosure, and at night there was inky darkness, for Jaeger seldom allowed a flashlight to be turned on or a candle to be lighted. If one of them had to crawl to the low anteroom to use the rusted bucket left by the builders, they were forced to do it by feel and with the knowledge that a lookout was at the viewing port five feet away, listening to their grunts and splashes. The foul-smelling pail was emptied each day, when Webb squirmed as far as possible into the extreme of one of several crawlways that extended into the mountain, and the stench within the living space grew worse with each emptying. Drinking water was dipped from a pool at the end of another crawlway, but it was foul-tasting and Webb suspected the waste somehow drained there.

They'd resealed the tunnel opening with carefully placed stones. At its top was a niche with a removable rock, which Jaeger called the viewing port, and one of them—usually Webb—manned it continuously to keep track of the searchers. By day the lookout used binoculars to scan the valley. At night he watched their lights and listened for their sounds. Helicopters and aircraft were constantly overhead, and several times they'd seen troops nearby and heard dogs baying, but Jaeger felt it was unlikely they could find them. Their spoor had been thoroughly mixed with that of the survivors and themselves, and now by the military searchers.

Twice daily Webb cautiously pushed a wire antenna through one of the vent holes so they could monitor the latest news from the Boise talk-radio station. So far there was absolutely nothing about them or the manhunt, which seemed eerie.

They had two weapons in the sanctuary: Jaeger's magnum and the rifle Webb had brought. Simon had borne only the leather folder, cradling it as if it held rare rubies. Before, Webb had had only a vague idea of the folder's contents, but in the tunnel Charbonneau talked freely about it and other things that seemed bizarre. Like how his greatuncle would take over Argentina, and within a short period they'd become the dominant power in South America. Provided with a fantastic base of natural resources and proper determination, they would replace the United States' vacillating leadership in the hemisphere.

That was a bunch of bull to Webb, but it was the other thing, the big thunder that another group of Simon's people were about to set off, that frightened the pee out of him. A lot of Americans, likely more than a thousand, would die in a single, great conflagration.

Charbonneau also talked about the Weyland Foundation—he spat out the words distastefully—and how he must get the folder to his uncle so he could eliminate their investigators. He also griped when the radio announcer said Frank Dubois had been taken from the valley alive. If Dubois recovered, Simon said he'd be able to identify a public official in Washington they'd bought off, and when he spoke the man's name Webb was astounded.

"Dubois can't identify anyone," Jaeger said after Charbonneau's diatribes.

The fact that Webb had overheard so much concerned him, for Jaeger never shared critical information. Jaeger's disdain for him was apparent. When they'd first arrived, he'd cautiously examined Jaeger's bloody hip, but after a moment, Jaeger had disgustedly pushed him away and tended it himself, burrowing out shotgun pellets with his pocket knife, pouring on disinfectant, sprinkling sulfa liberally into the wounds, and covering it with bandage material.

The medication had come from Webb's pack, which had also provided dried fruit, which they'd quickly devoured. Their only other food, a few pounds of jerky and bars of sweet chocolate, came from Jaeger's rucksack, which he'd stashed outside the camp in case of an emergency. Jaeger rationed the food, even that from Webb's pack, and gave him less than the other two. When he complained, Jaeger ignored him. Increasingly, Webb wondered what would become of himself when they got out—or whether Jaeger meant to let him out.

He was at the viewing port when Jaeger began to tell Charbonneau about his plan for their escape, so he moved into the anteroom to hear better.

When the searchers withdrew, the Hunter said he'd lead the way over the mountains. The map showed a road on the other side, as well as a number of scattered houses. They'd take an automobile from one of the families living there. Once they got to the airport they'd be free.

"I've got to pass on the information in the folder." Charbonneau pouted.

"They won't keep looking forever. As soon as they stop searching, we'll take our walk."

"There are only two more days until the *trueno*."

"Your people know to go ahead with it."

"Yes, but I want to *be* there." Charbonneau's voice was high and sulking.

Webb entered the chamber from the main crawlway. "The soldiers are walking through the forest fifty abreast, like they did yesterday."

Jaeger motioned tersely in the gloom. "Stay at the lookout for another hour."

Webb went without comment, thinking again about his vulnerability. Tomorrow they'd consume the last of their meager rations, and he was already growing weak from hunger. It was time to come up with an escape plan of his own.

27

THURSDAY, JUNE 20

8:10 A.M.—Arlington National Cemetery

The group gathered near the open grave of Jacqueline Ann Chang, once a U.S. Army lieutenant and recipient of the Distinguished Flying Cross and two Air Medals, was subdued. Lincoln Anderson felt it was an appropriate resting place, in the midst of the fine men and women who had offered their lives for their country. Jackie would fit in, for she'd been a patriot to the core.

Jackie's parents were seated at graveside, the mother in black dress and veil, the American flag from her daughter's casket held in her lap. Her husband was beside her, head bent low and back periodically convulsing in private mourning. Jackie's live-in boyfriend stood behind them, glaring morosely into space, as if angered that someone could so easily be taken from his life. There were two dozen others, including Henry Hoblit and several of the pilots and flight attendants from Executive Connections. The surprising attendee was Paula Dubois, who had arrived as the ceremony began. She looked on solemnly but unobtrusively.

As the honor guard did a snappy right-face and slow-marched away, Link remembered other such military ceremonies, for other friends. He stared for another moment, then turned and walked down the row of precisely positioned white markers to limber up after the prolonged inactivity, thinking about Jackie and how she'd endured brutal captivity by the Iraqis, only to die in a peacetime accident.

As he turned back, he was startled by Paula Dubois, who had quietly followed him.

"You appear to be in better condition than I'd thought."

"I've had good doctors and a mean therapist." But his leg still ached.

"How is your arm?"

"It's healing." He wore a lightweight cast on his forearm, but it offered no more protection than the one they'd fashioned from driftwood and gauze.

"Could we speak?"

"I've been trying to reach you for the past three days."

"It's been a difficult time."

He nodded, wondering why she'd come. "How are Frank and Katy?"

"There's little change in Frank's condition, but Katy's recovering. I'll be flying back today." She paused. "I've been asking about your Mr. Bowes. The hospital will release him this morning."

"I was told." He was surprised, for her concern seemed genuine.

"He's your friend, but we owe him a great deal."

"The FAA's about to suspend his commercial license."

"They were looking into your license too, Link, and I was outraged. Cyril spoke with the secretary of transportation. The FAA's been taken off the investigation, and it's been reassigned to the National Transportation Safety Board as a normal inquiry."

A heavy weight lifted from his shoulders.

"There's unfinished business in Idaho, Link. We need your help."

"To help find Jaeger?"

"There's also something else. Something much bigger and possibly very terrible."

"Are they still looking for them?"

"The authorities believe all three got out of the valley," she said. "The National Guard will begin withdrawing tomorrow. They'll make a final air survey, then call off the search."

"I warned Marshal Rodriguez." Link had been dreaming about the big man laughing at him from high on the hillside.

Link walked slowly along the row of white markers, careful not to tread on a burial place. He had tremendous respect for the men and women resting here.

Paula spoke from his side. "When they took me back to their camp, they left me with Frank. He was semi-lucid and passed on messages, but we don't understand what he meant. If you come with me, we'll explain everything."

Link looked back. Henry Hoblit was watching them closely.

"You'll be well paid for your time."

"No." The word emerged forcefully.

Paula did not understand, believed only that he had rejected her plea. She stopped walking and released a breath of resignation. "Checks are being prepared for Mr. Bowes and yourself. Frank's grandfather insisted that you be rewarded for what you've done."

"I don't want his money. What I did was between Frank and myself."

"You've more than proven your friendship."

"That's all the payment I need."

Paula stared for a moment. "Take care, Link." She started to turn away.

"When do you want me there?" He'd promised Frank to help when his family needed it.

She frowned, uncomprehending for a moment, then relief flooded into her face. "As soon as possible. Cyril believes it may already be too late."

"I'll go home to pick up some things." Link paused thoughtfully. "If you don't mind, I'll ask Henry to prepare one of our airplanes. We can use the business."

"No flight attendant. Just you, me, and another passenger in back, so we can talk privately."

"We'll want you to sign written instructions to that effect."

Airborne over Denver

They were at 37,000 feet, slicing cleanly through the clear sky, and Link was mulling over what Paula Dubois had told him. The Weyland Foundation was run by a group of patriots called the handful, whose underlying tenet was that democracy and capitalism were benevolent for all people, and that the United States, despite its problems, was a superb model. She'd explained how they'd saved nations from ruin, encouraged democracy, and kept a number of despots from assuming power. She'd also cited dismal failures, but it was apparent that the foundation had changed the turbulent world for the better.

"Frank had just been told he would take over as chairman," she concluded.

"I've been reading about the foundation in the *Washington Post*. Essentially the things you've told me, but the reporter writes about conspiracies, and how you purposefully set up industries in other countries to compete with American business."

"Except for our investigations, we've never done anything without the government's knowledge and encouragement." Paula went no further into the Weyland Foundation, except to add that Frank had brought a leather folder aboard the Gulfstream containing a brief showing their secretive activities. The last time she'd seen it had been at the camp, in the hands of the man called Charbonneau.

"I'm the reason he got the folder," she said. "I should never have told them about it. It was silly to imagine that they'd turn us loose."

There was a moment of silence, and Link looked out at distant clouds, thinking how vividly the details of the valley remained in his mind. Bad memories often fade quickly, yet he remembered every marsh and creek, every thicket and small rise.

"When we get there," he said, "I want to speak with Katy. I have something for her."

"There's something you don't know." Paula described Jaeger's attack on her daughter. As her words impacted, Link felt a gust of cold air sweeping over him. He'd heard their distant screams that night, but had not allowed himself to imagine their terror.

She finished and stared out the window.

"How is she doing now?" Link's voice was rough, his throat was lined with sandpaper.

"Katy has no recollection of that time, and very little of the past month. The psychologists call it a traumatic block. Don't be surprised when she doesn't recognize you." Paula scanned the sky with a narrow look, and her voice became a whisper. "They raped her. Not her body, perhaps, but her mind. Frank hasn't regained consciousness since Jaeger kicked him. My family was brutalized, Link."

The icy wind continued to sweep over him. Jaeger could not be allowed to escape. Link had turned the matter over to the authorities, but they'd let the big man elude them. Now another, louder voice, called for a darker solution.

"Who do Jaeger and Charbonneau work for?" he asked.

They were in the lounge, and she called forward the man she'd introduced earlier, who was seated in the rear section. He brought his briefcase, settled beside them, and began:

"You've been cleared for the briefing by Cyril," said the project leader, "but use the information discreetly. As you'll see, lives are at stake."

Link was told about Scarlet 277, the investigation of a financial institution called El Soleil, headquartered in Argentina. The bank's president, an ex-colonel named Salvator DiPalma, had used their funds to build weapons of mass destruction. While they hadn't fully developed a nuclear capability, they were close. He spoke about conventional-weapons programs they'd monitored at the Patagonian facility, and he removed a sheaf of photos from his briefcase. The top one was of a large rectangular trailer-van with stainless steel sides and smoke rising from one end.

Link stopped him. "Go on with the rest of it. I'll look at those later."

El Soleil was working to take over the Argentine government. Their elections would be in two months, and they'd eliminated a number of the opposition through a series of assassinations. The last had been the previous week, when five people had disappeared, then been found mutilated and horribly killed. Two had been U.S. businessmen, one of those a Weyland Foundation employee.

"The identities of our investigators were listed in the files in Frank's folder. If they're transmitted to Buenos Aires, they and our sources will be murdered."

"I take it the people in the valley worked for El Soleil?"

"One was Colonel DiPalma's grand-nephew." The project leader showed a photograph of a blond man. "His name is Diego DiPalma, but you heard him called Charbonneau."

Paula spoke. "He's Jaeger's paymaster."

"And Jaeger?"

The project leader showed a photo of an unsmiling man with a hawk's beak. "His father was an S.S. lieutenant colonel stationed in Paris, responsible for interrogating wealthy French Jews and recovering their fortunes. He was brutal and effective. When he escaped to Argentina, he took half a ton of gold bullion with him, but it was confiscated and he died in poverty a few years later. His son, the man you know as Jaeger, kills in the same manner as his father, by beating his victims to death. He's called the Hunter, and he's now the chief assassin for El Soleil."

"Do you have a psychiatric profile?" Link asked.

"Pages of them. Basically, Jaeger has a psychotic need to exhibit his superiority over others. Before he kills, he degrades his victims so they'll *know* they're weaker."

"What's his vulnerability?"

"He can't accept failure or proof of weakness in himself."

Link remembered Jaeger's gloating that he'd defeated him. He let that soak in for a moment, then changed the subject. "Will the reports in the *Post* damage your efforts?"

"They've bruised our credibility in Washington, but if the other projects in the folder are published, it's sure to be worse. Can you imagine the uproar when the public learns we've helped to finance almost *every* major economic rival ... and that *every* president since Franklin Roosevelt has approved? It wouldn't matter that those nations were transformed into peaceful democracies. It would be a bombshell, and in the uproar everyone would ignore anything we try to tell them about what DiPalma and El Soleil are doing."

"How's the *Post* reporter getting his information?"

"There's a highly placed American official involved. We don't have a name. All we know is that he's been bought off by Salvator DiPalma. We believe he's already told the press as much as he knows. He'll need the contents of the folder if he's going to give them more."

Paula nodded for emphasis. "Frank said to find the traitor, as if he's a key to everything. He had an idea about his identity, or at least *they* thought he did."

"So El Soleil wants Frank killed," Link said, "and they want the folder so they can stop the investigation."

"And the official will use the information to destroy the foundation."

"But it hasn't happened yet," Link mused. If they'd escaped, why hadn't Charbonneau turned the files over to El Soleil?

"Then there are the *truenos*," the project leader said. "Each time the assassinations occur in Argentina, they come on the heels of a news story here that overshadows it in our press. Three telephone calls of less than one minute's duration were made from Diego DiPalma's office in New York to the same Buenos Aires number—and those were the *only* calls to that number. The first was made the morning of the Oklahoma City bombing, the second the day the verdict came in on the Simpson trial, the third following our presidential election—when the attention of the world was focused. There were assassinations following all three telephone calls, but the news was lost in the noise of the *truenos*."

"What was the thunder last week?" Link asked.

"When their man in Washington leaked the story about the Weyland Foundation, it served two purposes: to destroy the foundation's credibility, and mask the news of more assassinations in Argentina."

"But the worst is to come, Link," said Paula.

The project leader nodded grimly. "Our sources say there'll be a final *trueno,* and that it will be soon. That same day they'll assassinate the Argentinean president and other leading candidates. Since the timing is critical, this time they'll generate the *trueno* themselves."

"What, and where?"

"We only know that it will happen in California, and will be so newsworthy that the entire world will watch. Remember the week of the Oklahoma City disaster? The nation was numbed and went into mourning. First our government looked for international culprits, then the President led a witch-hunt for right-wing organizations that weren't remotely associated. That's the sort of situation they'll create, where we're preoccupied and no one gives a damn about what happens in South America."

"You've got to warn the authorities."

"Cyril tried to tell the President," Paula said, "but he wouldn't listen."

"Surely someone will."

"Not any longer. Marshal Rodriguez was providing us with daily briefings about what was happening in the valley, but last night the President ordered all government contact with the Weyland Foundation to be severed."

"Can't you just send everything to the FBI?"

"And possibly to El Soleil's man in Washington?" Paula Dubois let the question dangle as she rose from her seat.

"Since we're left to our own devices, I'll get refreshments."

As Paula went to the galley, the captain announced they were passing over Ogden. They'd land on schedule—they would gain three hours during the flight—at 12:40 P.M..

Paula returned with a tray of Perrier water and sandwiches. "Before I left Boise, the weather people said another front should arrive by this weekend."

"Summer storms can be violent," Link said. "Warm air holds more moisture, and the towering cumulus buildups rise higher and get nastier."

"I've been through a big one, remember?"

Link recalled her fear of flying, which seemed to have diminished greatly. He sipped water from a bottle. "You said Frank spoke to you when they took you to their camp."

Paula frowned, concentrating. "First he told us not to trust them, and to try to escape. Then he said if something went wrong, they'd go somewhere that wasn't on the maps."

"Who?" Link asked.

"Jaeger and the others. Next he mentioned *trueno,* and how the final one would be terrible, but then Charbonneau came by and Frank slipped under, like he was purposefully sinking away. A while later he resurfaced and whispered the name Fay, and said to tell you she'd be on the Golden Gate."

"Fay?" Link could not think of anyone with that name.

"He'd mentioned her once before, and said to tell you they had her."

The project leader got up and stretched, then went back to the rest room, and Link went back to something Paula had said. "Frank told you if something went wrong, they'd go somewhere not shown on the maps. What maps?"

"He didn't say."

"Did they have charts or maps in the camp?"

"Jaeger had one that he looked at several times."

"Can you describe it?"

She pursed her lips reflectively. "It was about thirty inches square, and he'd drawn things on it with a black marker. I couldn't see any closer."

Fay, Link's mind suddenly whispered, and he tried to brush the thought away.

Paula was watching him closely. "What do you think?"

"I'll want you to do something for me. Have one of your people get hold of every detailed chart of the valley that's ever been printed."

Fay.

Paula wrote his request down, then grew a concerned look. "You're not thinking of going there, are you?"

"I'm . . ." He paused then, and frowned. *Fay!* his mind said, louder.

The project leader returned and sat down, holding a cinnamon bun in a napkin.

FAE!

He turned to the project leader. "Could I see the photographs of their weapons tests?"

Fuel and air.

The man picked up the topmost photo, but Link reached past him and took them all. "Go ahead and eat," he muttered, and began to leaf through them.

"Frank was interested in those," the project leader said around a bite of sticky bun.

The first photograph was the one Link had seen earlier, of the trailer with vapor rising from one end. *Air!* Something stirred within Link as he went to the next image, of a bright flash. *Fuel and air. Rapid combustion. Extreme heat. Vacuum. Implosion!* The following one was of a soaring mushroom cloud. He remembered the tremendous power released by FAE weapons. Like Frank, he'd learned about fuel-air explosives in classified military briefings.

His friend's tortured mind had conjured up the answer, and he'd tried to warn them. *"Tell Link about the FAE on the Golden Gate,"* he had told Paula, but she'd not understood.

He turned to her, words tumbling out anxiously. "Did either Charbonneau or Jaeger mention Fay or the Golden Gate Bridge?"

Paula shook her head, then brightened. "Charbonneau— Diego DiPalma—laughed and said he'd visit his favorite bridge next week."

"Next week?" Link's heart began to race faster.

"That was last Thursday."

Meaning *now.* He stared grimly at the next photo, of a huge crater of rubble.

"Meet FAE," he told the others.

Neither Paula nor the project leader breathed as they stared at the aftermath of the violent implosion in the photograph.

"I'll need to speak with Cyril Weyland as soon as possible," Link said.

The project leader was quickly on the in-flight telephone, first arranging transportation for when they landed, then calling his people in New York to have them dig through their files for any additional information they could find on the trailers.

Lincoln Anderson considered the enormity of what they'd discussed, and after a moment he made a call of his own, this one to General Paul "Lucky" Anderson, at their home in northern Virginia. While he could not tell him as much as he wanted to on the unsecure line, he relayed the importance of the situation.

"I'd say it's time to call on some help from our friends," his ailing stepfather said in his eternally tired voice. "I'll arrange something. Talk to Billy after you land."

As the airplane approached Boise and there was nothing further to be done, they grew silent, each lost in their individual, terrible thoughts.

28

12:00 noon—The Valley

They'd eaten the last of the food, and Webb was more miserable than ever.

Charbonneau had gone over names in the folder a dozen times now, telling how his great-uncle would deal with each, and how his people in San Rafael would carry out the big thunder he called the final *trueno*. A thousand people would die when it happened—perhaps a lot more. He'd picked the target well, and the structure would collapse in a single, great ball of fire. It was sturdy, but *nothing* could withstand the tremendous force they would generate.

"I'm needed there," Simon complained to Jaeger, but the Hunter seldom answered his carping, just remained in his corner and slept or exercised.

"I'm cold and hungry," Charbonneau said in his sulking tone. "You could go out and get clothes and food from the soldiers.

"No," was all Jaeger said.

"They can't have the *trueno* without me."

"Yes, they can."

"My grand-uncle will be concerned." When there was no answer, Charbonneau grumbled that Jaeger should have remembered to bring more food and warm clothing.

"They'll leave tomorrow," Jaeger said softly.

"The soldiers?" Webb asked.

"Yes. They've taken the heavy equipment. The soldiers will be next. Then we'll go."

"That will be after the *trueno*," Charbonneau sulked.

12:45 P.M.—Boise

When they landed at the airport, the Gulfstream III was taxied alongside a helicopter that bore the distinctive Weyland Foundation logo. As soon as they were aboard and slid the hatch closed, they were airborne. Minutes later they landed beside the converted medical building.

Cyril Weyland met them in the conference room, wearing a concerned expression. "I don't understand," he began, but without fanfare or introduction Link cut him off.

He used the photographs to explain the weapon, and had Paula repeat Frank's utterances at the camp. "Frank overheard them talking about it in the camp," Link said when she finished. "He wanted to warn us that they'd detonate a FAE weapon on the bridge."

The old man's mind was not slow. "My God," he whispered, staring at the photographs.

"Who can stop them?" Link asked.

"The President, certainly, but he's no longer listening to us."

"You can show him that El Soleil has developed the weapons."

"Yes, but there's nothing to prove that they've got one in California, or their intent. Frank can't tell what he overheard."

"Can you get in to *see* the President?"

"Normally there'd be no problem, but . . ." He brooded, then nodded. "I believe so, but it would be for the last time."

"If we prove the weapon's there, he'll have to take us seriously."

The project leader left them to answer a summons at the door. He returned a moment later with a single page, which he read intently. He looked up with a grim expression. "Five weeks ago a trailer like those used in the tests was transported from the campus to San Julian. Two ships were tied up, one bound for Santiago, Chile, the other for San Francisco, California."

"Could they transport a weapon like that?" Cyril asked Link.

"It would be too unstable. They'd have to ship the trailer empty, then fill it at the destination." He got to his feet. "I'll need the photograph of the trailer."

As the project leader handed it over, Link looked at Cyril. "I'm flying to the Bay Area to try to find it. How quickly can you get in to see the President?"

Cyril didn't hesitate. He gave orders, and his aide hurried toward a telephone.

Link glanced at his flying watch. It was well past one.

He used a free phone and punched in Leslie Rocklin's number.

Billy Bowes answered. "Lucky just called. He said to get yourself to San Francisco International, and he'll have things in motion."

"Who am I supposed to see there?"

"You'll be met at the airplane."

"I'll need a special camera, Billy. The kind newspapers use to transmit photographs over telephone lines."

Billy spoke off-line, then came back on. "Leslie will meet you with one at the airplane."

Link's second phone call was to an ex-Air Force friend, now the operations officer for the Air National Guard unit flying C-130's out of Reno, Nevada. His buddy said he'd meet him with the IR scanning devices on the taxiway at Reno-Tahoe International.

Finally he called flight operations at the airport and spoke with one of the Executive Connections pilots he'd told to stand by, and told him to file flight plans for the Gulfstream and the Baron, destination San Francisco International, with a brief stop at Reno for the Gulfstream.

Before he left the room, Cyril's aide gave him telephone numbers where they could be reached the following morning.

"I think we should go over everything again," said the project leader, but Link shook his head.

"There's no time. Charbonneau said it would be this week, and tomorrow's Friday."

He met the two Executive Connections pilots at the airport, and they briefed the flight as they walked across the tarmac. One would fly the Gulfstream with Link, the other the Baron.

Leslie Rocklin was waiting at the Gulfstream, a large canvas bag at her feet. "I brought two film cameras and two electronics ones, and plenty of batteries."

When he hefted the heavy bag, she followed him into the airplane.

"You're not going," Link said as he opened the main hatch.

"Like hell I'm not. I just stole those from the newspaper office. When I take them back they'll fire me, so I want *something* to show for it."

There was no time to argue. "Get in."

"Take the right seat," Link told the Gulfstream captain. "I'll fly the leg to Reno."

4:00 P.M.—San Francisco International Airport

They'd arrived over the bridge twenty minutes before, found it to be a good-weather day for flying, and made a circuit of the area to see what they faced. As they landed, Link wondered what kind of reception had been arranged.

They were directed to a parking spot immediately in front of flight operations, and shut down. When Link opened the hatch and stepped out, he was greeted by a sturdy gray-haired man wearing an expensive suit and a serious expression.

"Jerry Tiehl," he said. "You're General Anderson's son?"

"Yes." Link shook his hand.

"I was crew chief for your dad's jet in Thailand back in '67. Now I run maintenance for United Airlines here at SFO. The General said you'd need some help." He led the way toward the nearby building.

"We've got a comm setup inside so you can talk to the pilots at the five airports we'll be using. Your father, Colonel Bowes, and I have been calling airplane owners we know. Fourteen have shown up, and more are on their way. We thought twenty would be a good number."

It was far better than Link had dared hope for. He told him about the Beech Baron on its way and the two Executive Connections pilots who would be available.

"We'll make room for them," said Tiehl. "Next rotary-wing birds. The General felt helicopters would be useful in this situation, especially if we have to work in darkness. They've been more difficult to find—not many people own them privately—but we're trying for twenty of those too.

We'd like four fixed-wing birds and four choppers at each location."

"That would be great." *Definitely* more than Link had expected.

"So far I've got four United helicopters. Northwest's offering two at Oakland, and American has two in San Jose. Since we've got plenty of pilots, I found a local company that will rent us the other twelve."

Link was astounded. "Are all of these pilots Dad's friends?"

"Hell, no. They're ex-military, though, and when I got the word around that you needed help and a lot of civilian lives are at stake, they volunteered. And not only pilots. We've got mechanics, service crews, you name it."

"They know this is unofficial?"

"Yeah, but they've learned to have more faith in friends than Washington bureaucrats."

Link wondered about security. "What else did you tell them?"

"That's all the General told *me*. It's like the old days, Link. Trust your people, and they'll trust you. That's something your father taught us all."

They entered a large, twenty-by-twenty office with an assortment of telephones and radio equipment, where a small, wiry man waited.

"Will we have trouble getting flight clearances?" Link asked Tiehl.

"Nope. This is all Class B—congested airspace, and there are three major terminal-control areas involved. Clearance like we need would normally be impossible, but the FAA's regional manager's cooperating. Twenty years ago, he was a lieutenant working for your father."

"It seems everyone in the Bay Area's ex-military."

"The ones who count right now are."

"Everything's ready," said the wiry man. He explained the telephone setup: twenty lines, two connected to fax machines and two more to computer modems. Two headphone-equipped radio units were accessing VHF frequencies assigned by the FAA manager.

"I'll hang around in case there's a problem," he added.

Jerry Tiehl pulled over a local area map. Circled in red were the airfields at SFO, Oakland, San Jose, Rio Vista, and Santa Rosa, all in or just outside the Bay Area.

Link drew an arc that extended for fifty miles north, east, and south of the bridge, providing a total search area of some four thousand square miles. He divided that into five equal areas of responsibility and labeled each with the name of an airfield.

Ten minutes later, the wiry man set up a multiple-line conference call, connecting the pilots from the various airfields. He had faxed copies of the map, as well as the photograph of the van, to all five locations, and everyone involved had taken a look at both.

When they checked in, Link learned there were a total of twenty-two fixed-wing airplanes, all with pilots and observers—two more owners had heard about the request and insisted they participate—and twenty helicopters and crews.

Link began by asking that no one publicize the event. Regardless of how successful the venture, he wanted no names mentioned. "Amen," said a couple of voices, and everyone agreed.

Next he assigned understandable call signs. Oakland became Oscar, San Francisco was Frank, Rio Vista was Victor, San Jose was Joseph, and Santa Rosa was Rosie. Fixed-wing airplanes were Alphas and helicopters Hotels. Thus Rosie-Hotel-Three was the call sign of the third helicopter assigned to Santa Rosa, the one Leslie Rocklin had decided to board as an observer.

An air coordinator and an assistant were assigned at each location.

Link explained what they'd be looking for: (1) a secure area, likely fenced, (2) a building with white vapor rising from it, and (3) a trailer of the same shape and dimensions as the one in the photograph.

"What if the trailer's parked inside?" asked an observer in Joseph-Alpha-Two.

"That's doubtful since toxic chemicals are involved."

"What's the white vapor?" asked a helicopter pilot in Santa Rosa.

"It'll be from a liquid-oxygen plant, and the condensation may be hard to see. It's going to be dark in two hours," he told them, "and we'll have to cut back on the numbers of flights. I've only got three infrared scopes. Any ideas on how to distribute them?"

"Keep 'em," came a gruff voice. "I just hauled in thirty

sets of night-vision goggles with battery packs. Have your fly boys drop in at Rio Vista airport, and I'll explain how to use them."

"You have thirty sets of night goggles?" Link was astounded, for they were expensive and generally available only to the military. He started to ask gruff-voice how he'd gotten them, but Jerry Tiehl shook his head in a way that told him not to question his good fortune.

"This is Mike in San Jose," came another voice. "We don't have night-vision goggles, but my chief of police loaned us a dozen pair of I.R. binoculars."

Again Link did not ask. With the night-vision devices, everyone could remain airborne after dark, helicopters and light airplanes as well.

The FAA manager said his people would monitor them on radar and give blanket clearances where possible. He assigned the fixed-wing birds to altitudes from 1,500 to 5,000 feet, and asked that the helicopters remain beneath them.

Link told the pilots to fly a tight grid pattern, ensuring the fixed-wing birds had double coverage, and the slower helicopters single coverage, of all inhabited areas within their assigned domains each three hours.

The first birds were airborne by 5:05. By then four more light airplanes and two more helicopters had been added to the list, for their owners insisted on helping.

"You forgot something," Jerry Tiehl told him as they waited for the first reports to come in. "When they spot something, we'll need someone to check it out."

"Any ideas?"

Tiehl smiled. "The sergeant major's already got it covered."

Link frowned. "Who?"

"That's how you got your night-vision goggles. The division gunny for the local Marine Corps Reserve unit's the guy you talked to at Rio Vista. He's got ground teams standing by and monitoring the radios in all five zones. Young jarheads who won't mind going into tough areas."

"Who's the one who called himself Mike?"

"He's the new mayor of San Jose. Now, why don't we just sit back, have a cup of coffee, and you can tell me how your father's doing? I hear he's got a bad heart."

* * *

By 7:25 the aircrews had grown at ease with their call signs and duties, and had established a protocol. When they were not on the telephone with one of the airfields, the wiry communications expert would switch the radios onto speaker so they could listen in.

Over the Oakland frequency they heard:

"Oscar Central, this is Alpha One. I got a trucking company at One-Fifteenth and Lawrence. I don't see vapor, but there's trailers."

"Roger Alpha One. You got it in sight, Hotel Five?"

"I'm closing on it now." After a moment, "Yeah. It's fenced and there's three big trailers, but no smoke."

"Roger. We'll give that one a priority three. Label it P-three-seven."

"This is Oscar ground team. We copy on P-three-seven at One-Fifteenth Street and Lawrence."

Already the Oakland aircraft and helicopters had found twelve priority-fours sightings, seven priority-threes, six twos, and three priority-ones—a total of twenty-eight in their area of responsibility. The ground crew would check them in order of priority and proximity.

The communications expert switched to San Jose's frequency.

A moment later: "Joseph Central, this is Joseph Hotel Three. My observer just put on the N-V goggles. He says they're like looking through a bright green tunnel, and they'll take some getting used to."

Link was reminded that outside the sun had just dipped into the Pacific.

Hurry, he silently urged them.

By midnight the combined aircrews had located ninety-seven potential sites, all with fences, most with trailers of the general proportions shown in the photo, many with white vapor rising from nearby buildings. Ground teams had checked all but nineteen, and most of those were priority-fours. In most cases the effluvium was fog wafting from refrigeration units or smoke from chimneys, and closer observation showed the trailers were of the wrong size or shape.

Pilots were growing weary and observers eyesore, although there were enough qualified pilots that they were being rotated, replaced by others after every second flight.

It was going to be a long night, and Lincoln Anderson was not nearly as sure as he had been that they'd find what they were after.

"I'm going up for a look," he finally announced, getting to his feet and wearing a concerned expression, but Jerry Tiehl shook his head.

"You've got to show trust in your men. If it's out there, they'll find it."

One by one, reports of inspection arrived from the ground teams, and the nineteen suspect sites were eliminated. During that time announcements of fourteen more had come in.

29

Friday, June 21

5:30 A.M.—San Francisco International Airport

Link had rested his head in his arms on the desktop, and, despite his efforts to remain alert, fallen into a state of semi-sleep. He was awakened by the wiry communications expert's voice.

"You've got a phone call. It's Washington."

He shook his head to clear it. "Any new sightings?"

"Two, both in Oakland. They're checking them now."

Link took the telephone, and spoke with Cyril Weyland's aide.

"Nothing yet," he said. "It'll be light in a few minutes and we'll have better visibility." The night-vision equipment had been critical, but it was not nearly as good as daylight.

"We had trouble breaking into the President's schedule," said the aide. "They've finally agreed to slip us in at nine o'clock. That's half an hour from now."

Link released a tired breath. "Looks like Cyril will have to convince him without proof from here."

"He realizes that. You've got the phone numbers in case."

"Yeah." Link hung up. Reports of new sightings were coming in far less frequently. They'd examined a total of a hundred and seventy-two suspect sites.

He poured another cup of coffee, and raised it in salute to Jerry Tiehl, who had remained with him through the long night. "You put on a great effort," he told him.

"It's not over." Tiehl's voice reflected the edginess they'd all developed.

The wiry man had slipped on the earphones and was listening in on the pilots' radio chatter. He spoke conversationally. "The lady reporter's raising hell with a ground crew, trying to get them to check out a site again."

Leslie Rocklin was still in Rosie Hotel Three, the third helicopter assigned to Santa Rosa, and had to be dog-weary.

"Which one?" Link asked, pulling over the list.

"P-one-thirty-seven, the small one in San Rafael just off the freeway. The ground team checked and swears it's a re-frigeration outfit, but she's suspicious because there's only one trailer, the dimensions are right, and she feels the va-por's different from the others."

South Peninsula Refrigeration, the entry on the long list read.

The communications specialist grinned. "The argument's over. The gunny sergeant just told the guys in Rosie ground team to quit arguing and do as the lady says."

The White House

The President would not have allowed the meeting had they not agreed to come secretively.

Cyril Weyland had requested the presence of only the at-torney general and—by name—the FBI's top explosive weapons expert. He'd specifically asked that the secretary of state, their normal intermediary, not attend. The Presi-dent had finally agreed to meet with him this once, and made it clear that there'd be no more. They'd asked for an hour, but the President had granted only half of that time.

Weyland arrived with his aide and project leader, and the former remained outside as the others were escorted into the Oval Office. After a pointedly cool reception, the old man took his seat at one side of the President's desk, the project leader on the other, with a stack of papers and pho-tographs before him. The attorney general and the FBI expert—a corpulent man who taught explosives at the Bu-reau's academy at Quantico—were seated at the side of the room.

"I've got an engagement—" the President began, but Cyril abruptly cut him off. "We'll take very little of your time," he said. "Then you'll see no more of us."

Weyland was obviously unimpressed with his position,

but then the President remembered that he had dealt with every chief executive since F.D.R.

Cyril began speaking, and as he proceeded, the project leader provided documentation to back the aged chairman's words. The President remained impassive, for he'd been prewarned that the man had become senile and fanciful, that the tragic condition of his grandson had driven him to the edge.

Weyland explained rocket and nuclear programs in Argentina. He said physicists employed by El Soleil, a financial conglomerate controlled by Salvator DiPalma, were less than a year from nuclear capability, and had the means to deliver it. There were statements from scientists at the Patagonian campus, and photographs of test facilities and rockets on launchers.

The President had been told that Weyland would try to alarm him—that the CIA had no confirmation of weapons programs, and the experimentation and rockets were for peaceful use.

Cyril Weyland mentioned another weapon.

"Fay?" asked the attorney general, but the FBI expert's eyes narrowed at the word.

"It's spelled F-A-E." Weyland nodded to the project leader. "Please explain."

"In the seventies," the project leader said, "the U.S. Air Force developed experimental weapons called fuel-air explosives—involving fuel and oxidant. Once ignited, they created heat so intense that a tremendous vacuum was formed, followed by an *im*plosion. The destructive power was immense, but they proved unstable and too dangerous for operational use. The Soviets worked on a similar technology, but after a string of disasters they shut down their program too. When the Russian physicists arrived in Argentina, they were put to work improving the concept. Their goal was to create maximum temperatures and construct the most powerful implosive devices possible. After extensive trial and testing, they've succeeded."

The project leader showed photos. "They use reinforced trailers, with exterior shells lined with explosives as the igniter, and interior compartments alternately filled with nitrous oxide and benzene. Shortly before the devices are to be ignited, a central compartment is filled with liquid oxygen. The result is a very large, extremely volatile FAE, providing the equivalent force of a hundred tons of high explosives."

The FBI expert was leaning forward, listening intently.

The project leader showed photographs of a bright flash and a mushroom cloud, then of a tremendous crater. "A FAE is not a normal bomb. The tremendous heat and the implosive wave consume all sign of the device and the ingredients. There's little debris and no way to trace it."

"We have monitoring satellites," the President said. "No one briefed me about large-scale explosions in Argentina."

The project leader shook his head. "Those monitor for nuclear detonations. The FAE implosions emit no electromagnetic impulses, and leave no telltale traces of radioactivity."

The corpulent FBI expert agreed. "And our K-11 imaging satellites wouldn't have picked up the flashes unless they were parked overhead—which they were not."

Cyril Weyland went on, explaining a political takeover under way in Argentina, and the project leader showed statements by informants. Weyland told about *trueno*— thunder—and how DiPalma timed political assassinations to coincide with spectacular headlines.

The President knew better. He'd been told that Salvator DiPalma—who was friendly to the U.S.—was assisting the leaders of the troubled country.

"There's to be a final *trueno*," Cyril Weyland said. "This one will be the loudest of their thunders, and the news media, the nation, the world . . . will be preoccupied with the disaster."

"Is this the one you phoned me about?"

"Yes. DiPalma's people will detonate a FAE on the Golden Gate Bridge sometime this week, very possibly today. We assume they'll pick a peak rush hour, and that the trailer will be jackknifed so it can't be easily moved. The terrorists will probably try to escape in another vehicle, but I doubt they'll survive. DiPalma will want to make sure nothing can possibly be traced back to him."

"The equivalent of a hundred tons of explosive," said the project leader, "would sever the bridge, and the entire structure would collapse. Our analysts predict between seven hundred and two thousand people would perish, depending on the timing."

While he knew it was alarmist fantasy, the President's pulse quickened at the terrible vision.

"This week, you said?" asked the attorney general.

"Yes. The men who kidnapped my grandson were involved," said Cyril Weyland. "The timing may have been changed because of what happened in Idaho, but it's doubtful. Too many other factors are involved. We suggest you act quickly to stop them."

Despite his disbelief the President was increasingly concerned. But of course, he'd been told that was Weyland's intent.

Cyril Weyland cleared his throat with difficulty. "While we knew there was to be an atrocity, we learned about the FAE and the location only yesterday and felt the information should be provided to you immediately."

He was so convincing that the President wondered if he wasn't truly insane. "Do you have proof of *any* of this?" he asked.

"We know that a trailer was shipped from Patagonia—" Weyland began when the door was opened by the President's secretary.

"This gentleman *insists* that I interrupt you," said the secretary, and Cyril Weyland's white-haired aide slipped by her, bearing a manila folder that he handed to the project leader.

"This is damned irregular," said the President, unable to mask his displeasure.

Cyril Weyland ignored him, looking expectantly at his project leader.

"I have another meeting," the President said crisply, and started to rise.

"Here's your proof," said Cyril Weyland.

The project leader showed full-color photographs. "These were taken half an hour ago. The tractor-trailer is parked by a warehouse in San Rafael, California, seven miles from the bridge. You'll note that except for the color, the trailer is identical."

The President nodded tersely at the FBI expert. "Take a look."

"As I said," Cyril concluded, "the trailer is to be detonated on the Golden Gate Bridge, probably this morning.

The President ignored Weyland. "What do you think?"

he asked the expert, who was examining and comparing photographs.

"They were right about the FAE, and the trailer's precisely the same, down to the rivets and access doors. It's compelling enough to warrant investigation, sir."

Despite his reluctance the President could not afford to ignore a potential disaster. He turned to the attorney general. "Look into it," he said, masking his irritation.

The FBI explosives expert took the address and photographs, and followed the attorney general from the room.

"Please leave us," Cyril said to his project leader.

When they were alone, Weyland regarded him. "In the event you aren't able to stop them in time, I suggest you contact the governor of California and have him immediately prohibit all tractor-trailer traffic from crossing the bridge."

The President had been forewarned that Weyland would have outrageous revelations. He was not about to inconvenience so many voters and give credence to a pipe dream.

"I have one more item," Cyril Weyland said in his aging voice, "then I'll leave."

He revealed the identity of an American official who was in the employ of El Soleil, and showed computerized records of an account in a bank in Grand Cayman that had grown by thirty million dollars over the past months.

While the President had no recourse but to investigate the possibility that the bomb existed, he decided it was best to clear the air about this farce. His election had been, in large part, due to the Herculean efforts of the man Cyril Weyland accused.

"I was briefed," he said quietly, "that you're the one not to be trusted."

"That's what he was paid to say," said Cyril. "I suppose it's a matter of credibility as to which of us you believe." He rose painfully to his feet. "Our part of it is now over. I gave the order to evacuate our investigators from Argentina two days ago. They were in jeopardy, and it was apparent you wouldn't listen. I'm retiring, Mr. President, and I must say I have no regrets. The past few weeks have been painful to me and my family, and disastrous for the foundation."

The President also rose and extended his hand. It would

be their final meeting. The old man was as disturbed as he'd been told, and with the revelations about the foundation in the press, there must be no further connections to his administration.

Cyril Weyland stared at the hand for a moment, then shook it curtly with a surprisingly firm grasp, and left the room. His aide met him at the door.

"We're finished here," Weyland said distastefully as the aide took his arm.

A few blocks distant, Vern Calico sat in his large office at the Department of State building, reviewing his busy schedule.

He took a call, which his secretary announced was from the first secretary of the Argentinean embassy.

"Trueno." The word was softly spoken.

Calico replaced the receiver gingerly, as if it were fragile. This was the part he'd disliked most—the final big thunder to mask news from a country dismissed as trivial in the grand scope of things. American lives would be lost. This time many of them. He'd not planned it, he rationalized. He'd only gone along to complicate things for the Weyland Foundation, an organization that should not be allowed to continue.

In order to win the last election, he'd carefully positioned the President in the role of a moderate conservative, but that was not the politics of Vern Calico. He didn't give a diddley about the size of government, whether a great society spent themselves into bankruptcy succoring citizens or scrupulously paid their way. Political positions were dictated by the whimsical ebb and flow of public opinion, and he could easily adjust. There was only one firm maxim of American politics—to win—and he understood it well.

When Salvator DiPalma succeeded in Argentina, it would not be the end of things. America needed enemies to rally against. Perhaps he would even be the one to bring him down. There was the money in the Caymans, soon to be moved to a place where its source would be untraceable. In three years there'd be another election, and the President had been vulnerable the day he'd taken office. Winning in America took vast amounts of money, and Vern Calico now had enough to buy his way in. Things had taken a definite upturn since his youth on the Texas ranch, out in the middle of nowhere—a previous, disagreeable life that he scarcely remembered.

The deaths of so many Americans would be unfortunate, but there would be opportunity there too. He was viewed as a man of the people—the President's strong right arm. They'd fly to California together to view the tragedy, and he would be seen with a firm handle on things.

His thoughts were interrupted as his secretary called again from the outer office. "The President's on line two, Mr. Secretary."

He took his time answering.

"Sorry to bother you, Vern, but I believe you should come over. As you know, I was just visited by Cyril Weyland."

"Like I told you," Calico said in his carefully nurtured Texas twang, "the man's got more fantasies than a tom turkey that's just been invited to dinner."

"You hit on most of his subjects, but he had a couple others you'll want to hear."

"Then I'd better get right on over." He hung up, pleased that he'd anticipated Weyland and forewarned the President.

San Rafael, California

It was still early when the hastily assembled group of FBI agents gathered near the locked steel gate to the warehouse yard, remaining out of sight behind a small metal shack, and waited for the rest of the team to arrive.

The agent-in-charge, or AIC, of the operation was not at all sure what they were about to get into. There was no listed telephone number for the business shown on the sign at the gate as SOUTH PENINSULA REFRIGERATION, LTD.. He peered through the fence and motioned at a rig parked at a loading dock. "Is that it?" he asked.

One of the others examined the aerial photographs they'd received over the computer line. "There isn't a tractor in the photos, but the trailer's the same."

The trailer was connected by hoses that snaked out of a small warehouse, where billows of white condensation issued from vents.

"Where the hell are the people from ATF?" grumbled

the agent-in-charge. They knew more about this sort of thing, and he was hesitant to go inside without them. A team of specialists was also being flown in by the Air Force. If the attorney general's message was right, the trailer might contain the most destructive terrorist bomb ever assembled. Even if that was as doubtful as the AIC believed, he was reluctant to go charging in and chance his team being blown to hell.

Unless someone tried to move the trailer, it would be better to wait on the ATF.

Two vehicles were parked farther around the fence line. A dark-haired man carrying an oblong case and a woman with a camera emerged and walked toward them, then stopped a few feet distant. They looked rumpled, as if they'd gotten little sleep.

"Who the hell are you?" the AIC asked irritably.

"She's with the press," the man answered quietly.

The reporter was taking photos of the AIC and his men.

"Who told you about . . ."

"We've got movement inside," said an agent.

Two figures had emerged from the warehouse wearing heavy gauntlets and white protective overalls. One studied a gauge on the side of the trailer, then shut off a lever. They waited for a full minute, then decoupled the hoses, now white with hoarfrost, and carried them into the building.

"Damn!" muttered the AIC, peering at his watch. The ATF people were independent-minded but were necessary to the operation.

Three men emerged from a small office building. They stopped and talked; then one headed toward the back gate, and the other two walked toward the tractor-trailer combination.

"They're up early," said an agent, stifling a yawn.

"Truckers are like that," said another.

"So are terrorists," the dark-haired man said quietly. The AIC observed the oblong, hard case in his hand and wondered if it was what it appeared to be.

The agents had decided it was a wild-goose chase. They'd had no feedback from local informants about this or any other bomb, and had never heard of one containing liquid oxygen. The agent-in-charge believed they were probably right.

"You've got the search warrant?" he asked his assistant. The man nodded.

He huffed a sigh as the men inside reached the big truck. "Then we'll go in."

"Where the hell are the ATF?" asked an agent.

"Poor guys are probably tired," quipped another. "Likely spent the night confiscating stogies from little old ladies."

The agent-in-charge stepped into the open, held out his identification, and yelled to the two men beside the tractor-trailer.

"FBI," he called out. "We'd like to take a look inside."

Both men turned, startled, and immediately began running toward the third man, who was approaching the back gate, where several automobiles were parked.

The AIC motioned at his assistant. "Take one of the cars around and stop 'em."

"They're not going anywhere," the dark-haired man said in his quiet voice, and four men with determined expressions and shotguns raised to port arms appeared outside the back gate.

"Jesus," one of the agents muttered. "Who the hell are they?"

"Bring the bolt cutters over so we can get inside," barked the AIC.

The six-man squad from the Bureau of Alcohol, Tobacco and Firearms arrived fifteen minutes late. By then the FBI agents were inside, trying to talk with the reluctant men who'd been stopped as they'd tried to exit the rear gate, and others from inside the warehouse. An electronic device had been taken from one of the drivers, which the ATF supervisor said might be a remote triggering transmitter.

One of the drivers was led to the rear of the trailer. "Open it," demanded the agent-in-charge, but the man avidly shook his head. The ATF supervisor decided that discretion being the better part of valor—and since they didn't know screw-all about what they faced—they should wait on the military.

Throughout it all the woman from the sedan took notes and snapped rolls of film. The four men who'd appeared at the back gate had slipped away, and the dark-haired man had taken his rectangular case, which the AIC still believed contained a rifle, and departed.

It was another hour before the military-weapons experts arrived from Nellis Air Force Base, near Las Vegas, and took the first samples of the chemicals contained in the trailer. A few minutes later, the major in charge of the team advised the local police to evacuate all civilians within two miles of the warehouse.

1:15 P.M.—The White House

The President of the United States stared out the window as the attorney general briefed details of what had been found in San Rafael. His initial numbness was beginning to wear off, but not the enormity of the situation.

"How about the rest of it?" he asked. "The statements and photos Weyland gave us?"

"They appear to be valid."

"The bank records?"

"If they're contrived, they're damned good." The attorney general paused, then released a ragged sigh. "They're real. Calico was paid off by El Soleil."

The President continued to stare. "I told him everything Weyland said. I *trusted* the man."

"He didn't return to his office. His secretary says he's missed a luncheon meeting."

"Find him," exploded the President, "and bring the bastard here. I want to look him in the face and call him a goddamn terrorist animal before you lock him up."

"That would prejudice any case we may be able to build against him."

"*May* be able to build? He was going to stand by and let them kill *Americans*. I want the son of a bitch in jail!"

"On what charges? Passing information to the press? Keeping money in the Caymans?"

"Terrorism, damn it. It's a federal charge that carries the death penalty."

"Everything we've got is circumstantial, and there won't be any more if Weyland's pulled his investigators out of Argentina. A good lawyer would make us look foolish."

The President turned and stared angrily, then slowly deflated. "What *can* we do?"

"Fire him and assign a special prosecutor. Traditionally that's the way it's done."

The President's chief of staff spoke up from the back of the room. "If Vern's running, maybe he doesn't know how limited our options are."

"Don't bank on it," the President said bitterly. "The country boy act is bullshit. Vern's smart, and he'll have all the bases covered."

"Maybe not *all* the bases," said the attorney general. "I've got an idea about how to handle him, starting with a phone call to the Caymans to make sure he can't get his hands on the money. I'd also like to start freezing El Soleil's assets here in the States. Weyland gave us enough to show criminal intent."

"Go ahead."

As the attorney general left the room, the President regarded his chief of staff. "Get the president of Argentina on the line. We've got to talk. The man's in trouble."

As the chief of staff called the White House operators and gave instructions, the President huffed a sigh. The worst betrayals were those by a man's friends. He wondered if Cyril Weyland hadn't felt that way when he'd snubbed him.

30

Webb had pushed the wire antenna out a ventilation port so they could listen to the hourly news. Both Jaeger and Charbonneau waited expectantly, for it was the day of the final thunder, when the bomb was to destroy the Golden Gate Bridge and wipe out a few thousand people.

"The *truenos* were my idea," Charbonneau said proudly. "After the first one, my great-uncle believed I was brilliant, but I wasn't satisfied to wait for the Americans and their news. This one will be so loud we could take over all of South America and no one would notice."

It was the first thing covered by the announcer—but not at all what they'd expected.

The FBI had discovered a huge bomb in San Rafael, California, and military explosives experts were dismantling it. Citizens within a two-mile radius had been evacuated, and commuter traffic on highway 101 had been halted for the past hour.

"Oh, God!" Simon Charbonneau cried in his shrillest falsetto.

There was nothing about Argentina, only more about the bomb, described as far more sophisticated and powerful than the ones at the World Trade Center and Oklahoma City. An FBI spokesman said the discovery had been made possible by a tip from an informant. Seven people had already been taken into custody in San Rafael, and more arrests were anticipated. The announcer said they would break into normal programming as the story developed.

Webb was pleased that there'd been no atrocity. Now all he wanted was to get back to civilization. He hadn't eaten for two days. None of them had.

"Turn it off," Jaeger told him. "We'll listen hourly until we learn what's happening in Buenos Aires."

"*Nothing's* happening," Charbonneau cried. "There was no *trueno*."

Jaeger ignored him.

"If I'd been there, they wouldn't have found the trailer. It's your fault, Jaeger."

The Hunter sighed impatiently, then motioned at Webb. "Go back to the viewing port and see what they're doing. Come back in an hour so we can listen to the next broadcast."

As he left, the Hunter was sitting very still, and Charbonneau continued to complain.

Webb returned to the main chamber a few minutes before one and reported that the soldiers were gathering at the lake.

"They're preparing to leave." Jaeger's voice was becoming strained, as if he were riding the edge of a razor. Webb had heard the restlessness there before, and scarcely dared to breathe.

"Then we can go," Charbonneau said impatiently.

"Not until morning."

"I'm *hungry*," Simon pouted.

"Yes," Jaeger whispered, and the S sound was hissed.

Webb carefully pushed the wire antenna out the vent hole, then turned on the radio. They'd checked at eleven o'clock and then noon, and there'd been nothing except more news of the bomb. Two more people had been taken into custody.

After the last few seconds of an advertisement, the musical introduction to the newscast sounded. The first minutes were devoted to discovery of the bomb—then came a new announcement. Vernon Calico had been dismissed from his post as secretary of state by the President. There was no reason given, but rumors were circulating that he'd accepted a large bribe from a foreign source.

Simon Charbonneau drew in a sharp intake.

The announcer spoke of an upcoming black-power march on Washington, then turned to international news.

A coup attempt was under way in Argentina. First reports said the president remained in control in Buenos

Aires, but there was heavy fighting in the countryside. The arrests of several important figures had been reported.

Charbonneau began to whimper and curse.

Except for a rasping of breath, the Hunter remained quiet.

The newscast ended, and Webb asked if Jaeger wanted to hear more. There was no response, but when the Hunter turned his gaze on him, Webb cringed. He switched off the radio and scuttled to the anteroom, away from the terrible vision of Jaeger's fury.

"I'm *hungry*," Webb heard Charbonneau complain from the main chamber.

"Yes," came the ominous, hissing reply, and Webb heard the sounds of movement.

"What are you doing?" Charbonneau cried out, and then began to shriek in a voice that was hardly human.

4:20 P.M.—Boise

Link guided the Gulfstream onto the runway and touched down a hundred feet long. While it was not perfect, the landing was good enough to elicit a compliment from the pilot in the left seat.

When they'd taxied in and shut down, Link shook the captain's hand. "Thanks."

"My pleasure. I like happy endings, and the company out there was great."

The FAA regional director had called Link before he'd left, and said there'd never been anything quite like the previous night in the history of aviation in the Bay Area. A total of sixty-three aircraft had participated in the search, and there'd been not a single close call. It was the sort of professionalism he especially liked, since his primary job was flight safety.

"When the other pilot lands," Link told the captain, "both of you get a good night's rest, then head back to Washington. I'll fly the Baron out in a couple days."

Leslie Rocklin had stayed behind in California, sending photographs and one release after another to her newspaper and the nation's news services. She had her big story, this time with the cooperation of the FBI, the Weyland Foundation, and everyone else involved. As Link had requested, she'd agreed to keep his name out of it.

He went aft and opened the hatch, then hefted his bags and started for the terminal.

The Weyland Foundation helicopter was parked in front, and the pilot waved him over. "Mrs. Dubois said to bring you to the building, then take you wherever you want."

When he'd put his bags inside, the pilot handed him a folded note. "She also said to give you this."

FRANK'S AWAKE, the note read. HE'S BEEN ASKING FOR YOU. Link stared at the boldly printed words, then released a long sigh of relief.

When he arrived at the building, Paula was smiling so wide the expression looked as if it were painted there. "He's back with us," she told him happily.

"I can't think of better news."

Frank Dubois had come around twice that morning, and both times had been lucid. When they'd gotten the news of the success, Paula had told him what had transpired in California and with Cyril at the White House. He'd been extremely pleased.

When Link looked in, Frank was resting, but there was a vast difference between his present sleep and the previous condition.

They spoke in low voices, so he wouldn't be wakened.

"Anything new from Argentina?" Link asked Paula.

"Our investigators are still scrambling to get out of the country, so all we know is what we hear from the media."

"At least you're hearing about it."

"Yes," she said happily. "This time their damned *trueno* didn't work."

Link nodded at Frank. "Do you mind if I stay until he wakes up again?"

"Not at all. He wanted to talk to you." She nodded out at the hall. "I'll be with Katy. The bad memories are finally coming back. The doctors feel it's better to deal with them now rather than later, but I think it's best if I'm with her."

When she'd left, Link settled into a chair beside his friend, who remained an immobile swath of white. Except for an occasional nurse looking in, they were alone.

He read a magazine, then drifted off to sleep—and dreamed.

A distant, tall figure stood watching him from the rocky hillside.

"Link?" the word was softly spoken.

When he'd blinked his way back to awareness, Frank's eyes were on him.

He grinned. "Welcome back to the world, Pig-foot."

"I heard you found the FAE." Dubois' voice was weak but even.

"I had help. After you're up and about, there'll be a lot of folks out there to thank."

"That may be awhile."

"Try not to take too long. I want another contract from you. We need the business."

"I heard they gave your company a bad time. I'm sorry about that, Link."

They'd talked together for ten minutes when a nurse looked in. A moment later two doctors arrived with serious expressions, and Link rose to leave.

"How much longer will you be around?" Frank asked.

"Two or three days."

"Drop by before you leave."

"I will."

He met Paula in the hallway. "He's awake?" she asked.

"Yeah, but the doctors want a few minutes with him. Did you have a chance to send out for the maps of the valley?"

Paula led him to a conference room with a long, glistening table at its center, opened the top drawer of a file cabinet, and showed him dozens of charts in folders.

"There were more than I'd believed there'd be. Some are more detailed than others." She pulled a folder from the drawer. "These are current. The others are outdated."

She appeared anxious to get back to Frank.

"If you don't mind, I'll use the room for a bit."

"Go ahead." She frowned. "You're not thinking of going back there, are you?"

"I despise the place as much as you do."

Paula smiled. "I'll see what they're doing with Frank."

As the door closed, Link pulled more of the files from the drawer and took his seat.

He began with the current maps and found detailed ones issued by the U.S. Geodetic Survey. More useful were those issued by the Idaho Bureau of Mines. The familiar lowland between the mountains, measuring some forty by fifteen miles, was called the Valley of Wilderness.

It did not take him long to find what he was looking for. On the current charts, several pick and shovel mine symbols were shown in the valley. A Bureau of Mines map published in 1933 showed two such symbols that were not on the new one.

Why? Link wondered.

Perhaps a mistake, or the legal claim ran out and that was the way they did things then, or—had they been filled in?

He opened a brittle, badly yellowed chart with tear marks at the folds. Another Bureau of Mines chart, this one put out in 1912. On it he found a total of fourteen mines that weren't displayed on the new maps.

"If there's trouble," Jaeger had said, "we'll go to a place not shown on the map."

How would Jaeger know that?

Answer: He'd had a current chart, like Rodriguez's task force was using.

Twenty more minutes passed before Link refolded and replaced the charts in the file cabinet. He had a superb memory, and there was no reason to take one.

In the valley he'd seen several of the mineshafts shown on the old map. The one he'd fallen into was infested with rattlesnakes, and others were similarly unsuitable for Jaeger's use. He'd narrowed his selection to two, both in the foothills south of the lake.

He knew what he must do, but first he had to talk to the Weyland Foundation helicopter pilot, then make a few purchases.

By the time he left the building it was dusk, and black clouds were billowing in from the west. The summer storm had arrived.

The Valley

"Webb?" sounded the low rumble of Jaeger's voice.

He'd stayed out of the way, huddling in the passageway during the entire time of Charbonneau's bloodcurdling screams, and then through the long silence that was even more frightening. "Yeah?" he finally ventured in a low voice.

"Hungry?"

Webb swallowed. "No."

Jaeger chuckled.

Webb had not eaten properly in a week, and had had nothing at all for more than two days, yet his hunger had disappeared, and if he'd had anything in his stomach he would have lost it. The sounds of Charbonneau's bones being broken and his flesh being torn while he'd still lived and screamed had done that. Acrid odors of blood and bile emanated from the other room, mixing with those of the permeating stench.

Jaeger's voice wafted from the main chamber. It was calm, no longer filled with the restlessness. "My father was a great man, Webb. So is Colonel DiPalma. They learned the secret of power. In their religion, weakness is the great sin. As long as you're stronger and more powerful, and as long as weaker men have what you want, you never need to be without."

The Hunter released a blast of flatus and sighed contentedly. "Charbonneau was weak. I needed strength, so I took it from him. If he'd lived he would have told the colonel I wasn't worthy. Now I've got the folder, and Colonel DiPalma will give me the job in Argentina."

Webb remained silent.

"What's happening outside, Webb?" The Hunter's voice was sleepy.

He took a cautious breath. "They're leaving."

"They'll be gone by morning. We'll go then."

"Great," Webb said, but he did not feel good about anything. He remained utterly silent as he heard the Hunter stirring.

"You don't have to watch tonight. A storm's coming."

"I don't mind." He'd do about anything not to have to go to the main chamber.

"Do as you wish." Jaeger adjusted again and was quiet.

The darkness was absolute. Webb removed the rock and stared out the viewing port. There were many headlights, a necklace string of them going north from the lake.

A booming sound startled him; then he recognized it as thunder and slowly relaxed. A few minutes later it began to rain—lightly at first, then increasing in intensity. Webb was pleased, for the sound of precipitation would mask the noises he'd make.

The brutal treatment of the secretary in Wisconsin, then the young couple in the Volkswagen, even the woman and girl at the camp, had been straws that made the weight of his conscience too heavy to continue to carry. He'd decided that this was his last operation with Jaeger. But what the Hunter had done to Charbonneau was the most horrifying of all.

Quitting was out of the question. Jaeger had made that clear from the start. He'd get out of the damned tunnel, seal it behind himself, then run like hell until he was out of the valley.

Jaeger's big magnum never left his side, and he knew the Hunter might come after him. The thought of what would happen if he was caught nauseated him.

He took another look out the viewing port and found the vehicle lights obscured by rain. As the downpour continued, he heard water dripping into the main chamber. Webb prayed the sounds of the rain would continue, and that Jaeger would remain in his deep slumber.

31

SATURDAY, JUNE 22

5:50 A.M.—Airborne in Bell Jet-Ranger IV, Northeast of Boise

Link Anderson had no hard proof that Jaeger and the others were still in the valley. His only rationale was that if they'd escaped, they'd have already used the information in the folder, and the only clue to their hiding place were words Jaeger had uttered about going somewhere not shown on maps. Any jury worth its salt would have thrown his case out the door.

His case was further weakened by the fact that he wanted to find them so badly. The Weyland Foundation did not deserve the kind of abuse they'd get from the media. His friend needed his help, and as long as they went unapprehended, they might threaten his friend's family. He also thought of other rationales, but inside he knew that it had become a personal matter.

He *wanted* to find them.

And deal with them.

Revenge was seldom an honorable motivation, but he knew it was a more honest explanation than the others he'd come up with, and Lincoln Anderson never liked to delude himself when he was about to take a serious step.

He'd considered bringing Marshal Joe Rodriguez in on the possibility that the terrorists might still be in the valley. He had not rejected the idea, just hadn't taken the next step and called him before crawling into the helicopter in the early morning rain.

The other thing he'd not decided was how he would deal with the killers if he found them—but he had a seed of a plan, based on what he'd learned about Jaeger and what he knew about some of the fiercest people who had ever populated North America. A portion of his genealogical heritage—half the blood that ran in his veins—was from a tribe described by a French explorer two hundred years earlier as utterly fearless, devoutly proud, and displaying such bloody savagery that no man of reason should enter their domain without dread for his life.

In 1855 the Americans had placated the Blackfoot nation with a treaty that promised them sovereignty over their empire in perpetuity—and over the next two decades decimated them with starvation, whiskey, and disease—then bought their land for pennies.

The Piegan Blackfeet had never been defeated in a major confrontation with another nation, white or red. Their success had come from a display of ruthlessness, an invocation of fear, and their uncanny ability to move unseen among their enemy.

He'd asked himself what those ancestors would have done in his place. Then he'd remembered what he'd been told about Jaeger's psychological vulnerability—"He can't accept failure or proof of weakness in himself"—and knew what was appropriate.

Lincoln Anderson had decided to use the Piegan way, and although he'd resolved to come up with a more specific plan during the ride to the valley, it was the last thing on his mind.

We shouldn't be here! was Link's thought as he stared out at the high, craggy mountains, scarcely differentiated by their ghostly shapes and hues. The storm that had arrived during the night was at full fury. He was in the front, beside the stone-faced helicopter pilot, peering through rain that pelted relentlessly against the windscreen.

The pilot was good, was Link's other thought. He was an ex-Army rotary-wing pilot with combat experience in Vietnam and Desert Storm, now in charge of the Weyland Foundation's helicopter fleet. Paula had told him to transport Link wherever he wanted, and the pilot had not questioned when he'd approached him the previous evening. He wondered what kind of bonus he should give him for taking him up in the awful weather, and decided it could not be too much.

Link pointed toward a level area several hundred yards below a barely visible pass between two mountains. The helicopter pilot nodded and corrected their flight path. The valley lay just over the saddleback. It was unlikely the chopper could be heard on a calm day. In this weather it would be impossible.

As the aircraft flew lower they were sucked by a downdraft, but the pilot applied power and worked the collective like a maestro. The craft danced wildly, yet he stayed in control as they settled toward the spot a half mile from the rocky crest. A hundred feet above the ground he switched on landing lights that illuminated the rainswept earth beneath them.

As they approached, then briefly hovered, Link unbuckled and went back, then shoved a waterproof valise and rifle case toward the door. As soon as they touched down, he unlatched the door and was quickly outside.

He hauled the valise and case past the downdraft of the whipping blades into the rain, then waved the pilot away. The rotors churned and the helicopter lifted, then dipped and was quickly lost to view on its way back to Boise. Weather permitting, the pilot would continue to return at the different designated hours and, if he was there, transport him back.

The murky darkness was turning to lighter shades of gray.

"Chilly," he muttered to himself as he cinched the protective hood of the gray waterproof coveralls tighter around his face. It was the altitude. It would be warmer in the valley.

He moved out immediately, following the wide trail up the mountainside. The leg bothered him at first, stiff from the helicopter ride, so he walked slowly until the muscle relaxed. He took longer strides then and increased his pace.

Ten minutes passed before he arrived at the saddleback between the high mountains. The wind was brisk there, blowing the rain in relentless sheets as he observed directly below. A dark outcropping of granite jutted, glistening with wetness where he'd known it would be.

He descended for twenty-five minutes, until the knoll was to his immediate right. There he set down the rifle case and valise, and carefully looked about. He was alone. Link took only a small leather case with him, and as he climbed the side of the outcropping, he wondered if it wasn't an exercise in futility and whether the men weren't miles away, sleeping or eating breakfast . . . or whatever assassins did in the early morning.

The craggy knoll was as good a viewpoint as Link had thought it would be, but its surface was wet and slippery, and the dropoff to the rocks below was more than two hundred feet. He moved cautiously—for rapid movement might draw attention—and stopped near the ledge.

He positioned himself so due north was directly to his front. "Three-four-zero and zero-one-five degrees," he recited to himself. "Both at one and a quarter miles." He observed the two areas he'd picked the night before. From the distance there seemed to be nothing obvious, no sign that mine shafts had ever been dug at either location. The fact was not surprising. If Jaeger was there, he'd picked his location for that reason.

Link opened the case and removed a Bausch & Lomb monocular. It was only six-power magnification, but the optics were precisely ground and the image was exceptionally clear. He stood still, a sentinel on the mountainside, examining every tree and stone in the two areas. Except for a few wet birds, a deer, and a waddling porcupine, he saw nothing of interest.

Dogbone Lake was before him, the much larger one to his right, and when he peered hard he could discern both bodies of water in the rain-swept distance. He concentrated on the large lake, and during a short lull he saw that not all the searchers had left. There were still a couple of tents, with a single helicopter parked nearby.

How many are there? Link wondered, staring until the rain fell harder and the lake was obscured. Not many, he decided.

A howling gust threatened to blow him from the precipice, so he shifted slightly, widening his stance, and continued to observe the areas below.

"He's gone," Jaeger repeated incredulously for the third time. Webb had left during the night, taking only a rifle. Large stones had been piled outside, blocking the entrance.

The Hunter had slept late, sated, lulled by the steady sounds of the rain. He'd dreamed of his father, standing grandly before him in his splendid uniform as he'd done when he was a child, and the presence had been so powerful it was as if he were here, speaking to him from the shadows, admonishing him for allowing Webb to escape.

Jaeger returned to the main chamber, where rainwater had gathered and run off into the back reaches of the cave. The odors were so overpowering that a weak man would have gagged.

But the Hunter was in no way weak.

He ignored the bloody remains of Charbonneau, thinking about the restlessness that was fast overpowering him.

Webb could not go to the authorities, he tried to reason. "He's in too deep for that," the Hunter said to himself, speaking aloud so the trembling of his jaw would subside. "I made sure of it."

He told himself he needed Webb alive, so he could fly the airplane.

The rage threatened again to overpower him.

"Alive," he said aloud. "He must live until we get to Buenos Aires."

Jaeger picked up his coveted rifle and carried it into the tunnel, then felt the wall of stone Webb had created. He'd moved and replaced the rocks quietly, so it must have taken a long time. It was doubtful he'd gone far.

The Hunter placed the weapon safely to one side and began to remove the barrier, lugging the stones to the adjacent anteroom and depositing them.

He shouldn't have trusted him. Charbonneau had told him that.

He turned then, and scarcely breathed, thinking he'd heard movement from the main chamber. *Impossible,* he decided, but remained still until he realized it was sounds of wind and dripping water.

Jaeger worked faster, the sounds of his labored breathing loud in his ears. He had almost filled the antechamber when he thought of how he'd rush to Buenos Aires with the Weyland files and help the colonel destroy his enemies. The thought was reassuring, and Jaeger thought of the government position he'd hold, wondering if he shouldn't design a dress uniform like the one his father had worn.

He'd removed stones for a half hour and his fingers were raw when he finally saw the glimmer of light. The Hunter was tired, but he renewed his effort and thought of what he faced.

Getting Webb would be no challenge—unless he was

outside, lying in wait with the rifle. Jaeger cautiously removed the final rocks, then reached back for his rifle.

As Link continued to observe the mountainside, he was increasingly convinced that Jaeger and the others had escaped. While the valley was large, it seemed improbable that two hundred soldiers could not find them. He decided to forgo his plan—to simply descend to his left, check the westernmost tunnel, then cross the hillside to the other. When he was satisfied they were in neither, he'd return to the saddleback and leave.

He was shifting his vision, swinging the monocular slowly, when he stopped.

There was human movement in the sparse trees to his left, farther west than he'd expected. As he stared there a familiar figure came into the open—fleeing, stumbling and falling, scrambling upright and going on.

Webb was two miles distant, haphazardly carrying a rifle as he traversed a barren slope.

Link felt a jolt of adrenaline but then frowned. Webb was running from something, yet Link had seen no soldiers or agents in that area.

He observed the two old mines again, first pausing on the left one, then on the one below and right, and was about to shift back to Webb when a large stone tumbled down the rocky hillside. There were more, and then a pause—and the mountain was still.

A rockslide triggered by the rain? Link was still postulating when a human figure rolled out of the hillside and sought protection behind a boulder.

Link felt a tingling sensation as he watched Jaeger, lying utterly motionless with his rifle ready, then rising and staying low as he darted to a new location. Another full minute passed before the Hunter moved again, this time into the sparse trees below. Jaeger searched, found something, and began to walk, following Webb. When he broke into a trot, a wave of déjà vu swept over Link as he remembered the big man on his own trail.

A falling-out between murderers? In the contest Webb did not have a chance.

Link remembered the third man, the grand-nephew of Salvator DiPalma, but there was no sign of him. As he put the monocular away, the rain began anew, obscuring the men below. He felt a new quickening in his chest.

It would be done the Piegan way.

Link cupped his hands. "Jaeger!" he called in a voice that first blended with the stillness of the early morning, then rose higher and higher in intensity.

He smiled grimly to himself. *It was time.* A flutter of apprehension stirred. Then Lincoln Anderson took a resolute breath and descended from the crag.

At the bottom he unzipped the valise and knelt to shield it from the blowing rain as he pulled out three tubes of greasepaint and a roll of tape.

He daubed a narrow streak of white paint in a vertical stripe from his forehead onto his nose, then down to his chin. Next a black stripe on his right cheek, and a red one on his left, the holy colors of the ancient Piegan. The result, he knew, was a fierce mask.

Invoke fear. Move among the enemy like a spirit.

He taped the overalls at cuff and sleeve, then in spirals up each leg and arm, securing the fabric so nothing would be caught in foliage. After slipping a small metal flashlight into a breast pocket, then pulling on a pair of calfskin driving gloves, he closed the valise.

Finally he opened the rifle case and stared for a long moment.

Inside were two very different weapons.

One was a Remington model 700 BDL DM with bolt action and detachable magazine—in 7mm-magnum caliber. A variable 3X-9X Redfield scope was attached on oval, see-through mounts. A shooter could view through the magnification of the scope or drop his eye an inch and use the iron sights. It was a formidable choice.

The other was a sturdy hickory pole, two inches in diameter, thirty inches in length, and quite heavy.

"Give me strength, Old Man," he said, and drew out only the wooden club.

A moment later the valise and rifle case had been deposited behind a trailside bush.

Link was ready. He set out immediately, for there was no more time to moralize or consider alternatives.

The Hunter had been following the trail left by Webb when he'd heard his name echoing from the rain-swept mountainside. He'd slowed and stopped, and looked warily about, trying to determine the source, but it had come unexpectedly, seemingly from several sides.

Had it been Webb? he wondered. It had to be, Jaeger decided, although he'd believed the man was far too timid to challenge him.

He felt a new flash of anger, and the restlessness continued to grow inside.

"Don't kill him!" his mind argued. "You need him."

He continued his relentless pace, and as the downpour continued, he had the uneasy feeling that in his haste he'd forgotten something.

It came to him then that he'd left the leather folder in the mineshaft—but he did not dare turn back, for the rain would soon eliminate his quarry's tracks.

He'd go back for it after he caught up with Webb.

Link had set out in a course that would intercept Jaeger before he approached Webb.

This time there was no one to slow him, no one's safety to concern him but his own.

Wind howled across the mountainside, brought a new deluge that battered the landscape and made it impossible to see for more than a few yards. It did not matter. He knew where he wanted to go, and the obstacles he faced to get there. Lincoln Anderson crossed an area where it was impossible not to leave tracks, but it didn't concern him. He was now the stalker, and his prey was before him. He continued, hurrying but at a pace he could sustain.

In his right, gloved hand he carried the sturdy club.

He moved easily, quickly, and with confidence. With each step a new twinge of pain burned in his leg, but he ignored them and filled his mind with details of his surroundings.

The rain was falling in furious sheets as he entered the sparse foliage that covered the lower foothills, and found signs of both Webb's and Jaeger's passages. The latter's tracks were fresh and distinct, so he reduced his pace and became warier.

Ten minutes passed, and he was much closer. An impression left by Jaeger's boot was still unfilled by the steady rain.

Link was walking briskly, silently, staring into the downpour, when he sensed the familiar feral presence and stepped into the anonymity of the brush. He remained motionless for a full minute, knowing Jaeger was before him and also waiting.

The fact that the man carried a powerful firearm, that his own weapon was primitive in comparison, added to the emotion of the moment. His forebears had felt the same in their own tests of stealth and courage.

Silence permeated the thicket. Link moved only his eyes, studying the gray tones, looking for regularities in nature's world of random.

He saw slight movement.

The patch of cloth was only fifty feet distant. A shirtsleeve? Camouflaged fabric worked fine when it remained immobile, but was discernible when it shifted. Jaeger moved again, and Link had a fleeting glimpse of him. The front of his shirt was dark crimson, yet he moved with agility, not at all as if he was injured. Someone else's blood?

After a moment Link heard Jaeger's sounds from farther away. Link followed, and had gone no more than fifty yards when he heard a gunshot.

The Hunter had come upon Webb, but it had not been the booming sound of the magnum.

Link continued to the edge of the forest and looked out at the mountainside. Both men were hidden. After a moment he heard the low sound of distant sobbing.

Webb?

He eased forward and knelt in a small depression behind a rocky mound.

Jaeger called from the boulder-littered mountainside. "Put your gun down, Webb."

"Go away!"

"You're making me angry, Webb. I don't want to hurt you. Put it down and come out."

"Leave me *alone*."

"I need you to fly the airplane, Webb. We'll return to Buenos Aires. They need us there."

"You heard the news, Jaeger. They found the bomb, and everything's gone to hell. For God's sake, leave me alone." Webb's voice cracked on the last words.

As the rain diminished Link saw movement. Webb, two

hundred yards distant, had darted from behind a mound of rocks on the hillside.

"Come back!" Jaeger's commanding voice boomed across the mountainside.

Webb ran wildly for a few steps, then slipped and fell, and slid several feet down a sloped shale shelf. He remained immobile, mouth open and chest heaving from exertion. His rifle was several feet away, and he stared at it, then looked fearfully at a jagged outcropping.

It had begun to rain harder again as Link examined the rocks. The Hunter was on the other side, with part of his face and torso visible.

Jaeger left the security of the outcropping, then his form disappeared in the downpour as he continued toward Webb.

"Don't hurt me," Webb shrieked, but Link could no longer see him.

"You've made me angry." Jaeger's voice was strained, his accent thicker than usual.

Webb began to blubber helplessly.

Link rose and walked through the downpour, looking carefully as he advanced.

"No!" He heard Webb cry, then the sound of crumbling shale as he tried to escape.

Link got a wafting glimpse of the big man and began to run across the rocky mountainside toward him. The shape grew more distinct.

As the Hunter approached Webb, his face grew distorted, and his jaw began to tremble uncontrollably.

"I'll go with you," Webb pleaded.

Jaeger didn't respond, just crouched over him and stared, and the rage continued to grow until his vision was filled with crimson hatred. As the restlessness screamed ever louder in his head, he dropped the magnum and reached out.

He did not see the approaching shadow.

Something smashed into the side of his head, breaking bone and teeth, and he was knocked sprawling onto the shale.

The big man groaned loud and lost several long seconds of consciousness, then shook his head to dispel the symmetrical spots that danced and marred his vision. Sharp pain pulsed from the side of his face, and he spat blood.

When he was able, he pushed onto hands and knees, still dazed, and stared at the horrible streaked face that hovered before him.

Then the visage faded—and was gone.

Webb was crouched nearby, eyes wide as saucers.

Jaeger darted his eyes about, then looked back where the shadow figure had disappeared. The rage had evaporated—now his heart pounded mercilessly, and a new, alien emotion swept through him.

He grasped his big magnum and scrambled down the hillside—to get farther away from it. When he felt he was safe, he listened intently, the rifle held to his shoulder, but other than the sounds of Webb's crying he could hear nothing.

He heard a subtle noise from farther up the hill, and he shifted and fired toward the source. As the booming sound of the magnum still reverberated from the mountainside, he quickly descended, careful not to slide on the wet shale, and as he regained a degree of control his eyes methodically searched the murky shadows.

He reached the trees, then paused beside one to watch and listen again. The rain had diminished, and fog reached out in wispy fingers, rising like steam from the warmer earth.

"Jaeger." The word was a hardly audible whisper—and again he could not determine the direction from which it came.

"Who are you?" he called out, and immediately regretted that he'd done it. He was the Hunter, and could not show weakness.

Webb no longer mattered. He would escape, and if the damned—whatever it was—got in his way, he'd kill it. Then he cursed himself, for he'd left the leather folder in the mineshaft, and could not go over the mountain until he'd retrieved it.

Jaeger set out in the direction from which he'd come, rifle ready, eyes constantly shifting, searching as he went.

After walking for a half hour, he warily circled back, as was his practice, and knelt, waiting. The Hunter listened intently—fingering and testing the missing teeth, then the tender puffiness that had formed at the side of his face where the man-thing had struck him—and heard only the sounds of rain.

After a while he believed there was nothing behind him, yet he waited longer.

He tried to reason out what had attacked him, but could not, and a shudder of apprehension swept through him. Fear was an alien sensation, and he desperately wanted to reject it—it was weakness!—but he could not.

Hurry, his mind urged him, but he hesitated for more long seconds.

He rose cautiously, and as he turned saw a blur and was struck hard, this time in the other temple, the blow so severe that he dropped his weapon and groaned with new pain as he crumpled to his knees.

He fought unconsciousness, lest the creature kill him while he was helpless, but he wavered on the brink, although he sensed it was close by.

A shadow moved in his blurred vision. Then something struck him in the face again, hard! He cried out and recoiled, half in fear and half in fresh pain.

A moment later he'd revived enough to feel about on the ground and retrieve the rifle.

The man-thing had not taken it!

He checked and found that only a single round remained. He'd brought no more ammunition, had left it in his rucksack with the folder, in the mineshaft.

Jaeger rose unsteadily and began to walk again, even more slowly, more warily, trying hard to remain observant. Pain pulsed like waves from his battered face.

Link watched the Hunter leave his place of ambush, and knelt there, studying the pool of blood that had drained from the big man's wounds, already diluted to a pink color upon the wet earth.

He lifted his gaze. The big man was backtracking. Returning for Charbonneau? For the leather folder?

Neither Jaeger nor Webb had carried it.

The Piegan had called what he'd done to Jaeger "counting coup"—using stealth and audacity to get close enough to strike the enemy yet not dealing a lethal blow. It had been a sign of superior courage, and cast doubt and fear into one's enemies.

Did Jaeger know who pursued him? From his expressions Link doubted that was so.

It was just as well.

They were north of Dogbone Lake, where Link knew every thicket and clearing. He found and followed a game trail that paralleled Jaeger's route on the mountainside, then went faster, limping worse as his wounded leg rebelled from prolonged abuse.

After twenty minutes, Link came to a thicket of gnarled manzanita trees, the one he'd first paused at with Paula and Katy so they could rest, and he knew to proceed through it by following the narrow trail. He emerged on the other side and hurried on.

As he walked through the swirling fog, he remembered landmarks, and that the game trail ended not far ahead. He walked swiftly and without caution, for he'd heard Jaeger's sounds as he'd passed him a quarter mile back. The big man had circled again, in another attempt to waylay him. Link Anderson allowed himself to smile as he continued.

Twenty minutes later, the trail terminated as the forest thinned. The fog had lifted some, so he began to run again, to gain time for his next task.

Keep your eyes open for the third man, he told himself. Link maintained a steady, loping pace, measuring his breathing and ignoring lightning bolts that coursed through the leg. He was well ahead now, and the mineshaft from which he'd seen Jaeger emerge was not far.

The rain began anew, not the awful downpour of before but a persistent drizzle.

Link slowed again as he came to the treeline. Beyond a small expanse was a large tangle of brush growing against a rocky cliff side, and the tunnel was on the opposite side.

The thicket would have been easy to circle and avoid, but he did not.

Link approached it, then dropped low and pushed his way in, making little noise. When he was almost through, he stopped and went more cautiously. The rain pelted harder as Link kneed and elbowed his way to the edge and stared out.

The open maw of the mineshaft was less than fifty yards distant, and he still saw no sign of Simon Charbonneau. Link didn't like the idea that the man might surprise him, so he continued looking, but still saw nothing.

He returned his mind to the big man, and decided that Jaeger would take another ten minutes to arrive.

Link rose and trotted to the mouth of the mineshaft, where he pulled the small flashlight from his breast pocket and took a last good look around. He entered cautiously, holding the flashlight with his left hand, gripping the club with his right.

He emerged three minutes later, coughing and gagging at the stench, and almost lost the meager contents of his stomach. He breathed deeply, drawing precious fresh air into his lungs to displace the rotten, and looked skyward for a moment to drive away the vision of horror.

Diego DiPalma had been stripped naked, his face beaten into a bloody mass, his limbs twisted awry. A bloody, opened pocketknife lay next to the corpse. The muscles of a thigh and a biceps had been cut away, and the rocky floor was smeared with feces and thick, dried blood.

Link had tried to ignore it, had searched until he'd found what he'd come for.

He took another deep breath, then returned to the thicket, even more resolved than before, and resumed his former position to observe, refusing to let his mind linger on what he'd seen.

Jaeger took twenty more minutes, longer than Link had believed, and when he emerged from the forest he appeared skittish and nervous. His mouth was bloodied and his face badly battered. He peered about warily through a single slitted eye, for the other had swollen closed, and several times he started and aimed the magnum at nothing in particular.

The Hunter had become as fearful as Link had hoped.

Jaeger approached the mouth of the tunnel, took a last furtive look about, then ducked inside.

Link rose and walked closer, then waited, giving Jaeger time to search through the rucksack, and then to panic as he realized it was empty.

"Jaeger," he called out, but this time his tone was victorious. "I've beaten you."

"No!" The Hunter's voice shook in its intensity.

"Come out, Jaeger."

There was no response.

"Are you afraid of me?" He went closer and stood to one side of the tunnel's mouth so he would remain unseen.

The sound was subtle, but with it Link sensed the man's presence nearer the entrance.

Jaeger's puffed and swollen head appeared slowly—scanning carefully, although the second eye was now almost closed—his oversize weapon ready to bring to bear.

"Time to die, Jaeger," Link said calmly, and smacked the club hard into the bridge of the big man's nose. There was a howl of pain, and the head immediately withdrew. Then he heard the sounds of harsh breaths as Jaeger scrambled deeper into the mineshaft.

Link wondered if he shouldn't taunt him, tell the big man that he'd lost, that Frank Dubois was alive and he'd just taken the folder—but he waited and said none of those things.

Five long minutes passed.

"My . . . name . . . is Johann."

Link didn't respond.

"The Hunter's voice was subdued. "My . . . father . . . was powerful."

He sucked in a ragged breath. "I was strong . . . like . . . he told me to be."

Link spoke clearly, wanting him to hear. "I've never met a weaker man than you, Jaeger. You couldn't even control yourself. When you couldn't deal with people, you killed them."

Jaeger's voice was pleading. "I'm not weak."

Link laughed. "Come out, so I can show you."

He was answered by a long silence, then: "Who are you?" The voice trembled.

"Are both of your eyes swollen closed?"

There was no response.

"I'm coming in now, Jaeger, but you won't be able to see me. Do you know what I'm going to do to you?"

Link stepped farther from the tunnel, so he couldn't smell the stench, and lifted his eyes to look out over the valley. The rain had diminished to an occasional few windblown drops, and he could see the lake in the distance.

The rifle shot from inside the mine tunnel was muted, followed by the vague sounds of Jaeger's convulsions.

He heard the *clop-clop* sounds of distant blades, squinted toward the lake, and watched a helicopter lift off—a speck in the rain-swept sky. They'd waited until the weather had improved to respond to the sounds of gunfire.

"Only ducks and fools fly in a storm," Link said to no one.

He set out up the mountainside.

Two hours later Link watched from above as a helicopter crew finally sighted the mine entrance and searched for a place to land. They'd discover Jaeger's body and what remained of Charbonneau.

He felt not the slightest pity for them. When he thought of the carnage Jaeger had wrought—when he remembered what Charbonneau had tried to do—he knew it was just enough. Some couldn't be allowed to go on, or they'd continue to threaten the rest of them.

It was still misting, but the visibility had improved. He was near the saddleback between the mountains, looking out from under an overhang of rock, the rifle case and the valise set down nearby. He'd been careful to leave nothing behind.

As he started down the other side, he stopped and stared at a patch of exposed earth, and the human tracks there. He pursed his lips thoughtfully, then looked up the steep mountain slope to his left. Webb was above, hiding. Link's face remained stone hard as he examined the high rocks.

After a moment, he bled out a sigh and continued the steady pace down the hillside.

At two o'clock that afternoon, the Jet-Ranger returned for him. By then he'd wiped off the greasepaint and replaced the overalls with the second set of clothing he'd brought. He did not look back as the helicopter lifted off and turned toward Boise.

The rain had ceased and patches of blue sky showed though the clouds.

EPILOGUE

Boise

When Link had returned to the airport the previous afternoon, he had stowed the rifle and valise in the Beech Baron, and taken a taxi to the Riverwalk Hotel. He'd treated himself by renting a luxury suite, then sequestered himself with his thoughts and sore body. The physical miseries were easiest to deal with—a handful of painkillers and an hour in the Jacuzzi relaxed him to a slothful state—but the horrors in his mind did not leave so readily.

He'd called Marie, his ever patient fiancée, whose devotion could never be doubted, and told her he would stop over on his flight back to Washington. Her normalcy had made him feel better, for it proved that all of the world was not insane. Then he'd eaten in the dining room and observed ordinary citizens whose biggest problems were choices between the various entrees and whether to sample the dessert tray, and that too had helped. Finally he'd returned to his room and sat at the window, looking out over the lights of Boise and sipping Hennessey cognac until the urge to sleep was overpowering.

He hadn't awakened for twelve hours, and during that time the miracle occurred. In the light of the new morning the dark world that had threatened to turn into a great lunatic ward was transformed to a bright and cheerful one.

He turned on the television and the illusion was shattered. The President had spoken to the nation the previous day, and an analyst reviewed his words and provided commentary.

The President had opened by saying that he could not remain silent about the attacks on the Weyland Foundation, which had become a plaything of certain members of the media. He'd explained how years ago the wealthy founders of the institution had sacrificed their fortunes to ensure the betterment of mankind. Now, due to spectacular reports by irresponsible journalists, hate groups had targeted individual members of the institution.

The President had received word that the foundation would no longer fund projects requested by administrations. The hate mongers and the irresponsible press had prevailed. An arrow in the quiver of future presidents had been lost.

An example of the foundation's contributions had been their latest, to warn him about the trailer bomb in California that was to have been detonated on the Golden Gate Bridge. Estimates were that between 1,500 and 2,000 lives would have been lost, but the bomb had been disassembled and the bomb makers were in custody.

They'd told him about a South American bank called El Soleil, which in the past had funded Colombian drug cartels, and the bank's leader, who had planned the overthrow of the Argentinean government. Their warning had come just in time. When alerted, the Argentinean president had gathered his loyal military leaders and briefed them. They'd assigned units to protect him, and others to arrest Salvator DiPalma and dismantle his empire. It wasn't over, for a number of army units bought off by El Soleil continued to fight in Patagonia.

The President was sending a U.S. carrier group to the area, and if things went badly, he would order U.S. Marines ashore from a helicopter assault ship parked off the coast. Surveys showed that the American public overwhelmingly approved. After hearing about the atrocity planned by El Soleil, they were calling for blood.

In the same television address, the President had denounced his secretary of state, Vernon Calico, saying it was "suspected" that he'd been paid a large sum of money by Salvator DiPalma to deceive the President and discredit the Weyland Foundation.

Calico had gone into seclusion on his Texas ranch, where, on hearing the President's speech, his workers had quit en masse. Sources said he was close to bankruptcy, and might have to sell the family ranch to pay for his upcoming legal defense.

Thus far there'd been few rebuttals from the press about the President's speech. The only articles about the Weyland

Foundation were of praise for their warning about the bomb.

Link switched off the television, and took an hour with his shower and shave. It felt wonderful to have the luxury of time to be clean.

He checked out of the hotel and told a cab driver to take him to the medical building where the Dubois family had been relocated.

U.S. Marshal Joe Rodriguez emerged from the building wearing his western-cut suit, snakeskin boots, and Stetson with a lawman's triple crease. He'd noted the security guards posted inside and out, and fleetingly wondered what it would be like to be constantly wary that someone might want to kidnap your loved ones.

His contact with the foundation had been terminated four days before, then abruptly turned back on. Joe didn't know the rationales of his bosses, but he'd just provided what was likely to be their last briefing about matters in the Valley of Wilderness.

The bodies of the big man called Jaeger and an Argentinean citizen named Diego DiPalma had been located after the last agents at the lake had heard gunfire—and then found an opened mineshaft. The sight inside the tunnel had been awful. DiPalma had been partially dismembered, and Jaeger had blown his own head off.

They'd brought helicopters and ground teams back in, and after a few hours located the man called Webb, wandering aimlessly in the mountains. When they'd called for him to come down he'd run toward them, and since he'd carried the rifle, they'd had no alternative but to shoot him down. He'd lived for a few hours, regained consciousness long enough to croak a few words about someone being eaten alive, and being visited by a terrible angel of death.

Joe had his suspicions about the angel, but he'd not voiced them.

As he walked toward the parking area, he noticed Lincoln Anderson emerging from a taxi, carrying a package wrapped in plain brown paper.

As they approached, Anderson's eyes smiled. "Marshal."

"Good to see you again." They shook hands. "Going in to see the Dubois family?"

Anderson nodded. He was a man of few words.

"They're in," Joe said, measuring the man. He went on then, toward his car.

The previous afternoon Anderson had been seen dismounting from a Weyland Foundation helicopter, then stowing a rifle case and valise in his company's airplane. Later, when Webb raved about the angel of death visiting the valley, Rodriguez had considered investigating what Anderson had stored in the Beech Baron's baggage compartment.

Joe Rodriguez was no longer a real policeman, but he still had a cop's intuition. Lincoln Anderson had returned to the valley to settle things.

But Joe also had a policeman's sense of justice, and it gave him satisfaction when bad guys were taken down. There were times when they got away clean, and others when they were forced to pay their dues without the involvement of the judicial system. Like Old Gerald Rocklin had once told him about a man who'd cheated justice and was killed when a milk cow kicked him in the head: "It may not be correct, but it's *right*, and that's just as good."

The final deaths in the valley would be determined to be the result of an argument between the kidnappers. Not a scientific find, but a handy one they sometimes used to close a case. He felt the inner glow that things were *right*. Lincoln Anderson would stew, and might even wonder if Joe would discover the truth and come back at him. It was also *right* that he do that. People with consciences paid their debts with interest, a fact that kept society in check.

Old Gerald Rocklin had been a man of wisdom.

Speaking of Rocklins, he'd better hurry if he was going to see Leslie off at the airport. Her airplane would depart in an hour, bound for Washington, D.C., where she'd interview for a job with a large newspaper. Joe hated to see her leave—the city would lose a good reporter, and with the departure of the last ornery Rocklin, part of the state's heritage would be lost—but after her stories about flying with the good Samaritans and finding the trailer bomb in California, Leslie was big-time, and they'd hear more from her.

In another matter, she'd not been told about the Weyland Foundation's involvement, only that more than enough money had been found in her father's estate to pay off his debts, so she'd been able to keep the old Rocklin home. She'd return someday. They always did. The mountains,

fresh air, and good people of Idaho were hard things to
forget.

Joe Rodriguez had also been offered a job in Washington, involving a promotion and a position in the Department of Justice. His boss had called and said Joe's career
had taken a turn for the better in the last few days, when
someone had put words in with the man at the top. The
very top, he'd said. Joe had a promising future, if he so
wished. He'd talked it over with his wife and decided to
decline the move. They liked Boise and its slower pace of
life.

When Link arrived, Paula finally introduced him to Cyril
Weyland—they'd not had time for a proper introduction
before—and it was as if they'd known each other for a
long time. The two were separated by sixty years, but were
similar in that both were strong-willed men, sure of their
capabilities.

"We'll be seeing more of you," Cyril said enigmatically.
"At least I sincerely hope so."

When they left him, Link said he'd like to see Frank and
Katy.

Katy beamed as Paula presented Link Anderson, and a
rosy hue came to her cheeks. She'd recovered from the
physical damage, but while she still couldn't clearly remember what had happened, the tumultuous time in the
valley was surfacing. Not all of her memories were awful.
She'd mention the name Fuzz-butt and giggle about his
grumpiness, then ask about Link and grow a shy, private
smile. But now that the pilot was here, she seemed tongue-
tied.

Link spoke in his quiet voice, telling Katy he'd brought
something for her. He took out a bracelet made of braided
horsehair and porcupine quills, and told her it was an
amulet made by a woman of the Piegan Blackfoot Indians.
He said that some believed it held special powers.

"In the old days, when members of the tribe did something especially well," Link said, "they were given things.
It's my gift to you, for learning and helping so much."

"Thank you," Katy whispered in a state of awe.

When they were back in the hallway, Paula told him she
was touched by the gesture.

He took another bracelet from his shirt pocket. "This one's for the fisherman."

Paula started to laugh, then stopped herself and stared.

He dropped the bracelet into her hand. "The Piegan called things like this medicine because they made them feel good. You deserve it."

As they continued toward Frank's room, Paula grasped her gift as tightly as her daughter had just done.

When they arrived, Frank was speaking to a nurse. He was awake for longer periods of time and rested peacefully. The previous evening he and Cyril had talked about his role as chairman of the Weyland Foundation. Frank's injuries would take a long time to heal, but his mind was clear and they'd decided the transfer of power shouldn't be delayed.

"I'd like to speak with Link privately," Frank said, and Paula led the nurse out of the room.

Link unwrapped the package, then carefully laid the leather folder on the bedside table. Frank's eyes followed, and when he recognized it, he released a sigh of relief.

"I went back," Link told him quietly.

Frank regarded him. "Did you open it?"

"No. What's there is none of my business."

"I'd like you to read it. It explains everything the Weyland Foundation has done."

"The President announced that you're finished with secretive projects."

"That will have to be one of my decisions as chairman. The foundation was formed for good purpose, Link, and there's still much to be done. There'll be more countries that need a nudge toward democracy, and more Hitlers, Saddam Husseins, and Salvator DiPalmas to stop."

"It might be better if I don't hear any more."

"I want you to know everything, so you can make up your mind about something. I'll be convalescing for the next several months, and it's doubtful I'll ever walk without assistance. I need a strong right arm, Link. Someone who can travel and look into things. Someone I can talk things over with, and know I can trust."

Link let the words settle in. It was an interesting overture.

"I need you to help us make a difference in the world."

"What does Cyril think?" he asked.

"What you did in the valley, and then in California, impressed everyone in the foundation. Cyril and the others in the handful know what I'm asking of you, and have given their blessing."

"The timing's bad. I'm still trying to help my father's company out of a business slump."

"We talked about that too. The foundation has forty aircraft assigned to our various projects and operations, and we'd like to assign them to Executive Connections to manage. It would be a lucrative contract. That's regardless of your decision to join us, of course."

Link was stunned by the generosity of the offer.

"You don't have to decide right away. In three weeks I'll be well enough to be flown back to New York. I'd like you to take me there, and give your answers about both offers."

12 Days Later—Washington National Airport

Link was weary, for he'd just finished a long flying day. He'd brought in a new Gulfstream IV to replace the one retired to the wilderness lake.

Their new man was with him—a brash, young ex-Navy fighter pilot who had just received the first flight of his check-out. As they walked together across the tarmac toward the Executive Connections building, Link said the initial ride had gone well.

"I'll be away for a while," he told him. "In a few days Billy Bowes will be back as chief pilot and finish your check rides. If you have any questions, ask Henry Hoblit."

The young pilot grinned. "Henry's got a silver tongue. I heard him on the phone talking with a congressman, and he knew precisely how to handle him."

"Henry's sort of like baby shit," Link said. "Awfully smooth and easy to swallow, but sometimes there's a hell of an aftertaste."

The new pilot tried not to laugh.

"He's also a damned good man. You'll understand."

When they went inside, General Lucky Anderson and Billy Bowes were seated in the fancy foyer recently renovated by Henry Hoblit, regaling a group of company pilots with war stories Link had heard a dozen times—and which got better with each telling.

The new pilot went to join them, but Link continued toward the flight-planning room.

Henry emerged from his office, looking upset.

"Something wrong?" Link asked.

"We've got a reporter on the way over. I thought we were finished with that crap."

"Hell, Henry, you can handle a reporter."

"She's from the *Times* and insists she talk to Billy. Wouldn't give me a name, just said to tell him she was the best damned reporter in the world, and he'd better be ready for her." He looked concerned that Bowes might screw it up.

"Better get used to it, Henry. I believe she'll be around a lot." Link smiled as Henry continued toward the foyer.

He paused at the flight-operations desk and observed the revised flying schedule with mixed emotions, for Lincoln Anderson's name was not shown.

He planned to dead-head out to Montana, where he'd spend a week with his fiancée and make up his mind about his future. She was an anthropologist, and they'd spend their days hiking in the wild mountains around Glacier Park, looking for ancient Indian artifacts.

He'd insisted that they return every evening to a nearby Holiday Inn.

TERROR ... TO THE LAST DROP